Pemrose Key

McAuley Huffman

B. J. Huffman Publishing

Pemrose Key

ISBN-13: 9780692252321
ISBN-10: 0692252320
Library of Congress Control Number: 2014912425
B. J. Huffman, Birmingham, AL

Dedication

With love and gratitude to my family and friends who continue to offer encouragement and support of my efforts and have for a very long time.

To my siblings, Cindy, Donna and Glenn, and my mom, Dodie, I love you for instilling a can-do attitude in me, along with my late Pop, who was very proud of my work, but never had the chance to see it in print.

To Gage and Olivia, for the joy they've given BB.

Special love to Robert, my "Bobby Earl," my greatest fan, best friend, editor, and encourager. This is for you, sweetheart, until we meet again...rest in peace, My Love.

Above is my earthly dedication...my full gratitude goes to God, without Him, I would be nothing, do nothing, have nothing.

Acknowledgments

Appreciation goes to friends, Doris, Wanda, Deborah, Elizabeth, Elaine and Karen, who critiqued, applauded, offered suggestions and ego boosts and put up with my insistence they read and talk about my work. I especially thank LaRue and Paul for taking an interest in keeping me informed of available publishing options. I thank Jett for her valuable tips and Chief Wally for his esteemed judicial advice. To Donna for her ideas, and Cindy for her creative talents and hard work in designing my cover. Thank you many times over, little sisters.

Inspiration

My muse is in the beauty and majesty of the great Gulf of Mexico; the headiness of inhaling her sweet, salt air; the unique characters and their colorful, laid-back lifestyles that are embraced by villages and towns perched along the shores of the Gulf. The ribbon of silvery white sand that runs for miles along the Alabama coast and the Florida Panhandle is truly inspirational.

This fictional story *happens* in this magical place known as "The Miracle Strip."

Prologue

God Almighty, get me out of here! Dear Lord, please get me out of this place. Lucas Callaway looked down at the body he held in his arms—the still warm, blood spattered body of a soldier younger than himself. Moments before, the boy must surely have uttered that very same plea. God answers prayers, doesn't He? Maybe prayers couldn't be heard from the depths of hell.

Luke didn't even know the boy's name, but a couple of weeks ago, when Luke had been stunned by the blast of a nearby land mine, the boy saved his life. He had charged courageously through the ring of fire that encircled Luke and pulled him to safety mere seconds before another mine exploded a few feet away. While waiting for a rash of firing to cease, the boy told Luke April 30 was to be his lucky day, the day he'd finally be going home.

Luke gently lifted the boy from his lap and laid him on the ground. He placed his palm across the boy's eyes and pushed them closed, concealing the wide-open, piercing look that seemed to reflect profound disbelief. It was too bad about the boy. Today was April 27.

Luke watched as two men moved in and loaded the body on a stretcher. Before the medics carried him away Luke tugged on the chain of the boy's dog tag, loosening it from the soiled, bloody garments. His name was Teddy. Now Teddy would be going home three days sooner than he had planned.

Suddenly an explosion illuminated the night. *God, give me strength.* Men ran through the jungle, screaming in pain. Dismembered body parts flew through the air. Somebody's arm, fingers still intact, landed in a nearby bush—alongside a round, bloody clump. Outwardly Luke remained passive, but his insides reacted violently when he discovered the clump to be a detached head, recognizable as such by a bloody, matted tuft of hair that clung tenaciously to a piece of skin flapped across exposed skull.

I'll never get out of here. He had seen worse, but after nearly two years, this past week had been the hardest. The end was so close, yet so far away. For Teddy, even three days had proved to be too distant.

It was quiet in the jungle now. There was total darkness, save for the moonlight. Luke had only two weeks left in this place, if his prayers were answered.

1

$\mathcal{L}$ucas Callaway stood in the open doorway of the airplane, deliberately delaying his departure. "Cooper DeLaney...I want to go to Miami with you."

The stewardess laughed as though he were joking. If only he weren't so battle-weary he would follow her anywhere.

They met only hours ago in the coffee shop at O'Hare, but Luke knew there was something special about Cooper DeLaney. When he found himself stuck in Chicago due to a late-season, early-May snow, the beautiful airline stewardess pulled some strings and got him on her flight to Atlanta.

"If you hadn't convinced the captain to let me ride jump-seat, I'd still be sitting at O'Hare."

Her green eyes flashed passionately. "Consider it my contribution to the war, Luke. With the sacrifices made in Vietnam by you and many others, it's hardly enough." She touched the POW bracelet she wore on her wrist. "I'll be coming home to Mobile for a visit, maybe I'll look you up in Pemrose Key."

"I'd like to show you around when you do." *Perhaps they were destined to be together.*

"Daddy spends all his time in Washington since my mother died, but I still go back to visit friends."

"Promise you'll call me?" There was much he wanted to say to the beautiful copper-haired Cooper DeLaney, and there was a lot he wanted to know about her. Soon, too soon, the plane would be leaving and she would be gone.

"I promise…I've written my address down for you." She handed him a folded piece of airline stationery.

Luke couldn't take his eyes off of her as she continued to speak. How could he leave now, torn as he was between romantic possibilities and Pemrose Key. Realistically, Luke knew he couldn't allow himself to think seriously about a relationship at this time, particularly a long-distance romance. There was much to do before pursuing someone who was as geographically unavailable as Cooper DeLaney. It had been a long time since he'd been with a woman, but it had been even longer since he'd been home. He'd send her roses, white ones—clean and pure, like her, to thank her for her trouble, and later, when he had his life in order, he would arrange to see her.

Luke took Cooper's hand in his and peered into those wonderful, dancing eyes one last time. "Thanks, Cooper DeLaney, for everything. Maybe our paths will cross again."

She surprised him by raising herself on tiptoe and softly brushing his cheek with her lips. She looked at him sadly and her bubbly voice became soft, almost timid. "Good luck, Luke Callaway. I hope your life is wonderful and that everything works out the way you want it to." She pulled her hand away. "Guess you'd better go now, before you miss your flight to Eglin." Her gaze penetrated his soul, and Luke experienced a flood of emotion that he hadn't expected. The tall, sandy-haired Marine Captain descended the steps of the boarding ramp swiftly and walked towards the Atlanta terminal without looking back.

When Luke arrived at Eglin Air Force Base, he was lucky enough to get one of the last two rental cars available. He had a choice—a new 1968 Ford Mustang or an older model Chevrolet Corvair. He took the Mustang.

He had to hand it to the Marine Corps, they had timed his discharge just right, and his return to the panhandle was on the most perfect Gulf Coast kind of day. A mere hour-and-a-half drive lay between here and Pemrose Key. His insides fairly quivered with excitement as he walked briskly across the concrete ramp towards the little Mustang. A gentle, warm breeze flowed across the airfield from the Gulf of Mexico and he drank it in, inhaling deeply of the clean, salty air. He would take the beach road home, along Santa Rosa Island, through Mango Junction and on to Pemrose Key.

As the little Mustang topped the bridge to the island and Luke got his first glimpse of the dazzling white sands of Santa Rosa, his heart nearly skipped a beat. This entire route along the Gulf Coast, from Panama City, Florida, to Gulf Shores, Alabama, was called the "Miracle Strip," and rightfully so. Today, especially, God had done his handiwork. The sun shone brightly in a cloud-free, azure sky, and frisky little white-caps dappled the blue-green waters of the Gulf.

This was the place of his heart, the place he loved—the place of his dreams for the past four years and, like a beautiful and seductive woman, he never got her out of his mind. As he lay on his cot at night, she beckoned him. Lying on his belly in a field, covered with mud and holding in his arms the still warm, blood-spattered body of a soldier younger than himself, she had teased him and tempted him. Crouching behind sandbags behind enemy lines, bombs bursting in air, just as the song says, she had played in his mind over and over again, the vision helping drown the deafening sounds, the sparkling waters etched in his memory, her sometimes gentle waves, sometimes tumultuous currents, carrying him through the torments of hell.

He didn't ever want to leave Pemrose Key again. Why had he ever wanted to in the first place? Whatever had possessed him? Youth. Misdirected youth. How foolish he had been. How young and how foolish. When he first left home he had been ready to go. Not so much in anticipation of the military and Vietnam, but more or less as a way out, a way to get out on his own, and to find out what the rest of the world was like. He had been restless; had felt the call of the wild, so to speak, and just like every other twenty year old, he had felt invincible—death couldn't really touch him. It had been time to grow; time to experience life. So he enlisted in the Marines.

Now, four years later, he had lived a lifetime.

Luke belonged to Pemrose Key. Pemrose Key belonged to him. He couldn't wait to see her, the little village that lay just this side of the Alabama state line, nestled in like a tiny, perfect jewel, snug in the Florida panhandle.

Just as the Gulf of Mexico had beckoned him from afar, now Oyster Bay Marina was calling him as he neared Pemrose Key. He knew he should see his parents first, but they weren't expecting him until tomorrow. He was anxious to see them, but a little readjustment period was necessary and a stop by Oyster Bay would give him time to plan his strategy. What he had to tell his father wouldn't be well received.

It wouldn't be long now before Luke could see for himself, once again, his beloved Pemrose Key, and Oyster Bay. Like a homing pigeon with a mind of its own, the sleek Mustang sped along. It was as if he had no control over the direction the rented car took. Through Mango Junction, past old Perky Bittle's peanut stand and the decrepit, now defunct, Seafarer Boat plant. Past intermittently spaced luxury high-rise hotels and condominiums he flew, anxious to get to Oyster Bay, and barely noticing the high-rises that loomed mightily along the road.

Like sentinels the high-rises stood, guarding the beaches, themselves protected by high concrete walls, each wall painted in whatever soft, pastel hue matched each architecturally meticulous concrete and glass structure. Within these concrete walls, lush, semi-tropical landscaping confined itself, carefully manicured and maintained, the walls holding the salty sand at bay, enabling the grass to grow rich and green, and the brilliantly colored tropical flowers to bloom profusely. Opposite the beach and the high-rise hotels, weathered beach houses sit, perched on stilts, their paint peeling from the winds and the sands, their stilted legs thwarting the rising tides of the Gulf, looking as if they could turn and run from approaching hurricanes and storms. Brown grasses and sand spurs cover their sandy yards.

Luke focused his thoughts on Oyster Bay Marina and tried to reconstruct every detail in his mind. As happy as he was to be home, when he thought of Cooper DeLaney and what might have been, disappointment nagged at him. He wondered if Cooper had ever seen Oyster Bay and suddenly, he wished he had described it to her. Something told him she would have understood his feelings about the place. For Luke, it was the heart of Pemrose Key. It was the gathering spot for many of the local residents, as well as for tourists coming by land and by sea, and it was Luke's connection to life on the Gulf of Mexico.

The marina itself is not a marina in the true sense of the word. There is no shipyard or large marina facility, only a few tool sheds that the charter captains maintain, in which are stored small quantities of miscellaneous fishing supplies and yachting gear. The only commercial fishing boats docked at the marina are the charter boats, and their numbers are few.

The old Marina Cafe—half restaurant, half bar and lounge— sits perched on a shady bank beside the tall bridge that crosses over the Intracoastal Waterway and overlooks the twin piers that form the protective U of the docks. The boat slips inside the U contain what really makes Oyster Bay Marina a marina—dazzling white yachts in all lengths and sizes.

As Luke guided the car through the wide gates of Oyster Bay Marina, his heart raced, and for the time being he cast aside his regrets over leaving Cooper DeLaney behind. He was home at last.

2

"*L*uke? Hey! Luke Callaway! Where in the world did you come from?"

Luke spun around from his position on the end of the pier, recognizing the voice at once. Following the direction from which it had come, his eyes quickly scanned the long row of boats docked alongside the pier. There she was, the *Shady Lady* in all her splendor, sparkling white and gleaming under the brilliant afternoon sun of Pemrose Key. She had some age on her, but she was still a beauty.

From his vantage point on the pier, Luke looked down into the cockpit of the *Shady Lady*. A wide grin flashed up at him from a grease-streaked, sun-weathered face. Only head and shoulders were visible above the engine-room hold that encompassed the lean, muscular body of a man fairly slight in stature, but who Luke knew could be as mean as a stick of dynamite and quick as a snake.

"Trotter Blackwell, I thought you were either dead or still in Nam. When did you get back here?" Luke sat on the edge of the dock and lowered himself into the cockpit. Once aboard, he leaned over and extended his hand to the grease encrusted palm that reached up to him from the bowels of the boat.

"Shipped out more'n a year ago. Been back in Pemrose Key 'bout six months now." Trotter picked up a blackened rag from the cockpit floor and wiped his hands, blackening the rag more.

Luke shook his head and laughed. The marina was like home to Trotter. As a kid he'd worked long, hard hours at Oyster Bay, doing odd jobs and handy work for the harbor master and the charter captains, and with his wages, he'd helped his widowed mama.

The Blackwell's had been like Luke's second family up until the time Trotter's daddy died. After that, Francie Blackwell had to do what she could to make ends meet. Luke didn't understand until he was older what it was Trotter's mama had to do to make a living. Trotter never acted like he wanted to know, but Luke felt like he did know. Together, Trotter and his mama managed to get the four younger kids raised. They kept them clothed, fed and in school, with no money for extras, but that wasn't any worse than it was for half the other kids in school.

Trotter looked up at Luke through narrowed eyes, shielding them from the sun with his hand. "Man, I didn't know if I'd ever see you again. It's about time for you to be done, ain't it?"

Luke surveyed the long row of boats in the harbor and stared out across the channel before speaking. He whispered huskily, "I am done. Vietnam is history." With the realization sinking in, he laughed aloud, shook his head and shouted, "I am done. Hey! It feels good to say that. Everything about being home feels good. I haven't even seen the folks yet. I couldn't stay away from this place any longer, though. I had to see her. To find out for myself if she'd changed. I wanted to see if being here at Oyster Bay still felt the same. Know what I mean?"

It was as if they had never drifted apart; as if their friendship hadn't ebbed as their lives had taken different directions. Suddenly the years that had separated them seemed to melt away. They were two young boys again, one rich, one poor, standing on the dock at Oyster Bay with identical hopes and dreams, and the likelihood of anything and everything being a real possibility in their lives. They were going to buy a boat just like the *Shady Lady*, and they were going to sail around the world. They would catch only the fish they needed for nourishment, and they would land at tropical islands, where they would dine on the plumpest crabs and the sweetest tropical fruits. When they returned to Pemrose Key, they would both get rich writing a book about their travels and all their worldly experiences. And they would buy a great shipyard with their money, and build boats forever. They would build beautiful boats. Even now, Luke held on to that part of the dream.

For Luke, there were only good memories here. As a kid, he had worked here with Trotter for a couple of years, summers and after school. Then later, he spent every available minute here. His parents always knew where to look if they couldn't find him.

Trotter placed his palms on each side of the deck of the boat and hoisted himself up to the cockpit level. He dragged the rest of his body to the surface with his hands and swung his lower torso up and out of the hole that enveloped him.

"My God!" Luke stared in horror, stricken by what he saw. One leg of Trotter's trousers was gathered at the bottom and tied with a heavy elastic band. It dangled loosely below the knee of Trotter's leg, or what used to be a leg.

"That's why I'm not still in the Navy." Trotter slapped his thigh matter-of-factly. "Mine got me. Reckon I'm a heck of a lot luckier than most of 'em. They got three of our river boats at once. It was some mess. You never seen anything like it."

Luke tried not to stare.

"Yeah, I guess you've seen worse. Hey, how 'bout going for a cruise on the *Shady Lady* with me?" Trotter raised himself to a standing position with his good leg and a single crutch that had been laying in a corner of the cockpit.

Luke wondered how he had missed seeing the crutch.

Dangling a red and white buoy-shaped key chain from his fingertips, Trotter boasted, "I think I got her where she'll purr for me now."

Pulling himself together, but conspicuously ignoring Trotter's leg, Luke forced a smile and tried to sound natural. "What about old Captain Jack, he actually letting you take her out by yourself now that you're supposed to be all grown up?"

"Cap'n Jack ain't got nothing to say about this anymore. Nowadays, the *Shady Lady* belongs to one mean ol' ex-Navy, peg-leg, son-of-a-sailor named Trotter Blackwell. I may not be building boats like we always said we'd do—that's up to you, Luke, but I'm finally doing what my daddy was teaching me to do before he died."

Luke remembered. Henry Blackwell had wanted Trotter to be more than just a fisherman like himself. Henry fished all his life and knew all there was to know about fishing, but he didn't want his son to have to spend the rest of his life like him, sweating blood for somebody else, barely able to make ends meet. Henry vowed to see to it that Trotter would be captain of his own boat, but he died before that promise was fulfilled.

"I never thought I'd see the day, Trotter. How'd you ever get the old Captain to part with her?" Not waiting for an answer, Luke leaned over the port side of the *Shady Lady*, eye-balling her from stem to stern, appraising her full forty-six foot length. Her newly applied paint gleamed. She had clean, sleek lines and was the largest of the charter vessels in the marina. She had seen many years of service, but she had served Captain Jack well, and in return he had given her plenty of tender, loving care.

During their youth, Luke and Trotter had often crewed aboard the *Shady Lady*, and she was as much a part of their childhood experiences as anything in Pemrose Key.

"She looks good. She looks real good, Trotter. Be glad when I can get me one back on the water again." Luke didn't tell Trotter that it might be some time before he could afford to do that. "Right now, how about that cruise you promised me?" He longed to see Pemrose Key from the water.

After strapping on what looked to be little more than a stick with a tennis shoe attached at the bottom, Trotter climbed the ladder to the bridge with amazing dexterity. His arms were strong and he used them with the acquired skill of someone who might have been crippled all his life. After a few minutes of running the exhaust fan, he turned the key of the starboard engine.

Luke looked up from the cockpit, watching Trotter as he cocked his head to one side. He knew that even over the roar of the engines, Trotter's ears were so attuned to the heartbeat of the *Shady Lady* he perceived every uneven inflection she might make—every little cough and sputter.

Satisfied, Trotter turned the key on the port side and repeated his actions, head cocking the other way. He turned and looked down at Luke, grinning from ear-to-ear and giving him the thumbs-up.

As Luke ascended the ladder to the bridge, he was flooded with memories of the past and everything felt familiar, and Vietnam was a place that had never existed.

Trotter maneuvered the *Shady Lady* gingerly out of her slip, guiding her easily past the other charter boats and yachts, into the channel of the Intracoastal.

Pemrose Key banks one side of the Intracoastal and an undeveloped barrier peninsula the other. This peninsula is little more than a thin sliver of silvery white sand less than a quarter of a mile wide, stretching out for at least five miles parallel to the channel. That narrow ribbon of sand holds the Gulf at bay, creating a safe harbor for the big boats at Oyster Bay Marina.

The span of the channel runs narrow at this point, and the *Shady Lady* idled through impatiently, her powerful engines moaning and straining to be released as a horse might strain at his tether. As she approached the open waters of Oyster Bay, Trotter pushed her throttles forward and her bow gracefully rose into the air.

Luke felt the stiff salt air in his face, and he couldn't breathe deeply enough. He wanted to take it all in at once—the sun, the sand, the beautiful day. He wanted to be consumed by it, to wrap himself in it for eternity, and to glide smoothly across the clear, blue waters of Oyster Bay and the Gulf of Mexico forever, and to forget about Vietnam—forever.

Trotter motioned for Luke to take over the helm while he visited the head below. No words had to be spoken between them. Even though the years had separated them, the bond they shared remained strong. They had always been there for each other, except for Luke's college years—and Vietnam.

Luke slid into position and wrapped his hands around the cool stainless steel, squeezing his fingers tight against the wheel. It felt good to be at the helm again, the sun and the wind in his face, and the *Shady Lady* graciously accepting his guidance, obeying his every command with her movements.

He heard the opening and closing of the cabin door below and turned to see Trotter hoisting himself up the ladder to the bridge.

"Hey, Luke," Trotter hollered up to him. "Head for Mamie's Place."

Before Trotter got all the way up the ladder, Luke rotated the wheel only slightly. The water in the bay was as smooth as silk and effortlessly, the *Shady Lady* cut through it, her bow turning and pointing in the direction of the north shore of the bay, towards Pirate's Cove.

"How's the fishing business, Trotter? Get a lot of customers?" Luke raised his voice over the wail of the engines.

"Not bad, right now. Got some regulars that come around. Winter was pretty rough. Went out on the *Sea Horse* a couple of times, pullin' the nets. When things got real tough a few of us hardsalts worked the oyster beds for Mulligan's Seafood. Diving for oysters can be hell in the dead of winter. Sure makes a pants-pisser in a wetsuit a lucky son-of-a-gun. It ain't no picnic, but it helps pay the bills when there's nothing else. I ain't letting no grass grow under my feet, so to speak." Trotter grinned and rubbed the stump of his missing leg.

"Made the down payment on the *Lady* with my government pension here. Use this peg most of the time, except when I'm diving. I got to get the Lady paid for before I can hibernate for the winter or enjoy being disabled."

"I hate it about your leg, Trot. Nobody told me. I know you won't stand for any pity, and I won't bring it up again after this, but I just want you to know up front how I feel. I saw too much of that over there. I wanted to puke when I saw what they'd done to you. I wanted to go back and kill the SOB's, again and again. At the same time, I know I couldn't have stood being over there any longer. I served extra time. Who the hell knows why? I don't even know— made sense at the time, but if they hadn't let me out when they did, they would have had to ship me home in a straight-jacket." Luke's knuckles were white as he clutched the wheel. He stared straight ahead, masking his emotions.

"Yeah, I know what you mean." Trotter sat on the bench beside Luke. He leaned over and slapped him on the shoulder. "Hey, look, let's don't think about Nam anymore. We don't need to. We're in Pemrose Key, man, and we ain't going back. Look, there's Mamie's Place just ahead. Pull her in Skip Traylor's slip. I hear he's down in Mexico with the *Mari Jane Too*."

As they approached Pirate's Cove, Luke pulled back on the throttles and slowed the *Shady Lady* to idle speed. There was no wind, and he neatly eased her in between the finger piers at Skip Traylor's slip.

3

amie's Place sits protected at the mouth of Pirate's Cove, beside a narrow channel that feeds into the heart of the cove from the bay. The restaurant is a low-slung building of ancient, weathered-gray wood and a tin roof reddened with rust. Across the rear of the restaurant is a long screened porch that opens onto a dilapidated pier. The pier protrudes in a crooked line out into the bay and contains no more than six actual boat slips.

Inside Mamie's Place, picnic tables line the screened wall, and the sounds of music and laughter can always be heard drifting across the bay from within. In the winter, grease-encrusted, sliding glass windows can be pulled in front of the screens to block the chill of the wind, but you can still hear the music and frequently, Mamie's hearty, good natured laughter bubbling around the bay, mingling harmoniously with the lyrical sounds.

Just beyond Mamie's Place, at the water's edge, stands a row of ramshackle fishing cottages. Mamie owns these, too, and for a few dollars, or most of the time just for a share of their catch, she rents the shanties to some of the diehard, backwater fishermen who just want to get away with the guys—maybe get away from the little woman, drink a lot of beer, and eat a good meal at Mamie's Place.

Luke and Trotter secured their lines to the nearest pilings. Stepping around the missing boards of the skeletal pier, they proceeded to the front entrance of Mamie's Place, where a sign, hanging on the wooden panel across the middle of the screened door, proclaimed in crudely painted letters: NO FIREARMS ALLOWED INSIDE.

Mamie saw them coming and rushed to open the door, gushing joyously at their unexpected arrival, her large wooden spoon in hand, as usual.

"Lord, have mercy, looky what the cat done drug in my place today; both of you, and on the same day. I've surely got some good luck a'coming to me. Children, sit yourselves down right here and Mamie's gonna' feed you up real good. You both look a little undernourished. Billy Jack, bring these boys a beer, right away!" In her usual fashion, Mamie smacked the bowl of her spoon smartly against the palm of her hand, several times, a habit she had maintained ever since she opened Mamie's Place more than a dozen years ago. She was constantly patrolling the heavily laden picnic tables. Back and forth she would pace across the wooden floors, going from table to table, checking on the service, making sure her customers were happy and well fed. She would smack that long handled wooden spoon against her palm incessantly, much as a drill sergeant might smack a swagger stick for effect while inspecting his troops. Mamie was one of the most prosperous women in Pemrose Key, or so rumor had it. The restaurant had belonged to Scranton Peabody before he went into the weapons parts manufacturing business. Mamie had been his cook. As other business opportunities presented themselves, he began to lose interest in Peabody's Pub as it was known back then.

Mamie managed to get a loan—quite a feat for a black woman in the 1950's, or for any single woman, for that matter. She was proud of her business and the success she'd had with it. Gradually, she began to buy up available land around Pirate's Cove, until finally she owned a pretty sizable chunk of it. Her educational opportunities had not been the most advantageous, but she could read and she was smart, and her business expertise far outshone that of most of the other black or white women of Pemrose Key. Although she would never reveal where she had gotten her grubstake, she would sometimes brag that she had paid every penny back in five years, and with interest, too!

Mamie was a robust, ageless, black woman with an Aunt Jemima image that she herself propagated. Everybody loved Aunt Jemima, and image was important, she often stated; it was good for business. And plenty of business she had. Her patrons were widely diversified, from dressed up snowbird tourists to scudsy looking, sweat-stenched fishermen just off the boats. She knew how to handle them all and exactly who to sit where to keep everybody happy. Mamie's Place was renowned for having some of the freshest, tastiest seafood on the Gulf Coast.

When Luke was a kid Mamie always told him that the secret for everything she fixed was that it was all served up with a big, heaping helping of love, and if you ate everything on your plate you'd grow up to have a heart full of love and lots and lots of friends.

In spite of Luke's intelligence and good judgment, there were times when he rather suspected there might have been some truth to it. He had certainly eaten his share of Mamie's cooking in his lifetime, and numerous honors had been bestowed upon him by his classmates in school.

Many of the white kids around Pemrose Key had grown up knowing Mamie. Before she cooked for Peabody's Pub she used to watch folk's kids while she did their ironing. Nobody minded that she'd bring along her little boy, Toby, to play with the white kids while she ironed. Toby got on great with all of them and probably because of the self-respect Mamie had for herself, and in spite of there being racial turmoil in other parts of the deep south, Pemrose Key seemed colorblind and the fact that Toby was "colored'" was not mentioned, not noticed and no one cared. Nobody would've wanted to cross Mamie, anyway. She just had a way with people, young and old alike, black, white or purple, no matter. Mamie was Mamie, and everybody loved her.

Billy Jack reappeared with two frosty mugs brimming with the frothy-topped, golden draft that Mamie kept in large kegs in a back room.

"Okay, boys, drink up. You both look a bit thirsty," Mamie boomed in her loud, jovial voice, taking the mugs from Billy Jack and sitting them on the table in front of Luke and Trotter. "Mamie's going to bring y'all something good to eat while you just sit here and relax. Lucas Callaway, when did you get back from Vietnam? I know about this old renegade here," she placed her large palm on Trotter's shoulder and rubbed it affectionately, "but you must've just got back or Mamie would've heard about it by now."

"I did just get back, Mamie. I haven't even been home yet. Flew into Eglin this morning and stopped over at Oyster Bay, where I ran into this character here." Luke raised his mug to Trotter. "How could I refuse a cruise on the *Shady Lady*, especially with the opportunity of visiting this fine establishment of yours. Mamie, I gotta' tell you, I missed a lot of places around here while I was away, but yours was right up there on the top of the list. I've been thinking about a bowl of your seafood gumbo ever since I left Chicago this morning."

"Chicago! Is that as far as you missed me and my gumbo? Lord child, that's no good. You gonna' have to do better than that if you want to keep old Mamie happy."

"Mamie, I used to describe your gumbo to the mess sergeant. I told him that if I could ever get your secret recipe and he could finally learn how to cook, we could get rich selling it on the side over there. I said if we ever got out of that hell-hole he ought to come down to Pemrose Key and I'd take him to Mamie's Place so he could find out what good eating was all about."

Mamie beamed. "I sure am glad to have both my boys back safe and sound." She stood at the end of the table and rubbed both of their shoulders now, one with each palm, her wooden spoon momentarily parked in the pocket of her voluminous white apron. "Y'all going to have to come around a lot now, you hear, so old Mamie can keep up with you and make sure you're not getting into no scraps or nothing. You tell your mama and daddy old Mamie's been missing 'em, Lucas. Tell 'em to come on over here real soon and I'll fry your daddy up a big ol' batch of that fresh mullet he likes so much."

"I'll do that, Mamie. I know they'd like to see you, too. How's Toby these days? Army drafted him, right?"

"I don't want to talk about that rascal." A scowl darkened Mamie's face, replacing the smile that was usually present. "Toby got himself a medical discharge about a year ago. Back trouble he says. Hmpfh! Some back trouble. Only back trouble that boy's got is from laying around on his worthless backside too much. I can't never get him to come over here and help me and make an honest living like he's supposed to. He's the one ought to be thinking about taking care of his old Ma'm in her aging years, and here I don't do nothing but spend my hard earned money getting him out of trouble. He ain't done nothing but hang around with that shiftless bunch what docks their boats here since he got back. Reckon I'll go to my grave without ever seeing him grow up and make something of himself." In spite of not wanting to talk about it, Mamie had worked herself into an awful fret over Toby and was tapping her spoon rapidly against her palm now.

"Hey, Mamie, what about some of that gumbo Luke was talking about? Sure would be good right about now." Trotter tried to ease Mamie's thoughts over onto another subject.

In a quick turn, Mamie brought her mind back around to the fact that she was a business woman and had a restaurant to run. She pushed her shoulders back and took a deep breath, puffing her large breasts out even farther. She ceased the tapping of the spoon and placed it in her right pocket and with both hands, smoothed the folds of her apron. A wide grin reappeared on her face, white teeth standing out against her smooth, brown-sugar complexion, and she looked like Mamie once again.

"All right, honey, it's on its way. I did promise you Mamie was gonna' take care of you before I went off on my tangent. Just don't get me riled up over Toby no more. That's why it's best I just don't have nothing to say about him. Period!" She turned on her heels, very militarily and walked briskly back towards the kitchen.

"What's she talking about, Trotter? What's happened to Toby? Is he okay?" Luke huddled over his beer, leaning across the table so Trotter could hear him above the forlorn sounds of a hillbilly singer wailing a slow country tune on the jukebox. Neither of them paid any attention to the couple entwined as one and barely shuffling their feet in a far corner of the room designated as "the dance floor."

"Hell, he's got himself mixed up with Skipper Traylor and some of his thugs. Some say they're running dope. I think there's more to it than that. If Toby doesn't watch it he's going to get himself in trouble. Those guys are bad. Mamie can't do nothing with him. Said she won't dole out anymore money to him unless he earns it. You know how he is, I expect he thinks he's pretty hot stuff running with those sleazeballs. Can't nobody tell him nothing and I sure as hell ain't trying, much as I'd like to help Mamie."

"Where's Toby now...does anybody know?"

"I suppose he went down to Mexico with Skip. Like I said, he's in pretty thick with them."

Mamie breezed across the floor, her long skirt and apron swirling around her ankles. She carried a huge tray filled with her specialties. Puny little Billy Jack trotted along behind her, carrying two more frosted mugs, brew sloshing over the rims as he ran to keep up with her.

"Come on, Billy Jack, let's get these boys fed." Mamie, ever the business woman now, Toby packed neatly away in the crevices of her mind, was going about the business of feeding the townsfolk of Pemrose Key, and for all outward appearances, gave not a thought to anything else.

Luke couldn't shake from his mind the anguish he had witnessed on Mamie's face. Toby must really be pulling some stuff for Mamie to get this upset.

"Give my boys something good, now. Put those beers down, Billy Jack, and give me a hand. Here, take this tray," Mamie commanded in her clamorous voice.

Billy Jack nearly fell to his knees under the weight of the heavy tray. Mamie unloaded two steaming bowls of her famous gumbo and placed them before Luke and Trotter. The rich, dark concoction was served over a heaping scoop of fluffy, white rice. The stew was thick with okra, tomatoes and onions, and chocked full of the regional fruits of the sea: tender pink shrimp, sweet white crab meat and plump, juicy, oysters. The aroma of filé powder, the sassafras seasoning that was the ingredient that distinguished real filé gumbo from watery, soupy impostors, permeated their nostrils.

"I think I've died and gone to heaven, Mamie." Luke realized he had not eaten all day. He had been too busy and too smitten by Cooper to take time to eat on the flight down from Chicago and there had been no food service on the flight from Atlanta. He watched as Mamie finished unloading more mouth-watering morsels from the tray. She placed a heaping basket of crispy, fried crab claws on the table between them, along with a bowl of her spicy, horseradish-laced cocktail sauce for dipping, a platter of beer-batter cornmeal hush puppies, and an empty paper plate upon which to place the crab claw stems. Next came two large wedges of tangy Key lime pie.

"Well, go ahead and dive in, and I'll just leave you boys alone for now. Eat and enjoy." Mamie shuffled away this time, in no hurry now that her boys had been fed.

Luke held a large soup spoon in his hand and was poised to attack when an irritating, vaguely familiar, high-pitched voice confronted him.

"Well, if it isn't Lucas Callaway come back from the tropics. Hey Lukey, haven't seen you in a whole bunch of years." A tall girl with close-set eyes and a hawk-like nose stood before their table. Her features were homely, but she was well-built and wore expensive looking clothes.

"Don't you remember me, Luke Callaway?"

Trotter groaned.

Ignoring him, the girl flashed a barracuda-like, toothsome smile at Luke that triggered recognition. Somewhere between yesterday and tomorrow, Edna Sinclair had been filed away in the past, and without consciously thinking about it, that was where he once hoped she would stay.

"It's me, Edna Sinclair. Don't you remember? It has been a long time—ever since you went off to college in Mobile and left little old me behind. Next thing I heard, you were trotting off to Parris Island. Now here you are back home again, and you don't even recognize me. Guess I do look a little different these days. It is amazing how money and success can bring changes into people's lives." She examined her well-manicured nails and fingered the diamond rosette she wore on her hand, turning it advantageously to the light so that bright fragments of color flickered briefly across Luke's face. "Don't you agree, Luke? After all, look at Trotter here, doesn't he look successful?"

"Ouch, Witch!" Trotter flipped her a bird and turned back to his food.

"It has been a few years, Edna." Luke spoke cautiously, his voice a monotone. He didn't want to do or say anything she might misconstrue, remembering all too well how she had latched on to him his last two years in high school, making his life miserable. One day she just appeared at his side. She had developed a maniacal crush on him and took it upon herself to declare Lucas Callaway her steady boyfriend, in spite of the fact that he took other girls out and not her. She managed to make his life miserable, nonetheless, by persistently following him around wherever he went. He couldn't shake her. She was everywhere he turned, lurking at his locker, tagging along behind him at school dances, even when he was with a date. She pursued him doggedly. At first his buddies got a kick out of it. They rode him unmercifully about her. Once they even sneaked her into the dugout during a baseball game and hooted hysterically when he discovered she was sitting next to him. Later, they began to tire of her always being around, and then they really gave her a hard time. Frequently they were cruel, and many times she would run away in tears. Luke didn't encourage Edna's advances, and he didn't encourage his buddies' goading her. He just tried to ignore her, but she never relented. She was there till the day Luke graduated. She was just a kid, but she was goofy and persistent—a terrible combination.

On Luke's graduation day, Edna relinquished her undying love for him. She wouldn't be seeing him every day and she seemed resigned to the fact that there was obviously no hope that he would ever have the slightest bit of interest in her. She walked up to him before his graduation ceremony and with tears streaming down her cheeks, silently handed him a white envelope that appeared to be a graduation card. Luke even felt a momentary pang of compassion for her. She turned and ran away before he could say anything. That was the last he ever saw of Edna Sinclair...until this day.

"It's such a surprise running in to you, Luke. Actually, I'm here to see Mamie. We have some business to discuss. Very important business."

Mamie appeared at Edna's back. Her eyebrows formed a heavy, unbroken line above her eyes, and her lips were pursed in a severe pout. Her voice was low, and surprisingly for Mamie, somewhat threatening when she spoke over Edna's shoulder. "No ma'am, we surely do not have any business to discuss, Mizz Sinclair." Mamie fairly hissed the words. "Now, I ain't never had to throw too many folk out of this restaurant, but if you don't march yourself right back out that door, I aim to do just that, and honey, I'm a lot bigger'n you are. It grieves me to have to talk to you this way, but I done told you at least a dozen times that I ain't selling my place to you or your friends, whoever they might be. You might as well accept that and go on about your business. I ain't selling my land, I ain't selling my place, and I ain't going to listen no more to what you have to say. So just get on with you, now!"

Mamie turned and trod heavily to the door. She didn't open it, but she stood beside it with her arms folded across her bosom and stared silently at Edna.

Edna glanced nervously at Mamie. "I guess that old nigger woman thinks she's gotten the best of me. Ever since that Martin Luther King fella' got shot a few weeks ago, you can't reason with none of them! They are all getting uppity nowadays." Edna's obnoxious high-pitched voice was two octaves higher now, and twice as obnoxious. The care she had taken in enunciating her words and using proper grammar vanished, and in her agitation her backwater dialect surfaced. Suddenly, she changed her tactics in an obvious effort to rally support from Luke. "Maybe you can do something with her, Luke, honey. We're just trying to make her rich. You know I'm in real estate now, and I have a very prestigious client who would like to buy all Mamie's land at Pirate's Cove and make some wonderful improvements. He's willing to give her fair market value and everything. It can't do nothing but help Pemrose Key in the long run."

Trotter intervened, "Hey, Edna, Mamie's waiting for you, and that big wooden spoon of hers she's twirling around might near looks like a paddle."

"I'm on Mamie's side, Edna. It's her land, and her right not to sell if she doesn't want to. Like Trotter said, Mamie's waiting for you, and I wouldn't hold her up if I were you." Luke picked up his spoon and began eating slowly and deliberately, dismissing Edna once and for all.

"Kiss my precious ass, Luke Callaway!" Edna fairly shrieked, "Ain't you the high falootin' one. Like your daddy hasn't gotten rich or nothing building all those swanky high rises down at the beach. Guess you Callaways don't think anybody else ought to have anything around here. Damn you, *Mister* Callaway. I'm leaving all right, but it ain't because Mamie Washington's making me. I just have to be somewhere real soon, that's all. She'll sell, you just wait and see." Edna trying to depart with dignity was more comical than dignified. With her nose high in the air, her high heels clicking noisily across the wooden floor, she hastily retreated. She threw open the screened door with an exaggerated flourish and slammed it hard behind her.

Luke looked first at Mamie, then at Trotter, and they all three burst out laughing.

"Kiss mah PRECIOUS ass!" Trotter mimicked, producing a shriek every bit as shrill as Edna's. "Lord, that woman's ass ain't precious, and don't we all know it." Trotter hooted even louder.

Mamie covered her mouth with her hand, but her shoulders shook with mirth.

Luke had never laughed at Edna in high school as his friends had, but this time she deserved it, and he felt no qualms about it. She was white trash to the core, and no amount of money or success could alter that fact.

Luke and Trotter polished off the last crumb of hushpuppies and all that was left was a paper plate piled high with crab claw shells.

"Mamie, that was the best meal I've had in years. I'll be back soon. Don't let Edna talk you into selling this place unless you're sure you want to. I don't know what we'd do if we couldn't get any more of your good cooking. Now that I'm home I'm looking forward to a lot of it." Luke put his arm around Mamie's shoulder and squeezed it, with his other hand he stuffed some bills in her pocket. He cut her off as she opened her mouth to object. "Now don't you say a word. I know you don't need it, but as much as we ate I'm not going to let you put this on the house. So hush!"

"Luke Callaway, you're as bad as your daddy. Can't do nothing for you. Shame on you! Get on out of here, both of you. Your mama and daddy will have my head, Luke, when they find out you came to see me first." Mamie looked pleased that he had.

It was six o'clock and still light when Trotter docked the *Shady Lady* back at Oyster Bay Marina.

After promising to let Trotter know what he was up to as soon as he got settled in, Luke drove slowly along the beach road. He wasn't excited about what loomed ahead. He knew what he must tell his father. He glanced at the high-rises that blocked his view of the beach. He didn't like the structures, but he was used to them. It seemed they had been here forever, and he had actually been part of the construction of most of these swanky places when, at the age of sixteen, he went to work for Callaway Construction. Callaway Construction being one Ryan Callaway, Luke's father.

A few people raised a stink in the beginning about their beaches being taken over by the high-rises, but eventually the stink died down, and true to human nature, greed won out. There were too many poor people in Pemrose Key who welcomed the tourist trade and hoped they would profit by it. The problem was, the poor people had remained poor, and only the already affluent or middle-class had seen much monetary gain. Even the fishermen lost out to the slick, entrepreneurial fish market owners. The fishermen did all the work, but with the abundance of fish in the waters of the Gulf, coupled with the prolific competition in the fishing business and the expert price dickering skills of the fish mongers, most of the old-time fishermen barely eked out a living. It was a hard life, but it was a life many of them either wouldn't or couldn't have traded. It was a way of life that you didn't change. If you were born into it, you lived it, the way Trotter did. A fisherman fished, and that's the way it was.

And the rich got richer, including the Callaways. Specifically Ryan and Meg Callaway. Luke would have it made if he went back to work for his dad, but he had other plans. He had a dream he believed in and goals he wanted to accomplish on his own. He wasn't afraid of hard work. He was used to it. Many privileges had come his way because of his father's wealth, but Luke had always worked hard. That was an integral part of the Callaway's being, and something that came as natural to Luke as breathing. His father prided himself on the fact that he had instilled this in his son. Perhaps he had, but even in childhood, Luke could no more sit still than he could quiet his passion for the Gulf and Pemrose Key.

As Luke approached the long drive that led to his parent's home, he saw that the great wrought iron gates were swung open, as always, welcoming all who chose to enter the domain of the Callaway's and partake of their hospitality.

Luke guided the rental car between the brick columns that flanked the entrance of The Magnolias. His parent's estate was named in honor of the broad-leafed trees that yielded large, fragrant, creamy-white blossoms and grew profusely throughout the south. The trees lined each side of the crushed shell driveway that led to a magnificent antebellum style home. Before him, Luke could see the grand columns that graced the front veranda. The Magnolias sat on the bank of a broad slough that opened to an expansive section of Pemrose Bay. The front and rear of the house were identical, but on either side of the rear veranda, gigantic oak trees dripping with gray Spanish moss framed an unimpeded view of the scenic bay.

As Luke approached the house, his emotions ran the gamut—excitement, nervousness, anticipation, and dread. He wanted to see his parents. He had missed them, but he knew they wouldn't be pleased with what he had to tell them. He pulled the car to a halt in front of the wide front steps and sat for a moment, gathering his thoughts.

4

Meg Callaway opened the front door and peered out at the unfamiliar car parked in front of her house. Luke saw her at the same moment she realized who the stranger was in her driveway. She was a beautiful woman. She had maintained a youthful figure even after nearly thirty years of marriage. Sun-streaked hair framed soft, blue eyes and a kind face that was creased only by faint age lines. She was an active tennis and golf enthusiast, and her skin glowed with a year-round tan. Her eyes lit up when she saw her only son—home, and alive and well.

"Luke, oh Luke, you're home. Thank God you're home." She rushed to embrace him. Tears glistened in her eyes as she looked up at her handsome son. A prayer had been answered. "And you're okay. I would never believe it for sure until I could see you for myself."

"It's good to be home, Mom. You don't know how I've missed this place. Everything looks the way I remembered it, and I've thought about it every day for the last four years of my life." Luke looked over her shoulder as he returned her embrace, taking in every square inch of the magnificent home and the shady, St. Augustine-covered lawn that spread itself neatly beneath the moss-laden trees of The Magnolias. Memories of his childhood flickered through his mind. As a boy he had chased fireflies that twinkled beneath the darkness of these trees at twilight, and on a hot summer day, he would lay in the cool, thick grass, looking skyward, viewing the trees and the moss from a child's perspective, creating fantasy images from shapes of the cottony white clouds that drifted above grotesquely gnarled and wind-weathered tree limbs. It all came back to him—the skiing parties and cookouts for his friends down by the water; the cotillion parties, when all the doors of The Magnolias were flung open to the verandas. On a still summer evening, the music and the laughter of teenage boys and girls could be heard lilting across the moonlit grounds, the boys in coats and ties, trying to mind their manners and behave like perfect gentlemen, so the young ladies in their fancy, ruffled dresses might be impressed. Those days were gone, but The Magnolias still stood in splendor, and the memories would always be there in his mind and in his heart—along with his memories of Vietnam.

"Your father's not home yet, Luke. We didn't expect you this soon. When you called from San Francisco yesterday, you said you wouldn't be here until tomorrow. Your father is going to be so excited to see you. Oh, Honey! I just can't believe you're really here. It's like a dream come true, and all my prayers have been answered."

They walked into the house arm-in-arm. Inside, every elegant appointment was meticulously in place, just as Luke remembered. In the foyer, freshly cut gardenias filled an ancient blue and gold oriental bowl that sat atop an antique French console. The perfumed fragrance of the flowers greeted him and mingled nicely with the lemon-scented furniture polish that had always been used in caring for the many cherished antiques that adorned the rooms of The Magnolias. Elaborate millwork and deep moldings and trim embellished the high ceilings and doorways, and the highly polished hardwood floors gleamed spotlessly.

In the expansive kitchen, dinner simmered on the stove. It was dusk out now. Through tall French doors that graced the rear wall of the kitchen, the sky glowed pink and gold, and all was calm on the horizon of the bay. Serenity...to Luke, this place was perfect bliss and the epitome of serenity.

"Are you starving, Luke? I know you must be. Why don't you let me fix you a plate?"

"I'm not hungry, Mom. I just ate, over at Mamie's Place. I stopped by Oyster Bay on the way home and ran into Trotter. As it turned out, we grabbed a bite at Mamie's. I hope your feelings aren't hurt, but I needed a little time before I saw Dad."

Meg silently set two wine glasses on the table. She pulled a chilled bottle of white wine from the refrigerator and filled the two glasses. She sipped from one and handed Luke the other, then she sat down at the big oak table across from him and folded her hands before her. Still, she did not speak.

"Mom, I may as well get this out in the open. I don't want to go back to work for Callaway Construction, and I don't want to go back to school and get my Engineering degree. I got my undergraduate degree; did the ROTC thing; did the Marine Corp., made Captain and survived Vietnam. I'm ready, now, to live my life my way."

Meg waited.

"There are other things I want to do. I'm lucky to even be back here. A lot has happened. Anyway, I've got this life that's been spared, it's the only life I've got. I came out ahead, and I don't want to spend my life doing something I don't want to do. I know you understand, but I'm not sure Dad will. I'm glad to have this chance to talk to you first."

Meg looked at him intently, her blue eyes brimming with the love of a mother. It was evident in her face that this child of hers, this man-child, could do no wrong in her eyes. "Your father will understand, Luke. He won't like it or agree with it, but he will understand." She reached across the table and gave his hand a squeeze. "You see, once upon a time when your father was a young man, he was very much like you, but his father, your Grandfather Callaway, he wasn't anything like the two of you. He wasn't the outdoors type at all. He was a good man, a humble man, and a hard worker. You probably don't remember too much about him, you were very young when he died. He was an accountant. He worked independently for large companies keeping their records and managing their books. He made a good living at it, and he provided a comfortable home for his family." She looked around the room and gestured with her hand. "It wasn't The Magnolias, and I say this not pretentiously, Luke, you know that, but merely to serve as an illustration in point. Well, he wanted your father to study accounting and join him in his business. Your father was good with numbers, too, but he refused. He said he would suffocate having to work indoors behind a desk. Grandfather Callaway thought he knew what was best for your dad, because he loved him. A huge disagreement ensued. One trait they did have in common was their stubbornness, and many years of heartache and estrangement followed that disagreement."

Luke waited for his mother to continue.

"His father had planned it for years, and his son would have a secure future. Excellent accounts had been established through his years of painstaking diligence, and father and son could work together. When his father retired, Ryan would take over the business. It was the perfect plan. He magnanimously offered this gift to his son, and fully expected his grateful appreciation in return. Remarkably, little did he know about this son of his. He had worked with his nose to the grindstone for so many years to get to this point, he failed to recognize the boy who rose up against him in defiance of the structured path that had been mapped out for his emerging journey through life.

"You know what a rugged outdoorsman your father is. Could you really see big, brawny, Ryan Callaway stifled in a tiny office with no windows, a stack of ledger books balanced on his knees?" Meg took a sip of her wine.

Luke smiled at this image of his father.

"Well, neither could your dad," Meg continued, "so he defied his father, got himself a job on a construction crew in New Orleans and the rest is history. Oh, except for one thing, in Grandfather Callaway's anger and disappointment, he lashed out at your father. He told him he would never amount to anything. He said Ryan was passing up a fantastic opportunity, and for such stupidity he would disown him." Meg contemplatively ran the tip of her index finger around the rim of her wine glass until it sang.

She took another sip of wine and continued her story. "Lawrence Callaway was crushed, and Ryan Callaway was angry. Neither understood the other, and they didn't speak for twelve years. During that time your father had something to prove. He was determined he was going to make his father proud. He would show him that he wasn't stupid. Opportunities presented themselves, and Callaway Construction was born. Your dad worked very, very hard, Luke. You know that. Harder than he would've ever had to work for his father. That's why The Magnolias and Callaway Construction mean so much to him. They are living proof of what he has done with his own two hands, in spite of his father's warnings and observations. He surpassed his father's dreams for himself, and proved his father's predictions wrong.

"In time they buried the past, but it was almost too late. Many good years had been lost. The point is, Luke, your father does want you to come in with him. He wants to give you so much. Callaway Construction is a very successful business, and it can be yours if you want it. He feels very strongly about this, but I don't think history will repeat itself. I think he will accept what you want to do since he knows the consequences of a father trying to live his son's life for him. I'm not saying he will accept it readily, but in time I think he will reconcile himself to it."

Meg pushed her chair back and stood, looking at her son, "You look tired, sweetheart. Here you are just home from the war, and already you're worrying about what you're going to do with the rest of your life."

The side entry door opened and closed loudly, and Ryan Callaway made his presence known. His deep, gravelly voice could be heard clearly in the kitchen, booming from the little anteroom. "I'm home, Mrs. Callaway. That supper sure smells good...I'm starving. Who's car is that out front?"

Luke looked at Meg, then took an exaggeratedly deep breath and mimed a look of panic. She laughed at his antics, then walked across the kitchen and opened the door to the utility room from which Ryan would soon appear.

They heard the thud of his boots drop against the linoleum floor as he removed them, and then, a moment later, his hulking frame filled the doorway. His shock of yellow hair was more white than yellow—whiter than when Luke had last seen him.

When Ryan saw Luke he just stood there for a moment, apparently trying to come to grips with his emotions.

"Dad...how've you been?" Luke grinned at his father's immobility. He walked across the room to his father and extended his hand.

Ryan ignored it. Instead, he gripped Luke's broad shoulders with his coarse hands and pulled him close in an affectionate bear hug, and Luke responded. They had always been close, but never very expressive of their love and affection for each other. It was unspoken and understood between them. Now, neither wanted the other to see what was in his face.

Meg was laughing, but tears streamed down her cheeks as she stood aside and watched her two burly men embrace each other.

"My God, it's good to have you home, boy!" Ryan resounded. He was in control now. He backed away from Luke, his hands still braced on Luke's shoulders. "You sure as hell threw me, I thought you weren't coming home until tomorrow. Let me look at you, I guess you're a little worse for the wear, but it won't take long to get you fattened back up. At least you're still in one piece."

"Come on in you two and sit down." Meg put an arm around both their waists and herded them in the direction of the table. "I think we have a lot to talk about, if Luke is up to it. I know you must be tired, Luke. Just tell us when you've had enough. Your old room is ready for you, just like you left it. Maria put fresh towels out and clean linens on the bed. She was nearly as excited as we were when we told her you were coming home." Turning to her husband, "He's seen Trotter, Ryan."

"Tell us how you've been, son. I know it hasn't been any picnic. We've seen Trotter a few times since he got out of the hospital and back to Pemrose Key." Ryan opened the cupboard and took down a bottle of sour mash. He turned to Luke. "You kind of glossed over things when we met you out in California last year. You know your mother and I could hardly stand it when you went back for that second tour of duty. We figured you had your reasons, though, and we had to respect that. We knew it was too good to be true when you didn't have to go to Vietnam your first two years in. We should've known with all that top-secret stuff you were involved in they'd be using you over there sooner or later. I know you didn't want your mother to worry, but the news on TV hasn't exactly pulled any punches."

Ryan poured two glasses half full of the whiskey and dropped three ice cubes in each. Taking a seat at the table, he pushed one of the glasses towards Luke, then took a long swig from his own glass.

"I wasn't particularly excited about going back over, either. Without going into any detail, I can tell you they had me pretty qualified for the job I was doing over there, and the job just wasn't finished. I was strongly encouraged to re-up."

They were sizing each other up, skirting the real issue. Ryan rarely wasted any time in getting to the point, but he was warming Luke up first, mellowing him. Thus, the whiskey.

When Luke emptied his glass, Ryan seemed to take that as his cue. "I hope you're going to re-up at Callaway Construction, Luke. I need you. We've got some pretty big projects going right now. I figure you can go back to school part-time over in Pensacola and it wouldn't take long with the courses you already have to get another degree in Engineering, while getting cranked up at Callaway. I want to make you project manager of the East Shore condominium job we're getting ready to start." Ryan offered it up as a gift, as his father before him had offered him a career. Perhaps forgetting what his own response had been, he seemingly expected Luke to be as excited about a future with Callaway Construction as he was.

"You'll like it, boy. Being out on the job, right on the beach. I got you an office ready, too. Got a drawing board for you—everything you need. You take some time off first and get rested up, then I'll tell you about other projects I want you to get involved in." His blue eyes were like a kid's, all round and lit up with excitement.

The pressure was on. Luke watched as his father stood up, glass in hand. Ryan removed something from his pocket.

"Come outside with me, son. Got something to show you."

Luke followed his father out through the utility room door. Ryan paused long enough to stuff his size twelve feet into a pair of muddy canvas slip-ons that were sitting beside the screened door, then he continued on into the side yard.

"Look here, Luke." Ryan held a set of car keys in his hand.

In the side drive sat a shiny, baby-blue, Thunderbird with a white convertible top. It was a bribe. It was the most beautiful car Luke had ever seen, but he couldn't accept it.

"Here, let's go for a spin." Ryan thrust the keys into the palm of Luke's hand. You'll have a company truck on the job, but this is just a little incentive for you. Advance bonus, we'll say. You'll need a way to get around after hours."

Meg stood in the doorway behind them, watching through the screen and sipping from her wine glass.

Luke handed the keys back to Ryan. "I can't take it, Dad. I'm not going back to Callaway Construction, and I'm not going back to school. I wanted to talk to you about it, but I haven't had a chance. Guess now is as good a time as any."

It seemed as though a great cloud moved across Ryan's face. He was silent for a moment, then he pushed his hand towards Luke again. "Take the keys," he said somberly, in that great, gravelly voice. "We'll talk inside." He turned back towards the house.

Luke stood for a moment and watched his father's retreat. Suddenly Ryan's great, rugged frame looked smaller, his shoulders narrower. A wave of compassion rose from Luke's guts. His father wasn't getting any younger, and Luke understood how much Ryan needed him—how much it would mean to him to have his only son working by his side in the business he had built with his own two hands, so that his son could have all the advantages that had in fact been Luke's to enjoy. The only way to please his father would be to go to work with him. Luke would be miserable. He had his own dreams—his own goals. His mother had been right, his father would eventually understand, but he would have a terrible time accepting it.

Luke respected his father's accomplishments. Over the years Ryan had used his wits and his brawn to build up one of the largest commercial construction firms in the southeast. His company had built nearly every major structure erected in south Alabama and northern Florida. His honesty and hard work had earned him choice contracts, now his money earned him prestige and valuable contacts in private enterprise and government circles. He was a powerful man, and he had earned the respect of many a good man by maintaining a high level of personal integrity in spite of his success. Luke knew his father just could not understand how his son—his smart, intelligent, hard-working son—could possibly pass up such an opportunity. All his life his father had worked hard, and mostly it had been for his son.

When Luke came back into the kitchen, Ryan was already seated at the table again, pouring himself a full glass of whiskey, this time with no ice. Meg busied herself at the stove, stirring and rapping spoons on the sides of pots and not looking up from what she was doing.

"Sit down," Ryan commanded of Luke.

The command and Ryan's tone of voice were not typical of Ryan Callaway. He appeared to be gruff and grizzly, but he gave orders with much more finesse than that, even to his construction crews.

Luke complied. He was sympathetic to Ryan's inner struggle, but he would remain firm in his convictions.

"Now, what's this all about? I never thought there was any question about your coming back to work for Callaway Construction. What happened over there to make you change your mind? Maybe you just need a break. You know you've been gone a long time. I don't mean for you to start right away. Take some time off, play a little." Ryan was desperately seeking hope, looking for some sign of encouragement from Luke.

Luke laid the keys in the middle of the table. They now took on the symbolism of a pawn being played in a game of chess.

"Dad, I tried to explain this to Mom earlier. We're just passing through. I saw so many young lives snuffed out. Boys younger than me. They never even had a chance to do what they wanted to do. They never got to see much of the world, other than their own hometown, and a jungle called Vietnam. And that was it! Their lives were over—gone! I made it through, Dad. I survived the biggest hell-hole I've ever seen. I've got things I want to do, before my time is up. Your dreams aren't necessarily my dreams."

Ryan grimaced, and it was plain it all sounded familiar to him. Not the words. The words were different, but the tune was the same. He put his hand over the keys and once more, it was his move. He pushed the keys across the table.

"I want you to have the car, Luke. It's yours. I bought it for you. It doesn't matter that you're not coming back to Callaway Construction, it's yours anyway. Hell, it's a good tax write-off. My daddy did teach me something on that end. Consider it a 'welcome-home-and-thank-God-you're-alive' gift. I want you to have it, so don't argue with me." He looked defeated, but he was trying to moderate his feelings, Luke could see that, and Luke knew better than to move the pawn one last time.

The game was over. They had both lost. An uneasiness hung in the air. Meg rapped the sides of the pots again, stirring the food with vigor, scraping the bottoms and noisily clearing her throat. Luke understood his mother. She had known better than to interfere, and that this was something Ryan and Luke had to work out for themselves. Luke knew she must surely ache for Ryan, knowing how important it was to him that Luke work with him, but that she must also know that in hurting his father, Luke hurt, too. Luke felt an urgency to do what he had to do. He couldn't help his feelings, anymore than Ryan could when he defied his father in search of his own happiness—his own road to travel.

With a sudden reversal of temperament, Ryan seemed to accept. "Drink up, everybody!" He raised his glass in a toast. "Welcome home, son. We sure as hell are glad to have you back, no matter what it is you want to do. I just got to accept it. You know what they say, the sins of the father..." He didn't complete the sentence, instead, he raised his glass to his lips and drank heartily.

Luke toasted his father. Meg breathed a sigh of relief.

5

Luke cruised slowly down the tree-lined boulevard of Ponce de León Place. Long shadows, painted by the low afternoon sun playing through the trees, dappled the pavement. Crape Myrtles filled the center of the boulevard, their branches heavy with lacy blossoms of watermelon reds and flamingo pinks.

To Luke, it seemed time had stood still here. Houses, whitewashed sparklingly clean, stood behind giant oaks that lined the streets in town, shading the sidewalks on both sides. As always this time of year, tropical breezes maintained a brisk pace across the Gulf of Mexico, offering relief from the usually relentless Florida sun.

Luke drove with the top down, enjoying the weather and the peacefulness of Pemrose Key. Thoughts of Cooper DeLaney played in his mind. Thinking of her was a pleasant pastime he often indulged in since his return. The longer he was home, the more he thought about her. He recalled the vision of her lovely smile and the exact shade of green in her sparkling eyes. It was disturbing that he'd been unable to reach her by phone. He had ordered roses for her, but several delivery attempts by the florist found no one home.

Today was the first chance he'd had to get out on his own and savor his new-found freedom. He was adjusting to all the comforts of home once again, and being back in civilization didn't feel so awkward.

Luke's thoughts were suddenly interrupted. Standing on the sidewalk in front of March Keefer's drugstore and waving her arms wildly in the air, was Edna Sinclair.

"Luke...Luke! Stop, Luke! It's me, Edna!" Her piercing screech was audible over the radio's rhythm and the hum of the engine.

Luke reluctantly slowed his car in front of the drugstore. The day had been so pleasurable until now. As the car came to a halt, he noticed Edna was not alone.

"Luke, imagine seeing you again so soon! Who would've expected it? Hey, I like your new car."

"Hello, Edna, what can I do for you?"

"Have you met my cousin, Lisa Logan? Of course you haven't... Lisa just moved here two years ago...and I almost forgot, you've been gone all this time."

Didn't she ever come up for air? Either Edna had forgotten about their confrontation at Mamie's, or she had an ulterior motive for choosing to ignore it.

"Will you take us for a ride, Luke?" Without waiting for an answer, Edna opened the passenger door and pushed her cousin in beside Luke, then she slid in behind her, slamming the door and flashing that toothsome smile that had tortured Luke for so long.

"This is Lisa." Edna put her hand on Lisa's arm and gave her a nudge in Luke's direction. "Lisa, this is Luke Callaway."

Caught in the midst of Edna's whirlwind performance, Luke had not paid full attention to Lisa. With an uneasy feeling, he turned to look directly at her. *Pleased to meet you* or some other such phrase of cordiality was what he intended to utter, but the words wouldn't come. Lisa was stunning.

Lisa turned in the seat and peered at Luke with dark, smoldering eyes.

Damn! How could this beautiful creature be related to Edna? Since he sat there frozen, unable to speak, Lisa spoke first.

"How do you do, Luke Callaway." Her voice alone was seductive, and the words oozed from her lips, like golden honey.

"Hello, Lisa...uh, where can I take you ladies, Edna?"

"Oh, it doesn't matter, I just thought we might take a short spin. Let's see how your T-Bird stacks up against mine, Luke." Edna bared her teeth again.

Her brashness grated on Luke's nerves. There was a hardness about her, an underlying character trait that Luke couldn't quite put his finger on. Whatever it was, it made him feel uncomfortable.

He drove a short distance down Ponce de León and took a right on Main Street. All the same shops were there, along with a new shopping center at the end of the third block.

"There's something new. When did that happen?" Luke queried.

"Oh, that's my shopping center." Edna waved her arm in the direction of the long, low building that filled half the block.

"Your shopping center?" Luke was surprised.

"Well, I...I, it's not really all mine, but I do own a small part of it. I was responsible for the developers acquiring the land for it, and for my commission, they gave me a percentage of this place. I figured in the long run it'd be a pretty smart business move. I've learned a lot about that stuff," Edna crowed.

Lisa interjected in a soft southern drawl, "Edna is such a smart business woman, Luke, she has been quite successful in real estate, you know. Isn't that right, Edna?" Lisa reached over and gave Edna's arm an affectionate squeeze. Edna ignored her.

Lisa's voice was exciting to Luke. It was breathy and sexy, and seemed to hold a promise of surprise, as if one listened long enough, they might discover hidden secrets. He was acutely aware of the shapely figure pressed against his side, and of the fact that he'd been in the trenches far too long—and that he may never see Cooper DeLaney again.

Luke pulled into the parking lot of the shopping center. He knew his dad would have said something in his letters if Callaway

Construction had built it. During Luke's absence, Ryan kept him faithfully apprised of all the Callaway projects in anticipation of Luke's return to the family business.

"Who was the contractor?" Luke turned in his seat to face Edna.

"Well, uh...I..." Edna squinted her eyes and gazed off into the distance as though deep thought were required in producing the answer. "...let me see, actually, it was Jeremy Mason Builders, from Montgomery. It was. It was Jeremy Mason. They came in with an eleventh hour bid that was lower than anybody else's. Of course everybody wanted your daddy to build it, Luke," Edna quickly added. "But it just wasn't monetarily advantageous." She glanced over at Luke, then looked down and gave her long, scarlet-painted fingernails an intense study.

Luke wheeled the car around sharply, heading back out to Main Street, turning left towards Ponce de León Place. It wasn't that he minded someone else getting the contract, that's free-enterprise, and what America is all about. It was the annoying way Edna had of telling him about it, goadingly. Maybe he was just imagining it. She did make him irritable, even after all these years. Although he didn't want to make Callaway Construction his life's work, family loyalty ran deep, and he took a great deal of pride in his father's business.

"Take me back to my car," Edna ordered. "I have an appointment soon and I only have a few minutes to spare."

Luke stopped in front of Keefer's Drugs, and noticed the bright red Thunderbird parked around the corner on the side of the building. Edna got out and left Lisa sitting in the car beside Luke.

"By the way, Luke, would you mind terribly giving Lisa a ride back to my house?"

Lisa looked from one to the other, awaiting her fate.

"I wouldn't mind, Edna. It would be my pleasure." Outwardly maintaining a calm demeanor, he tried not to look at Lisa as he spoke, hoping to conceal his overanxious, hormonally induced thoughts since meeting her. The prospect of being alone with such a voluptuous creature stimulated his masculine desires—desires that had been relegated, out of necessity, to the very bottom of his brain far too long.

"I do appreciate it, Luke. You two have fun. Bye, now. You be a good girl, Lisa." Edna winked at her cousin, then turned and prissed across the sidewalk towards her bright red car.

It puzzled Luke that Edna was pushing her cousin at him, practically leading the lamb to the slaughter. It occurred to him that the question of who was the lamb and who was the slaughterer remained to be seen. There was still something about Edna that caused him uneasiness. Being Lisa's victim couldn't be all bad, though. The way she moved her body—the way she looked at him beneath those long lashes—caused him to wonder if she was a *good* girl.

Luke cleared his throat while he searched for words. "Is there something you'd like to do, Lisa? Go for a ride or get a bite to eat before I take you home?" He failed at disguising the quiver in his voice and the excitement he felt.

"You bet ah would, Shugah," Lisa cooed, drawing each word out slowly, adding emphasis to her already pronounced drawl.

Her breasts were straining at her blouse.

Luke put his car in gear and nervously guided it away from the curb and back into the light flow of traffic. The evening air was balmy as they drove along Ponce de León. Front porch lights were flickering on, and the scent of gardenias in bloom drifted from the front yards, filling the air with a heady, sweet fragrance and contributing to the romantic setting of Pemrose at twilight.

Lisa slid a short distance across the seat, away from Luke. "Let's go to the beach, Luke, if that's okay with you."

He nearly drove off the road when he saw, out of the corner of his eye, Lisa raise the hem of her skirt above her knees and unfasten her garter clasps. What she did next made it extremely difficult for him to keep his eyes on the road. Slowly and deliberately she slipped her silky nylons, one at a time, down long, slender legs, her long-lashed eyes steady on him as she did so.

"It's so hot out tonight. Ah think the breeze has already died down. Don't you, Luke?" She fanned herself with one hand. "I'd like to feel the cool, wet sand between my toes. Surely it'll be much more pleasant at the beach." Her breasts peeked flirtatiously above her low-cut, pale-yellow peasant blouse. She tilted her chin up and ran the fingertips of one hand slowly down the front of her throat and across her chest, following the rise and fall of the swell of her breasts. She closed her eyes as she stroked herself, and appeared to be deriving pleasure from the stimulation of her own fingertips.

"Yeah." Luke took a deep breath. "It is a pretty steamy night. You're right, the breeze has died down. I'm sure it'll be much cooler at the beach." Luke's stomach churned and he experienced the heat.

Lisa's sensuality overwhelmed him. At least she didn't seem to be terribly interested in good conversation for now. She seemed so calm and relaxed; so cool; so totally in contrast with his nervous tension.

Lisa reached to the floorboard for her purse. She stuffed her rolled up nylons inside and pulled out a small silver flask. After removing the top, she leaned over and waved the bottle back and forth beneath Luke's nose. He caught an unmistakable whiff of sour mash.

"Want some?" Lisa asked him sweetly. "Good ol' Tennessee whiskey." Not waiting for his answer, she turned the bottle up to her lips and took a long sip. "Ahhhh, kinda' like a mint julep." She closed her eyes, savoring the flavor. "We just don't have any mint, and you're the only shugah. No muss, no fuss. Don't you agree, SHUGAH?" She giggled, and the whiskey glistened on her full lips. She tilted her head slightly, giving him a sideways glance, and extended the bottle to him.

He took the flask and downed a swig. The whiskey burned as it trickled down his throat, warming up his insides.

He was a Marine just home from the service. She was everything he had missed in a woman for the long years he had been away. Her brown eyes were dreamlike, kind of wistfully distant. The moonlight highlighted her long, dark hair and illuminated the strand of iridescent pearls that shimmered at her throat, contrasting with her dark, tanned skin.

Damn! You lucky son-of-a-gun! Luke marveled at his good fortune. He sucked in his breath and took another swallow of the whiskey. He had a feeling she knew how vulnerable he was. She was ripe with womanhood and brimming with sensuality—a dangerous combination. An inner voice told him to be careful.

Lisa leaned her back against the car door on her side. She stretched her long, bare legs across Luke's lap as he drove. Her familiarity surprised him, but he wasn't complaining. Was she like this with all men? She seemed to know how to please a man in every way, at least to the limits he had witnessed thus far. With keen appreciation he took note of every seductive detail, from her polished, pink frosted toenails and bronzed skin, to the pale yellow blouse that teasingly revealed a shaded valley between her bosom.

Nearing the beach, Luke could hear the rushing roar of the ocean, and the waves breaking against the sand. It never failed to excite him, especially now, with Lisa so close beside him, her bare legs pressing against his thighs. It had been so long since he'd been with a woman, and she was sweet and sexy. The quickened tempo of his pulse could be likened to drums beating rhythmically within his being.

He wanted her in the worst way. It was as basic as that. He had not yet tasted the wine, and already he was drunk.

He slowed the car and pulled off to the side of the road. Before he could put the brakes on or cut the ignition, Lisa was out of the car and racing barefoot towards the beach. Halfway there, she turned and extended her arms to him, playfully beckoning him to her. She pulled the flask out of the pocket of her full, white skirt and paused long enough to turn the silver bottle up to her lips.

Luke kept his eyes on her as he removed his shoes. She was a vision of enticement silhouetted against the ocean, her billowing skirt translucent in the moonlight; her dark, silky, hair dancing with the gentle ocean breeze. She was a temptress.

He raised his arms and pulled his shirt over his head. The chilly night air felt good against his bare skin. With long strides he ran to her, feet pounding against cool, hard sand, his muscular body moving fluidly across the beach, reaching her before she got to the water's edge.

He took her small hand in his and together, they ran along the beach like children, splashing in the water as the waves lapped at their feet. They moved in one smooth motion as they ran, their bodies perfectly synchronized. It was exhilarating. Suddenly, as if reading one another's mind, they slowed at the same moment and turned to face each other. Without speaking, Lisa reached to her waist and slowly pulled the soft fabric of her blouse up over her head, revealing round, white breasts that stood out against her bathing suit tan. She put her arms around Luke's waist and pulled him to her, pressing her body firmly against his chest.

"Mmm, you're warm, Luke," she purred against his bare skin. Her arms surrounded him and she hugged his body tightly to hers. When he lowered his head, his lips brushed against her fragrant hair. Her sweet scent contrasted pleasantly with the heavy, salty, night air.

Lisa looked up at him through dreamy, half-closed eyes. "Kiss me..." Her voice was low and husky. The words and the faint scent of bourbon lingered on her lips.

He felt a tightness in his chest and his knees grew weak. He tasted her lips—they were slightly salty from the ocean spray and still wet with whiskey.

"Lisa," he moaned softly into her ear. The drums were pounding in his head. He began to devour her with his mouth, nibbling gently at her neck, tasting the saltiness of her skin.

She pressed her body closer to him, chiseling away at any honorable resistance or thoughts of chivalry he may have momentarily entertained. He wanted her so badly. The muscles in his calves contracted in knots, and his breathing came harder so that he felt he was suffocating. He ached for her. She was wicked and wild and wonderful, and he was succumbing to all of her womanly charms. Luke could tell she was used to being in control. Her own excitement seemed to surprise her. She pressed her mouth against his and surrounded his waist with her arms, pulling him ever closer, moaning sensuously as she kissed him. Her heightened excitement aroused in him an all-consuming desire. The pleasure she seemed to derive from the physical control she could exert over him was something he had not experienced with a woman before. She was so uninhibited, so wild and so free. He suddenly felt as a man powerless in his ability to control his own destiny. He could have her now, a hasty one-night stand to satisfy his urges. The uneasiness he had felt when Edna was present returned. He hesitated for a moment and tilted Lisa's chin upward with his fingertips. Her big brown eyes stared passively into his. Luke spoke softly, "I want to be sure this is what you want, Lisa." His keen sense of timing and cautiousness and knowing when not to act in haste was what had saved him in fearful, deadly situations time and again in Vietnam. Now, in the heat of passion, why did he have to compare those times with this? Even though he knew he must have her, that underlying fear in the pit of his gut was gnawing at him and playing in his mind. Who was this woman? What was it about her that he couldn't quite define? He searched her face for answers and asked, "Who are you, little girl?"

Instantly, wild anger flashed in those dark eyes. It was clear to Luke that she took his hesitation as rejection, and she was not used to having her advances rejected. Her face was flushed and moist with perspiration, her nostrils flared slightly as she breathed short, angry breaths, and then suddenly, her anger ebbed as quickly as it had erupted. Without ever having spoken a word, her eyes and her attitude reflected complete indifference. When she did speak, her voice was controlled; her composure intact. "You want to know who I am, Luke, honey? I'm just little old Lisa, but I'll tell you this, I can work my magic on you and make you feel like you never felt before. I KNOW what I want. Oh, you'll get to know me in time. That's a promise."

She pulled him to her and kissed him again, a slow, lingering kiss at first, then more intensely, absorbing them both in her passion. As she kissed him, she slid her hand across his chest, then down to his hard, bare belly, purposefully rubbing the flat of her cool palm against him. He held his breath.

She pressed her hand harder against his skin, teasing him with her touch. Luke emitted an involuntary moan. Lisa tilted her head back and looked up at him, watching his face intently. Her kisses sought to consume him body and soul. She knew what she was doing, and for Luke, there was no turning back. He'd given her a chance to stop before they went too far, but she had rejected his attempt to acknowledge and respect her innocence. Now he found himself powerless to resist her determination to have her way with him. He chastised himself for his weakness. Lisa was in complete control, and she seemed to know the exact moment the last shreds of his resistance dissolved. No man could withstand the delicious pleasures this lustful temptress offered. He placed his hands on each side of her face and kissed her fiercely, the constraints of his fears dissipating with the acknowledgment and resignation of his weakness.

Without warning, she abruptly freed herself from his grasp, and with tremendous might from those small, capable hands, shoved her palms hard against his belly, deep into his gut.

"Damn!" He gasped at the thrust of her hands. At least now he knew what he was up against and why he had feared her.

He stood motionless, trying to recover, and stared in amazement as she nonchalantly leaned to pick her blouse up. She turned on her heels and dashed off in front of him, her skirt swaying as she skipped along in the sand. She dangled her blouse beside her, holding it just high enough out of the water's edge to keep it from getting wet. She stopped and furtively looked back, reminding him of a criminal returning to the scene of the crime. Albeit a beautiful criminal, and a calculating one. He watched as she pulled her blouse on over her head. His skin crawled, and that uneasy feeling returned as he witnessed the satisfaction in her face over her accurate assessment of the effect her actions had on him, then she winked and flashed him an innocent looking, playful smile.

"Touché," he conceded in a loud whisper. Damn this girl! He had never seen anybody like her. What gumption she had. What a tease. He grudgingly admitted she had given him a dose of his own medicine. He could handle it. The gauntlet had been tossed. He would accept the challenge. He ran to catch up with her and when he did, he turned her to him and gave her a long, assertive kiss. Emotionally and physically drained, he took her hand and they walked in silence to the car.

6

*L*uke took the long route from the beach and drove slowly in the direction of Cole's Bayou. Lisa positioned herself snugly against his side. After their shared passion on the beach, her familiarity seemed more natural than it had before, but she still puzzled him. What was she after? Why did she behave this way? He looked down at her, briefly studying her face. She was an odd one, beautiful, but different, unlike any of the girls or women that had ever been a part of his life.

"Tell me about yourself, Lisa...and your family."

"What's to tell? My daddy's in the Navy. He stays overseas mostly, and the Navy has been his entire life." She shrugged her shoulders as if it was unimportant, then took a sip from the silver flask clutched tightly in her hand. She sighed deeply before continuing her story. "That's why I stay with Edna and her mama. That's why I came to Pensacola. One day when I was a baby, my mama went away. We lived in San Diego then. She never came back. She just went away. Daddy never would talk about it, but one day, when I kept asking him why I didn't have a mama, he said she was in an automobile accident. He said she went away one day and he never saw her after that. An automobile accident, that's what it was. I didn't see my daddy much when I was a little girl, he was always sailing away on some ship." Lisa told the story mechanically, with no feeling or emotion in her voice, as if she had explained her own life to herself many times over, and perhaps to other people, too.

Luke sensed more than saw the hurt little girl hiding inside the aloof facade she presented to him. A little insight into her psyche began to slowly dawn from within, or so he thought. A pang of tender emotion that was somewhat foreign to him after years on the battlefield, stirred within his soul. This strange, sexy, sensuously naughty woman created a conflicting combination of emotions, and for a moment he ached for the little girl sitting beside him. He wanted to shield her from harm. He pulled her closer to him and gave her shoulder a protective squeeze. She looked up at him, her eyes as distant as ever, and gave him a generous smile.

"When I was ten Daddy got based in Newport News and we moved from California...I know you can't tell it, but I wasn't really born a southerner...not like Edna was...she was born right here in Pemrose Key...out at Cole's Bayou." Without further encouragement from Luke, Lisa continued on in the same monotone, her thick accent and the sexy huskiness of her voice that excited him earlier, now vanished. She sounded more like a little girl.

"Before we went back to Newport News, Daddy said it was going to be like going home. It wasn't like going home for me. I didn't have any friends there. Daddy just had a bunch of girl friends. I did have one friend there, she helped take care of me, sort of like a nanny. Yeah, Matilda was my nanny!" The way she said it, as though an idea had suddenly dawned, sounded as though she had, at that very moment, acquired the term *nanny* in her vocabulary.

"We used to have these great parties while Daddy was gone, and Matilda would invite all her girl friends over, and a bunch of sailors from the base would always come over. She would fix my hair and put makeup on me just like hers. When I was fifteen everybody thought I was at least twenty. I've always been real mature for my age." At this she glanced down at her chest. "Some of Matilda's girl friends would even get jealous because the boys would pay more attention to me than to them. It was fun, 'till Matilda ran away with a sailor." Lisa paused, and for a moment she looked like she had just buried Matilda.

"After Matilda left, I had to come here to stay with Edna and her mama. I think Matilda really had her eye set on Daddy to start with, but he was gone so much, and she said she just had to have a man around all the time to feel like a complete woman. Aunt Ruth is old, and she doesn't care what we do." At this she looked meaningfully up at Luke. "It's okay staying at her house. I can go where I want to, and stay out as late as I like. Edna's my best friend now, even though she is six years older than me. I would do anything for Edna, she's so smart'n'all." She looked hard at Luke. "Don't you think Edna's wonderful, Luke? She's so sweet and nice."

"You know her a lot better than I do," Luke conceded. If you say she's a nice girl, she must be a nice girl." Give Edna the benefit of the doubt. Maybe she's changed, right?

Lisa's story shed some light on why she was the way the was. She'd not had a mother to guide her into her teen years; no one to impart wisdom in the art of becoming a lady; no instructions on behaving with genteel restraint around men, as the privileged and pampered girls of his youth had.

As for the story about the sailors always being around, that would explain her uninhibitedness around men. Regardless of what the previous eighteen years of her life had been, she was the most sensuous woman he had ever known. How many sailors had she been with? Too sure that he might know the answer, he allowed himself to wonder briefly. This was a subject he did not want to dwell on.

As they neared Cole's Bayou, Luke pulled the car onto the dirt road that led to Shank's Landing. He had always known—not that he had ever been interested, but merely as a matter of common knowledge typical among kids in a small town—that Edna lived out by Shank's Landing. Luke had been to Shank's Landing only once before, and that was by boat. One day he and Trotter drifted into the mouth of the bayou while doing some inland fishing. They docked at the pier long enough to get an icy-cold Grapico from the rusty soft drink machine that was beside the entrance to the old boathouse.

Cole's Bayou was a secluded fishing settlement on the outskirts of Pemrose Key, and Shank's Landing was a dilapidated fishery where the fishermen and shrimpers could come to clean, weigh, and package their fresh catch. There had been rumors back then that Cole's Bayou wasn't the safest place to get stuck in after dark, but for young boys, it held a certain fascination. It had a reputation not only for being a bit on the rough side, but also as a den of iniquity. Some even had it that prison escapees and pirates found refuge at Shank's Landing, trying to make a living as best they could while hiding out for one reason or another.

As his car hobbled the ruts in the sparsely covered crushed-shell lane, Luke wondered why Edna had not taken a place of her own in town by now. What with all the success she boasted, she surely could afford it. Why would a single girl stay out here in the boon-docks if she didn't have to? Seems like her mama would have liked being in town, too, but Luke didn't know her mama.

The road began to narrow and the foliage grew thicker and closer to the road. Vines and branches formed a natural arch overhead.

"This is like going through the jungle, Lisa. Is it very far to the Landing?" Luke asked, keeping his eyes on the road and both hands on the steering wheel as he attempted to dodge the potholes.

"No, it's just ahead, Luke, just a little ways up the road. We're almost there." Lisa leaned forward and brushed the sand off her feet. She slipped her sandals back on and turned sideways in her seat, facing Luke. When she spoke, the sexy drawl was back. Vanished was the little girl that sat beside him only minutes before. "Luke, I had a wonderful time tonight." She leaned towards him, her breasts straining against her blouse, pushing the curvaceous swells to their fullest above the low-cut neckline, and deepening the dark valley in-between. She was a daring thrill seeker, and it was evident that she knew all too well the titillating effect her body and her actions had on men. She maneuvered her position so that her chest brushed against Luke's arm. He was aware by now that she was indeed experienced in the art of achieving power and control over the opposite sex through the use of her body. Even so, her nearness nearly drove him to distraction. She was certainly doing a number on him. With her index finger she slowly traced an invisible line down the side of his face, from his pulsing temple and downward, along his jawbone, to the cleft in the center of his chin. At the bottom of his chin she lifted her finger and started at the temple again, this time tracing a bead of perspiration that trickled from his forehead.

"Next time, Luke, I promise." She whispered the words, moving her mouth closer to his ear, blowing her warm breath gently across the side of his face and pressing her breasts against his arm. "And it'll be so-o-o good." She fairly purred now, drawing out the word *so* and placing emphasis on the word *good*.

Rounding a curve, they emerged into an expansive clearing. A light fog hung over the bayou. It wasn't enough to greatly impair vision, but the drifting, sub-tropical haze that eerily enveloped the shoreline cast a mystical aura about the bayou. Luke shivered involuntarily. The main road ended, if you could call it a main road, and separate lanes forked out in all directions. The glow of several small campfires shimmered along the banks, reflecting abstractedly in the water. It was so dark in the bayou, and the headlights were so mud-spattered and dim, Luke could only faintly see the dirt lanes ahead. Luckily, the light of the campfires guided him away from the water's edge.

"There's where I live, over there. You see, Luke. Go right past the Landing and you'll see it. It's that quaint little brick cottage over there just on the other side." Lisa straightened herself up and moved back to her side of the seat.

So much for finding a place to park. Only moments before, Luke had considered pulling off to the side of the road, prompted by a desire to re-enact the earlier events of the evening. Now, however, finding their way in the dark became a priority.

Quaint little cottage? From the looks of it there wasn't anything quaint about Cole's Bayou. As he drove past the Landing, the moonlight reflecting off the water provided him with a hazy view of the fishery. It looked old and dilapidated now.

"Guess the fishery's not doing much business these days." As he got the words out, he caught sight of what appeared to be a flashlight moving about towards the end of the boathouse pier. He saw three distinct flashes of the light before it went dark, and then in the blinking of an eye, across the water and very low on the horizon, he detected a rapid flash. For a moment he was reminded of the war. His jungle training facilitated his night vision. If not for that, he probably wouldn't even have seen the single, acknowledging flash through the haze, but he knew its purpose instantly, and it piqued his curiosity. Why would someone, God only knows who out in this wilderness, be signaling a landing at a broken down old fishery? To heck with it, it wasn't his business.

He wasn't sure whether Lisa had noticed or whether she just pretended she hadn't. Secluded as it was from the rest of the world, Cole's Bayou was very close in itself and geographically small. In Luke's estimation, anyone who lived here would know exactly what transpired at any given time, and in all likelihood know the reason why, or make it their business to find out. He drove past the ramshackle fishery without mention of the signaling lights.

"There, see! There it is." Lisa pointed to what was indeed a small, quaint, brick cottage that sat about fifty yards past the landing. A dull, yellow-ish light warmed the entrance to the cottage, and the faint glow enabled Luke to distinguish which way the ruts ran through the tall, marshy grasses. As they approached the cottage, Luke saw Edna's red Thunderbird parked between the house and a thickly covered, unkempt, scuppernong arbor. The arbor, with the car wedged in beside it, added to the mystique that had permeated the entire evening. It was all too surreal—like something out of a book or a movie. Perhaps it was just his imagination. Whatever it was, it was more than he wanted to deal with at this moment. He was tired. Lisa had worn him out, his manhood and his passions had worn him out; fighting the dark and dodging the ruts in Cole's Bayou had worn him out. He would see Lisa to the door and head for home. This could all be sorted out later. There was too much to try and absorb tonight.

Just as Luke halted the car in front of the house, the front door opened slowly. He could barely make out a figure standing in the dimly lit opening. Lisa glanced nervously towards the entrance. She quickly opened her car door and hopped out.

"Bye, Luke. Nice meeting you, Shugah. I'll be seeing you." She blew him a kiss and was gone.

Before he even had a chance to say goodbye, the front door had closed behind her.

"What the...? Now what the heck do you suppose that was all about?" Luke muttered, perplexed by her speedy departure. He shifted the car into gear. Nothing to do now but try to find his way out of here. He bumped along making a wide swing and headed out of the clearing towards the shadowy tree-line where he hoped he would find the dirt road that would lead him back to the highway.

At the edge of the clearing he spotted the narrow parting of the trees where the road began. He slowed the car, attempting to avoid scratches from the vicious, road-hugging tree branches. He navigated his shiny new car onto the road between the wildly over-grown trees.

Startled by a loud thud, Luke brought his foot down hard on the brakes. The upper torso of a man sprawled across the hood of Luke's car. His head rested in the middle of the hood and his arms were spread-eagle on each side, as if to halt the progress of the car with his embrace—a feat he had certainly accomplished. Luckily for the man, Luke had been driving at a snail's pace. The man's feet were still planted firmly on the ground beside the right front tire. With the braking of the car, the man's body slid across the hood, closer to the windshield. As he slid, a wide, reddish-brown streak followed the path of his head. Inches from the windshield, the man raised his head slightly and through half-closed eyes, he peered in across the dash at Luke.

Face to face with his perpetrator, Luke could see that the man was badly wounded, his skin was streaked with dirt and clay, and his face glistened with sweat. A nasty looking gash slashed through his left eyebrow. It oozed with blood and pus, and appeared to be infected, an indication that it was not a fresh wound, but perhaps several days old. The man's lips were badly crusted over with scabby, peeling skin. His filthy clothes clung to his emaciated body, and he was in dire need of medical attention.

Luke moved into action. Once over the initial shock of having a body slammed against his car, and seeing that the man was inca-pable of posing any threat to him, Luke's military training came into full play. His mind and his body worked together in rapid-fire action. He knew what he had to do. In one fluid movement he was out of the car and around to the other side where the man lay sprawled across the hood. He had to get the man to a doctor as soon as possible, but first he would see if he could give him some relief. He put his arms around the stranger's waist and gently lowered the skeletal frame to the ground. Laying the man on his back, Luke straightened out the skinny, limp legs and began unbuttoning the front of his clinging shirt. He took a handkerchief from his own pocket and gently patted all around the gaping wound, wiping some of the dirt and perspiration from the man's face. He was a light skinned black man who looked to be in his twenties, maybe around Luke's age. It was hard to tell for sure. The man was hot with fever, but he began to slowly open his eyes again, and a hollow, barely audible moan rattled in his chest. Through partially parted lips he muttered what Luke could have sworn sounded like his own name. Luke leaned closer to the man's face, to better hear what he was trying to say. It was something he saw in those eyes and the cheekbones. A wave of nausea welled up within Luke as recognition dawned.

"Toby! My God, Toby. What has happened to you? Lie still. I'm going to get you into the car, and get you to a doctor. Don't try to say anything, just take it easy. It'll be okay." Luke tried to mask his skepticism. All he could think about was Mamie, her jovial image presented itself in his mind. She was such a good woman, she didn't deserve this. What HAD Toby been up to? What had he gotten himself into? He remembered what Trotter had told him just a few nights ago at Mamie's Place and he ruled out going back to Edna's for help. He could get Toby to a doctor sooner than a doctor could find his way out to Cole's Bayou. He would take him to old Doc Bauchet, a couple of miles past Pirate's Cove. That would be the quickest, and it was close to Mamie's. Besides, Doc Bauchet was good at keeping his mouth shut. Luke and his buddies found that out in high school when Jamie Flaherty filled their bottoms with buckshot for stealing watermelons out of his field. They all had to go to the doctor's then, and good old Doc Bauchét never breathed a word. Guess he figured they'd all suffered enough by the time he got through with them.

"No doctor..." Toby's voice trailed off and he shut his eyes again. "No doctor...Luke." Luke could barely decipher his words.

"It's okay, Toby, you have to see somebody. You're sick. You know Doc Bauchet. You won't have to worry, he won't say anything. He won't cause you any trouble." Ignoring Toby's feeble pleas, Luke placed one arm under Toby's neck, the other under the back of his knees. His strong arms lifted Toby's feverish body with ease. He positioned Toby in the passenger seat and tried to make him as comfortable as possible. Slowly, he made his way back out to the highway. Once on the smoother asphalt, Luke pushed the gas pedal to the floor. It seemed an eternity, but in reality was only a matter of minutes before he was pulling into the circular driveway that led to the front door of Doc Bauchet's modest, white-frame cottage.

The porch light came on, and Doc Bauchet himself opened the door. He was a large, balding man with a protruding gut. The robe he wore over his pajamas just did meet in his middle, and his chin met his chest as he peered out over the rim of a pair of reading glasses perched on the tip of his nose. His eyes wandered down the front of Luke's dirty, bloody shirt.

"What brings you here, young man? Luke Callaway, isn't it? Thought you were off soldiering somewhere. You don't look sick to me. What's the problem?" His words had a slight Cajun cadence.

"It's not me, Doc. It's Mamie Washington's boy, Toby. He's been hurt. I don't know exactly what happened, I just know he needs your help, real bad."

"Bring him in here." The doctor spoke sharply, his usually stern face was now grim. He held the screened door open while Luke went to the car and returned with Toby cradled in his arms.

"Lay him down in there." He nodded towards a small room that opened off the living room. Against the wall was positioned a small cot that was made into a bed, with a pillow and crisp white sheets. A few medical supplies lay neatly on a small round table at the head of the bed. Doc Bauchet was semi-retired and he didn't maintain an office. He was used to patients calling on him at home, and he was always prepared.

Luke lowered Toby onto the cot. Doc Bauchet covered him with a lightweight blanket that had been folded in a neat square at the foot of the bed. Luke stood back and watched as the doctor leaned over Toby and tenderly placed his palm flat against Toby's forehead just above his wound.

"I'm glad you brought him here, Luke. Mamie doesn't know, does she?"

"No, and I'm not going to be the one to tell her. I was hoping you could get him on his feet first..." Luke lowered his voice to a whisper "...if he doesn't die."

The doctor snapped angrily, "He isn't going to die. I won't let him die, you hear, Luke? So don't you go talking that way. Toby's not going to die. Now you go on home and don't worry about him. He's in good hands. I'll take care of him. He will not die."

Strange behavior for a doctor. Luke knew Doc Bauchet knew the facts—people die—people get sick and die. Luke had seen plenty of it, and if ever anybody looked like they might not make it, it was Toby. Why, then, this strange behavior? Had Doc Bauchet gotten so old now he was losing touch with reality, or was it something else? To Luke's way of thinking, this emotional outburst and this denial of the danger Toby was in demonstrated a profound lack of professionalism.

Luke backed out of the room. As he was leaving, he glanced around the living room. It looked to be spotlessly clean, but terribly cluttered. It was a comfortable, cozy looking room, but it was a room void of a woman's touch. A big, over-stuffed chair sat at an angle in the corner and looked well used, as did the stuffed ottoman that sat before it. The green plaid fabric on both was worn. A floor lamp with a tacky, yellowed shade stood beside the chair and newspapers lay scattered on the ottoman and on the floor around it. On one wall was a massive bookcase that rose to the ceiling. Every inch on every shelf was stuffed with books. In one corner was a large, square-topped oak desk, its surface barely visible under the clutter of papers strewn across the top. Luke took one final look at Toby and saw Doc beginning to dress the wound on Toby's forehead. He quietly let himself out the front door.

7

Nearly a week passed before Luke decided to call Lisa. His evening with her left some confusing images in his mind. He thought it best if he never saw her again, but somewhere in the recesses of his subconscious was the certainty that he would, especially since he'd tried again to reach Cooper and once more, his efforts had been unsuccessful. He recognized that calling Cooper was like grasping at a final straw—an antidote for succumbing to Lisa's charms.

The events that transpired the evening he met Lisa took on a bit saner perspective once day had dawned and he had gotten some rest—except for the part about Toby.

Luke intended to pay a visit to Doc Bauchet today. He hoped to find out what had happened to Toby. Where had he been to get himself so mangled? When Luke phoned Doc the day after, he requested that Luke hold off on informing Mamie until he had a more accurate prognosis on Toby's condition. Against Luke's better judgement, he complied, and when he called back a few days later the good news was that Toby was going to make it. If Doc Bauchet knew any details, he wasn't sharing the information with anybody and again, he requested Luke not mention Toby to anyone. Luke felt like a heel and a traitor to Mamie, but he would continue to comply with Doc's request since it looked like Toby was going to be okay now. Doc must have his reasons. If Luke went out there today, maybe Toby would enlighten him on what happened and why he was out at Cole's Bayou that night? What were the signaling lights Luke had seen at the Landing? Most importantly, did Toby know if Lisa was involved in whatever secrets were being harbored in Cole's Bayou? He suspected Toby could supply some of the answers.

As for Lisa, he thought he had her figured out. She was simply a gorgeous creature with overactive hormones, and no red-blooded American male could fault her for that. She was the most sexually desirable female he had ever known, and even though it might not be the best thing to do, he decided to get to know her better, perhaps beginning tonight. Before leaving for Doc Bauchet's, Luke picked up the phone and dialed the number Lisa had written on the corner of a Biloxi Bar and Grill cocktail napkin she pulled from her purse the other evening. The girl does get around, he noted.

She seemed to be happy to hear from him and promptly accepted his dinner invitation.

For the second time in little more than a week, Luke pulled his car into Doc Bauchet's driveway. Other than the recent experience of Doc's emotionalism in the face of an emergency, he'd never had any reason to doubt Doc's professional competence. Now, given Toby's dramatic recovery, he maintained a much keener appreciation for the good doctor's abilities than he had last week. Enlightened now regarding the doctor's dedication to his practice and his patients, he was still puzzled by Doc's strong convictions the other night that Toby was not going to die—this before he ever examined Toby. The reaction had not been clinical nor professional, but from the heart—very emotional. Who could figure it? Luke decided he wouldn't try to analyze it. Lisa was enough of a puzzle to ponder.

When Doc Bauchet opened the door this time, he was very cordial, even jovial. "Luke, good to see you, son. Come on in and take a look at our ward, here. Quite a difference, wouldn't you say? You didn't give him much of a chance of making it this time last week.

Tell you the truth, neither did I. Oh, I can talk a good game. I guess I'm a great believer in the healing powers of the human spirit, and the power of the mind over the will to live—or the will to die—medicine alone didn't get this young fella' on his feet."

Looking past Doc Bauchet, Luke saw a hollow-cheeked Toby with crutches propped under each arm, supporting an injured, bandaged foot—an injury that had escaped Luke's notice the night he and Toby's paths had crossed out at Cole's Bayou. His immediate concern had been for Toby's near comatose state and the nasty, festering, head wound that was now surrounded by a gauze wrap that came down low over one brow, nearly covering his eye.

"Toby…" Luke sidestepped past the doctor and extended his hand to Toby. "…it's good to see you alive, even if you do still look like you've been tangling with a 'gator." Luke inclined his head towards Toby's bandaged foot. "What happened to you out there to get you in this shape?"

Toby's eyes widened, and his lips started moving, but before he could get his words out, Doc Bauchet intercepted. "Oh, I'm sure Toby doesn't want to relive a bad accident right now, Luke. I 'spect you'll hear all about it in time. Why don't you boys have a seat here, and I'll get us a pitcher of iced tea." Doc Bauchet fussed around like a mother hen, moving newspapers and plumping pillows.

Toby, propped on his crutches, had not moved from his position. He held his right crutch securely under his arm, freeing his hand to clasp Luke's. He didn't say anything until Doc Bauchet finished having his say and headed for the kitchen.

"These crutches are just for show, it ain't too bad. I reckon I owe you some thanks, Luke. I reckon I owe my life to you, even though it ain't worth much. I'm glad I get to stay around a spell longer." He didn't volunteer any information about what had caused his infirmities. "I know I need to let Mama know I'm back in town. I haven't wanted to worry her none, Luke. How about not saying anything to her yet. I might ought to wait 'till I ain't so banged up. That way I won't have to listen to her griping at me for not helping her at Mamie's Place." As Toby spoke, he appeared nervous and seemed to be gauging Luke's reactions, looking for some kind of a sign from Luke, something that would tell him he could trust him.

Luke realized it would do no good to press Toby to tell him what happened.

"I'm gonna' get out of the Doc's hair, Luke. Got one of Mama's fishing shanties I stay at sometimes. I'll heal real good out there on the bay. Won't be imposing on Doc none, either. I don't reckon you'd mind giving me a lift out to Pirates Cove, would you, Luke?" Apparently Toby had decided to trust him.

"I don't mind, Toby. I can't tell you what to do, but it seems to me like Doc can take better care of you than you will yourself."

Doc Bauchet entered the room carrying a tray that contained a frosty pitcher of iced tea and three plastic glasses. "Here you go, boys, just what the doctor ordered on a warm day like this. Make yourself comfortable, Luke." Doc gestured to one of the chairs with the plumped pillows. "Go on, Luke, have a seat." He poured the iced tea and handed each of them a glass.

Toby turned his glass up and gulped it down all at once. "I'm leaving, Doc. Luke here is gonna' take me out to Pirate's Cove. I'll do okay out there. Don't want to see Mama yet, but at least she'll be close by if I do need anything."

A scowl crossed Doc Bauchet's face. "Toby, I don't think that's a very good idea. You need to stay here a while longer and let me doctor you. That wound's not healed and needs to be cleaned regularly, and it's not easy for you to get around on that foot. Now take the doctor's advice and listen to what I say. The best thing for you right now is to just stay put."

"Can't, Doc. I got to move on. I can't sit still no longer. There's people I gotta' see and stuff I gotta' do. You don't understand and I can't explain it to you, but I got to go. I appreciate what you've done for me. I don't have any money to pay you right now, but somebody owes me, and I'll be getting it real soon. If I don't, Mama will make it good. Don't you worry."

Doc Bauchet's voice boomed. "Boy, don't you talk to me about money. I didn't do this for money. You couldn't ever afford to pay me for the kind of care I've given you this past week. Nor Luke for what he's done, or your mama, God love her. You're nothing but an ingrate—a lazy, worthless bum. I've wanted to get to know you better, to give you the benefit of the doubt. When the heck are you going to straighten yourself out? You've been nothing but a heartache to your poor mama since you got out of high school. Oh, I've kept up. I know the kind of trouble you've been in." Doc suddenly seemed to remember Luke's presence. He picked up the iced tea tray and retreated towards the kitchen, then turned in the doorway. "Go on, get out of here. Take him, Luke, take him wherever it is he wants to go. I'm done with him."

Luke and Toby both stared in amazement at Doc Bauchet's back as he left the room. At least Toby had the decency to look a bit sheepish—for the moment, anyway.

Assisted by his crutches, Toby promptly raised himself from the sofa. "Come on, Luke, let's get out of this place." Toby couldn't get out of there fast enough, it seemed. Making his way to the screened door, he clumsily let himself out.

Luke, standing in the middle of the living room, turned his glass up and finished his tea. In an effort to neutralize any embarrassment on Doc's part, he tried to act as if nothing out of the ordinary had happened. He called out towards the kitchen, "Thanks for the tea, Doc. Be seeing you."

Nope, there just wasn't any analyzing Doc Bauchet.

Once in the car, Toby seemed anxious to explain himself. "Hey, man, I appreciate what the doc has done for me. I just wanted him to know that I appreciate it and that I got some money coming. I can pay him like everybody else does."

"I know, Toby. I understand. Doc Bauchet did behave strangely, even if he was insulted over your offer to pay. I can't figure it, either. You know him better than I do. How is it he knows so much about you?"

"Aw, man, he don't know nothin' about me. He just thinks he does. When I was a kid, I remember him coming around sometimes to get Mama to do his laundry like everybody else did. He'd always bring me a present. Rich guy doing his good deed, helping the poor kids in the slums. Guess it made him feel fine, alright. Don't know where he gets off telling me how to live my life."

"Toby, whatever you're up to is none of my business. How you got hurt is none of my business, but I've known you and your mama a long time, and I don't like seeing either one of you hurt. Your mama's been like family to me, you know that, and whatever you're mixed up in, I just hope it's legitimate and has nothing to do with what happened the other night. If it does, somebody's going to get hurt for keeps."

"It ain't nothing, man. Don't worry about it. Everything will be fine. You see, some people done me wrong, and I just got to take care of it. You would too, Luke, if it was you."

Luke saw that Toby wasn't going to see things his way, so he let it rest.

Before turning onto the road that led to Pirate's Cove, Luke pulled into the parking lot of Maxwell's Food Mart. "You'll need some supplies if you're not going to let your mama know you're home. You wait here."

Luke returned with a brown paper sack cradled in each arm. "I don't have to tell you what a mistake this is going to be if your mama finds out. She would run me to the far side of the county and beat me to a pulp with that big wooden spoon of hers if she thought I had anything to do with this."

For the first time, Toby smiled. "Oh, it hurts to laugh." He held his sides and laughed. "Everything still hurts."

A private, two-lane, dirt drive led to the cabins from Mamie's Place. As they bumped along past Mamie's, Toby scooted down a bit lower in the front seat. Riddled with guilt, Luke caught himself furtively slinking lower in his seat, too, as if he could hide from Mamie if she saw his car. There was nothing he liked about being placed in this position. It made him feel like a fugitive.

Toby directed Luke to the last shanty in the row, the one farthest from Mamie's Place. He left the car running in front of the cabin while he helped Toby out and carried the groceries in.

Once Toby was situated, Luke was anxious to get away from there. The day had gotten on. He had just enough time to get home, get cleaned up and get over to Cole's Bayou to pick Lisa up.

8

uke stood before the dresser in his room and fastened his crisply pressed khaki trousers. Before putting on the light-blue shirt Maria had laid out for him, he passed a comb through his damp hair and scrutinized his appearance in the mirror. Taking his good looks in stride and not given to vanity, he did realize the importance of keeping himself in shape for reasons other than appearance. While in the jungle, the litheness of his body enabled him to move quickly, and having always been active in sports, he liked the feeling of being in control of his body. He sucked in his breath and patted his rock-hard stomach with the flat of his palm—mustn't get soft around the middle from all this good life. His upper torso was lean and bronze.

A few days ago, time spent on the *Shady Lady* with Trotter had yielded more sunshine than fish. They spent a couple of relaxing days, talking about old times and reliving past adventures. Trotter even broke his own hard-fast rule of never allowing alcohol on board the *Lady* while at sea and had iced down a cooler of beer. Maria packed some sandwiches for them and on two of Trotter's slow days, they took off. One day they drifted around over Neptune's Reef, lazily wetting a hook and doing a little bottom fishing, but mostly enjoying the weather, not much caring to exert themselves. The second day was spent cruising along the shoreline, trolling for

Spanish mackerel. It had been good to relax. Those couple of days were long and lazy and pleasurable, something Luke had needed.

After a final pass of the comb, and a quick call to Oyster Bay for dinner reservations, Luke was off. There was an hour or two of daylight left when he turned off the main road and headed for Cole's Bayou.

The drive into the Bayou was a bit less foreboding now, given the fact that he wasn't trying to make his way into strange territory after dark. The limbs of the trees that lined the narrow road still came dangerously close to scratching the finish on his new car as he straddled the ruts and made it to the front of the cottage, but the going was a lot easier by light of day.

The earlier hour disclosed other revelations, such as a cottage that was somewhat shabbier looking and less *quaint* than before. The yard was unkempt and scraggly grass grew in patches. Some roofing shingles needed replacing and bare, weathered wood showed through the peeling paint of the cornice. There might as well not have been a screened door given all the holes that pocked the rusty screen. With all the existing decay, Luke found the most curious revelation to be a shiny, red and blue, children's swing set in the yard behind the scuppernong arbor.

Before Luke had a chance to get his car door open, Lisa appeared on the front stoop. As he stepped out of the car, he involuntarily emitted a long, low whistle at the sight of her. Her softness and femininity contrasted starkly with the backdrop of the dingy cottage. She was deceptively innocent looking, almost angelic. Tonight her silken black hair was pulled back with a clasp at the nape of her neck and fell in thick curls down her back. The white, priest-collar blouse she wore was slightly sheer, revealing lacy lingerie beneath that barely covered her breasts. Luke's pulse quickened and he recalled how it had felt to explore her body, and the smoothness of her skin beneath his calloused hands. The slim, navy-blue skirt she wore conformed to the lines of her shapely hips and did not leave much to the imagination.

Lisa smiled shyly at Luke as he approached the front stoop.

"You look beautiful, Lisa." He smiled his admiration. Her shyness was becoming. "I've made reservations for us at Oyster Bay. I hope that suits you." He now had second thoughts over making plans without consulting her. He hoped he had not been in error in assuming she would want him to plan the evening. Some women liked that, he had found, but some didn't. Lisa didn't seem to necessarily be a take-charge type of woman, but where intimacy was concerned, he already had discovered she liked being in control. The way she looked tonight, he would go anywhere she wanted him to.

"The food is good," Luke continued, persuasively. "I thought it'd be nice to go somewhere on the water. That is, if you want to," he added for good measure. "I guess you've been there? I suppose everyone in Pemrose Key has been to Oyster Bay at one time or another."

"Well, of course I have, Luke. I've been to Oyster Bay lots of times." The breathy southern accent was back.

When she spoke, Luke was once again reminded of the last time they were together. He had relived many times during the past week the events of that evening. It had been an evening of lust and passions misspent with this woman-child-seductress. What a fool he'd been. Would tonight be different? He was undeniably "in lust" with her.

Few words were spoken on the way to Oyster Bay. Luke liked the fact that Lisa was quiet and her silence even gave him a comfortable feeling. He was keenly aware of her sensuality as she sat beside him in the front seat of his car, and the quiet allowed him to reflect on what might possibly transpire.

Luke drove through the familiar gates of Oyster Bay and pulled around to the rear, where he knew there would be a few vacant parking spots that the general public didn't know about. As the most popular place in Pemrose Key, the restaurant was always crowded with an even mix of tourists, locals, and Navy personnel.

Lisa pulled a lipstick from her purse and when Luke stopped the car, she reached up and adjusted the rear-view mirror so she might view herself. She pursed her lips and dabbed on a touch of color, sensuously alternating between running the tip of the lipstick and the tip of her tongue across pouty lips. She turned away from the mirror and gave Luke an inviting look, one that blatantly seemed to say, *take me, I'm yours*. She had a way about her of making the simple act of applying lipstick look like an invitation to slip between the sheets.

"I'll be the envy of every man here tonight, Lisa." Luke eyed her appreciatively.

He opened the car door for her and as she got out, she made no attempt to conceal the immodest portion of shapely thigh her short skirt revealed.

He would let nature take its course tonight. First, a nice leisurely dinner, a couple of drinks, and from there...? Lisa had said that Edna's mother didn't care what she did. After that message and the signals she's been sending tonight, who knew what might happen? He felt a stirring of arousal as his mind raced ahead to his plans for the evening. Past the dinner...past the drinks...past the casual conversation, and on to the *Shady Lady*, where Trotter had invited Luke to spend a little time after dinner with his lovely lady friend. Just a short stroll down to the end of the pier to the door of the *Shady Lady*'s cabin—a little music, soft lights, the gentle rocking of the boat. So what if he was a drowning man? He couldn't think of a better way to go.

Luke guided Lisa past the many people milling about on the dock. He led her up the wide wooden steps to the lounge. His plan was to have a drink while waiting to be seated.

Even with reservations there was always a wait for a table in the dining room at Oyster Bay. Guess you could say it was *tradition*. The tourists expected it. Serenaded by music blaring from well-positioned loudspeakers, they strolled up and down the pier, yacht-watching and doing their own bit of daydreaming. They sipped from tall plastic glasses filled with fruit-laden tropical drinks while waiting to be called.

A group of sailors sat at the bar and as Luke and Lisa walked past, the sailor's catcalls began. Drunken young men whistled and nudged one another, elbowing each other in the sides as Lisa passed. Luke bristled and stopped dead in his tracks.

Lisa turned and smiled at the boys at the bar, and with a thick-as-molasses drawl, greeted them congenially. "Hi, boys. How are y'all this fine evening?" She seemed to forget Luke's presence. She winked at the sailors flirtatiously and waved the tips of her fingers at them. Luke was distressed to witness this unladylike response, but he was even more stricken when they called her by name and responded in kind with much familiarity.

To make matters worse, Lisa began to roll their names off the tip of her tongue in recognition of so many old friends. Her attention finally turned to Luke. "I want y'all to meet someone, fellas." She reached for Luke's hand and pulled him closer. "This is Luke, boys, Mr. Lucas Callaway. Now y'all be nice to him, y'hear?"

The one sitting at the bar closest to Luke slapped him on the back. He closed one eye in a pathetic effort at focusing and placed a heavy arm across Luke's shoulders. "Luke, how ya' doing? Good to see ya', ol' buddy."

The entire group greeted Luke in unison, waving their drinks in the air with gusto, sloshing them towards Luke in a sloppy toast and reaching to shake his hand with much the same familiarity, but not as much enthusiasm, with which they had greeted Lisa.

They were just a bunch of kids still wet behind the ears, but their familiarity with Lisa made Luke uncomfortable. He extended his hand to the one who embraced him.

"Joey, right? He didn't think this guy knew whether he was *Joey* or not, nor did he seem to care.

Having made a congenial showing, Luke tried to move along smoothly, past this uninvited interruption and on to his evening with Lisa.

"See you boys later." Luke placed his hand firmly around Lisa's waist at the small of her back and nudged her gently, attempting to finally guide her away from the bar. "There's a table for us over there, Lisa, by the window." As he spoke the words, Joey leaned over and grabbed for Lisa, ignoring Luke's hand at her waist. He cupped his palm around Lisa's rump and patted it fondly, and to Luke's outrage, with too much intimacy. Lisa giggled and squealed, not minding Joey's audacity at all.

Luke took hold of Joey's wrist and squeezed forcibly until the sailor's hand went limp, forcing it away from Lisa's derrière. His arm twisted in Luke's grasp and his body rose involuntarily off his bar stool. "Don't EVER do that again!" Luke demanded venomously through clenched teeth, his nostrils flared and his eyes reflected an intensity of anger that he had not frequently experienced as he thrust Joey's wrist aside forcibly.

That was the last thing Luke remembered clearly.

Though the pain was vivid, what happened next was a bit hazy. He saw a beer mug coming at his head, and his guts suddenly felt like they had been ripped open. He couldn't breathe. Six drunken sailors lunged at him and tried their best to beat him to death before he lost consciousness.

When Luke came to, he lay on the floor in a watery puddle of blood and booze. Jake, the bartender, was kneeling over him with a dish towel packed with crushed ice, dabbing at one of his eyes. The young sailors were nowhere in sight. "Hey, Luke, one minute into it you knocked two guys out cold. The one that started it got a broken arm and there were enough teeth scattered around here to make a set of dentures. You were pretty rough on them."

"Owww! I feel like I've been run through the meat grinder." Luke massaged his aching jaw. "Where's Lisa?" he moaned. Through the pain, he remembered how the evening began. He pushed at Jake's arm and tried to raise his head. When he did, everything began to sway, including the fisherman's netting and painted life preservers that decorated the walls of the lounge. He lowered his head back to the floor.

"Stay put." Jake applied a slight bit of pressure to Luke's shoulder to hold him in place against the floor.

Searing pain shot down Luke's elbow and up across his shoulder.

"Let me see that." Jake expertly probed Luke's shoulder, gently maneuvering and feeling with his fingertips and the flat of his palm. "Your shoulder's dislocated, Luke. You do double time in Vietnam without a scratch, but all it takes is one night at Oyster Bay for you to get mangled like an old pole cat in an alley fight. You did do most of the mangling, though. I never saw anything like it, the way you took on all six of those fellows at once."

"Yeah? Well, I'm glad you know what happened to get me in this shape, because I sure don't remember. I feel like a brick wall fell on me." Luke turned his head to the side and looked around the room. Now that the excitement was over, everybody had gone back to the more serious business of eating and drinking. In spite of excruciating pain, he had to know. "Where's my date? Did anybody see where Lisa went?"

"Lisa split when it started getting rough. When you grabbed Joey, one of his buddies came at you with a beer mug. All I got to say is it's a good thing you're hard-headed, Luke. While you still had hold of Joey's arm, the fellow next to him came at you head first, right into your guts like a battering ram. He caught you off guard, alright, then the rest of them got in on the action. You started swinging and might near took all of them out with one swipe. I never saw anything like it, Luke. You just about killed 'em. They were ready to run home to Mama. At the first sign of trouble I called the Shore Patrol, but by the time I hung up and was coming to help you, you'd pretty much taken care of the situation. They rounded up those boys and herded them out like a bunch of sheep. Those sailors won't be feeling any pain tonight, but by the time that alcohol wears off tomorrow, they'll be suffering plenty. Looky here, got me a couple of souvenirs." Jake grinned and opened his palm to display two small white objects tinged with blood.

"Damn! They're not mine, are they?" Luke explored his mouth with his tongue.

"Naw, I already checked. Thought I'd save these just to show you who fared the worst. C'mon, I think we can move you now." Jake gripped Luke's good arm and helped him to a sitting position.

Luke winced and fought back a wave of nausea. "Feels like they worked me over pretty good."

"Hold still, Luke." Jake made one swift movement.

Intense pain wracked Luke's body. "Son-of-a-gun, Jake!" He sucked his breath in and held it for a moment. "What are you doing to me?" he demanded, still trembling from the pain. Luke knew, but it happened so fast he was unable to stop him. He also knew it had to be done. Thank God it was over quickly. He was sore, but he could move his shoulder and arm now.

"Had to put your shoulder back in place. I was a medic in Nam. Took care of several like this, Luke. Don't worry, you'll be as good as new as soon as those claw marks on your face heal and that knot on your head goes down."

"Well, thank the Lord for that." Luke rubbed his shoulder. With Jake's assistance, he picked himself up off the floor.

The evening had been a huge disappointment. Not only had he been beaten up by a bunch of kids, but in a final blow to his ego, the lady of his life hadn't cared enough to hang around and administer first-aid. Where could Lisa have disappeared to in such a hurry? He was curious, but at the moment, he didn't feel like trying to find out.

9

*O*n a few days Luke was as good as new. He was young, strong and resilient. As soon as he healed, he hit the road running. Aside from the pain, what bothered him about his injuries was the delay incurred in his quest for instituting his master plan. He had already invested endless hours at the drawing board, blueprinting his ideas, investigating all avenues of possibilities for financing, personnel requirements, location availability—all things needed for the eventual attainment of his goals. He was excited about a location out at Mango Junction, the old Seafarer boat plant, but he needed cash to secure a lease on it.

As relentless as he was in the pursuit of his dream, time was running out on him. He was depleting his financial resources and he needed machinery and tools, and employees, and a place to work. He needed money. The little he had been able to save while in Vietnam was only enough to pay deposits and down-payments on some of his equipment. It barely made a dent in what he needed, but it was a start. He felt like he was doing something, and those little "somethings" might serve to lend validity to his long-held ambition of designing and building the boats of his dreams, thus influencing an investor.

Luke was probably more handicapped in his efforts to borrow or find an investor because of who he was than if he had been your average John-Doe-with-a-good-idea type of guy. Ryan knew every potential investor in the area and Luke, knowing the pain his father had suffered over the rejection of his job offer, could not pour salt into the wound by going to one of his father's friends.

Luke did acquiesce to his parents wishes that he stay on at The Magnolias for awhile, the advantage being that it helped him save on living expenses. He'd lived lean in the military in order to save money and he could do it again. His parents insisted he stay, and there was no conceivable reason why he shouldn't.

Living at home did have one drawback—it cramped his style some-what where Lisa was concerned. In the weeks that followed, he and Lisa continued to see each other. Their evenings were uneventful. Edna was frequently present, and he often felt that she and Lisa had planned things that way. Lisa continued to frustrate him and hold him at bay.

The more he saw of her, the more his feelings for her intensi-fied. The longer he did without her, the more obsessive his desire for her. He couldn't stand to think about her with another man now. He wanted her for himself. The depth of his emotions surprised him. His reaction a few weeks ago to Joey fondling Lisa had sprung from where? Why had he reacted so strongly when he hardly knew the woman? Where had those feelings come from? All questions he needed answers to. In order for their relationship to progress, he had to persuade her to spend some time alone with him. Perhaps she was getting all she wanted out of the relationship. Perhaps he was wast-ing his time. Tonight he intended to find out.

Edna's mother answered when he called.

"Mrs. Sinclair? This is Luke Callaway. Is Lisa in?"

"Who? Who do you want to talk to?" She sounded like Edna when she screeched the words.

"Lisa...your niece...Lisa Logan."

There was a pause; Luke thought she had hung up.

"I know who you are, boy...I know who you are. What are you doing calling here? You hurt her. You hurt my baby. You did, you hurt my..."

There was a muffled sound, then Lisa's voice was on the other end of the line. Mrs. Sinclair never finished the sentence.

"Hello...this is Lisa."

"Lisa, it's Luke. What does she mean, Lisa? Are you okay?"

"Everything's fine, Luke. She gets confused. She was talking about something else. How are you doing, Shugah? I'm so glad you called me. I was just thinking about you." The words tumbled out in a soft, breathless rush.

"Lisa, would you like to go out tonight, just the two of us for a change?"

"I would love to, Luke. Maybe we could try Oyster Bay again."

"Oyster Bay it is. Pick you up at six?"

"Six o'clock is fine, Luke. I can't wait to see you."

The playful hint of what was perhaps to come helped put his fears to rest.

Luke pulled up in front of Lisa's house at precisely six o'clock. Just as before, she was out the door the minute he came to a stop, this time even before he had a chance to get out of the car.

Tonight she had on a red dress with a low-cut ruffled neckline, a tight fitting bodice, and a full skirt that fell in red swirls around her knees. Bright red, polished toenails peeked out from the end of dainty, red, high-heeled sandals. She was a bewitching gypsy with flowing black hair. Her dark eyes danced playfully when she saw him, and he knew she could read every emotion reflected in his face—awe, approval, excitement, anticipation. How was he going to get through another evening with any degree of self-control? She was mysterious. Exciting. That's what drew him to her, like a firefly to a flame. It wasn't entirely about sex. He wanted her more than ever, but it was her complexity that presented him with the challenge. She puzzled him and delighted him and scared him to death, and he loved being with her, he was discovering. She was pulling him in, bit by bit, and he had become a willing captive.

The night was warm and muggy. It was one of those still, summer evenings when nothing moved, not a breeze stirred. They drove along the beach road with the top down. The hot air ruffled their hair and the heat and humidity dampened their skin. Across the still waters of the Gulf, the moon reflected in a smooth, unbroken line; a sheer, glassy pathway shooting straight into the night, all the way to infinity and narrowing into a silvery thread on the horizon, creating the illusion that one could easily walk across the glassy waters, for as far as the eye could see.

Lisa interrupted the stillness of the night with her soft drawl. "Luke, I know it hasn't been long since we started seeing each other..." Sitting close beside him, she watched his face as she spoke. "...but I just have this feeling about you. I want to marry you and be with you forever. You may not know it yet, but you want to marry me, too. At least you will, when you really, really understand how happy I can make you."

Lisa's left hand rested comfortably on Luke's leg and she began to rub back and forth along his thigh in a slow...steady...motion. Starting at his kneecap and sliding her hand up his leg far enough to tease, but not too far—back and forth she rubbed, with a comfortable familiarity—a hypnotic, repetitive-type motion, back... and...forth.

It was not her words, nor the stimulation of the motion of her hand upon him, but her voice that held him spellbound. "I know it surely must sound crazy to you, but I just have this feeling, you know, like it's going to happen. I know it will."

There. She had done more than plant the seed. She had cast a spell. This gypsy-woman beside him spoke with an intuitiveness that made him nervous. When he glanced down at her for a moment, her dark eyes revealed a worldliness beyond her years. That made him more nervous, but he didn't protest, something told him she was right. And she was right about something else—it was crazy! It was absolutely insane! How could he be allowing this to happen? He had determined a couple of months ago, when he had met Cooper DeLaney, that marriage and romance would have to be put on hold until he had straightened a few things out in his life, such as his career. Marriage was the last thing he wanted to think about. Why was he having such a difficult time controlling his emotions and his life? He had already determined he was not in love with Lisa, in lust maybe, but not in love. Particularly not to the degree of already making plans to marry her. He barely knew her. What was she doing to him? Every time he saw her, the situation became more serious. She had gotten under his skin, that was certain. His own choices seemed to be becoming less of an option as he found himself succumbing to her provocative charms.

Luke pulled the car off to the side of the road. He looked out across the smooth waters of his beloved Gulf, at the moon's straight and silvery path. Strange feelings he had, the silvery path suddenly represented an escape route. Escape from what? His fate seemed so certain now, and something told him his choices had narrowed to two: The only way he would not marry Lisa would be to walk out across the water and follow the silvery path straight to eternity. That summed up his choices. Life with this beautiful creature could not be as fatal as all that. In a matter of minutes, the course Luke's life would take had been altered. Despite his fears, he felt a sense of composure that he had not experienced in the weeks since meeting Lisa. The inexplicable, nagging sense of urgency that had been his constant companion of late dissipated with this new and sudden resolve, this unexpected twist of fate. It dispelled all his fears and relieved all his anxiety, and suddenly, just having sex with Lisa wasn't so urgent...he would marry her.

He pulled her to him and gazed deeply into her eyes. The tender kiss he gave her was more than a kiss, it was a promise.

He held Lisa's hand in his as he drove the rest of the way to Oyster Bay in silence.

Tonight, Luke had Lisa all to himself. The waitress poured from an expensive bottle of wine Luke selected and when she turned away, they toasted their happiness and good fortune at finding one another. Everything was going well. They had a good table next to the window—an excellent vantage point for viewing the channel and watching the activity of the boats coming and going, and the scuttle of tourists meandering up and down the docks.

Luke saw Tommy Granger walking towards them. Following closely behind were Scotty Dillard and Peyton Fuller, all old-time regulars from the Oyster Bay days of their youth.

"Uh-oh, here comes trouble." He set his wine glass down and eyed their approach.

Peyton was a few years older than Luke, but they had known each other from Oyster Bay summers even before Luke's family moved to Pemrose Key. Peyton was a walking contradiction. He was short and fat and dumb looking, with a good disposition. He was a brilliant attorney, though. Perhaps attributable to his deceptively mild appearance and jovial personality, he was able to slip in slowly for the kill, disabling many a more experienced attorney when the odds were stacked heavily against him. His daddy was one of Florida's most revered senators and a personal acquaintance of Ryan Callaway. In just a few short years Peyton had built quite a reputation for himself in Escambia County based on his own merit, and only slightly advantaged by the benefit of his father's name and contacts in Washington. Peyton seemed determined to achieve success in his own right. His father was bullish and blustery, and cast a large shadow. He cut quite a wide swath for Peyton to make his way through, but now, with an eye on a future in politics himself,

Peyton was making every effort to cut his own path. He had graduated from high school at sixteen and completed college and law school in record time. With a good shot at being elected Circuit Judge in November, he seemed to be well on his way to following in Daddy's large footprints.

Scotty and Tommy had crewed aboard the *King Fisher* at Oyster Bay when they were kids. The *Shady Lady* and the *King Fisher* had been sister boats. They frequently went out together on offshore trips, and their captains built their "beds" together, the manmade reefs they created by hauling trees and old cars and various other large items of debris and dumping them overboard. These offshore landfills then became their designated, private fishing holes. The captains of the other boats respected this and everybody stayed away from everybody else's "hole."

Scotty and Tommy were "good ol' boys" and never seemed to change. Scotty was a slob. He took no pride in his appearance. His wide-eyed, innocent expression and youthful features were always masked by his eternal need for a shave. A full-grown beard would have been a vast improvement over the unkempt, scruffy, in-between look he sported. The stubble of dark hair against his fair skin looked much like soot smeared across his cherubic cheeks, dirtying his face and hiding potentially good looks. Scotty didn't have a great deal of ambition, and he was happy to occupy his time as a "sometimes" inland fishing guide. Had he a bit more initiative it could have been a fairly lucrative business for him, but it just wasn't in him. He only fished when he wanted to fish, and not always when he had customers that wanted to. He relied heavily on the support of Odessa Barlew. She was more like an adopted mama to him than his lady friend. Odessa was a good bit older than Scotty and had no children of her own. Scotty was her "baby." The man had just never grown up, and he fell into the role with ease. He was a natural for it.

Tommy was something else again. He had tough good looks and was very vain. The women would die for him. He was with a new one every week. He called them his "Broadies" or "Broads," not a great showing of respect for the female gender, but he loved women. Of course the women that tended "to die" for him did resemble his terminology. He was still a "good ol' boy." His vanity didn't interfere with his friendship and loyalty to his buddies, and they all kidded him about his looks and his weakness for the women. Tommy was a supervisor at the paper mill with ambitions of one day becoming captain of his own charter boat, as Trotter had, but he never expressed an urgency to accomplish this. It appeared it would be a long row for him to hoe. Boats were expensive, and he didn't have the advantage of "severance" pay as Trotter called it.

Tommy gave Luke a rousing whack on the shoulder as he passed, and for a moment Luke thought he was going to pass on by. Instead, he stopped, and he and Peyton and Scotty gathered around Luke and Lisa's table. Tommy Granger spoke first, "Hey, Lucas, you in here looking for trouble again?"

"C'mon, Luke, don't you go stirring up no trouble with the Navy tonight, you hear now?" Peyton Fuller grinned from ear to ear and gave Luke the thumbs up sign.

"Odessa Barlew said you told her you was going to join the Navy, Lucas. What you gon' do a thing like that for?" Scotty Dillard chuckled at his own joke.

"That's right, Scotty. What do you think that fight was all about? You know those Navy boys just wouldn't take 'no' for an answer. They said I'd be an asset to the U.S. Navy, and when I told them I was partial to the Marines they just got a little upset, that's all." Luke winked at Lisa. Everybody in Pemrose Key knew about the bar-room brawl.

Scotty hooted. "Pardon us for hornin' in, Ma'am, but we haven't seen this old scoundrel in years. We was about to forget all about him 'till we heard he showed his ugly face in here again last week."

"What's this about Odessa Barlew, Scotty? You still seeing that woman? I thought for sure you two would've gotten hitched by now. You're not chicken, are you?" Luke knew Scotty had vowed to never marry.

"Yeah, I'm chicken. I ain't letting no woman put a noose around my neck. The good Lord gave me better sense than that. I was single when I came into this world and that's how I aim to go to my glory. A wife might make me shave!"

Lisa's sandaled foot found Luke's leg under the table. She began to rub it up and down along the back of his calf. Luke struggled to maintain a poker face and not let these jokers get an inkling something serious might be brewing. His brain must be defective for him to think they couldn't read him like a book. When he looked at Lisa he nearly lost it. She sat across from him, maintaining a chaste demeanor, while rubbing his leg and drawing him in with a look of secrecy and seduction. How did she do that? Concealment of the development in their relationship was hopeless when Lisa reached across the table and placed her hand on top of Luke's, smiling at the men as she did so.

"Wait a minute! What's this all about? What we been missing here, boys? Looks like Luke and Lisa know something we don't." Nothing escaped Peyton's keen legal eye.

Luke couldn't protest. He felt like a kid caught with his hand in the cookie jar, but strangely enough, he didn't care.

Lisa batted her eyelashes. "What are you boys talking about?" Her hand in Luke's, she secretively tickled the center of his palm, and looked with wide-eyed innocence at Scotty, Tommy and Peyton.

Luke spread the fingers of his left hand apart slowly and rubbed his ring finger with his thumb. Caught up in the banter and gazing across the table at Lisa's exquisite features, he verbalized his earlier realization. "Meet the future Mrs. Lucas Callaway, gentlemen. We probably would've set the date by now if you hadn't come along and interrupted this private dinner party." Luke joked good-naturedly. He would have to tell his parents immediately now that his newly-laid plans had been exposed.

A familiar voice greeted the bartender. They all turned at once to see Trotter making his way across the hardwood floor, being careful not to bump his artificial leg into any chair legs that stuck out in the aisle.

"Trotter Blackwell..." Tommy stopped mid-sentence when he saw the grim look on Trotter's face.

Trotter spoke not a word as he neared the group. When he reached them, he retrieved a chair from a nearby table and dragged it across the floor. Using the chair back for support, he continued to stand while he made his announcement.

"There's been some trouble at Mamie's. Somebody blew up one of her cabins. Mamie said she got an anonymous phone call yesterday and somebody told her she was fixing to lose something valuable. She thought it was a prank until this happened tonight. God only knows why anybody would do this to Mamie. She never hurt anybody. That's what ticks me off. Thing she can't figure, they said 'something valuable,' and those shanties aren't worth squat. The cabin nearest the restaurant was the only one occupied. Some fishermen are staying there and they were over at Mamie's when it happened, so nobody was hurt. The worry is, were they really trying to kill somebody?"

A nauseous knot welled up in the pit of Luke's gut. He smacked his hands against the table and raised himself to a standing position.

"WHICH cabin, Trotter? Which one got it?" Luke demanded, anxiously. Out of the six cabins, Trotter had confirmed that the one next to Mamie's Place was okay. That gave Toby a one-in-five chance.

"It was the last one in the row, down on the far end. Why?" Trotter raised an eyebrow. "That's why the restaurant wasn't damaged. What's the matter, Luke? You look like you've seen a ghost."

"We have to get over there." Luke pulled his car keys from his pocket. "How long ago did it happen, Trotter? Were you there?"

"I was there. Just a few hours ago I stopped by to get a bite to eat. As soon as I sat down at the table it felt like judgement day coming on us. For a few seconds there I relived a whole year of Vietnam. Mamie has closed the place down for the night. She's pretty shook up. I came over here as soon as the dust settled. There's not really much we can do over there now."

"Toby's been staying in that cabin." The impact of Luke's revelation was clearly translated in the expressions of the four men.

"Why wasn't he at his mama's? That's where he always stays when he's not running with that bunch of bums he hangs out with." Scotty sounded like the pot calling the kettle black. His round eyes widened naively when the others looked at him.

"Let's take the *Lady*. It'll be quicker by water," Trotter volunteered.

"I have to take Lisa home." Luke motioned for the waitress to bring their check. "I'll meet you over there afterwards."

Lisa had remained silent throughout the conversation, looking from one to the other. Luke wasn't sure she understood what it meant about Toby being in the cabin, but he was grateful that she seemed to understand what he must do.

"That's alright, Luke, darlin.' Edna will be here after 'while and she can take me home. You go on. We'll see each other later. Go on now. I'll be alright."

So his evening alone with Lisa was to have included Edna after all. "Let's go." Luke angrily stuffed his own keys back in his pocket.

Trotter viewed their exchange wordlessly. His lips were taut as he dangled the keys of the *Shady Lady* from his fingers.

Trotter brought up the rear as the five men clattered down the wooden steps that led from the restaurant to the dock. Before descending the steps, Luke turned to glance through the glass picture-window. Lisa was nowhere in sight.

10

he men converged on the *Shady Lady*'s slip, and Luke's thoughts of Lisa were temporarily tucked away in the back of his mind. Once aboard, all five men moved into action. Trotter at the helm, Luke and the others each taking a line and releasing the *Shady Lady* from her restraints. Boating was second nature to all of them. They could go through the motions of launching a boat in their sleep. Luke looked around at the five of them together once again. There were no four men on earth he would trust his life to more than these four scalawags.

The sky was hazing over and the moonlight only peeked through the clouds intermittently now. Luke stood alone on the bow of the boat as she cut through the night, heading out into the blackness of the open channel. There was almost total darkness, save for a few lights twinkling along the shore. Luke's heart was heavy with grief, knowing that Toby must have been in the cabin. The few times Luke had checked on him, Toby was still laying low. His nasty wounds required time to heal and he refused to let Doc take another look at them.

Just beyond the marina, the shoreline of the narrow channel was sparsely populated. To an unknowing soul it would have seemed an impossibility to find their way through the dark waters at night, even under the glow of an occasional moonbeam, and the *Shady Lady* was not equipped with radar. Each of the men aboard the

Lady relied on exceptional navigational abilities, and an uncanny "sixth-sense" that a lifetime on the water had equipped them with.

Once the *Shady Lady* was well underway, Scotty, Tommy and Peyton sat outside the cabin in a close circle in the cockpit, talking loudly over the noise of the engines, speculating over the possibilities that Luke could be wrong, that maybe Toby was no longer staying at the cabin. With Toby foremost on their minds, they reminisced about childhood escapades.

Luke stood apart and listened as they talked about the trouble they used to get into with Toby, and how they always used him for a scapegoat because he was a couple of years younger and smaller than the others. He tried so hard to please the older boys and he wanted to be as big as them. It had been fun to play jokes on him. When Toby would realize he'd been duped, he sputtered comically and tried to lash out at them with his fists, but invariably, he was too small to do any damage. How badly they would feel now if he were dead. After all these years, they felt a little guilty about how they often lead him into thinking it was okay to do something. Before he caught on, they had him going in as the ringleader in whatever scheme they dreamed up. Toby would be the one to get in trouble over the things the other boys instigated, and he would be the one left holding the bag. They always ran off ahead, leaving Toby to face some neighbor lady wielding a broom, or someone else screaming and yelling at him about his gang of hoodlums and troublemakers.

Toby was a likable kid—a good sport, agreeable and always ready to please the older white boys. It had all been good-natured teasing. Toby was a friend, a little brother to them all. Thing about it was, the adult Toby never seemed to realize that those boys didn't think in terms of black or white. They liked him back then, just for being Toby. They never thought of him or his mama, or any of the other Negro families in town as being a different color than they were. There were a few exceptions, but for the most part, that was the kind of community Pemrose Key was. People were just people. They were either good or bad, not black or white. Mamie was wise enough to know this, but Toby thought in terms of black and white as he grew older. That's what hurt him. He seemed to become a little bitter and resentful of white people who had never done anything but try to be his friend. As a grown man, he still seemed to think he needed to strive for acceptance by white folks on the one hand, while resenting them on the other. The resentment didn't manifest itself until he was older, though, when he lost his innocence. That might be what kept him in trouble. The resentment began to fester and grow and served no purpose but to make him miserable, and create much heartache for his mama. Everyone knew Mamie had so hoped the military would help.

With Trotter behind the wheel, the *Shady Lady* raced across the motionless bay, swiftly arriving a short distance offshore from Mamie's Place. Trotter pulled back on the throttles, slowing the boat to idle speed. Tonight there was no music wafting across the water from Mamie's Place. No dancing shadows. No lively crowd; no laughter or merriment echoing across the bay. There were bright lights—plenty of lights—spotlights, red flashing police lights, flashlights, lights that focused brightly on the vacant lot where the cabin once stood.

Luke looked with sickening disbelief at the charred ruins and the rubble that littered the narrow strip of beach in front of Mamie's Place. Blackened debris floated in the water all around them. He began to tremble. The scene reminded him of the ravages of war.

One small trace of moonlight found its way through the clouds and reflected on the water. Luke's disbelief turned to horror when he saw, about twenty feet out, the mangled remains of a man's body floating face down in the water. He turned to holler out to Trotter, but he held his words when he saw the split-second glistening of the stainless steel wheel turning sharply in Trotter's hands. From Trotter's vantage point high up on the bridge, he, too, had seen.

In the face of disaster, Luke's trembling subsided. There was work to do. He moved into action before the other three were even aware of what he and Trotter had seen. He moved quickly from the bow and stood poised over the safety railing at the stern of the boat, gaff in hand, while Trotter carefully maneuvered the *Shady Lady* closer to the body.

Finally, aware of Luke's intentions, the three men sitting in the cockpit rose to their feet.

"Oh, man! Would you look at that. I think I'm gonna' puke!" Scotty gagged and covered his mouth with his hand.

"My gosh! Do you think it's Toby?" Tommy got no response. Perhaps nobody else wanted to put their fears into words just yet.

"Let's just everybody stay calm. We don't have any facts on what's happened here. We don't know for a fact that this is Toby. We don't even know for sure that this poor old fella' was even in the explosion." Arms outstretched, palms flattened to the air, Peyton's courtroom body-language came into play as he tried to take control of the situation.

"Oh, hell, Peyton. Would you quit being a dad-gummed lawyer for a few minutes. Good Lord knows, we ain't got no facts on nothing yet. Nobody said we did. What we got here's a dad-blamed dead body, for cripe's sake." Tommy turned his head in disgust and spat a brown stream of tobacco juice over the railing.

"I ain't never seen a dead body before, 'cept at a funeral. Neither have you, Peyton, and I bet you haven't either, Tommy." Scotty's round eyes were twice their normal size.

"Trotter and Luke have, you can bet your precious ass on that one." Peyton had dropped the lawyer bit.

"You boys get that hatch cover and bring it over here." It was Luke's turn to give orders. "Tommy, how about getting those spare lines off the bridge. Trotter will hand them down to you. We're going to use the winch to hoist him up once I get him on the hatch cover. That'll be our stretcher. Go ahead and tie a line on for me. It's going to be pretty heavy, but I think that with the winch in position, and the right kind of help from all of you, we can do it." Luke removed his shoes and trousers. Before anybody could answer, he climbed over the railing and dove into the dark waters while Trotter held a beam of light on the body.

Luke swam the distance, then gave instructions from the water. "Okay, lower the hatch cover. Easy...don't make any waves, just lower it gently. That's good, that's good. Now, hold it right there until I get this fellow over there," Luke directed from the water. He mentally removed himself from any personal connection with the situation, focusing solely on the task at hand. Vietnam...in Luke's mind there was no difference. All disasters and casualties were the same. He couldn't allow himself to think in real terms about the body, and the fact that a few short hours ago this was a living, breathing being, possibly his friend, Toby.

Luke moved mechanically. He took one arm and positioned it over his own shoulder, pulling the body along as he paddled. When the hatch cover was at arm's length, he pulled it slowly towards him, then worked his way around to the other side of the body, positioning it between himself and the hatch cover, which he wedged in under the edge of the swim platform that ran the full width of the transom. With the hatch cover pushed against the boat, it gave him some leverage. Tommy stepped over the safety rail and onto the swim platform. He was able to lean over and help hold the cover in place while Luke began lifting the body, bit by bit, onto the cover; first an arm, then the head and another arm, then the torso. The legs were last. One foot was missing. For a moment Luke's intensely applied concentration waned when he saw the bloody stump where a foot had been. His eyes darted to the bridge and for one brief moment, focused on Trotter's face, which was faintly illuminated by the green glow of the control panel lights. Trotter was handling it. He was tough, and there wasn't a shred of self-pity in him.

Luke grimly went back to the task at hand, his eyes now as distant as cold, hard steel. He watched from the water as his friends took over and did their part. They rigged the winch, hoisted up the hatch cover containing the body, and slowly lowered it to the cockpit floor.

Trotter was still at the controls. Luke washed the blood off his arms and the front of his shirt. None of the three who stood in the cockpit wanted to be the one to roll the body over. They stood there quietly, looking down at the dead man and waiting for Luke to climb back aboard.

Luke grasped hold of the swim platform and swung himself up to a sitting position. He rested his back against the transom while he garnered the fortitude to face what was on board the boat. Was it Toby? He stood and stepped over the transom into the cockpit. He unbuttoned and removed his soggy shirt, then pulled his trousers on over his wet skivvies. Every movement was slow and measured, delaying the moment of truth. He felt a heaviness in his chest. No one else was going to do it. He had all the time in the world. Trotter would have done it, but he was still holding the boat in position, maneuvering the controls.

Damn! I don't like these feelings. He rubbed at the ache in his chest. I don't want to feel. It's Lisa. She's awakened feelings in me again. When he thought of her these days, an unfulfilled hunger gnawed incessantly at him and filled him with an ache similar to the one now pressing on his chest. The ache generated by thoughts of Lisa was more tolerable than this. He would think about her now. Not where he was or what he was doing, or about who this was lying here, blown to bits. Thinking of her made his head stop spinning. Normally, thoughts of her made his head spin.

Luke clenched his hands into a fist and knelt beside the body. He hesitated before turning it on its side. As horrible as the sight, he was almost relieved at what he saw. There was no way to tell by looking at this face who it might be—there wasn't enough face left to distinguish facial features. No use checking pockets for identification, either. The garments were in shreds, and there were no pockets to check. The only thing they could do was continue to speculate until the coroner did his part.

Scotty leaned over the railing, sick to his stomach for real now. Tommy chewed his cud rapidly, spitting three consecutive streams into the water. Surprisingly, Peyton had more of a stomach for it than these two. He began to espouse his legal jargon again, nervously, for sure, but maintaining a fairly cool head.

"Alright, we still don't know for certain who this is. We gotta' stay calm—everybody stay calm. Let me do the talking to the police. Here's what they'll do—they'll keep us all night questioning us about every little detail—they'll want to know what position he was in when we found him; what condition he was in; how we happened to find him; what we saw in the water near him; what we think happened to him...and so on and so forth."

"Hell, Peyton, what kind of condition do you think they're going to think he was in? You think they'll think we did this to the poor guy when there's been a major explosion a few hundred yards away? You think they'll say we tore his face off after we found him floating around out here all by himself? Maybe they'll think we played tug-o-war with his foot, too." Tommy chewed furiously now.

"Oh, man! Don't...don't talk like that, Tommy. That's gross. Of course Peyton knows they're not going to think we did this, are they Peyton?" Scotty anxiously awaited reassurance from Peyton.

"'Course not. I'm just carrying on. Guess I been spending too much time in the courtroom lately." Peyton wiped at the sweat on his forehead with the back of his hand. "Damn! It's not even June yet and it's already hotter'n a blast furnace. Whew! Not a breeze stirring. Looks like we might get a little rain, though. Maybe it'll cool things off some."

Luke tilted his head up and peered into the night sky. He had remained quiet, taking it all in. Now he had his own observations to make. "I think we're all overreacting. It's obvious this fellow was hit in the explosion. I thought at first it might be Toby, but who knows, it might've been somebody walking along the beach, or a fisherman out in a dinghy right off shore. No sense getting in too big a sweat over it being Toby, yet." Luke fervently wished he could believe his own words. Whoever it was, it was too bad, but he hoped it was someone he didn't know. "Can't even tell whether this fellow's black or white. We need to stay calm, like Peyton said. We can't change anything that's happened. All we can do is see if there is anything we can do to help out."

In the debris-ridden waters, Trotter headed the *Shady Lady* up the beach, opposite the current's direction. He steered clear of the bulk of the rafters, siding, and roofing tin floating around, threatening damage to his boat. The water along the beach was shallow, but there were the rickety remains of a pier a couple of hundred yards up the beach from the cabins. Trotter nosed the *Lady* in neatly at the end. The other four men acted quickly in securing the lines, fastening the *Lady* snugly into position.

Luke led the way. Scotty and Peyton followed closely on his heels, making their way down the beach, stepping over and around driftwood and debris, towards the flashing lights. Trotter and Tommy stayed behind with the body.

As they neared the site, they could see there were only a few uniformed deputies poking around in the rubbish. By now, the small throng of sightseers that had gathered earlier in the evening, according to Trotter, had disbursed. There really hadn't been much to see. There was nothing left to see, actually, just a pile of smoldering wood and tin.

"Finding anything, boys?" Peyton spoke authoritatively and rummaged in his pocket for a business card. At the sound of his voice, one of the deputies turned a spotlight on them.

"Who's that? What do y'all want?" It wasn't necessary, but the officer spoke through a hand-held megaphone. He was awfully young and seemingly wet behind the ears, and the megaphone had more the effect of making him look like a cheerleader than an officer of the law.

"This here is Peyton Fuller, Attorney at Law, at your service." Peyton bowed with exaggeration and extended his business card credentials to the young deputy. "And this is Lucas Callaway, Esquire." Peyton waved his hand grandiosely in Luke's direction.

At the title Peyton had bestowed on him, Luke furrowed both brows and looked skeptically at Peyton.

Unabashed, Peyton continued on in the same vein. "And this here is Scotty Dillard, man-about-town, jack-of-all-trades, master of none!" Without waiting for any response from Scotty or the deputy, Peyton forged ahead, "And whom might we be addressing?"

The young, clean-shaven, deputy couldn't have been more than nineteen or twenty. He was about as wide-eyed as Scotty usually was and appeared to be taken a bit off guard by Peyton's humorous eloquence. Behind the authority of his badge and the gun he wore in the holster on his hip, he had been prepared to take control of the situation.

The deputy recognized Peyton's name instantly, as nearly all of Escambia County's law officers would have. Not really knowing much about Peyton, but evidently thinking that merely because his name was recognizable, the counselor must be a pretty important lawyer, so he gave the three men his utmost respect.

"I'm Maynard Skinner, Mr. Fuller. A buddy of mine was in court with you one day last week. What can I do for y'all?" the young fellow offered eagerly. "We got a mess here we're trying to take care of."

"So we see. However, it's not what you can do for us, Officer, it's what we can do for you—namely, produce a body that seems to have met with a most unfortunate accident, such as this here explosion."

Luke remained quiet, letting Peyton have the floor, even though he found Peyton's banter on such a solemn matter reprehensible. This was Peyton's style, and apparently it had served him well in court and in various tense situations. It wasn't Luke's way, but he was tired. Let Peyton handle things. It had been a long day, and having to cut short the much anticipated evening with Lisa, once again, had created much tension and stress and intensified his desire to be with her.

As Peyton babbled, Luke absently stared down the beach towards Mamie's Place, allowing his mind to wander through the events of the evening. He had been standing there in a semi-trance, wrapped up in his own thoughts and halfway listening to Peyton's ramblings. What he was looking at did not immediately register. Beyond the shanties that were still standing, parked just on the outskirts of the parking lot of Mamie's Place, was a shiny red Thunderbird. What had jogged his mind to a more conscious level of awareness was the figure he saw dart from the restaurant to the waiting car. The figure was clad in a flowing red dress. Before the red-clad figure could get the passenger car door completely closed, the driver had revved the engines and sped away, rapidly placing a great deal of distance between themselves and Mamie's Place. The figure had been too far away for Luke to make out details, but she definitely wore a red dress, that much was clear. So had Lisa.

You couldn't mistake Edna's red T-bird, but what would they be doing at Mamie's Place? Mamie had closed for the evening, Trotter said. Luke remembered earlier when he had turned to look for Lisa as he was leaving the Marina Cafe, she had been nowhere in sight.

"Luke! You coming?" Peyton called over his shoulder. He and Scotty and young Maynard were already headed back down the beach, towards the *Shady Lady*.

Luke turned his attention away from Mamie's parking lot, and quickly closed the gap between himself and the boys.

Maynard apparently had little experience as a law officer, and it seemed likely that he had never encountered a dead body before. Aboard the *Shady Lady*, he tried to cover up his inexperience. That only made things worse. Putting on a brave front, he walked right up to the body, rolled it over and peered directly into the faceless face. Nobody had thought to tell him, either intentionally or accidentally. At any rate, the shock sent him reeling. He stumbled on the edge of the hatch cover, lost his balance and fell right across the body, as prone as the dead man.

Maybe they were in shock themselves, or maybe the experience of the evening had just left them numb. Whatever it was, Peyton, Scotty and Tommy broke up. The harder they tried not to laugh, the more hysterically they did so. Trotter removed himself from the situation. He sat alone, resting on the transom and quietly taking long tugs off a cigarette he held between his fingers. Luke kept his senses about him; with a straight face he stretched his hand out to Maynard and helped him to his feet. By the time Maynard had collected himself, the three laughing hyenas had pulled themselves together. All three proceeded to exhibit a modicum of composure.

Maynard brushed nervously at the front of his bloody, damp uniform. "Well, that's a body alright. That's sure a body. We'll get some help here." He put the walky-talky, which was clipped to one side of his holster belt, to his mouth, pressed the transmitter button, and began clearing his throat directly into the mouthpiece. Finally, he spoke. "Cliff, this here's Maynard. You over there? Cliff, this is Maynard. Do you read me?"

"Yeah, I read you, but just barely with all that damned static you got going on."

"Shhh, Cliff! You're not supposed to cuss on this thing. I got people here with me, anyway, so just listen."

"Well, you listen...where'd you go, anyway? I thought you were right over here by all this mess. I don't see you anywhere."

"That's what I'm trying to tell you, Cliff. We gotta' call somebody. There must've been somebody in that cabin. We're gonna' need some help over here."

"Well, I ask you again, where the heck are you? And what do you mean there was somebody in that cabin? Make some sense, fella'."

"Cliff, I'm over here. Look over to your right. I'm aboard the *Shady Lady*. She's docked right over here about a city block down the beach. Look at this light." He turned the plastic surround of his flashlight to the red side and began waving it wildly in the air, signaling Cliff.

"That you, Maynard? I see you now. Well, what's up, buddy? Who you want me to call? What you doing aboard the *Shady Lady*, anyway?"

"I've been trying to tell you, Cliff, there was somebody in that cabin, but he's dead now, and he's out here onboard the *Shady Lady*. Bunch of fella's found him floating around out in the water and brought him in to us. Guess you better call an ambulance...and the coroner. Well, maybe we don't need an ambulance. Just call the coroner and see what he says."

"Done."

Maynard clipped the walky-talky back on his belt. He rubbed his hands together and rocked to and fro on his heels and the balls of his feet, trying to look like he was in control again. He had it all taken care of. Nothing to do but wait.

When the coroner arrived, so did two more patrol cars full of Sheriff's deputies. Luke climbed the ladder to the bridge and waited with Trotter while the body was bagged and tagged and carried away. The boat remained docked a short distance down the beach from Mamie's Place. With the arrival of much more senior and decidedly more experienced law enforcement officials, the questioning Peyton had anticipated began in earnest. It went on into the wee hours of the morning, and with Trotter brewing pot after pot of coffee, the solemn interrogation evolved into a social gathering aboard the *Shady Lady*. There was no suspicion cast on the crew of the *Shady Lady* at all, especially with the involvement of such a highly esteemed citizen as Peyton Fuller. For lack of anything better to do, though, and just on the chance there might be commendation medals awarded when the case was solved, the deputies thought it best to go through the motions of conducting a thorough investigation.

The *Shady Lady* eased into her slip back at Oyster Bay around four A.M. With the coffee wearing off, the five men bid each other a sober farewell. There was a lot to absorb, and Luke was sure a lot of rehashing would be done tomorrow. Personally, he had a lot of questions for Lisa.

11

The morning sun streamed through the great French doors that graced the rear wall of the kitchen. After only a few hours sleep, Luke stood bleary-eyed at the kitchen counter and filled an oversized mug with steaming coffee. He turned and squinted his eyes at the sunlight playing across the rippling waters of the bay. The time between last night and this morning seemed like an eternity. It seemed as though it had been a bad dream.

His thoughts drifted to Mamie in remembering that after the explosion he had seen Lisa at Mamie's Place. He allowed his mind to dwell on Mamie only for a moment. He had to sort this out about Lisa and how she might figure into the whole scenario without letting himself get besieged with sympathy and sorrow for something that was too late to do anything about...that is, if it was Toby's body they fished from the bay.

There was something else he had not had time to digest—had he really committed to marrying Lisa, someone he had known for only a couple of months? Had he lost his mind? Perhaps. No other woman had ever had such a disturbing effect on him. Her mystique provided a challenge he couldn't walk away from, but there was still that question that lingered in his mind. *Had there been many others?* He didn't want to know the answer, but on the chance there were, he wanted to extinguish whatever it was that might make her want other men, whatever it was in her that bred the familiarity of the sailors that night. He would not share her. He must marry her. If he didn't, there might be too many others, and then he wouldn't marry her. He had to know her, to know how to satisfy her so that she needed no other man.

For a time after he returned home to Pemrose Key, Cooper DeLaney had fueled a passion in him and thoughts of her had been most pleasant. His attempts to send her roses and to get in touch with her always met with failure. She was never there. She was as beautiful as Lisa, perhaps even more so, but her's was also the kind of beauty that radiated from within, making her altogether different. He had known instantly she had the qualities a man should look for in a woman he wanted to spend his life with. There just hadn't been enough time to find out if it might be right with her. It seemed as though they were kindred spirits, but then suddenly, there was Lisa.

Lisa's naughtiness intrigued him and presented him with the thrill of a challenge far different from those he had confronted and conquered in the past. God knows, he was a Callaway through and through, and that thread of inner conflict, vying with one's self to win, was woven throughout his being. Part of his very nature was to seek and be captivated by that which was more difficult. The path less traveled seemed to always be the road he chose.

How could he expect to help Lisa choose the right road? How could he save her? It did seem as though she so needed help. She needed saving from the big bad wolves of the world—in truth, she needed saving from herself. He thought of the little girl that sat beside him that night after their passion at beach, sadly, yet so nonchalantly, reciting the tragedies of her life.

So much to think about. Luke closed his eyes and rubbed his forehead with the palm of his hand. He got a headache thinking about his parents and what their reaction would be when they found out about this new turn of events that would alter his life forever.

They had no idea he'd even been seeing any one person. He'd break it to his mother first. Whatever the problem, telling her was always the rehearsal he needed for telling his father.

As Luke pondered how he would begin—and when—the answer to "when" presented itself. At that moment, Meg appeared on the rear veranda, a bouquet of multicolored snapdragons cradled in one arm.

Luke stood transfixed at his place by the counter, clutching the mug that was now only half full, watching his mother struggle to open one of the great French doors with her free hand, and almost hoping that she would stay outside.

As Meg entered the kitchen she expressed her surprise at finding Luke standing there, immobile and bleary-eyed.

"Luke, darling, I didn't know you were up yet. I know you were out late, or early, depending on one's perspective," she chided him good-naturedly with a look of mock reproach. "You should have stayed in bed a bit longer." She looked down at her flowers, "Pretty, aren't they?" she said as she placed the colorful bouquet on the counter next to the sink.

"They're pretty, Mom." Luke wasn't interested in snapdragons. He took a swig of coffee, then set his mug down. He gripped the back of one of the ladder-back chairs, and with both hands pulled it away from the table. "Why don't you have a seat, Mom, and leave those flowers for a minute. I have something I want to tell you."

"What is it, Luke?"

Try as he might to conceal it, his mother knew him all too well, and he knew his edginess had not escaped her.

Meg braced her hands on the table top and lowered her slim figure slowly into the chair Luke held for her. Fearing what was to come, she fixed her gaze across the room and avoided looking at him.

Luke took a seat opposite her. Despite her efforts to dodge his scrutiny, he studied her face closely. He really hadn't looked at her since he had been home. She was beautiful. Life had been good to her. Her sun-kissed face was only faintly creased with a few tiny lines. Her blue eyes were clear and steady, as always, and as always, her face reflected serenity. Competitive as she was, she always appeared to be unruffled, even in the midst of a heated tennis match or a close round of golf.

Meg waited silently for Luke to begin; silent but for the tapping of closely clipped, well-manicured nails on the tabletop. Luke knew she tapped to still the trembling of her hands, though her face was a mask of composure. He had forgotten how her hands always trembled when she feared for his own or his dad's safety. With two such daredevil men as Luke and Ryan, she had experienced many confrontations with fear over the years, but through it all, she would never interfere. Luke appreciated that she had always let her men make their own decisions, and she had put her faith in God—quietly, prayerfully. She always joked that with either of her men, she never knew what to expect. Outwardly, she had the faith and patience of a saint, but in her heart, Luke knew, she had the fears and concerns of a wife and mother.

Luke leaned over the table and cupped his right hand over his mother's, to still the tapping. "It's not bad news, Mom. Don't be nervous. At least I hope you don't perceive it as such." He wouldn't tell her the part about Toby until it was known for certain that it was Toby.

There was no sense in beating around the bush. His decision had been made and there would be no turning back. That was just one more thread in his being. The Callaways stood by their decisions, hard and fast, with no thought or time for regrets or recriminations. No, Meg never interfered. Perhaps she knew it wouldn't do any good, she was like that, too, and the Callaways were always prepared to take responsibility for their own actions. They were ready to take their medicine if the decision was a bad calculation, and they would neither make excuses nor blame anyone but themselves for their mistakes.

Luke squeezed Meg's hand before releasing it. "You know you've always been the most beautiful girl in the world to me, Meg Callaway. Problem is, you're spoken for. Dad was a lucky man the day he met you." He winked at his mother affectionately. "Think you could see your way clear to letting another woman share a little space in my heart?"

Meg breathed a visible sigh of relief, and the finger tapping ceased. "Oh, Luke, is that what this is all about? I think it's wonderful that you've met someone. I'm happy for you, sweetheart. Who is this lucky lady?"

"Her name is Lisa Logan, Mom."

Meg was by no means a stupid woman. Luke read her reaction. It was evident she knew instantly there was more, and that she had spoken too soon.

"What else is on your mind? I do know my son better than that. What happened last night, Luke?"

"We're getting married." The words fell to the table between them with a verbal thud.

Meg's face was as nonplussed as ever. She got up from the table and walked briskly across the highly polished black-and-white-checked linoleum floor to the kitchen sink. She removed a pair of garden snips from a drawer, pulled a crystal vase from a cabinet, and began to snip tips off snapdragon stems. Slowly and meticulously she began to arrange them in the vase, pulling one out here, placing a particular color there, measuring the stems beside the vase before she cut, and deliberately ignoring Luke.

Snip. Snip. Snip.

He had to break the silence. "What are you thinking? Don't you want to know anything about her, or what my reasons are?"

Meg returned to the table and took her place opposite Luke. She leaned across the table and unwaveringly met his blue eyes with her own. "Oh, Luke, I'm thinking so many things that you don't want to hear. I'm thinking, Meaghan Callaway, you didn't raise a fool. I'm thinking, I'm responsible for the kind of man you've become. I'm responsible for always allowing you to make your own decisions, even when you were young. I'm thinking, don't do this, my precious son. I don't even know her, and I know it's not right. It can't be right. You couldn't have known her long, you've been home such a short time. Oh, I want you to get married and have a wonderful life as your father and I have, but I know you, and I know whatever your reasons, they can't be right. Not this time. Not for marriage. You haven't been with a woman for awhile. Maybe you have lust and love confused. It's easy, it can happen. She's captivated your heart, and marriage is an aspiration. It's what the relationship can develop into, but it's not something you have to decide after such a short time with someone. What's your rush, Luke?"

"She hasn't only captivated me, Mom, and marriage isn't just an aspiration. I have my life to get on with. I have four years to make up for. Life is short, and I don't want to risk losing Lisa." He couldn't tell his mother about his fears of Lisa being with other men, of losing her that way. If time passed and she had a chance to do the things he imagined she would do, it would be too late, she would be lost to him and it would be of his own doing. If he knew too much, he wouldn't want her...and perhaps then, he would always want her.

Now Meg fidgeted. One hand began to tap slowly. quietly. She clutched at her throat with the other hand, her fingers toying nervously with the cameo brooch that clasped the collar of her white linen blouse.

"Luke, help me understand, please. You haven't mentioned 'love' through all this talk of marriage. Not once have you mentioned the word 'love'." She spoke tenderly, now. "My darling, darling son, it's the single most important ingredient in a marriage. In any lasting relationship there must be love. Surely you know that.

I've been young and in love, too, and I am still very much in love with your father...love...it's what life is made of. Your old mom is a romanticist, and I could never have lived life without love. But you, you seem to be so smitten by this girl and you're normally so practical, yet you shy away from the word 'love.' Why is that, Luke? That makes me worry."

"You're right, I have not mentioned love. I don't know why. That must be what I feel for Lisa. I know that whatever it is, it's powerful enough to make me want to marry her, and not feel that it's a mistake. Maybe that's what love is."

Did he really say that? Listening to himself under his mother's scrutiny, Luke knew it must appear he had gone stark-raving mad. He shifted uncomfortably in his chair. He was miserable under this inquisition. He felt like a little boy again—a little boy who had done something stupid. He was not accustomed to having to explain his actions to anyone, least of all his mother.

"Well, as I said, I don't make your decisions for you. I never have, and for a parent, even a parent of an intelligent, adult child, that's not always easy. Granted, your father has tried to be...let's say 'persuasive,' on occasion, but only when he thought it was in your best interest. I have never tried to tell you what to do—unless you asked for my advice, which I'm happy to say you have from time to time. But Luke, honey, this is a major step in your life, the most important step you will ever take—but then you know all that—so I can't understand...I cannot for the life of me understand this. It's not like you to do something like this, so spur-of-the-moment, with no more regard for the consequences." Meg's voice was strained. Her face still possessed the serenity of still waters on a windless day, unwavering, dauntless, but her voice was deeply troubled and belied her calm demeanor. Her tone indicated that she knew to take whatever her son had to say seriously. This was not just a passing, trivial whim.

Luke felt a keen emotional unsettling when he noticed for the first time a frailty—no, that wasn't the right word—a fragility, an underlying fragility that he had never noticed in his mother's face. She was always so active, so healthy-looking from the sun, but underneath it all she really was a delicate woman, and at this moment Luke saw beyond her fearless facade to the trembling beneath. She appeared to be very vulnerable. He didn't want to hurt his parents, but this was the only life he had, and he was the one who had to live it. He couldn't see living it without Lisa. He was certain that to wait too long would mean losing her. He wouldn't risk that. She had become too important to him. Try as he might to deny it outwardly, the rational side of his mind knew he had an irrational obsession to be with her, to make her a part of his life. His parents would come around when they met her. They would surely be as smitten with her as he was.

As if right on cue in the midst of an uncomfortable conversa-tional pause, the phone that hung on the inside wall of the butler's pantry jangled insistently. Meg moved to answer it, but Luke was on his feet first.

"Hello? ...Yes, Sheriff Gravlee, this is Luke Callaway...that's too bad...I hate to hear that...Thanks for letting me know. Thank you, now. I'll do what I can to help."

"What is it, Luke? Is something wrong? What did Sheriff Gravlee want?" She called out to him.

Luke stood at the phone for a moment before going back into the kitchen.

"There was an explosion last night, over by Mamie's Place. The sheriff said it was a bomb. It was one of those old cabins she keeps down on the water. Toby was in the cabin. We fished his body out of the bay last night, what was left of it. The sheriff just got the cor-oner's report confirming that it was Toby...we couldn't tell." Luke poured himself another cup of coffee. He stared out the window for a long moment before risking looking at his mother. Vietnam had hardened him, but there were some things he knew he couldn't hide from her.

Meg loved Mamie. At this tragic news, her valiant front wavered. Tiny furrows creased her brow and her eyes reflected deeply the sorrow she felt. With the grace of acceptance, she asked no further questions of Luke, and for this he was thankful.

"I'm going to go to Mamie. There must be something I can do, some way I can comfort her. God knows, losing a child has to be the greatest tragedy a mother can suffer. I don't know what I'm going to say to her. Thank God my child has come home safely to me." She looked at Luke with gratitude for his safe return, tears for Mamie brimming in her eyes. "But at least I can be there for her. Let her know she's loved."

12

The very day Toby's death was confirmed by the coroner, Luke accompanied his mother to Mamie's. They spent the remainder of the day at her side. Ryan met them there late in the afternoon, and Doc Bauchet was there, administering to Mamie's needs, calming her nerves with an occasional sedative. Mamie moved about mechanically, dazed, but still making rational decisions regarding the arrangements for Toby's funeral. She didn't want to wait. She wanted the funeral to be over and done with as soon as possible. Someone had murdered her son, but perhaps not intentionally.

Luke read the typewritten note that had been found on the premises at Mamie's Place that morning. Typed on a typewriter with a red ribbon, it read: *Next time it might be Mamie's Place instead of one of the shacks, and somebody just might get hurt.* No demands had been made, but Mamie said she felt certain it was meant to force her to sell. She didn't want anyone to get hurt at Mamie's Place, but she had a stubborn streak in her and now, more than ever, she was determined to stay put.

Initially, Luke suspected that the sole purpose of the blast had been to kill Toby, but the note confused that notion, and indicated that the perpetrator had been unaware anyone would be hurt—or killed. He remembered Edna pressuring Mamie. She had even tried to get him to side with her, and coerce Mamie into selling. Surely she wasn't capable of anything like this. The way the note was worded, it couldn't really be connected to Edna's harassing Mamie to sell. Whenever he tried to convince himself, he remembered the red car and the red clad figure he had seen at Mamie's Place after the explosion.

Luke and Ryan arranged the release of the body from the coroner's office, and the funeral was planned for the following day. They both made phone calls and spread the word around Pemrose Key. Friends were many, family was almost non-existent, save for an old aunt of Mamie's who was at least a hundred years old, and her eighty-three year old daughter, Mamie's only cousin. Mamie wanted to tell them herself. She wasn't sure the cousin would comprehend what had happened, but her aunt was still as clear-minded as she had been from the day Mamie was brought into this world.

Mamie's mama had died giving her birth, and old Aunt Connela had been the one to take Mamie as her own. She raised her up around Mobile, on the banks of Dog River, after her own family was grown and gone from those parts. They had seen poverty such as most Negroes in the rural south during those times had rarely seen. They lived off the river, catching catfish mostly, the mainstay of their meals. They salvaged discarded vegetables from the vegetable wagon that parked up on the main road, thanks to the generosity of the old farmer that tended it. He peddled the seasonal fresh fruits and vegetables to the local city folk who frequented the highway, and on a slow day, he considered it his bounden duty to feed the poor rather than take the unsold goods home to rot. That old man's kindness had surely helped kindle Mamie's generous spirit and goodness of heart. Mamie never recognized the hardships and poverty they endured as such. That was just life, and she was happy to be in this world and to be the recipient of the wonderful gifts God did send her way. Such had been Mamie's early years.

Mamie said her old Aunt Connela had seemed old even back then, having lived through much hardship. She taught Mamie all about the water and how to fish, and everything there was to know about sea-food and how to cook up the old recipes that she used to cooked for some of the rich Mobile families in her younger days. Mamie learned from her how to can and put up the vegetables, making the most of the scraps they were able to scavenge off the vegetable wagon, provid-ing nourishment during the few cold months Mobile saw each win-ter. They lived among other Negroes along the river bank, helping each other in times of need. Their small cluster of cabins were really no more than a few sticks and boards thrown together atop four pil-lars of rock and stone that had been cemented together for pilings, with sheets of tin nailed on for a roof. These places couldn't really be called houses. You could barely call them cabins, but with Mamie's outlook on life, she had always called it home.

When Mamie was a young teenager, her cooking skills fetched her a job in town, cooking for a white family of modest means, and the boarders they took in. They couldn't pay her a great deal of money—but it was enough to get by. It was more than Mamie had ever seen in her life, and she got free room and board. Other than that, her needs were few. There was an apartment that served as the servant's quarters over an old garage out back, it had a clean bed and a tiny kitchenette and heat in the winter time. To Mamie, it was a mansion.

The family let Mamie have the apartment as her own, and she moved Aunt Connela in with her. They were good to Mamie. They had a son a couple of years younger than her. The boy spent his time teaching Mamie what he was learning in school about math and reading. Mamie, in turn, herself possessed with an innate wis-dom about people, taught him much about life and the goodness of people, and all about fishing and the ways of the world, and they became very good friends. The young boy's name was Ryan Callaway.

The sky was a brilliant blue and the sun shone brightly in Pemrose Key on the morning of Toby Washington's funeral. It was a morning fraught with emotion, and the weather rendered a stark contradiction for all who knew Toby and Mamie. It was a beautiful, frisky-winded day, but the prevalent mood around the Key was one of heavy heartache. The air was emotionally thick with a foreboding dread. Nothing like this had ever happened in Pemrose Key before. Murder was not a common occurrence.

Luke shifted the car into low gear as he neared the dirt road that led to Mamie's church. The little whitewashed chapel had seen many a funeral in its day, along with weddings and baptisms and dinners-on-the-grounds. A white cross topped a disproportionately tall steeple and the tiny church, situated about a quarter of a mile off the main road, sat just beyond a rippling green sea of soybean plants. With simplistic purity the church stood with open doors to welcome mourners and provide solace to all who entered the little sanctuary. Behind the church, a thicket of dark green pine trees provided a contrasting backdrop for the stark white chapel. Under the bright sunshine, the pine needles and fields of green glistened and shimmered.

From the main road, Luke could make out the distant figures moving about the church grounds, all dark and shadowy. He couldn't distinguish white from black with everyone dressed in mourning clothes. On a day like this everyone should be wearing bright colors and floral prints. The women should be in sundresses, and the men should be sporting white shirts and shoes and straw summer hats.

Luke could tell there were many people already there, clumped together in small groups and milling about individually. The dirt road was smooth and well-worn. The soybean plants grew low to the ground and ran right up next to the clean-swept, sandy dirt of the church yard. It didn't seem right, going to Toby's funeral. He shouldn't be dead. Luke had seen much death and destruction in the war, but that was war, that was to be expected. He had learned then to desensitize himself. His own form of self-preservation had been to erect a psychological shield, a fortress of sorts, to dwell in for the duration of the war. He found in this instance that the shield was ineffective.

The time he had spent with Toby only weeks before made his death harder to take. He never got the chance to have that talk with Toby, to find out what happened that night he found him out at Cole's Bayou. Luke had intended to let him know that the world wasn't against him, and that he had no reason to be so angry all the time. He knew Toby would grow up and come to his senses. Toby could have a good life if he could get over all that anger. Luke was Toby's friend, and he had intended to try and impress that upon him. Toby was alright. He just hadn't given life a chance—that was yet to come. Now he wouldn't have that chance. Another short life was over.

Though Luke had made no progress in discovering why Toby had been out at Cole's Bayou, or what had happened the night Luke found him on the brink of death, he intended to find out.

Just as the book was closed on Toby Washington's life, so his casket remained closed. Even Mamie had not viewed the body. It had been determined that it would serve no purpose for anyone to see the faceless remains of what had once been Toby Washington.

Ryan got to meet Lisa sooner than Luke had planned. When Luke got out of the car in front of the church, the first person he saw was Lisa, strolling towards him arm-in-arm with Ryan Callaway. With Toby's death, Luke's plans to tell his father about Lisa had been put on hold, and his mother had not mentioned it again. Luke had not expected to see Lisa at Toby's funeral. Toby had been away most of the few short years Lisa had been in Pemrose Key, and given the friction between Edna and Mamie, he didn't think Lisa knew Mamie very well.

"Hi, Dad. Lisa, how are you?"

"Ah'm fine, Luke, and I've so enjoyed meeting your daddy here. He's so much like you, Luke." She looked up at Ryan and gave him a radiant smile. Lisa was dressed appropriately, but in spite of wearing a demure, basic black dress, she looked like she had just stepped out of the pages of a fashion magazine. Atop her head was perched a black straw, pillbox hat with a veil of fine lace netting that came down over her face, barely reaching to the tip of her nose. The veil imparted an air of mystery and gave her dark eyes a smoky, smoldering, sensuality.

"And I've enjoyed meeting your young lady, here. I understand there's a lot we haven't had a chance to talk about, Luke. For now, though, I'm going to go find Mamie and your mother. I'll see you two inside." He transferred Lisa's hand from his own arm to Luke's, giving her hand a pat as he placed it at the crook of Luke's elbow.

Lisa leaned in close after Ryan left and further entwined her arm around Luke's. "I've missed you, Luke." She stood on tiptoe and whispered the words in his ear, pressing her body against his arm.

His imagination must be playing tricks on him. He thought he detected the faintest scent of bourbon on her breath. He wished she hadn't come to Toby's funeral. As much as he wanted to be with her, now was not the time or the place. For some reason, it felt as though he was being disrespectful to Mamie by being with Lisa on this grievous occasion.

"I need to see Mamie, Lisa. Let's go inside." With Lisa still firmly attached to Luke's arm, he guided her through the throngs of people that had now gathered in the church yard.

At the front of the church, positioned just beneath the altar and looking much too big and out of place in the small sanctuary, stood a large, pewter colored casket, ornately embellished with brass filigrees. Masses of floral arrangements and wreaths surrounded the casket. Nearly covering the top of it was a large spray of deep, wine colored roses—from the Callaway family. The casket was closed.

The church was quiet. It was still early. A few individuals and small groups of two or three were scattered throughout the small chapel, some already sitting in their pews, some standing near the back of the church. Luke followed the muffled voices he heard through a door that led to a small anteroom behind and to the side of the pulpit.

What he found was unnerving.

Mamie sat in an armless chair, trance-like, mumbling to a framed photograph of Toby that lay on her lap. Toby was dressed in his military uniform. His hat was perched at a cocky angle and he was smiling up at his mother.

"My precious baby, Mama loves you. You just can't leave me. What will I do without you?" She touched the picture with her fingertip and traced his lips, then brushed her fingers across his cheek. "I wanted everything for you, baby, and I gave you so little. I didn't even give you a daddy. Now it's too late." She mumbled the words between sobs, but Luke was close enough to hear.

Mamie hugged the photo to her chest and rocked her body to and fro. She didn't seem to recognize Luke, though she looked directly at him with swollen, reddened eyes. Continuous moans were coming from her, audible pain from deep inside that great, loving heart of hers, and tears streamed incessantly down her face.

"Mamie." Luke reached out and touched Mamie's shoulder. He wanted to console her, to ease her anguish, but she didn't seem to see, or feel, or hear at all. He looked away. His mother sat nearby, her face composed, but sorrow and pity reflected deeply in her eyes. Off to one side Luke saw his father speaking quietly with the minister and Doc Bauchet.

Luke turned on his heel, placed his hands on Lisa's shoulders, and guided her out the door ahead of him. He couldn't bear witnessing Mamie's pain, and he felt guilty that he never told her Toby had come home. Had Mamie known, it's likely Toby would not have been staying at the shanty.

"I'll find out who's responsible for this and I will kill them." The words were spoken quietly, as an affirmation to himself, a verbal confirmation of what he intended to do.

Lisa walked ahead of Luke, but she heard what he said. "Luke! You do have a temper, don't you? I haven't seen you this angry since you fought Joey and his friends over me." Lisa looked back at him with wide-eyed innocence and mock fear.

All the pews were filled now, and many people were left standing, crowding the doorway at the rear of the church. Doc Bauchet, Ryan, and Meg all entered the chapel from the anteroom and took a seat on the front pew on one side of Aunt Connela and her eighty-three-year-old daughter.

All were there because of Mamie. Toby had put so much distance between himself and Pemrose Key in the few adult years of his life, they hardly knew him anymore. They still thought of him as the little Toby he used to be. The thought crossed Luke's mind that it was probably fortunate that most of them had not known the angry, adult Toby.

The low buzz of the congregation's murmurings ceased when Mamie entered the sanctuary, supported by the arm of Reverend Thornton. She took her place beside Aunt Connela. The moaning had ceased, but the pain appeared to be etched in her face permanently and the tears continued to flow.

With some distance between Mamie and himself, Luke was better able to handle his own grief. Reverend Thornton took his place at the pulpit. He solemnly bowed his head before beginning a short sermon on the advisability of accepting Christ as our Savior and living our lives admirably enough to be allowed to enter the gates of heaven. No speculation was made as to whether he thought Toby might have entered those pearly gates.

At the completion of his sermon, Reverend Thornton introduced Doc Bauchet, though an introduction was hardly necessary. Everyone there had been attended by Doc at one time or another. Doc Bauchet delivered the eulogy. With Toby's infirmity, he had actually spent more time with Toby-the-adult than anyone else in Pemrose Key, besides Mamie. The eulogy began with kind words for the deceased, as all eulogies do for the dearly departed. Then, in an unconventional twist, Doc began eulogizing Mamie, as if she was the one who had departed. He himself appeared to be in a dazed state as he droned on in a monotone about Toby having been like a son to him, and about the grievances Mamie had suffered at the hands of those miserable unknowns responsible for her loss. He talked about what a wonderful woman Mamie was, and how she loved everyone so tremendously. As he spoke, tears streamed down his face. Then, in the same monotone, "Let's go bury a friend—one we will all miss." He stepped down from the pulpit and it was over.

Luke was one of the pallbearers. He helped carry Toby outside to the gravesite behind the church, beside the grove of pine trees. They sang Swing Low, Sweet Chariot. The preacher offered a prayer, and the casket was lowered into the ground.

"That's it. My boy's gone. Can't nothing be done about it." Mamie looked at Toby's picture she still carried in her arms. "I done grieved enough. My heart can't stand no more grieving." As they turned and walked away from the grave, the first shovelful of dirt clattered against the coffin. Mamie flinched and drew her back up stiffly, but she kept going, never looking back, moving with a sense of purpose and stoic determination. Her eyes were dry now. "Everybody's coming to Mamie's Place. I'm gon' feed all of y'all."

"Mamie, please don't do that. You can't be up to it. Why don't you come over to The Magnolias and stay with us for a little while, so that you're not alone. You need some time. I'll go over and see that Billy Jack takes good care of things at Mamie's Place," Meg offered. She had not left Mamie's side for two days.

"No'm, I done put it to rest. We're gonna' play some music on the jukebox and eat some fried mullet and get on with the business of living. Life is for the living, Meg Callaway, you know that. I got to do this."

When they arrived at Mamie's Place, Billy Jack and the rest of Mamie's employees had already placed heaping platters of fish, french fries and hushpuppies in the middle of each table. The jukebox blared loudly. People were everywhere.

Mamie sat this one out. She took a table for herself right in the middle of the room, where she could watch all her friends, old and new, young and old, black and white, eating her good food and enjoying themselves—all because they had come to share her grief with her, and mourn for her boy, Toby.

They gave him a fine send off.

13

There was going to be a wedding. Tomorrow was the day. Lisa had been bound and determined to be a September bride. Luke agreed. He was ready to get on with their life together. Their courtship and engagement had not been easy. Thank God it had been brief. Sexually, things got hot and heavy from time to time, but in the end, Lisa always backed down. He got mad about it, in fact at times he was furious, but Lisa would have her way.

On several occasions Luke even had second thoughts. When that happened, one glimpse of Lisa and he would once again be lost in his lust for her, and the certain pleasures that lay ahead. She was his weakness, his Achilles heel, but even with this affliction, for the most part he was able to outwardly maintain his composure. Tomorrow, the frustration would be over.

No one knew of the extreme conflict within, of the pain and anguish that tormented him nights when he lay awake for hours, refusing to acknowledge any regrets over his decision.

His plans to marry Lisa had gone pretty smoothly, too smoothly upon reflection—frighteningly so. It was scary that changes that would affect his life so profoundly were so easy to come by, such as Lisa's readiness to marry him, and his father's willing compliance with his desire to do so.

The only visible wailing and gnashing of teeth had been his mother's. In truth, there hadn't been much of that. Mostly just in the beginning, when Luke first told her of his intentions. Ryan refreshed her memory on how swiftly his own passion for her had blossomed. Their's had been love at first sight, and in a matter of months, ripened into a mature, life-long love and friendship. At Ryan's insistence, Meg reluctantly offered her blessings. If Ryan foresaw happiness there for Luke, Meg said she was willing to re-evaluate her position, but she was quick to add that still she worried about what kind of wife Lisa would make for her son.

Luke stood before the mirror at his dresser and adjusted his tie. Tonight was the rehearsal and the "After Rehearsal" party. He was calm, outwardly. He would be glad to get the wedding behind them. He didn't go in for all the hoopla and *gala affairs* given in the bride and groom's honor, but he had tried to be a good sport about it, for both Lisa's and his mother's sake.

What was troublesome to Luke was that with all the rush and flurry of the wedding preparations, Lisa's personality seemed to change. It was an almost imperceptible change. Probably no one else even noticed, but Luke thought there was a small loss of naiveté there. Lisa drank a little more than he felt she should at some of the parties and when she did, she got irritable. This he attributed to the stress and nervousness of going through the motions of preparing for a wedding. There was a vague tugging at his mind about it that bothered him, though. It was probably a fault of his, something he had to work on. Through the sleepless nights, he had come to terms with his feelings. He loved her, didn't he? And surely the change in her was merely attributable to the hectic schedule they had maintained. She just didn't seem like her usual sweet self. He hated to admit it, but at times she seemed frighteningly like Edna. This did worry him. God knows, it had to be his imagination. There was no comparison between the two.

Luke leaned in closer to the mirror and studied his face. His eyes looked weary, and there was a tautness around his mouth. The pace they'd kept was telling on him, too. There was something else that bothered him besides the change in Lisa. He tried to ignore it, but it gnawed at him. It was the grief he felt for the loss of a dream he had held close for many years. That dream had evolved in his mind since childhood, from a mere glimmer of an idea to a full-blown vision with its own independent compulsion, hell-bent on becoming a reality. It affected every aspect of his life, until he met Lisa.

To have her, he was giving up all he ever imagined he was destined to become. Ryan's ulterior motives in promoting Luke's marriage to Lisa were quite obvious. He indicated he knew the potential for problems was there, but nonetheless, he strongly encouraged the relationship. Ryan reinstated his offer to Luke. With a young wife to support, it was likely Luke would more readily reconsider. Lisa was Ryan's willing ally. Ryan's cause was her cause. Rarely could Ryan be duped by anyone, not even one blessed with Lisa's abundant charm, but where Luke and Callaway Construction were concerned, he suffered from first degree tunnel vision.

Filled with skepticism, Luke agreed to accept the position. Admittedly, he'd made no headway in securing financing for his venture, crippled as he was by his father's connections. If he went to work for Callaway it would delay his plans, but maybe he could put some money aside and one day have a shot at achieving his goals.

It seemed that the pieces were coming together. He was getting exactly what he wanted in Lisa. So why did he feel so out of control of his own life at times.

Luke gave his tie one final tug. Prenuptial jitters, that's all.

14

"Who gives this woman in marriage?" The question lingered in the air and for a moment, no one spoke. Father Mallory's resonant voice filled the nearly empty sanctuary and bounced off the tall, cathedral ceiling of the Episcopal church.

Commander Thomas Logan stepped forward, belatedly realizing this was his cue. He smoothed the trousers of his formal uniform and cleared his throat dramatically. He made a great showing of picking a piece of imaginary lint from the front of his jacket, and spoke the words "I do" as if they were the opening lines in a movie or play, in which he was the star. His voice was in keeping with his uniform, crisp and snappy.

The wedding rehearsal went as wedding rehearsals go, with some confusion on timing, but with everyone involved knowing their role and their cue.

At the conclusion of the rehearsal, Ryan minced no words in expounding to Luke and Meg his extreme dislike for Logan. Having met the man for the first time only two hours earlier, he now expressed serious misgivings about having so eagerly bestowed his blessings upon this marriage. Everything had gone so well—Luke and Lisa's engagement, their wedding plans, and Luke's return to Callaway Construction. Ryan told Luke it had all been too easy, he should have known there had to be a hitch. There was—in the persona of Thomas Logan!

The after-rehearsal party was held at the Bay Water Yacht Club. Commander Thomas Logan appeared on the scene only hours before the rehearsal, one day ahead of the wedding, barely in time to see his only child take her vows of matrimony. He had been scheduled to arrive in Pemrose Key three weeks prior to the wedding, to spend some time with his daughter, whom he hadn't seen in over a year, get to know his future son-in-law, and attend some of the parties given in their honor. Other things apparently took precedence in his life, such as running into old friends in Newport News upon his arrival back in the States. He had called Lisa and told her he would soon be there. She was to convey his apologies to the Callaways. He would stop over in Newport News for a few days before catching a flight south. A few days turned into a few weeks, and he arrived in Pemrose Key the night before the wedding.

At the after-rehearsal party, Ryan again expressed his contempt for this obnoxious little man who would soon become Luke's father-in-law. Three times in less than two hours, Logan had given him an enthusiastic slap on the back and proclaimed in his crisp, nasal tone, "I'm pleased to have my little girl marry into such a fine family as yours, Callaway. Yes-sir, I'm glad to see my little girl taken care of." Slap! Three times! Then, grinning like a Cheshire cat, he flashed his sparkling white teeth obnoxiously at Ryan, then looked around the room to see if his charming smile had been noticed by all the women present.

He was a much smaller man than Ryan Callaway, but even Meg conceded that he did cut a lean, dapper figure in his dress uniform and Hollywood-like tan.

"Hell! He's a sure 'nuff dandy—and a jackass!" Ryan told Meg and Luke when he was able to get them aside, out of earshot of the rest of the wedding party. He could see right through the man, he said. "An opportunist if I ever saw one. Why doesn't he take care of his own daughter? Why does he need someone else to take care of her for him?"

Luke listened to this exchange with wry amusement.

Ryan didn't hold back. "I see how he politic-ed his way to the top of the heap and got command of his own little ship. He must've charmed more than a few of the brass on the way up instead of taking care of business at home."

"Ryan! Please! The man is going to be our son's father-in-law. Don't do this, now. Please, let's enjoy the party. He's probably not as bad as all that. Give him the benefit of the doubt," Meg pleaded with her husband. Looking ill with the whole scene, she said she fully understood her husband's misgivings, but she gave Luke her *you know how your father is* look, hoping to minimize Ryan's emotional outburst.

"Your father's just nervous for you, Luke. I think *he* has prenuptial jitters."

Luke was indifferent to Ryan's rantings. He knew his father well. He didn't like Thomas Logan either, but he wouldn't have to see much of him. Lisa never had. Why should he expect Logan to suddenly become an attentive father?

The Admiral's Room at the yacht club was overflowing with people when the wedding party arrived—all well-wishers for Luke and Lisa's happiness—all interested in having a good time, partaking of the food the tables were laden with, and drinking their fill from the freely flowing bar. The conversation was loud and the crowd swayed in motion to lively jazz tunes played by a Dixieland band. It had been one continuous party since the engagement. The Reception tomorrow would be more of the same, but that was a party Luke looked forward to with anticipation, because it would be the last of the parties, and then he would have Lisa to himself.

Finally they would be together, alone, and there would be no more denying him. Tomorrow they would be wed in holy matrimony, and afterwards they would consummate their vows. Just thinking about that part these long months past had given him pleasure and helped him get through the sleepless nights and the trying times—all the wedding trivia, the parties and the people—going to work everyday at a job he didn't really want to be doing. The anticipation of that first sweet moment when he would finally satisfy his longing made him glad they had waited.

"May I have this dance?" Thomas Logan held his arms out to Lisa. "Do you mind, young man?...Son." Apparently testing his father-in-law terminology, Logan displayed his teeth and gave Luke a solid whack on the back.

"Not at all, Sir." Luke looked down at the little man and made a mental note to always keep his face forward when in Thomas Logan's presence.

Lisa giggled nervously and left Luke's side, dancing into her father's arms.

Over Logan's shoulder, Luke had a clear view of his own father across the room, eyes bulging, struggling to swallow a mouthful of champagne after witnessing Logan whacking upon his big, grown son. Luke smiled wryly and lifted his glass to his father in a toast. The band shifted gears from a jazz tune to a waltz.

Luke heard the little-girl voice return just before she waltzed away across the dance floor, "Daddy, you're just never going to grow up, are you?"

"Why should I? Your dearly departed mother never did, and you're just like her, my darling daughter."

That was all Luke heard before Thomas Logan spun Lisa away in rapid circles around the dance floor. He saw Logan narrow his eyes at his daughter. The corners of his mouth were turned down, in an ugly, vicious leer. Luke wanted to rescue Lisa. In that instant he gleaned what kind of father Thomas Logan must have been, and he experienced the immense dislike his father had expressed.

So intense was the conversation between father and daughter, they seemed oblivious to others around them. As Lisa's father led her around the dance floor, they passed within earshot of Luke. He couldn't make out all they said, but the words that passed between them held him riveted in his place.

Lisa spoke shrilly, and could easily be heard above the music. "Is that why you hate me, Daddy? Because I remind you of Mommy? Are you sure I don't remind you of yourself?"

Luke didn't take his eyes off the two of them as Commander Logan held his daughter tighter and spun her faster than before, at what appeared to be a dizzying pace.

Lisa's cheeks were red and her dark eyes flashed, matching her father's, and Luke wished he could hear more of her words. When Logan tightened his grip on his daughter's hand and bent her fingers back, Luke started across the dance floor towards them, but he stopped in his tracks as they began to dance once more in his direction. The waltz was nearly over.

They waltzed up to Luke and Thomas Logan transferred Lisa's hand to his. "Thank you, my darling," he said to Lisa as he kept moving, gliding across the dance floor alone to the far corner of the room where Peyton Fuller stood. Peyton was surrounded by a small gathering of people, his round mouth wide open in obvious oratory bliss at having a captive audience.

Luke's curiosity was piqued when he saw Peyton cease his lecturing long enough to extend his palm to Thomas Logan in a friendly greeting, as though they were already acquainted.

Luke turned his attention to Lisa, who stared at him without seeming to recognize him and looking to be on the verge of tears.

Luke puzzled over what the words could have been that put her in this state, but he tried to keep things light. "May I have this dance now, Madam?"

What he said jogged Lisa out of her trance-like state. "What do you mean, Madam?" she shrieked, in a totally irrational manner. "I'm not your MADAM. A Madam is a whore. Why did you call me that?"

"Lisa, what is wrong with you? Quiet, before somebody hears you. I only want to dance with you. 'Madam' means Ma'am, Lisa. A term of respect, Ma'am. Do you understand?" With that explanation, she calmed down and became his sweet Lisa again.

Luke was baffled, but then, most women baffled him, it seemed. They were both tired. The confrontation with her father had put her on the defensive. To Luke, the lack of time they'd had together had frustrated him and created tension. He supposed it might have had the same effect on Lisa. He had worked long hours and most weekends since going back to work for Callaway Construction, partly to avoid Edna as Lisa's constant companion, would-be-mother, and planner-of-weddings. The rest of the time, they had either been with his family or at parties. Flare-ups such as this had not been uncommon in the weeks past, but surely, this too would pass. Pre-nuptial jitters.

The wedding itself was merely a pause between parties. Last night's after-rehearsal party had lasted into the early hours of the morning, with time only to get a few hours sleep before the wedding brunch.

On the day of the wedding, The Magnolias was decked in splendor, welcoming all the out-of-town guests to the wedding brunch. Round tables skirted with long white tablecloths were spaced comfortably apart along the wide, rear veranda, and on the spacious patio beyond. A single magnolia blossom floated in a water-filled crystal bowl in the center of each table. White paddle fans that hung from the veranda's ceiling rotated lazily, stirring the already warm air.

Guests wandered around seeking the shade provided by the tall magnolia trees that grew along the outer perimeter of the patio. Most of the guests were not used to the white-hot Florida sun. A warm bay breeze barely rustled the large, thick leaves of the magnolia trees, but even a warm breeze was welcomed relief to those who ambled around the tables, champagne glasses casually held between their fingers.

Luke was required to make an appearance at the brunch, which was customarily held for the out-of-town guests. The groom's appearance was protocol, so he had been informed by the wedding-planners, which included Lisa, Edna, his mother and the wedding director who owned the local flower shop.

Luke had never set eyes on most of the people here. Lisa was not at the brunch. It was supposed to be bad luck for the groom to see the bride before the wedding. It seemed to Luke that the bad luck was that he was the one who had to be present at this brunch thing. He didn't know these people. They were mostly friends and acquaintances of Commander Logan. Some of them didn't seem to be very good friends at that, and a few looked a bit surly and unscrupulous.

At Luke's insistence, Trotter showed up. Luke needed him there for moral support.

"I'm sure glad to see you here, Trotter."

"Yeah, you owe me." Trotter looked about as happy to be here as a flounder at a fish fry. When an aproned server passed a silver tray filled with glasses of champagne, Trotter took two.

"I overheard a strange conversation last night at your party, Luke. I don't remember the exact words." He tossed off one of the glasses of champagne with one gulp.

"What do you mean, Trotter?"

"I heard that dandy father-in-law of yours talking to Edna." Without heeding the other guests, Trotter turned and spat on the ground to the left of his only foot. "He told her that the idea she had of getting Lisa hitched up with a Callaway just might pay off. He said something about it helping their cause, whatever their 'cause' is." Trotter glanced around and lowered his voice. "With Edna involved, I thought it might be something worth mentioning."

"Is that all you heard, Trotter?" Luke wished Trotter had heard the conversation between Lisa and her father, the parts he had missed.

"No," Trotter hesitated. "He told Edna the little tramp wouldn't let up asking questions about that whore mother of hers. I guess he was talking about Lisa."

"Is that what he called his own daughter? A little tramp?"

"I don't know Lisa that well, Luke, but I know that having a whore for a mama doesn't make a kid love her any less. Knowing about it just makes it hurt more inside." His eyes were narrowed slits.

"The guy's sick. Thanks for telling me, Trotter."

It was clear Thomas Logan's opinion of Lisa's mother must have precipitated Lisa's outburst last night. It appeared Lisa needed Luke more than ever. Today she would become his wife.

"Who gives this woman in marriage?" As he had at the rehearsal, Father Mallory once again asked the question, this time in earnest. His voice rang loud and clear throughout the sanctuary. The final vows were spoken. Luke lifted Lisa's veil. His tired eyes caressed her, he wanted to consume her here and now, but he held himself in check. Just a few more hours to get through and they would be on their own.

Lisa was a vision in white—virginal and pure. How could he ever have had any doubts about her. She was his wife. He pulled her to him and in front of those present, kissed her very respectably on the mouth.

The reception was grand and took place at the Officer's Club at Pensacola Naval Air Station. Thomas Logan was in his glory. This was his shindig and even though Lisa, Edna and Meg had planned everything down to the last elaborate detail, he took full credit. He crudely let it be known he was footing the bill. He was the father of the bride.

Luke watched his own father as he stood watching Thomas Logan make a fool of himself. With only a brief pause between gulps, Ryan quickly polished off a stiff bourbon and water, then shook his head in ill-concealed disgust. He raised his bushy eyebrows over the rim of his glass and stared hard at Luke.

Luke shrugged his shoulders, he knew full-well the meaning of his father's expression.

"For better or worse…" Luke didn't complete the sentence, and he didn't smile as he raised his own glass in a silent toast. Everything will be all right, he reassured himself. For better or worse, Lisa was his. That is what he had wanted these long months past.

15

"Miss, oh Missth! Come here!" Lisa slurred the command. She leaned over the armrest of her first-class seat aboard the DC-8 and extended her arm, glass in hand, into the aisle. "Stewardess!" She waved the glass vigorously, trying to get the stewardess' attention.

"Lisa!" Luke reached across Lisa from his seat by the window, grabbing at her arm in an attempt to stop her. "You don't need anymore. Give me the glass." He was able to stretch far enough to get a grip on her forearm, and with just a little bit of applied pressure, he managed to force her arm back onto the tray-table in front of her.

"Ow! You're hurting me! Get your big hands off of me. I want another drink and I'm gonna' get it, so leave me alone!"

"Lisa, don't cause a scene! You've had too much to drink. At this altitude it gets to you before you know it." When Luke saw the airline stewardess coming down the aisle towards them, champagne bottle in hand, he tried to signal her to discourage her approach.

It was too late. Lisa had already seen her, and her arm shot back into the aisle, glass in hand, ready for a refill. "Here, Stewardess...I'd like some more, please."

The stewardess looked at Luke apologetically. She realized too late what was happening. In trying to smooth things over, things only got worse. "What seems to be the problem here, Mrs. Callaway?"

"There's no problem, except that my glass is empty, and I want a refill." Lisa jabbed her elbow hard at Luke's side. "Don't pay any attention to him. If I want a drink, I'm gonna' have one."

The stewardess was obviously embarrassed. Lisa's actions had put her in a predicament. Airline regulations prohibited serving alcohol to anyone who was intoxicated.

The stewardess gave Luke a pitying "poor fellow" look and tried to channel the conversation away from the booze. "Hey, by the way, congratulations, you two. My manifest says you're on your honeymoon. Well, Hawaii is the perfect place. So romantic!"

Lisa wasn't buying it. She was persistent. "Drink, please." She shoved her glass towards the stewardess once again.

"I'm sorry, Mrs. Callaway, I see you're having bourbon. I'll have to take your glass and replenish it in the galley. All I brought with me is champagne. Give me a few more minutes and I'll see if I can't get to you shortly."

Luke winced. It hadn't taken him long to catch on to this other side of Lisa.

"I will NOT wait a few more minutes, and don't you expect me to. I'll get it myself if you won't help me." Lisa struggled to get her table raised so she could get up from her seat. She upset her glass and it rolled to the floor and down the aisle in the direction of the tourist section behind first class.

"Lisa, sit still! You're not going anywhere." Luke pulled the tray back down in front of Lisa to hold her in place at her seat.

"No, I'll not sit still. I want a drink!"

"I'm sorry, Mrs. Callaway, I'm afraid you've had a bit too much, already. I'm not allowed to serve you anymore," the stewardess stood her ground.

All it took was one swift motion, Lisa pushed her tray to the upright position and she was out of her seat, arms flailing. Before the stewardess had a chance to back away, Lisa had swung her right arm. She brought it forward with full force. Her hand centered with a loud smack against the side of the stewardess' face.

The stewardess looked for a moment like she was going to cry.

Lisa reared back for another swing. "You can't tell me what to do!"

Luke was horrified. He lunged out of his seat, grabbed Lisa's wrist, and yanked her forcefully down into his seat by the window. "Sit!" he commanded furiously, as he took the aisle seat for himself, wedging her in beside him.

Lisa's demeanor changed instantly with Luke's show of force. As if she suddenly realized the import of what had happened, she slapped her hand over her mouth and her eyes widened.

"I didn't mean to…I didn't mean to." Lisa slumped down low in her seat, turned her face to the window and began to sob.

Luke felt like he could cry, too. He was appalled at the monster his bride had become. He was beyond embarrassment. All the other first class passengers had witnessed the scene. The close quarters of the cabin disallowed discreet glances, though most of the passengers around them politely made a pretense of ignoring Lisa's actions.

"Is she alright?" the stewardess asked kindly. The left side of her face was red where Lisa's hand had left its impression, but she ignored it. She was a professional. She reached above her head into the overhead bin for a pillow and blanket and handed them to Luke.

Through the entire experience, Luke found the pitying look the stewardess gave him to be more humiliating than anything. If she could but know the real Lisa, the one he had married only yesterday, the one he so recently promised to "love, honor and cherish… in sickness and in health."

The realization that Lisa had serious problems had not just begun to dawn with these events, Luke now realized.

"Are you alright, Miss? I can't apologize to you enough. I don't know what came over her." Luke was still mortified. He glanced at Lisa, afraid his words might prompt another flare-up.

"I'm fine, Mr. Callaway. It's not your fault. I'm sure your wife will be okay."

Lisa was curled up in the corner of her seat, her head against the window, sound asleep. Luke eased the pillow beneath her head, to cushion it against the vinyl-clad fuselage. He placed the blanket over her lap and pulled the edge of it up under her chin, then turned back to the stewardess who still stood beside his seat.

"I don't know...I don't understand it. Our wedding was yesterday. I suppose planning the wedding, with so much to do, must've been pretty stressful on her, and I guess she's not used to drinking at this altitude, either. I'm just real sorry this happened. I don't know what else to say." Luke didn't know what else to say.

"Don't worry. You have your hands full. You needn't worry about me. Not much damage done here." She smiled kindly at Luke.

Luke looked beyond her to the front of the airplane, where another stewardess was emerging from the cockpit, followed by the captain. The captain strolled down the aisle and stopped where Luke and the stewardess stood.

"Is everything okay here?" He put his hand on the stewardess' shoulder and patted it twice when he saw Lisa sound asleep in her corner.

"Everything's fine," the stewardess assured him.

The captain continued his stroll, moving on towards the rear of the airplane, and the stewardess went about her business.

When it was announced that they were about to land in Honolulu, Luke was relieved. Lisa continued to sleep.

"Welcome to Honolulu, Ladies and Gentlemen. If you're visiting, we hope you enjoy your stay in beautiful Hawaii. Before you leave, please check around your seat for any personal belongings you may have brought on board. Thank you for flying with us today. We hope we have the opportunity to serve you again in the future." The microphone clicked off.

Luke decided it would be best to stay seated while the other passengers deplaned. When the cabin was clear, he pulled their carry-on bags from beneath the seats in front of them. He turned to wake Lisa, touching her shoulder tentatively, dreading her awakening, not knowing which Lisa he would confront. She didn't wake up at first, so he gave her shoulder a gentle shake. "Lisa, we're here. Wake up, now."

"...M-mmm, I'm awake, Luke, I'm awake." She was docile.

Luke was relieved.

Lisa rubbed her eyes and stretched her arms out in front of her, much like a little girl awakening in the morning. "Oh, hi, Luke, darlin.'" She turned to face him, smiling as though she had just gotten a full night's sleep and nothing out of the ordinary had happened. Suddenly something seemed to click, and she smacked both hands over her mouth. Her eyes widened and she sucked in her cheeks. "Oh, Luke, oh no...what have ah done?"

"You had too much to drink, Lisa. I've never seen you like that before. What you did was inexcusable." He wanted to shake her. He wanted her to know just how reprehensible her actions were, hoping that perhaps she would curtail her drinking in the future. He still adored her, though, didn't he?

At the bottom of the boarding steps, an airline Customer Service supervisor stood beside two men in white, short-sleeved shirts. As Luke and Lisa neared the bottom of the steps, the two men approached them.

"Mr. Callaway, I'm Joe Lianoho...FBI, Honolulu. This is Mr. Kip Kuamohe. The captain of this flight reported there was a little trouble on board, and we boys get called to check it out whenever the airlines or their crews are involved in any way."

Luke supported Lisa's elbow with a tight grip. "How do you do, gentlemen. I know there's no excuse for what happened, but we're on our honeymoon, and my wife had a little too much to drink. I'm terribly sorry for the stewardess. Although there's no excuse for my wife's actions, I can only tell you that the past few weeks have been stressful for her, and I hope you'll take that into consideration." Luke hated having to make excuses for Lisa. He hated the fact that the entire episode had transpired, and a small part of him even hated Lisa for creating the problem in the first place.

"Of course, Mr. Callaway, but there are laws. Striking a crew member is a Federal offense, and I'm afraid we're going to have to take your wife in for questioning. Would you like to come along?"

Lisa had remained silent while Luke made apologies, but now she evidently decided it was time to intervene on her own behalf. She pulled her arm free from Luke's grasp, took a step towards Mr. Lianoho and lowered her eyelids contritely. She pushed her lips out in a pout and directed her best smoldering gaze at Mr. Lianoho. "Ah nevah, evah…" she was good, she drew the words out long and slow, raising her left shoulder in a sexy roll for added emphasis and gyrating her upper torso, somehow managing to make it look natural. "Nevah did I evah intend to hurt that stewardess, Mr. Lianoho. Ah just don't know whatever came over me. You see, I've never flown before, and I've never even really drank alcohol before. It must've just made me plain ol' crazy. It scared me when I realized what had happened. I don't think I will evah, evah take another drink again, as long as I live."

Lisa wasn't through yet. "Haven't you ever accidentally had a wee, little bit too much to drink, Mr. Kuamohe?" She turned her sultry gaze to him now, expertly weaving her web.

Luke looked on, astonished. Before his very eyes, these two grown men—tough, hardened, professionals in their field—seemed to succumb to Lisa's seduction.

She was totally absorbed in herself and her theatrics now, oblivious to Luke and all others in the vicinity, concentrating only on her audience, Mr. Lianoho and Mr. Kuamohe, and dedicated to delivering to them a perfect performance.

"Please, please, I don't know whatever came over me. This is my honeymoon. I would never hurt anyone intentionally. Please believe me." She boldly placed her palm flat against Mr. Kuamohe's chest, right over his heart. The gesture was brief, but long enough for effect. One needn't have a hand on his chest to see that he was breathing a bit heavier now.

With a look of satisfaction, Lisa turned to the other man. In a blatantly forward act of familiarity, she fingered one of the buttons on the front of his shirt.

Only Lisa could pull this off.

"Oh, Mr. Lianoho, can't you see I'm not a bad girl at all. Luke will take care of me, and I promise this will never happen again."

The older man seemed slightly amused, and less taken with her charms.

As Luke looked on, an uncontrollable, internal trembling possessed him, and even as the heat rose in waves from the concrete of the Honolulu Airport ramp, he felt cold. His head was spinning.

Lisa had lied to these men, shamelessly, and with ease. Everything she told them was a lie. He knew she had flown many times, and in thinking about it, he had never been out with her when she wasn't drinking. In fact, on a few occasions she had practically guzzled the stuff, but he'd never seen her so out of control as she had been today. Where her drinking had been a small worry to him before, something he hoped would go away, it now appeared that Lisa was a lush, with a problem that must be dealt with.

Luke closed his eyes, and in that one instant he saw clearly what had happened to him, how Lisa had possessed him body and soul, just as she had appeared to wrap these two grown men around her little finger, she had beguiled and entrapped Luke—and he had allowed it. When he looked at Lisa, for the first time since he had known her, he saw her for what she really was. He wanted to love her, but could he? The reality of that question scared him. He wanted her terribly, but thus far, love had escaped him. The acknowledgement of that reality had come far too late.

Distantly, Luke heard the stewardess approach their little group.

"I'm Anna Kirkpatrick, gentlemen. I was the senior stewardess aboard Mr. and Mrs. Callaway's flight. I'm the one Mrs. Callaway had the little altercation with and I can assure you, it was nothing. Sometimes emotions can set the pace for ill-chosen actions. No harm done, really. I realize the Captain was obligated to report the incident, but truly, it wasn't as bad as all that. I hope you will allow Mr. and Mrs. Callaway to continue with their honeymoon with no further hindrance."

No one but Luke noticed the flash of fire in Lisa's eyes as she turned to Miss Kirkpatrick. Vengeance was written all over her face. The little green monster had reared its ugly head. Jealousy was another facet of Lisa's personality he had only recently begun to notice.

Thank God Mr. Lianoho spoke before Lisa had a chance to. "The airline has left it up to you, Miss, since you're the only one who was involved, and there was no real threat to the airplane or any of the passengers. If you aren't going to press charges, I suppose we have nothing further to do here."

The FBI agents seemed to be relieved that the situation was going to be resolved in this manner. It was evident they didn't really want to arrest Lisa.

"We're sorry this happened, Mrs. Callaway." Mr. Lianoho touched the brim of his hat and nodded at the two women. He ignored Luke. Both men turned and walked back towards the terminal.

Luke couldn't get over it. Somehow Lisa had gotten an apology out of these two experienced professionals, when she was the one who had committed a crime, and her victim ends up getting her off the hook.

It was a matter of minutes before Luke discovered why Miss Kirkpatrick so readily dismissed the charges against Lisa. Beyond the fact that she seemed to be a remarkable young woman with a very kind heart, it soon became apparent that someone else had also intervened on Lisa's behalf. Out of the corner of his eye, Luke saw an approaching figure and when he turned to look, he came face-to-face with Cooper DeLaney. He was astounded. He had never expected to see her again.

"Hello, Lucas Callaway." She extended her hand in friendship. "Congratulations." The dimples played across her face, and she laughed aloud at his surprise at seeing her.

She looked good. She looked healthy and wholesome and happy. Her coppery blonde hair glistened in the Honolulu sunshine and to Luke, she looked like an angel.

Cooper and Lisa were exact opposites. Lisa, with her dark, exotic beauty, scowled at Cooper and eyed her suspiciously. Cooper, with a sprinkling of freckles across her fair skin, bubbled with enthusiasm and exuberantly took both Lisa's hands in her own.

"You're a lucky lady, Mrs. Callaway, to have such a fine man as Luke. I wish you both the best." There was sincerity in Cooper's words. She released Lisa's hands and turned to Luke. "I just got in from San Francisco about thirty minutes ago. I'm here for a few days R & R. Anna and I planned on getting together while she's here on her layover, so I came out to meet her. What a surprise it was when I discovered that you had been on her flight."

Anna revealed what Cooper wouldn't. "Actually, it's lucky for you two Cooper came along. I'm afraid without her intervention I wouldn't have been so merciful. She pointed out that having Mrs.

Callaway arrested would serve no purpose. I had to agree with her."

"Thank you for being so understanding. I apologize again, Miss Kirkpatrick." Luke wished Lisa would make her own apologies, but thus far she had remained silent.

"Don't mention it...Cooper and I go way back...anything to help a friend of hers. I know Mrs. Callaway didn't intend for it to happen. It's not like she's a dangerous character or anything."

Luke let that remark pass. He wasn't too sure about that at this point.

"Anna's leaving tomorrow afternoon, but maybe the three of us can have lunch together one day, Luke. How about it, Lisa? You two give me a call at the Ilikai."

"I tell you what, since Anna's leaving tomorrow, why don't Lisa and I take both of you to dinner this evening? To show our appreciation."

"But you're on your honeymoon. Taking the two of us to dinner wouldn't be very romantic. Anna and I couldn't impose like that."

"We'll make it an early dinner. Lisa and I have two full weeks here. This is our only chance to repay both of you. What do you say?" He assumed Lisa would be appreciative enough to want to share one evening with them.

Anna shrugged her shoulders at Cooper. "What do you think, Cooper? I think it would be terrific. You didn't have anything else planned for us, did you?"

"No, not really. Anna and I haven't seen each other in awhile, but we can still catch up, and you can fill me in on your life since your return to Pemrose Key, Luke." Cooper looked at Lisa, giving her an approving appraisal. "It looks like wonderful things have happened for you. You have a beautiful wife. I'd like to get to know you, too, Lisa."

Luke knew she meant it. That was Cooper DeLaney.

Lisa ignored Cooper's friendly gesture—and that was Lisa. She continued to scowl angrily between Luke and the other two women. After arrangements for the evening had been agreed upon and they parted company, Lisa still had not uttered a word to either Cooper or Anna.

On the ride from the airport to their hotel, Luke had time to reflect on the events of the day while Lisa sulked in her corner of the back seat of the taxi. He realized he'd had difficulty taking his eyes off Cooper. Her personality was so magnetic; her warmth so genuine. The intensity of his attraction to her surprised him. It also scared him a little, but he attributed the attraction to his own disillusionment over the beginning of his marriage. Lisa's silence and disagreeable personality only served to magnify the contrast between Cooper and her. Perhaps when they had a chance to relax, they could begin anew and have a real honeymoon. With all the turmoil behind them, Lisa would once again be the woman he'd first been attracted to. He was sure of it.

It was late in the day. Luke decided it best not to disturb the peace by trying to make conversation with Lisa, so he stared out the taxi window at the sights they passed between the airport and the Royal Hawaiian. Honolulu was beautiful, a fantasyland of scenic blue skies and fluffy, white clouds reflecting on turquoise waters. Tall palm trees, fronds rippling in the wind, waved their greeting. This was the perfect place for a honeymoon. Everything was going to be fine.

16

$\mathcal{L}$uke's hopes of a fresh start quickly faded once he and Lisa settled into their suite.

"I'm not going to dinner with those two women along, Luke."

"Why not, Lisa? We've already invited them."

"No, Luke, you invited them. I'm not going, and you're not either."

"I understand your feelings, Lisa. We haven't even become man and wife yet." Luke knew diplomacy was his best tactic. "Why don't we do something about that right now." He took Lisa in his arms and pulled her to him, his romantic hopes rising as he moved to kiss her.

She pulled away from him. "No, Luke. I don't believe you do understand. I'll not be going, and we'll not be having any sex if you do."

With great effort, Luke held his temper. "You're my wife, Lisa. We're supposed to make love. I was patient with you last night when you got drunk and passed out on me, or pretended to pass out. I understand the stress you've been under."

"We'll not be going to dinner with them, Luke Callaway." Lisa left the room in a huff.

Luke spent the afternoon walking Waikiki Beach alone until sunset. He agonized that he had been wrong to set up the dinner engagement, and he felt guilty for expecting Lisa to spend the first evening of their Hawaiian honeymoon out with two other women, both total strangers to her.

When Luke returned to their room to shower and shave, Lisa was dressed and willing to go with him to meet Anna and Cooper at the *Top of the I,* the mutually agreed upon restaurant that sat high atop the Ilikai, overlooking Waikiki Beach. She was devastatingly beautiful and ever the southern belle, all sweetness and light again. Luke was pleasantly surprised.

The best way to handle her moods, it seemed, was to leave her alone and let her work things out for herself. He put a fresh blade in his razor and hummed a tune while he shaved. He felt better now. However, he was convinced he would never understand women.

The shower rejuvenated him. After dressing, he fixed himself a scotch and soda. Lisa already had a drink in hand, no ice.

Luke was delighted with the change in her. He spoke softly, inviting a reconciliation, "You look wonderful, Lisa." He placed his hands on her bare shoulders and pulled her to him, cradling her head gently against his chest and tenderly stroking her hair. He held her close for a long, quiet moment, relieved that she was calmer now. He was anxious for them to assume a normal relationship. He placed his fingertips on her chin and tilted her face up to his. Her eyes were closed, and she looked so innocent. Her lips were parted sensuously, waiting for his mouth to cover hers. He obliged her, and she responded passionately. He savored the taste of her lips and wanted to caress every inch of her body with his kisses. She was soft and yielding. He breathed deeply of her scent. He buried his face in the thick, shiny hair that fell around her shoulders. It felt so good to be holding her—touching her. His arousal was powerful. He'd waited a long time. He couldn't stop now. He moved his fingers to the zipper at the back of her dress. She was his wife, and he was certain he could make her happy. She would know there could never be any other man for her, ever again. Soon, now, they would truly be husband and wife.

Lisa nibbled gently, playfully at his neck. She blew her warm breath in his ear and whispered softly, "Luke, you can have me under one condition, and I'll make it so good for you. But only under one condition, Luke."

His body tensed. "What's your condition, Lisa?"

"Cancel our dinner plans with those two women. Those...those two witches!"

He tightened his grip on her arms and pulled her closer, determined to resume the mutual play of seduction they had begun, refusing to believe what he had heard. He ran his fingers through her hair and roughly sought her lips with his mouth.

"Stop, Luke! Stop it this minute!" Lisa squealed loudly. She pulled back, wriggling herself free of his embrace. "We're not going to do this. Not now! Not ever! Not unless you cancel this dinner engagement with those two." She was screaming now, and glaring fiercely at him. Her lower lip protruded like a pouting child.

Luke tried to control his voice and contain his fury. "Lisa, I know I was wrong to invite them to dinner on our first night in Hawaii. I admit it, and I apologize for it. Believe me, if I had known you would feel this way about it I would never have done it. It was a spontaneous reaction—a show of gratitude for their help. A mistake, yes, but it's done now. Don't ruin the rest of our time here because of it. Tonight will be over soon enough, and we'll have the rest of our lives together. If they hadn't helped us you would be spending your first night here in jail instead of having dinner at the Top of the I. We'll have two weeks together without them. Let them know you appreciate what they did."

"I don't appreciate what they did! I handled those two FBI cops myself. They liked me. It was because of me—not because of them!"

He lashed out at her with his words, no longer attempting to control his anger. "What you did to that stewardess aboard that airplane was inexcusable, yet she had the dignity and class to virtually ignore your actions. Now try having a little class yourself."

"I hate you, Luke!" Lisa spat the words viciously in his face. She spun around and snatched her evening bag from the sofa. When she faced Luke again, fury flashed in her eyes. Above her strapless gown her chest rose and fell visibly with heavy, angry breathing. Was it anger, or a glint of full hatred Luke saw in her eyes? Whatever it was, the intensity of it perplexed him.

As quickly as it had erupted, her anger subsided. She instantly regained her composure and changed her tactics midstream. Appearing calmer, she enunciated every word slowly and singularly through clenched teeth. The words, nonetheless, were venomous. "I'll go, Lucas Callaway, but you will regret this later. That's a promise. Just wait and see."

Her threat didn't scare him, even though he was quite confident of her potential for making the threat good. The look he witnessed in her eyes was quite a different story. He was stricken with the horror that she would never be any different. This was Lisa, the woman he had married. The truth hit him full force. Beneath the beautiful veneer of this temptress dwelt the same family traits and characteristics that her cousin, Edna Sinclair, possessed.

Luke's skin crawled with a flash of deja'vu. Edna stood before him, and the words were the same. *"You will regret this, Lucas Callaway. I promise. Just you wait and see."* The experience was dizzying. He searched his mind. Had Edna really said this to him before, on some long ago day when he had rejected her? Absurd as the idea seemed, a tingling chill crept across his skin. *What in God's name have I done?*

Luke held the door open and let Lisa lead the way to the elevator. She was beautiful, there was no denying that. Heads turned as she strode through the corridor and as his anger over the unsettling turn of events lulled a bit, he marveled at the degree of pride he experienced walking a pace or two behind her. He should have his head examined.

At the hotel's entrance a taxi awaited their departure.

Once Luke and Lisa were situated in the taxi, Lisa removed her ever-present little silver flask from her purse and took two long swigs. They sat apart. She was still pouting and like a child, had drawn an imaginary line between them. She made it clear Luke was not to cross over to her side, but as a means of sanctioning her own indulgence, she leaned over to Luke and passed the bottle under the tip of his nose. "Want some?"

Luke looked away, ignoring her offer.

The taxi driver maneuvered through the traffic and pulled to a stop directly at the front entrance of the Ilikai. He got out and opened the car door for Lisa. When Luke came around from the other side and offered his hand, Lisa stubbornly remained seated.

"Come on, Lisa, let's go in."

She refused to budge. She stared straight ahead, ignoring Luke's plea.

"Lisa, get out of the cab." Luke's patience was wearing thin.

She raised the flask to her lips and continued to stare straight ahead.

People milling around the entrance stared at them. There would not be another public scene. Luke looked at the taxi's meter. "Is that what I owe you?"

"Yes, Boss." The driver looked nervously at his meter again to make sure.

Luke dug into his pocket, pulled out a fistful of bills, and shoved them into the driver's palm. "That's more than double the fare. Take her back to the Royal Hawaiian."

Without another word, Luke turned and opened the heavy glass doors before him and strode into the lobby of the Ilikai alone, without looking back. It was only a moment before he heard a commotion behind him.

It was Lisa, shrieking and running and stumbling as she cleared a path through the lobby.

"Luke! Lucas Callaway, you stop this instant. Stop! Stop it right now I said, and wait for me." Lisa ran towards him, hollering at the top of her lungs, arms all akimbo, clutching her evening bag in one hand and waving it wildly before her.

He cringed at the sound of her voice and closed his eyes in exasperation, but still he didn't look back. He slowed his pace to allow Lisa to catch up with him, hoping that would quiet her screams.

Lisa grabbed hard at his elbow with both hands, yanking him around to face her. Abruptly she released his arm, and her eyes widened at something she saw behind Luke's back. With her mouth hanging open, she squinted her eyes now as if attempting to focus. After a moment she exclaimed loudly, "Skip Traylor, what are YOU doing here?"

Luke quickly turned to follow her gaze, but only in time to catch a glimpse of a rapidly retreating bald spot on the back side of a redheaded man. The man wore a boldly colored Hawaiian print shirt. Luke had not turned in time to see the man's face, but he did see Mr. Kuamohe and Mr. Lianoho standing a short distance away. At the sound of Lisa's shrieking, they glanced sharply in her direction and with no acknowledgment or seeming recognition, they turned and quickly followed the Hawaiian shirt out an exit door on the far side of the lobby. Luke thought it strange that they seemed to be following the presumed Skip Traylor. He also thought it strange that Skip Traylor would be in Honolulu. As a crusty, weathered, old sea captain, it didn't seem likely that Skip would be vacationing leisurely in this tropical resort. If it were Skip Traylor, his hasty retreat at the sight of Lisa was a curious act.

"Lisa, how well do you know Skip Traylor?"

At least for the moment, Lisa's anger at Luke appeared to have subsided. She now seemed to be only halfway snockered and a whole lot puzzled. Apparently she didn't hear Luke's question. She stood still, staring at the spot where the balding red-headed man in the Hawaiian shirt had been. Her brown eyes reflected fear, and she shook her head emphatically when she spoke. "Uh-oh, maybe that wasn't Skip Traylor, Luke. Yeah, maybe it wasn't him at all. Actually, I don't think it was."

Yes, it was. Luke knew with a certainty it was. And it possibly had something to do with everything that had happened since his return to Pemrose Key.

When they emerged from the elevator at the Top of the I, Luke instantly spotted Cooper and Anna at a table midway across the room. When Cooper saw them, she raised herself halfway out of her chair and waved them over. Luke felt his heart quiver, but it was somewhere out of place. It seemed to have slipped down to the pit of his stomach.

Cooper was every bit a match for Lisa in the looks department. He had seen Cooper in her uniform and in casual attire. Now, dressed for the occasion, her coppery-blonde hair shimmered softly in the candlelight and fell in lustrous waves across bare, fair-skinned shoulders. She wore a cream colored, strapless sarong that wrapped around her slender waist, the fitted bodice accenting an incredible figure. When Luke and Lisa reached the table, Cooper's radiant smile welcomed them with all the warmth that was Cooper's to give. Her luminous personality, the blending of her fair skin with the cream colored fabric, and the shimmering highlights of her hair, truly gave her the aura of an angel, his special angel.

Dear God, it's Cooper I'm in love with! The realization struck with such force and so completely unnerved him he had to struggle to speak. He stammered and stuttered and for one suffocating moment, he couldn't catch his breath.

Finally, when he found his voice, he spoke with a tense formality, which was all he could manage, and he made a concerted effort to mask his true feelings.

"Ladies, how are you this evening?" His heart pounded so furiously he thought they might hear. "You both look lovely and rested after your flights today." He avoided looking directly at Cooper, and he was cautious not to single her out with his words, but then, realizing his avoidance may be too conspicuous, he tried to assume a relaxed demeanor.

Lisa greeted the ladies tersely. In fact, she greeted the waiter with much greater enthusiasm when he came around and took their drink orders. Luke surprised himself by ordering a double martini, something he rarely fancied, but something he hoped would now calm his jitters.

Thankfully, Lisa was pouting still and had very little to contribute to the conversation. She sulked, and Luke was aware of her watching his every move, which made him all the more nervous. Lisa's sullen eyes bore into him, and she glanced back and forth between him and Cooper when he at last trusted himself enough to engage in congenial small talk with her. The waiter brought their drinks. *Please, God, let Lisa continue to keep her mouth shut. Don't let her cause another scene, not now, not tonight.*

Tonight. What connotations that had held earlier. He had wanted tonight to be special. He had wanted to come home and make love to his new bride. He had imagined that things would work out for them, but now he feared they never would. Now he wasn't sure he wanted her at all, this Edna-in-disguise, this little wanton winch that he had been so hell-bent on making his wife. He would get an annulment. They would go home immediately. He would try to get a flight out for them tomorrow.

He finished his martini in just a few gulps and motioned for the waiter to replenish his glass.

"Here's to Cooper—and Anna—thanks for all your help, ladies." He was feeling more courageous now. He waved his glass in a toast to them. "Salud." He didn't care anymore about placating Lisa. He was tired of trying to appease her.

Cooper responded first by touching the rim of her glass to his. Anna followed suit. Then the two women toasted each other. Now Cooper raised her glass towards Lisa. It came without warning. Lisa stood and brought the palm of her hand up smack-dab under the bottom of Cooper's glass of Chardonnay.

The cold splash in her face startled Cooper into action. She was angelic and sweet, but she wasn't a stupid woman by any means, and evidently she wasn't a coward. She silently blotted her face with her napkin, then stood and came around to Lisa's side of the table. In a most ladylike, non-threatening manner, she placed her hand firmly on Lisa's upper arm, forcing her to her feet. In one brief moment, a moment Luke found himself relishing, Cooper managed to bring Lisa to the most subdued state Luke had witnessed thus far on their honeymoon.

Cooper leveled her gaze at Lisa and in a soft, controlled voice, commanded with more grace than Luke could have imagined anyone to have possessed in such a situation, "Come with me, young lady, I would like to have a word with you." When Cooper firmly curled her fingers around Lisa's upper arm, outward appearances indicated only that she was requesting that a friend accompany her to the ladies room.

"Let me go!" Lisa hissed as they left the table, making a feeble attempt to wriggle her arm free. Surprisingly, she didn't raise her voice or react violently. Tonight she was outnumbered.

At a closer glance, the pressure marks Cooper's fingers made on Lisa's bare arm told the whole truth. Cooper wasn't fooling, and she very proficiently proceeded to guide Lisa around the tables towards the powder room.

Just two best friends sharing secrets as they strolled arm-in-arm through the restaurant. Luke watched in awe. He suspected none of Lisa's victims had ever stood up to her, and she actually seemed a bit cowed, like a child who welcomed a scolding because she knew she had been bad.

Anna pushed her chair back and stood. "I'll be back." Her smile spread across her face mischievously as she winked at Luke and hurried off after Cooper and Lisa. Anna was a tall, thin, angular woman with a mid-western accent, high cheekbones and short, fluffy brown hair. Not a beautiful woman by any means, but she had a broad, infectious smile that enhanced her looks and endowed her with a genuine attractiveness. She had a sincerity about her, a no-bull kind of personality that made you know she was someone you could trust. She was the sort of friend one would expect Cooper to have, a good girl, with a wholesome outlook, unlike the Edna's of the world, and the Lisas.

Luke had no doubt that Cooper and Anna were capable of handling the situation. He was confident Lisa was in good hands, and maybe getting one of life's little lessons thrown in to boot. He could only sit and imagine what might be transpiring behind the closed door of the ladies room. Granted, were it not for the martinis, he would not be taking this in such stride. Cooper seemed to have a way about her of diminishing the importance of seemingly major catastrophes. Luke took another sip of his martini. He had slowed his pace a bit. We make a good pair, he thought to himself as he lined up two olives on his napkin and pushed them around together with a swizzle stick. His brief marriage was over.

Luke waited. He played with the olives. He toyed with the gold engraved matchbooks that had been at their places when they arrived. He snorted a half-smile. The words *Luke and Lisa* were inscribed in gold across the glossy white, matchbook covers. Classy place. It was a sure bet Lisa had never been in a place like this, a far cry from the Biloxi Bar and Grill. He looked around the room. The tables were all meticulously set, fresh flowers in crystal vases centered on every one atop the crisp white table cloths. Through the glass that lined a portion of the outer wall of the Top of the I, the lights of Honolulu flickered romantically. Not too many diners had arrived yet and it didn't appear that anyone had witnessed the scene. The evening had begun early as they were still running on mainland time.

Luke glanced at the Maître d's station. He was taken aback when he saw Mr. Lianoho and Mr. Kuamohe standing there, leaning against the wall, their arms folded across their chests. They smiled, and nodded recognition at Luke. Luke looked around to see if they were, indeed, smiling at him. There was no one else around, and yes, they must surely have witnessed the scene with Lisa. Were he and Lisa being followed? They'd been in the lobby when he had been skirmishing with Lisa and now, here they were again.

They started towards him, threading their way past the immaculate white tables, getting closer, smiling at him all the while. Damn! He wished he hadn't sucked down those martinis so fast. He shook his head in an effort to clear his mind. What if Lisa should reappear with Cooper and Anna? She would likely start doing a number on these guys again, or worse. What could they want now, anyway? To see Lisa again? Maybe she'll unbutton their shirts—or better yet, hers, or maybe she'll go for their fly's this time—that would be a kick.

"Mr. Callaway, so nice to see you again, and under such…different circumstances." Mr. Lianoho extended his hand and bowed melodramatically.

The implication was not lost on Luke. The circumstances of Lisa's attack were the same, only here, off the airplane, it wasn't a federal offense, and Lisa had only to reckon with the ladies themselves. The men had no jurisdiction over what Lisa did to the off-duty airline stewardesses. So why were they here?

Luke stood. "Gentlemen, can I buy you a drink?" Luke hoped the words sounded a bit less martinized to them than they did to him.

"No, thank you, Mr. Callaway." Mr. Lianoho looked over his shoulder towards the Ladies Room. Although no one was around, he lowered his voice. "Actually, Mr. Callaway, we have something very important we would like to discuss with you." The banter was gone. "Could you meet us at noon tomorrow at Fort DeRussy, near Battery Randolph?"

Luke was puzzled. He shook his head. The martinis had really gotten to him. Did these FBI men really want to have a clandestine meeting with him? Sure, he had done some pretty high security stuff in Vietnam, but that was over. This couldn't be about that. "I can do that, but can you give me a clue?"

"No, sorry, there's no time right now. It's just something we have to discuss with you, and don't worry, it has nothing to do with what your wife did today—or tonight!" Mr. Kuamohe grinned.

"Oh, yes, and one more thing, Mr. Callaway." Mr. Lianoho spoke, "Please don't mention our meeting to anyone. Not your wife, or the airline stewardesses. Not anyone. This is extremely important." He looked serious. This time he didn't preface what he said with a grin.

They both turned and walked across the room and out the door. What was going on? So much for getting a flight out tomorrow.

As if on cue, the minute the two gentlemen disappeared from the room, Cooper and Anna reappeared, a very subdued Lisa in tow. Right away Lisa contritely informed Luke that she was going back to the hotel. She wasn't feeling too well, but she insisted Luke stay and have dinner with Cooper and Anna. No need for him to miss dinner merely because she wasn't up to par.

Luke knew Lisa well enough by now to know the meek front was a sham. She wouldn't be leaving unless she wanted to. She had to be up to something. There was no way even Cooper and Anna could have persuaded Lisa to leave if it hadn't been her own idea.

When Lisa left, Luke turned his attention to Cooper and Anna. Not once did he glance in the direction of Lisa's shapely, departing rear.

"I'm sorry for this, ladies. Are you alright, Cooper?" He was past the point of being embarrassed. Lisa's shenanigans were taking their toll. He reached for the unfinished bottle of wine and motioned for the waiter to bring another bottle, along with a fresh wine glass for Cooper. He filled the glasses himself, and proposed a simple toast, "To health, wealth, happiness and longevity!"

The remainder of the evening was pleasant. Dinner was delicious, Cooper was beautiful, and Anna was entertaining. No mention was made of what had transpired in the ladies room.

Though it wasn't the conventional way to spend one's honeymoon, Luke's self-imposed marital protocol was impeccable. His married-man facade as the ever-faithful husband was in place, although he hadn't had much practice at being a married man. He knew he must avoid revealing his attraction to Cooper, and his re-awakened desire for her remained where it belonged, in a hidden corner of his heart and an obscure crevice of his mind. The vision he held of himself and Cooper someday being together in a healthy, happy relationship, must remain just that for now—a vision.

His relationship with Lisa and yes, even his marriage to her, had been not a relationship of love and trust and mutual interests, but rather one based purely on lust and sex, and God forgive him, he had been wrong. It was easy in hindsight to see how he should have listened to what his mother had to say, and to his own warning signs—that inner voice that had cautioned him. The warning signs had been in place, but he had shoved them aside for mere wanton lust. Where had it gotten him? Into the biggest mess of his life, and into an unconsummated marriage with a very sick girl.

17

It was only 10:00 p.m. when Luke returned to the hotel. He dreaded having to face Lisa. His internal clock was still on Central time, and based on that it was extremely late. Even so, one nightcap in the bar might do him some good. Actually, it just might give him the courage he needed to go upstairs and confront the situation with Lisa, tell her they were leaving as soon as he could arrange it, and that their marriage was over before it had begun. Tomorrow he would move his things out and into another room until they could leave.

Luke navigated his way through the lobby of the Royal Hawaiian, making the turn to the long corridor that led outside to the open-air restaurant and bar, past the shops, past the chairs that lined the corridor.

A man wearing a bright, multi-colored Hawaiian shirt came through the open entrance of the corridor. As he walked, he was preoccupied with a shiny, silvery object he held in his hands which Luke identified as a snuff box when he saw the man's pinched fingers go from the box to his lips. Luke stepped aside to avoid colliding with him.

"Watch it," the man snarled as he side-stepped the spot where Luke had been, never looking up.

The man appeared to be in his mid-forties. He had a tuft of carrot-red hair over each ear, and he was bald on top. Luke turned and viewed him from the rear. It was Skip Traylor. By the time this registered in Luke's exhausted brain, the man was halfway down the corridor and heading towards the lobby of the hotel. The last time Luke had seen Skip Traylor in Pemrose Key was before Luke went off to college. At that time Skip still had a fair amount of bright red hair, and he didn't wear glasses as this man did. Without a doubt, though, this was Skip Traylor.

When Luke reached the bar, the first thing he recognized was Lisa's shapely bottom perched on a chair at the end of the bar.

He started to leave, then realized Lisa must have been with Skip Traylor. He wanted to know why. Skip was more than twice Lisa's age, and his reputation was rank. Rumors were rampant of drug running, pimping, illegal gambling trips on the water. In fact, everything Luke had ever heard about Skip Traylor had a strong stench to it.

Lisa was drunk. It was evident even from this rear perspective. Admittedly, he wasn't much better off himself. At least now he could meet her on common ground.

As much as he wanted to, leaving tomorrow was out now that he had to meet with the FBI. He supposed he could have told them his plans, but in spite of what his brain told him to do, burning dimly within his heart was a flicker of hope that Lisa was really the most wonderful woman in the world. The agony of failure nagged and deceived him into believing that tiny glimmer that it might simply be a bad dream, and that as soon as Lisa grew up, she would make him a wonderful wife. To be in love with Cooper was too complicated.

"Oops! Oh, my, look what I've done," Lisa giggled about the glass she overturned. The unamused bartender scowled and silently mopped up the spilled contents with a towel.

Luke's image of Lisa as a wonderful wife evaporated as quickly as the thirsty towel absorbed the liquid off the bar. The reality of it was, his marriage was over.

"More, please, Mr. Bartender. The same."

Despite his obvious disgust, the bartender set a full glass, no ice, in front of Lisa, which she instantly lifted to her lips.

"My darling wife, fancy meeting you here. Couldn't sleep?" Luke placed his hand on the back of Lisa's neck, and his fingers sensed her back stiffen at his touch, like an arching, bristling cat.

"Luke! Where did you come from? How long have you been standing there?" There was fear in her eyes. Her glass was already half empty and she turned it up at once and drank the contents to the finish.

Luke had given her no reason to fear him—yet. How easy it would be to tighten his fingers around her tiny neck and squeeze. Instead, he removed his hand and ordered a brandy from the bartender.

"I just got here. Thought I'd get a nightcap before turning in. We can have one together. How about it?"

Lisa hesitated. She turned in her seat and looked around towards the corridor entrance. Satisfied there was no one there, her fear seemed to subside. "Okay, that might be nice. Ah'm so sorry I misbehaved, Luke. I was a bad girl again. Will you forgive me?" She pleaded innocently.

He wanted to smack her, but he maintained his composure. The girl just wasn't normal.

"Cooper and Anna made me feel so bad I just didn't want to stay and ruin your party. I wouldn't have been very good company. They did tell me how much you loved me, Lukey, and that I was a lucky lady to have you. I realize now they were right. I've just been sitting here all night thinking about everything that has happened since we got married, and you know what, Luke? I think I've just been in shock. Yeah! Shock. That happens sometimes to people, right? Especially when they go through a big change. Anna and Cooper helped me see that alright. You see, otherwise I never would have done the things I did. I just haven't been myself at all.

Cooper said I'd just been through too much, too fast." She paused, breathlessly, overcome by her own dramatics.

Amazing. She was trying to work him, just as she had Joe Lianoho and Kip Kuamohe.

"Luke, let's go up to our room now. Ah'm so tired, aren't you?" Though she enunciated with a slur, she sure could bat those eyelashes, and they effected an unspoken promise.

"I guess I am at that. Let's turn in." It would be interesting to see how far she would go. His fascination with her was far different now than when he first met her. Luke didn't finish his brandy. He left some bills on the bar to cover his tab, and asked no questions when Lisa told him hers had already been taken care of. With that, there was nothing left to do but retire to their suite.

Once upstairs, Lisa retreated to the bathroom. A half-hour later she still hadn't come out. Luke watched the local news on TV. When it ended, he stared at the television test pattern for a full five minutes, then finally gave up on Lisa and stretched out across the bed. He kicked his shoes to the floor and fell asleep fully dressed.

Upon awaking in the morning, the first thing Luke saw when he opened his eyes was Lisa stretched out in the overstuffed chair across the room. She was stiff as a board, arms flopped out on each side and dangling over the sides of the armchair. Her legs were stretched out stiffly in front of her, and her heels were planted on the floor, toes peeping out from beneath the ruffled edge of a pale pink satin gown and pointing upwards towards the ceiling. With gaping mouth and tightly closed eyes, her head was thrown back against the chair cushion in what looked like a terribly uncomfortable position.

Luke was startled by the sight. He raised his head to get a better look. Was she dead? No, not judging by the snores emitting from her opened mouth. Lisa didn't look too desirable or glamorous from this angle. He laughed aloud and shook his head. If he didn't view his whole predicament with a little humor, the tragedy of it would be overwhelming.

Luke rolled his body over and raised himself to a sitting position on the edge of the bed, placing his feet solidly on the floor before attempting to stand. "Oops, oh boy! Did I really do this to myself last night?" He groaned aloud, with no fear of waking Lisa. He rubbed both palms across his face. "Whew! No more martinis for me."

He headed for the shower, closing the door to the bathroom gently behind him. On the vanity sat Lisa's empty silver flask. The top to it lay in the sink and in the trash container beside the vanity was an empty Jim Beam bottle. Man! She must have had a real party for herself after I went to sleep. Sadly, it dawned on Luke that she must've been trying to get up her courage to be with him. *Well, Skip Traylor, looks like you win the prize—the booby prize.*

Luke remembered the night he first met Lisa, her passion had been so fervent. She played her little game, the power play, but there had been no question in his mind that she had been as consumed by desire as he had. It seemed now as though she had no desire to even be near him. Lisa was totally absorbed in Lisa. She used sex, or the promise of it, only when she wanted or needed something from somebody—like Luke's wedding band on her finger. Now, rather than sleep with him, she got drunk! After that charade at the bar and Luke called her bluff, she just couldn't bring herself to follow through.

In the beginning, part of the turn-on to Luke had been her unbridled passion for him, as it would have been for most any man. She was good at it. What he'd mistaken for passion had been no more than an act in a play. She was a tease. She was beautiful and exotic, but she had exhausted him. The lure of the challenge no longer enticed him.

He let the steaming water penetrate his pores. If it could only wash away the mistakes he had made. He focused his mind on

Cooper while he showered and shaved and allowed her to absorb his thoughts. It felt good to think about her, about her freshness, which was as fresh and clean as the water that washed over him now. *Cooper...Cooper...I have made a terrible mistake. It's you I want.*

The reality of being with Cooper seemed so distant now, at least until he could take care of this business with Lisa. Even then, Cooper might not want him the way he wanted her. What a terrible mistake he had made.

His thoughts were interrupted when he heard, through the closed bathroom door, Lisa stirring around in the other room. She coughed, then cleared her throat and coughed again, and Luke heard drawers opening and closing and the closet door slam shut. A moment later Lisa pounded on the locked bathroom door.

"Luke, let me in. Are you in there? I want to get in there, hurry!"

He knew what she was looking for. The condition she must have been in when she finally passed out in the chair last night told him she had to have a drink to function this morning. He wasn't going to stay around and watch the same kind of self-destruction he had witnessed since they had left Pemrose Key.

Luke pushed his way out of the bathroom door, Lisa crowding to get in as he did. Good, maybe she'd stay in there long enough for him to get his clothes on and get away. He wanted no confrontations this morning. All he wanted was out, in more ways than one.

Lisa looked like hell; like she had aged ten years overnight. Her face was screwed up and swollen and her eyes were half closed, and she looked as though she couldn't mobilize her lips enough to speak. She squinted at him and emitted something that was half grunt and half squeak, a noise she must have thought sufficed as a greeting.

"Got things to do, Lisa. See you later." Luke owed her no explanations and he offered none. He buttoned his shirt on the run. Lisa still stood at the threshold of the bathroom door as he exited their honeymoon suite.

Luke had nearly overslept and he needed to hustle if he didn't want to be late. He knew his way around Waikiki Beach. He'd spent some family vacations here when he was younger and more recently, R & R between his Vietnam stints. This place had once seemed like paradise and a brief respite from hell. These islands had represented comfort and succor at a time in his life when something had been desperately needed to bring relief from the insanity that was war. He wanted to leave this morning in time to walk to nearby Fort DeRussy. He wanted to relish the sights and the sounds and to see if this was the utopia he remembered it to be.

18

The walk to Fort Derussy Park was refreshing. Besides allowing time for remembering—and forgetting—it felt good to move his body. The time gave him a chance to reflect on his present situation and it occurred to him that perhaps he'd been temporarily insane as a result of wartime stress.

When Luke reached the park, he looked around for Joe Lianoho and Kip Kuamohe. He'd been instructed to meet them at Battery Randolph. There was some site construction going on and things looked a bit different since Luke's last visit. In the middle of all the activity he finally spotted them, not more than a hundred yards away, talking animatedly to two construction workers. All four men were gesturing with their hands and appeared to be shouting above the noise of a nearby backhoe.

As Luke neared the group and got a closer look at the men, he slowed his pace a bit. Mr. Kuamohe saw him and motioned energetically for Luke to come on over. Luke hesitated in disbelief. One of the construction workers was Skip Traylor. Luke's initial reaction had been to back off until he could find out what this was all about. Skip Traylor couldn't be on a construction crew in Honolulu unless he was leading a double life.

Mr. Lianoho extended his hand. "Luke. Thanks for coming. This is Munsen Wales...and this is Stephen Pau. Gentlemen...Luke Callaway."

The two looked to be anything but gentlemen, in Luke's estimation.

"Mr. Pau, Mr...Wales, did you say?"

"Yeah, hey, how ya' doin'? Munsen Wales here." The accent was English, cockney English, but the red tufts, the balding head and all the facial features were the same. He thrust a freckled, pudgy palm forward. The third finger, right hand, was missing. His fingers were so thick and dense the missing finger didn't seem to leave much of a gap, not one that was noticeable by his handshake, anyway.

This man wasn't Skip Traylor—not when he spoke. But the two rogues had the same face, same build.

Luke maintained a poker-face, concealing his surprise.

Mr. Lianoho forged ahead. "Luke...hope you don't mind my informality...I have a feeling we're going to be staying in pretty close contact with one another for awhile. That is, if you agree to coop-erate with us. We need your help. There is a degree of coincidence here, but it's not all coincidence. The coincidence is that you were to be approached by the FBI in Pemrose Key when you returned home from your honeymoon, but when your wife created that little, uh, incident, your name cross-referenced with our records instantly. We knew of your plans to honeymoon here in Honolulu, but we weren't going to bother you, until your wife expedited our meeting. Your wife's actions created more of an urgency to meet with you sooner. It's important to our objective that you not tire of your wife too prematurely, Luke," he stated as though he had read Luke's mind.

"I don't believe that's any of your..."

"Please, let me finish." He held his hand up, halting Luke's words. "Besides your high security clearance in the Marines, who you are married to has something to do with why we need you. Thanks to your new bride, you just played right into our hands, so to speak. You see, you have been the subject of an intense, shall we say 'review,' of late. We happen to know you had one of the highest security clearances in Vietnam because of your duties, and you quite possibly have the highest security clearance in history of anyone connected with Pemrose Key, barring key Navy personnel at Pensacola, of course. We already know you can be trusted for good of country. Your country needs you again, and you don't have to re-enlist for this job. However, this may even be a bit more dangerous than what you did in Vietnam."

Nothing could be more dangerous. With an ominous feeling, Luke knew he would never fully get away from Vietnam. He would never be able to forget. Never! He'd served his time. Uncle Sam had swallowed up four years of his life. Now what did they want of him?

"Well, I can't say that I fathom what you're saying." No one this side of Saigon was supposed to know what he had actually done over there. Did these men?

"What does my marrying Lisa Logan have to do with anything I did in Vietnam? I can't imagine why you might be even remotely interested in my personal life. You're not with the Marine Corps, the State Department, the CIA or the Defense Department, or even the Secret Service. So what gives? The FBI didn't have anything to do with what I did in Vietnam. Why the interest in my life?"

"The FBI investigation centers around Pemrose Key and illegal interstate activities, Luke."

"What could my wife possibly have to do with any of this? I'm afraid you need to be more explicit, Mr. Lianoho." Luke was exasperated. The blood rushed to his head and he could feel it pulsating in his temple. His jawbone tightened and protruded as he clenched his teeth. His anger was at himself, not at these men. He knew that whatever suspicions they cast on Lisa could be true. No, he did not know much about her or just what he might have gotten himself into with that woman.

"Slow down, Luke, don't worry so fast. We didn't say your wife is personally involved...not that we can prove, anyway. We don't have much, but we know she has ties to the Navy...she knows a lot of Navy personnel in Pemrose Key, right? We've had our eye on her for awhile."

Luke wanted to slug him. Did he know about the night at Oyster Bay, too, when he tried to wipe out half the Navy? Did he also know why? Was there nothing about his military or private life that had not been examined under their microscope?

"I mean, Luke, her father is in the Navy. I believe you have recently become acquainted with your father-in-law, Commander Thomas Logan?"

Luke was momentarily taken aback. Lisa was a Navy brat. So those were the connections they meant. They might mean the others, too. He'd wondered himself how many Navy "connections" Lisa had, but never had he suspected any of those she knew would be of interest to the FBI. "Exactly what is it you want of me, gentlemen?"

"We will tell you exactly—in time. Mr. Pau and Mr. Wales here are ex-Navy. They both served their time in Vietnam. Because of each of their individual circumstances and military history, they have been recruited for this project, too. You see, Mr. Pau served on a frigate once under the command of Thomas Logan. Mr. Wales was stationed here in Honolulu, as well as San Diego and Vietnam. He has a brother in Pemrose Key, a twin brother. I think you know his brother, Luke. Skip Traylor is his name. Even though Mr. Traylor is his brother, Mr. Wales has agreed to help us. The two of them have not communicated in twenty-five years. Mr. Traylor does enter into this scenario. To what degree will be explained to you upon confirmation of your cooperation in this investigation. Mr. Wales has expressed his gratitude to the United States for the opportunities given him here, and he assures us there is no love lost for his brother. He received commendation medals in Vietnam and he has served his country well. We do not question his loyalties." Joe Lianoho placed his hand on Munsen Wales' shoulder in a gesture that seemed to indicate to Luke that Mr. Wales might need a little more persuasion. Perhaps they hadn't offered him enough money.

"In other words, I'm a fink!" Munsen Wales looked down and spat brown tobacco juice, making a little wet indention in the sand between his feet, then he looked at Luke with a broad display of teeth. There was a gap between the two front incisors, and Luke couldn't discern whether the man meant to exhibit a grin or a snarl. Whichever, it was evident there was an unpleasant sarcasm intended.

Luke considered his words carefully before speaking. He wasn't sure what he was or wasn't supposed to know, and he recalled Toby's association with Skip Traylor, though he never really knew the extent of that since his intended conversation with Toby had never transpired. Maybe this would be a way to find out more, and maybe somehow there would be a way to vindicate Toby, for Mamie's sake, as he had privately sworn to do.

"I don't know Skip Traylor very well. Years ago, as a kid, I knew who he was from hanging around the marina docks back home. Traylor was a sometimes-charter-captain, and some of the other boys would crew for him once in awhile. I never had much to do with him. He was an unfriendly sort. I was just a kid who worked at the marina. I had my own job that kept me busy enough, crewing for another captain. I still don't know what all this has to do with anything."

"Luke, I know you need to know more and you need to know how you figure into this whole scheme. Right now we don't have the time to tell you everything. We mainly wanted to find out if you will cooperate with us. We have every reason to believe you will maintain the highest degree of confidence, and we wanted you to meet the men who will be working on our side. Are you with us?"

Once again the gauntlet had been tossed. Luke wouldn't back down. Whatever they needed from him, he was their man. He felt the blood rushing again; the excitement; the compelling challenge; the danger of it all. He had thought himself to be tired of it. He had thought himself to be happy to be at peace in Pemrose Key again, but when he allowed himself to examine all that had happened since his return, he realized everything he had done had created strife: His initial refusal to take the easy road and go to work for his father; his relationship with Lisa, which in itself had been his chosen path to perpetual misery. He narrowed his eyes and looked out across the waters of the great ocean that surrounded the island of Oahu, not so different on this day from the waters of his beloved Gulf. The wind was not as brisk as usual, the palm fronds overhead ruffled only slightly in the gentle breeze. There was tranquility here. The deep blue sea was relatively calm today. Diamond Head loomed magnificently before him, a sentinel guarding the island. It couldn't keep the Skip Traylors of the world away, nor could the spirit of King Kamehemehe banish them from this world of exquisite, ancient geological beauty.

"I'll help you." The words were spoken. The blood ceased to rush. The world around him stopped spinning, and everything seemed to move in slow motion now. He felt relaxed, and an underlying sense of happiness pervaded his mood, attributable to the prospect of participating in this mission that Mr. Lianoho had warned could be more dangerous than Vietnam. Danger, to Luke, was akin to a drug addict's fix. It was that inherent Callaway trait of never being able to back away from danger or a challenge that had been the thorn in his side.

"When will you return to Pemrose Key?" Mr. Lianoho squinted his eyes in the bright sunlight that was to Luke's back.

"You mean you don't already know my full itinerary?"

With brow raised, Mr. Lianoho gave Luke a piercing look.

"I was planning on leaving today. My marriage is not likely to last much longer, but then I am sure you have already deduced that from witnessing my bride's unorthodox behavior on several occasions since arriving in Honolulu." Luke felt uneasy explaining his personal life to these strangers. He had always been a very private person in regards to his activities and his emotions. If they were going to trust him, though, it seemed necessary at this point to totally disarm himself, to lay his cards on the table.

"Take a good look at Steve and Munsen, Luke. You will need to remember them, for it is likely you will cross paths again, and the circumstances may not allow for so leisurely a pace as to study their features. You may need to recognize them instantly, and to know they are on our side." Mr. Lianoho watched Luke closely, his own face reflected confidence in Luke and his capabilities.

Stephen Pau had not spoken the entire time. He must be Hawaiian as his name implied. His dark features were finely chiseled. His shiny black hair looked as if it had been cut with a bowl placed over his head, kind of Buster Brown-ish. He was slight of build and innocent looking. Very young. His big, brown eyes reminded Luke of Scotty Dillard. He didn't look to have been old enough or tough enough to have already served his time in Vietnam. When he did speak, he spoke quietly and his words were few, but he spoke them with conviction, "I already have memorized your face, Lucas Callaway. It is an easy face to remember, and when I see you again, I will know you."

"And I will know you, Stephen." There was a connection there, and Luke knew he could trust Stephen Pau.

"Yeah, I'll know you, too. I always work alone, though, just don't nobody get in my way when I'm busy." Munsen Wales was another story.

Luke decided to reserve his opinion on trusting Munsen Wales. He valued his own judgement in trust, and he didn't take it lightly. Trust in Munsen Wales would have to be earned by Munsen Wales.

"I think that's enough for one day, gentlemen. Luke, we will be contacting you shortly. We would appreciate your remaining in Honolulu until you hear from us."

"That's not a problem. I had planned to stay for two weeks. Only last night did I decide to go home, but then I guess you already know that." Luke shook hands all around, then turned and quickly walked across the park to the street.

When he reached the sidewalk he stood for a minute, digesting what had just transpired. It appeared his father's mistrust for Logan had been well-founded. Luke could only wonder what this was all about. He'd have to bide his time until they chose to tell him more. Bide his time and abide his bride. What other surprises might Lisa have in store for him? Luke had a clearer vision now of what had happened at the airport yesterday. It was not just the appearance of Cooper or the twisting of the men around Lisa's little finger that had inclined them not to arrest her. They couldn't, and they needed an excuse not to. Lisa's arrest could possibly impair their investigation by compelling those who were being investigated, including her father and Skip Traylor, to distance themselves from her, making themselves more inaccessible.

19

*L*uke had not been blessed at birth with the gift of patience. It was something that did not come easy for him. Patience was an acquired virtue and one that he had to constantly hone to maintain. Strength and endurance, yes—patience, no. Their values were decidedly different. Strength and endurance were for the more important things in life, thank God. Patience, though, was for everyday living, and the lack of it sometimes made daily survival more difficult. He did painstakingly strive to master the art of it, frequently in vain, but often he succeeded.

For three days following his meeting at Fort DeRussy, Luke had to have patience to endure his existence with Lisa. She drank incessantly. She griped. She moaned. Once she didn't come back to the room until four a.m., red-eyed and stumbling, falling into the overstuffed chair without even changing out of her clothes, passing out until two o'clock in the afternoon. Luke avoided any arguments with her by not speaking to her at all. If she ate, he didn't know about it. He ordered room service for her and then left. Going out to dinner wasn't even an option. Lisa stayed so crocked it was easy to go his own way. It wasn't so easy to ignore her, though, and he winced every time he saw her in this condition. She was so beautiful, and to see what she was doing to herself was painful. He knew the driving force behind her actions must have been her father and whatever "illegal interstate activities" he was involved in that might concern the government. The FBI had not accused her of being directly involved, but with her obvious acquaintance with Skip Traylor and his presumed involvement, it seemed likely to Luke that even at a minimum level she must be privileged to certain inside information. Ultimately, if this were the case, she would have to be responsible for her own actions. Whatever mess Logan got himself into, he would have to answer for, but whatever mess his actions got his daughter into, she would have to answer for herself. She would be nineteen next week, and past the age of consent. Already she was considered an adult, but she was still a child in many ways, and she was ruining her life. Too bad her mother had died when she was so young, at such a critical time in a child's life. If she wasn't what Thomas Logan had implied, perhaps she could have guided her daughter into womanhood with a little more love than her absentee father had.

Luke waited, patiently. Hawaii was a beautiful place, and he occupied his time visiting the sights he had missed when he had been here before. He spent time at the beach and dined alone in the evenings. He didn't encourage Lisa's companionship. In no condition to join him most of the time, she spent her evenings in hotel bars. She left the telltale signs of logo imprinted matchbooks around like so many personal calling cards. Luke missed Pemrose Key and the Gulf of Mexico. He was ready to go home.

One day, purely by accident, he ran into Cooper at the International Market Place. The joy he experienced at seeing her inclined him to deem the encounter to have been one of fate rather than accident. He had decided against any further contact with her while in Hawaii, but this chance meeting buoyed his belief that a life with Cooper must surely be his destiny.

"Have lunch with me, Cooper. I won't take 'no' for an answer." At first, the impact of seeing her unexpectedly so intensified his yearnings for her, he did not even attempt to cover up his desire to be with her.

"I would love to, Luke, but I can't. Really, I can't. I'm on a fiercely tight schedule. I'm leaving this evening, you know. I have some shopping to do, and then I have to get back to the hotel and pack." The disappointment in her voice sounded sincere.

He pressed harder, "I told you, I won't take 'no' for an answer. I won't let you leave until you at least agree to a quick lunch. Who knows—we may never see each other again." He placed his hand across his chest, feigning heartache. Had he really believed this, he could never have voiced that fear. He continued the banter, "Declining my offer might be something you regret forever." He had to be careful, lest he reveal the intensity of his feelings. He was still a married man, to the rest of the world. He took the package she was carrying and placed it under one arm, then grasped her elbow and guided her in the direction of a coffee shop he had passed a few minutes ago. "Come on, that looks like a 'fast' food joint over there."

"Well, okay, you win. How can I say no to such irresistible charm? Are you always this persuasive?"

"Always."

"That's what I figured. 'Fast' is all I have time for though, Luke...truly."

"Understood."

Once seated at a booth in the restaurant, Luke indulged himself one long, intense look across the table. She would be gone soon, and he had to carry something with him. He wanted to absorb every detail—to etch indelibly in his mind the exact spot where her dimples deepened, the way the corners of her eyes crinkled when she smiled, and the precise shade of green that flickered in those eyes that had so captivated him from the first moment he met her in Chicago. He wanted to retain the vision that sat before him for however long it took to get through this thing with Lisa. He wanted to remember the melody in her voice, and her joyous smile, and the pleasure she seemed to inject in everything she did.

Cooper ordered a salad. Luke ordered a hamburger. Neither ate a bite.

"You're staring at me, Luke. What is the matter?" She pushed the lettuce around on her plate a bit, then smiled charmingly at him. "Do I have a smudge on my face, or something?" She rubbed at her chin, then glanced across the room, conspicuously avoiding his stare.

"Cooper…" No. He couldn't do this to her. He wouldn't tell her. It wasn't fair. Small talk was all he could muster.

A short time was all she would allow. Before she dashed away, she briefly took his hand in hers, and then it seemed to him that she peered more deeply into his soul than anyone ever had before. "Be happy, Luke, with your life. That's so important. Have patience with Lisa. She's young." Solid words of wisdom. She sincerely cared.

Cooper turned abruptly, leaving Luke standing beside the table.

Only when she had reached the exit, establishing a well-defined degree of distance between them, did Cooper look his way. Her parting smile lit the room as she waved her palm in a wide arc. "Please, stay in touch from time to time." Her words floated across the room. She then touched her fingertips to her lips and blew him a kiss, piercing his heart with precise accuracy.

Was it just Cooper's way, or could he interpret her gesture as he longed to, with the belief that there was meaning and a promise there? Decidedly not. That was just Cooper, and it was part of why he loved her.

Though greatly disappointed at her departure, it was also all the time he could allow. How close he'd come to baring his soul.

He felt that Cooper was unaware of his feelings and if there were any feelings on her part, other than platonic, she hid them well.

Three days after his meeting with the FBI, Luke rented a car and drove around to the other side of the island, whiling his time sightseeing and watching the surfers. On his return to his hotel, he was met just outside the entrance by a man wearing a white, short-sleeved shirt and black trousers. His attire was pretty much a give-away amidst all the brightly colored tourist garb. With his closely cropped hair and clean-shaven, youthful face, he looked exactly like a government employee, and had he worn a tie he would resemble the secret service men found in the President's entourage.

"Mr. Callaway...Mr. Lucas Callaway?"

"That's me." Luke knew instantly this was the message he had been waiting for.

He was handed a barely legible note, hand-scrawled on a *Things To Do Today* note-sheet: Meet me at Michel's at the Colony Surf— 4:00 p.m.—today—cocktails—J.L.

Luke took the pen the messenger offered and evidenced his response with a single word and his initials in the white space on the bottom of the note. He handed the note back. "Here you go. Thanks."

The young man nodded and he was gone before Luke had a chance to cross the threshold of the Royal Hawaiian.

When Luke walked into Michel's at four o'clock sharp, Mr. Lianoho was already seated at a window table.

"Here you are, sir. Scotch and soda." The waiter handed Luke his drink of choice even before he had pulled his chair in close to the table.

Luke raised his scotch to Mr. Lianoho. "How did you know? Never mind."

Mr. Lianoho inclined his head politely. "You're welcome, Luke. Now, there is a lot to tell you and very little time to tell it. This place will be mobbed in a couple of hours. Sunset, you know, best place to watch it."

"I know. Very romantic place, if you have someone to be romantic with. Here's to you, Mr. Lianoho, guess we're it for now. Wouldn't be a bad idea to get the heck out of here before sunset."

Mr. Lianoho leaned back in his chair and laughed loudly, good-naturedly. "You're right, Luke, I didn't think about what it would look like, a couple of grizzlies like us rendezvousing in a place like this. The food is good, and no one would think to look for us here, that's for sure. Enough of this, though, you need to know what this is all about."

"I do. That would be nice, considering the implications that have been made, particularly about my wife's father."

"Yes, there have been some inferences made. Okay, let me see how to begin. First, we don't know everything, so that's the reason for the investigation. I will pull no punches with you, but you do understand the confidentiality of this?"

"Understood....no need for you to worry. There hasn't exactly been a close bond formed with my wife, as I mentioned before, and as I am sure you have surmised."

"We understand each other, then." He raised his glass in a toast to Luke. "To your good health, Luke, and your safety."

Luke hesitated before raising his glass. He felt the familiar rush he always experienced with the threat of danger. The glasses pinged when they touched, the deal was sealed, he belonged to the FBI.

"The illegal activity I referred to the other day has to do with the smuggling of illegal weapons into Vietnam. Somebody is placing a unique kind of automatic rifle and a particular type of handgun into the hands of the Communists. The FBI is involved because of the interstate shipping activity prior to the weapons leaving this country. Your father-in-law and Skip Traylor have been implicated. I do not say they are directly involved, but there have been suspicions cast upon them. Skip Traylor, in particular. We haven't been able to figure out who he is working for, who the godfather of the operation is, so to speak. About Commander Logan, we don't know for sure the extent of his involvement. Thanks to Stephen Pau's cooperation, we have good reason to believe he is directly involved. There are many more involved, and it would serve no ultimate purpose to bring an indictment solely against Commander Logan or Skip Traylor, should they be found guilty of any wrongdoing against our government. There are some high ranking government officials spearheading the investigation, the Secretary of the Navy, for one. A Senator from Washington is heading up the investigative task force. Because of the possible involvement of other high-ranking government officials, confidentiality is of the utmost importance. I know you understand this, Luke, and will comply."

"You've done your homework, sir. Tell me more."

"Pemrose Key is your home. It's a low profile area, the ideal place for illegal weapons smuggling to be instituted. It's in close proximity to a Naval base, where some of the principal players may be headquartered. Also, Mexico is easily accessed across the Gulf, and a suspect weapons-parts manufacturer with government contracts is located near Pemrose Key. What more can I tell you? It's happening. We've documented some of the activity, but we don't have all the specifics, nor do we have all of the key figures. We know for a fact that Navy personnel are heavily involved. The inside players are our prime targets. They're the ones that infiltrate our system and undermine our strategies. They're the ones responsible for the loss of so many of the lives of our young men.

"Also, I have a personal vendetta. My son was killed in Vietnam two years ago, by Viet Cong with illegal weapons in their possession. American-made weapons. The Cong were captured, but my son was already dead."

"I'm sorry." Luke didn't know what else to say. He never knew what to say. Save for the grace of God Almighty, he might not have survived and he almost felt guilty that he had.

"We can help those who are still there by eliminating the slime...the scum of the earth. Maybe it will be in time to save other lives...some other mother's son." His voice rose an octave. "My wife has never been the same since we lost him. It's been hard on her." He wiped his mouth with the linen napkin that lay at his place on the table, then closed his eyes momentarily and took a deep breath before speaking, "I apologize. I try not to let my personal feelings influence my professional perspective. Sometimes I do not do such a good job."

"You're doing fine, Mr. Lianoho." Luke felt sympathy for the man, but there were a lot of others he felt sorry for, too.

"Luke, call me Joe. Mr. Lianoho can get weary. I call you Luke, you call me Joe."

"It's a deal. Now, what gives? What do you want me to do, and how do Stephen Pau and Munsen Wales figure into this?"

"You know Cole's Bayou? We think that's a point of departure. So far they've escaped us. We have to be careful, we would be easy to spot at the mouth of the bayou, and Cole's Bayou is so secluded in itself no one has been able to get up in there to perform any significant surveillance. We have to be careful not to scare them off. We don't want to screw things up before we get to the top. We've had people out there trying to infiltrate their ranks, but we haven't met with much success. When Stephen Pau was with Commander Logan on the frigate, he didn't document any evidence, but he has reason to believe there was a transference of questionable cargo to the Communist. More than that I cannot tell you. His suspicions are complicated, and we have to be a little careful with him lest he pleads the Fifth.

"Munsen Wales—he has several reasons for wanting to help us. He retired after twenty-five years in the Navy. His daddy met his mother, an English gal, during the war and brought her to America. He got her pregnant, without the benefit of marriage, and she had twins, Skip and Munsen. When they were eight years old she finally realized that Traylor was never going to marry her. She split...took one of the kids, he kept the other one. That's about all she got out of ten years of tenure with Mr. Traylor. Bitter and broke, she took Munsen back to England with her. Two years later she died, leaving Munsen to run the streets of London and fend for himself.

"Skip was raised by his father in Pensacola, where his father retired from the Navy. For ten years after his mother's death Munsen carried a letter with him that his mother wrote before she died, telling him where to find his father and his brother. She told him that he was a U.S. citizen, and if anything ever happened to her he was to find his way back to America and lay claim to what was rightfully his. It was ten years before he could do that. When Munsen was twenty he decided to come back to America and find his father and his twin brother. When he finally got to Pensacola he discovered that his brother was, indeed, still nearby in Pemrose Key, but his father had died only weeks before. Skip was left a small inheritance, some government bonds, a little shack on the waterfront, not much, but it gave him a grubstake for buying his first boat. To Munsen, it seemed like a fortune. His long-lost brother refused to share anything with him. Full of anguish and disappointment, finding himself in a strange country and having little education and no money, he had nowhere to turn.

"The United States Navy recruiting office in nearby Pensacola offered him the best opportunity he had ever known. Perhaps it provided him with a link to the father he barely remembered. The Navy put bread on the table and gave him the chance he would have never had otherwise. The Navy literally saved his life. He feels indebted, and he has no love lost for his brother. He would like nothing better than to get even with him for denying him his rightful claim to his inheritance. His motives are to our advantage. We don't question them. What information we have given him is limited, though, just in case blood proves to be thicker than water."

"The entire situation sounds complicated. How do you figure Skip Traylor into the whole mess?"

"Skip Traylor makes frequent trips to Honolulu and Mexico, and he has been observed meeting with Navy personnel on many occasions, in spite of the fact that he was a conscientious objector, and never served in the military. He has also been known to frequent Cole's Bayou."

In one split second Luke's mind's eye replayed the light signals he had wondered about, the ones he had seen at Cole's Bayou the night he first met Lisa, the same night Toby sprawled near death across the hood of his car. What Joe now offered could reveal answers.

"And…" Luke filled in the blanks, "…I have easy access to Cole's Bayou and to Commander Thomas Logan, via his daughter. There's just one small problem, I do not intend to remain married to his daughter upon my return to Pemrose Key. Considering the status of our relationship, an annulment will be forthcoming and very easily obtained. There should be no wait at all, or do you propose I maintain my marriage in name only, simply to facilitate this investigation?"

"We can't tell you what to do about that, Luke. You can only do what you have to do. We are merely posing the problem, and however you achieve the solution is up to you. Soon we will be able to keep a close eye on Commander Logan from right here in Hawaii. He is being transferred to Pearl Harbor—at his request. Toby Washington was a friend of yours, right?"

Luke knew the question shouldn't have surprised him, but it did. "You obviously know he was. Toby's mother is a friend of mine, and yes, I know he was in some way mixed up with Skip Traylor, and that this very likely contributed to his death. I never discovered exactly what happened, or the reasons for the events leading up to his death. I intend to do all that I can to find out, though. That's one of the primary reasons I want to work with you on this."

"Whatever reason you choose to act on is of no consequence to me, only the fact that you will be working with us. We value your assistance, Luke. The first step is to determine whether you are going to stay married to Lisa Logan...uh, Callaway. Your value to us, in part, depends on that."

"I'll stay married for an indeterminate period of time—for however long is necessary. If she doesn't kill herself with alcohol." Damn this unquenchable thirst for the thrill danger presented.

"Best wishes to you." Joe touched the rim of Luke's glass with his own. Their eyes met and held for a moment, signifying a mutual understanding of their unwritten agreement.

20

*L*uke's suitcase lay open atop the colorful, floral-print bedspread that covered the unchristened marital bed. Meticulously he folded his socks in half and laid each matching pair at one end of his suitcase. Just as carefully, he folded his bleached white jocks and placed them on the other side, golf shirts and shorts neatly folded and fastidiously placed in the middle, allowing ample spacing between socks and shorts. He wasn't obsessive about it, but he did notice that a certain propensity for organization and cleanliness had arisen since his return from Vietnam. The fact that Lisa was a slob was the catalyst that intensified Luke's mild neatness fetish, which contrasted with the orb of squalor that surrounded her.

"I still don't see why we have to leave Honolulu almost a full week ahead of schedule, Luke. I've been having so much fun. Haven't you?" Lisa lounged in the armchair. She popped a piece of gum in her mouth, letting the silver wrapper slip between her fingers and fall to the floor beside the chair.

Luke turned away in disgust. "Yeah, a blast, Lisa. We need to do it again."

"Well, Luke, you don't have to be so sarcastic, do you? I know it hasn't been the perfect honeymoon, but I won't be so nervous when we get back to Pemrose Key, ya' know? Besides, we do have the rest of our lives together. You said so yourself, ya' know?" She smacked and slurped on her gum. At least she didn't have a drink in her hand, for the moment, anyway.

Somehow, with all the patience he could muster, Luke managed to keep his thoughts to himself. *No, we don't have the rest of our lives together. Not on your life, woman!*

"Lisa, have you got all your bags ready? I'm going to call the bell captain if you do. Our flight is at 8:30 and I don't want to be late."

"Yes, Lucas, my bags are ready, and you could be a little nicer to me, ya' know?"

"Yes, Lisa, I KNOW! I'll try to do better. Now let's get out of here, okay?"

Thankfully, the flight to Los Angeles was on time and uneventful. After only three drinks she passed out and was not heard from for the duration of the flight. Her silence allowed Luke to immerse himself in his own thoughts. For hours he thumbed through the pages of a magazine, never focusing on the words. Cooper's face was an ever present vision in his mind, and his thoughts were absorbed in trying to recall every word he had ever heard her speak.

When they landed in Los Angeles, Lisa insisted on phoning Edna while they waited for the plane to Atlanta and Pemrose Key. Luke found a seat in the boarding area close to the phone. He stretched his legs out comfortably and scanned the abandoned newspaper left in the seat beside him. After perusing the front page, his eyes wandered up and down across page three. Something he saw there registered in his mind, and his eyes darted back across the page and focused on one photograph that featured a group of young people. The accompanying article told of the inception of an organization being formed to honor the memory of Dr. Martin Luther King, who had been shot and killed in Memphis only months before. Amidst the small group of young people in that photo, a familiar face stared back at him. "It can't be," he whispered. Then, remembering Lisa's close proximity, he looked over his shoulder, verifying that she had not heard him. She remained by the pay phone, babbling with her cousin, Edna.

Luke folded page three into a small square, making sure not to crease the photo portion of the page. He thought about it a moment then unfolded it and looked at it again. The banner on the front page told him it was the Washington Post. He would contact that newspaper when he returned to Pemrose Key. He refolded the paper and slipped it into his jacket pocket.

Of the two-hour interval between flights, Lisa spent the better part of an hour on the phone. It would be an expensive phone call, but better Edna entertain Lisa than him.

When their flight from Atlanta landed in Pensacola, it was nearly two in the morning. Edna was there to greet them, red lips parted broadly, exposing all those white teeth. She surely did remind him of Thomas Logan and his white toothy smile. Funny he'd never noticed the resemblance before.

"Hi, Luke. Lisa...Precious, I do declare, you have a pallor about you. I would have thought you would come back with your tan intact. Why, look at Luke, he's just our gorgeous, golden, fair-haired boy," Edna trilled. "How is it that he's sporting such a tan, and you've lost what you had before you went to paradise?"

"Not much sunshine in a bar, not even in Honolulu," Luke muttered. "I'll get the bags and meet you two out front."

"What is this I detect from you two newlyweds? Is there trouble in paradise already?" She sounded smug to Luke, with a touch too much satisfaction in her voice.

Luke moved along several feet ahead of them, making his way towards the front of the terminal to the baggage area, not lingering long enough to have to respond to Edna's remark.

At Edna's next words, he slowed his pace a bit, staying just far enough ahead of them to feign inattention, but close enough to be within earshot of Edna's shrill pitched voice. "What the heck are you trying to do?" Edna had attached herself to Lisa's arm and was hissing at her, speaking well above a whisper so to be heard above the airport noises, and not realizing just how distinguishable her voice was from the scant flow of people moving along the terminal corridor with them.

"Do you want to ruin your marriage before it's even begun? Are you stupid or something? I thought I had you straightened out before you left," Edna chided. "You know you can't control your actions when you get soused! If you mess things up, do you know what's going to happen to you? They'll take care of you. Not to mention what I'll do to you, Cousin."

"Owww, you're hurting my arm. Let me go!" Lisa didn't try to whisper. "I can do what I want."

"You think? I've worked too hard to get you in this position. He would've never married you if I hadn't helped you. Who taught you how to act like a lady, you little tramp, even if it is just on the surface, and apparently only for brief intervals?"

"Edna, don't be mad at me, please," Lisa whined. "I promise I'll do better. We were just so far from home, and I was scared. Skip was there. He doesn't like that I married Luke. He said he'd kill me if I went to bed with him. The only way I could keep from it was to stay drunk. I guess I'm gonna' have to give in to Luke sooner or later, though. Sex with him might not be too bad, if Skipper doesn't find out."

"You stupid, stupid child. You're supposed to go to bed with him. He's your husband, you idiot! To heck with Skip Traylor. You've done a lot better marrying Luke Callaway—if you don't mess it up. You mean you never even consummated your marriage?"

"Huh?"

"Had sex...S-E-X...something I know you're more than familiar with."

"Well, no. With Skip right there and all it made me scared. I think he really would've killed me."

"Well, he is capable of it, but now you've set yourself up for an annulment. It'll be like it never even happened, and all my efforts will have been wasted."

"Oh. I guess I better do something about it, huh?"

Consumed with anger, Luke fought to maintain self control. Every nerve in his body tensed as he restrained himself from turning around to face them, to let them know he knew, and had heard every word. He and Lisa never had a chance. It was all part of Edna's plan, whatever the grand scheme of it might be, for whatever warped reasons she fostered. Forget the personal, he had a lot to do now. Joe had said this could be dangerous. "Danger" was two cunning females such as these manipulating your life! "Stupidity" was allowing it to happen. What a fool he'd been.

Luke was silent as he arranged their bags in the trunk of Edna's car. Edna and Lisa chatted incessantly, all girl-talk now, Edna's admonishments aside. Given a few minutes to recover, his anger over the initial shock subsided. Perhaps he could use the knowledge he had gained to his advantage. Might be interesting to see what would happen next. He would play along, since he seemed to be a key figure in Edna's intriguing scheme. Her revealing words seemed to verify many of the things Joe told him regarding Lisa's family's involvement. Someone else had to be behind this operation. Commander Logan, perhaps? The tiny pieces were starting to come together. They weren't boulders, they weren't even chunks yet, just tiny little pieces, and eventually they would all fit together, he knew, like so many pieces in a jigsaw puzzle.

Luke drove the distance from Pensacola to Pemrose Key while Lisa and Edna sat in the back seat, perpetuating their scam, giggling and catching up on the local gossip, mostly about people Luke had never heard of. Their social circle seemed to be oriented in a completely different galaxy than his. He didn't know these people. He didn't know Lisa, and had never cared for her cousin.

He pulled the car to a stop at the entrance to the newlywed's new address, the little love-nest his parents gave them as a wedding gift. Their first "home" was in the high-rise condominium, Pemrose Pinnacle.

"Thanks for the lift, Edna." Luke loaded their bags on the luggage cart he obtained from the lobby and wheeled it onto the elevator. There was no one else in sight. Lisa bid her farewells to Edna and ran to wedge her way in behind the luggage cart before the elevator door closed.

"Luke…" She spoke softly, using the same lusty voice he'd been attracted to before he married her.

He turned to face her. There she stood, at three in the morning, naked as a jaybird, on a slow elevator to the thirteenth floor. She reached for his hand. He started to withdraw, to rebuke her, then thought better. Her body was flawless, from a strictly physiological point of view—tiny waist, shapely hips, the dark V beneath her abdomen pointing to the middle of slender, perfectly shaped thighs.

She took his hand and guided it across her silken skin to her hip. He could barely stand it. His physical being was in conflict with his mind. He hated this woman. Didn't he? He hated what she represented, but her body held the promise of fulfillment that up until now had been flaunted teasingly before him. Right now this voluptuous creature was as sober as he had seen her since marrying her. His pent-up frustrations and the possibility of succumbing to her charms in a potentially public place heightened his excitement. The door could open on any floor. It wasn't likely at three in the morning, but it could, and they would be caught. The hilarity of the image of his neighbors finding him in such a "pubic" place, brought him to his senses. It was too risky. As much as he wanted it, Lisa wasn't worth it anymore.

"Come on, Lisa, put your clothes on, quickly. This is our floor."

It only took a second for her to slip back into the little summer sundress she had donned for comfort for the long flight home. It was a quick zip number and she wore no lingerie, only sandals and the Hawaiian shift.

"Chicken!" she goaded as she stepped from the elevator.

Inside their condo, everything was in place—little touches that spelled "romance." His mother was a self-confessed romanticist, and she had evidently been here. There were candles everywhere, waiting to be lit, and fresh flowers. Satin sheets adorned the bed and laying atop the sheets was a lacy teddy tied in silk ribbon. Luke suspected that his father had a hand in that. He knew that Ryan Callaway's envisioning Lisa enticing his son with such frilly garments wouldn't be beyond his imagination, and his motive was obvious. He had already expressed his desire to be a grandfather, and wouldn't hesitate to openly encourage that likelihood.

"Oh! Looky, Luke, this is nice!" Lisa trilled as she held the sheer bit of lingerie across the front of her body, flaunting her image in the full-length mirror.

"Yeah, it is." Luke reluctantly agreed with her. He walked to the sliding glass doors that led to the terrace. He needed some air. The sounds of the ocean filled the uncomfortable space in the room. The sounds of the ocean he had always known comforted him now—calmed him—allowed him to recapture a fragment of sanity. He tried to understand his feelings. Something about what he overheard between Lisa and Edna presented an unknown challenge, yet it warned him more than ever to be careful.

He would let Lisa call the shots tonight. Her antics on the elevator had amused and aroused him, so why not have fun with it after all, as long as he was on guard? The anticipation of what he sensed the evening held excited him, from a purely physical standpoint.

The condominium had been stocked with wine and champagne and Lisa could not resist the temptation to imbibe. In an act of revenge, Luke poured the champagne freely. "To my beautiful wife." He did not lie, she was beautiful—to behold. Let the fun begin.

They drank. They toasted. For Luke's part, with an underlying, angry vengeance, and he knew Lisa's reasons. From the balcony they observed the moon casting its silvery shimmer across the rippling water, and Luke thought wryly of the night he decided to marry Lisa. They played the game well, equals in their thespian endeavors. Luke had fun observing Lisa and participating in her "passion" play. She played well, giving the performance of her life, and he had not misjudged her intentions. He experienced absolutely no guilt for contributing to her weakness. She had intentionally deceived him, and at this very moment continued to do so. His callousness helped appease his anger.

"Oh, Luke, I love you. I really, really do. I'm so sorry about Hawaii. Please let me make it up to you. I promise I can." She was laying it on thick, and Luke found himself succumbing. Mentally, he was on guard, alert to her every move, and with his senses thus heightened, it almost made it more fun. Physically, he allowed himself to enjoy the moment, and the game.

Lisa orchestrated the dance. Admittedly, he was turned on. He had sure paid the price for it. Once when he thought about what he had overheard at the airport, he withdrew, only to be brought back to the threshold of gratification as she sought to control him with her body. Yes, she'd had some experience. Based on her remarkable skills, she was very obviously experienced in all sexual areas. How could a woman satisfy a man so completely and leave him so empty inside?

Afterwards, Luke lay exhausted upon the bed, the ocean breeze cooling his dampened skin. She lay beside him, perspiration glistening on her belly and her face, her eyes closed, her moist lips parted sensually. He had let her have complete control, and all she had cared about was seducing and satisfying him, which, in her mind, meant bonding him permanently to her—in *her* mind. It was evident she was greatly impressed with her own sexual prowess. He loved the mockery of it. He enjoyed allowing her to have her way with him, never suspecting that he knew her motives. But he hated his reasons for loving this bit of revenge. Before falling asleep, he contemplated the irony—there was no marriage, but it had finally been consummated. He fell asleep without speaking a word to her.

The October sun painted the room with its brilliance and gently aroused Luke from a restful sleep. His mind, still lingering in a semi-twilight state, began to slowly regain consciousness and assimilate the events. He had been vulnerable. That could have been dangerous had he not struggled to maintain a mental vigil, but it had been oh, so stimulating, and served to alleviate much of the tension incurred by the past few month's sexual frustrations. When the moment of truth had finally arrived, the mere physical act had been gratifying, but the emptiness inside him left him more psychologically drained than before. He didn't love her, and the sex that occurred fell far short of the expectations he'd had during those long months of antic-ipation, when he mistakenly identified being in lust as being in love. Sobriety brought with it a degree of guilt.

To his surprise, Luke smelled fresh coffee and heard breakfast sounds coming from the kitchen. Had last night been a turning point?

"Morning, Luke. I trust you slept well. I surely did. Your mama put eggs and bacon in the refrigerator, and milk and juice and all sorts of goodies."

Lisa entered the room carrying two icy glasses of orange juice and wearing nothing. Yeah, she still looked as good as she had only hours before. She was friendly this morning, the sex must've had a sobering effect.

Poor Lisa. She was so lost. He didn't hate her this morning. He pitied her. He wondered if there was anything he could do to help her. He couldn't stay married to her. There was no love there, for either of them. But perhaps he could talk to her, maybe she would consent to counseling. Maybe there was something that could be done to help her salvage her life before she made too big a mess of it.

Lisa handed Luke one of the glasses. He tasted of the sweet Florida nectar and set it on the nightstand. He raised himself to a more upright position, propping against a couple of pillows. "Is that bacon I smell?"

"Yeah, it is. Oh, and I better check it." Lisa set her glass on the nightstand and hurried into the kitchen.

Luke reached for the nearest glass and took a big swig. He grimaced. "Ooh, what is this?" He smelled of it. Gin! It was only nine o'clock in the morning. He held the glass up to the light. Instead of the rich Florida gold that his glass held, this one contained a liquid that was barely tinted yellow. By mistake he'd picked up Lisa's glass and it was almost straight gin. There appeared to be no hope for her.

Disgusted, Luke jumped out of bed, threw on some shorts and headed for the door. "Think I'll take a run before breakfast," he called towards the kitchen, not caring if Lisa heard him or not. He was gone before she had a chance to respond, leaving her to her breakfast preparations and her bottle of gin.

Luke jogged along the beach at the water's edge. The impact of each foot coming down on the white, powdery sand infused his soul with renewed energies. Last night had been physically beneficial in spite of his guilt. There was no beauty in what had transpired. It had been sex, pure and simple, and a release for him. He knew that his thoughts of rehabilitating Lisa were sheer fantasy.

He would put the guilt behind him and get on with the next phase of his life. He needed a plan of action. How was he to discover the secrets of Pemrose Key and Pirate's Cove? Who was the mastermind behind the smuggling operation? Who was responsible for Toby's death? How involved was Lisa, and how much did she know? Edna seemed to have a strong hold on Lisa, and there was something about their relationship that piqued his curiosity.

He ran faster, the rushing, whirring sounds of the ocean spurring him on as the waves tripped over themselves, clamoring to reach the shore, only to fade quickly into frothy obscurity in the sand. Is that what was happening to him by staying married to Lisa? Diminishing himself; sacrificing his goals; fading into obscurity as he became a nonperson, doing what he didn't want to do? He wasn't going to stay married to her, he reminded himself. He was going to help in this investigation, and that would be that.

He closed his eyes for a moment as he ran, trying to conjure up an image of Cooper. Damn his weaknesses! He ran faster.

He noticed two boats on the not-too-distant horizon. One was a sailboat, the other a white fishing vessel with a black stripe adorning its hull and a black Bimini top over the flybridge. They appeared to be rendezvousing. The sailboat was approaching from out in the Gulf and the fishing boat was coming from the direction of the inland pass. Luke slowed his pace and watched with mild curiosity as the fishing boat raced towards the sailing vessel at breakneck speed. As the gap between them narrowed, the sailboat lowered a bright turquoise spinnaker. Even as the spinnaker was being lowered by a single figure, and only moments before the black and white boat reached the sailboat, Luke was amazed to see two figures at the stern of the sailboat toss a long, dark object overboard. He stopped running altogether and stood gazing out toward the boats, his curiosity more than just a little aroused now.

Luke glanced around at the sparsely populated beach. There was a woman and a small toddler picking up shells off the sand not too far from where he stood. About fifty yards away, a surf fisherman was leaning over a plastic bucket, and judging by his stance, all he was concerned with was getting his hook baited and back in the water. Had no one else seen? Luke hated the direction his speculation took, but the object looked to have the same length and girth of a man. He wondered if the black and white boat had seen. Had the object been tossed from the sailboat because of the rapid approach of the other boat? From the direction of its approach to the sailboat, it appeared not to have a clear view of the stern.

Luke turned and walked back towards the condominium, keeping his eye on the two boats. The fishing boat finally pulled alongside the sailboat and they tied on to each other, rocking and bobbing in sync. He was close enough to the condo now to look up and see the balcony of his unit on the thirteenth floor. There was Lisa, standing at the balcony's railing, her long hair billowing around her face in the gusty wind. She must have seen the two boats. From her vantage point, she very likely saw the sailboat relieve itself of the suspicious looking cargo. He waved at her, but she didn't see him. She was immobile, staring out to sea in the direction of the boats. She had seen, but she didn't know he had.

When Luke arrived upstairs, Lisa still stood on the balcony, wearing the skimpy Hawaiian frock she had worn on the flight home last night. He looked in disgust at the mess she had made of breakfast. The bacon was burned and still floating in a skillet of blackened grease. At least she'd had the presence of mind to set the skillet off to one side of the stove, away from the heat. A broken egg was on the floor by the sink, and an empty gin bottle sat on the counter beside an almost full bottle. Would it have been any different had he stayed? He had been gone an hour, maybe. He could be generous and take the blame for this one. He supposed she did have a right to be mad at him, leaving in the middle of her breakfast efforts. He walked to the glass door. "Lisa, do you want me to fix breakfast?"

"No, thank you Luke, I'm not hungry. I'm having a milkshake for breakfast. See?" She held her glassful of clear liquid up. It contained no ice or orange juice. Only gin.

He decided not to mention the boats to her. He stepped out on the balcony in time to see both boats clearing the pass, the sailboat operating under motor power and following the fishing boat in at a slower pace.

"Your mama called, Luke. She said they would like for us to meet them at Mamie's Place this afternoon. Your daddy's been real hungry for some of Mamie's fried mullet. Oh, yeah, and she's glad we're back. I told them if we couldn't go we'd let them know."

"That's good Lisa, you told them right. I'd like to go, wouldn't you?"

"I don't think so, Luke. I'm going to see Edna this afternoon."

He felt relief that Lisa wasn't going. He didn't want his parents to suspect anything.

21

amie's Place was jumping, overflowing with people laughing and enjoying themselves. Mamie bustled about, feeding them all. They were mostly locals bidding farewell to the last lingering days of summer. They were here to enjoy a carefree afternoon, the music of the jukebox, and the fresh bounty the still-warm waters of the Gulf offered up. The crab, the shrimp and the mullet would soon be out of season. There was already a chill in the evening air. Before too many weeks passed, the winds would stiffen and the waters would become icy cold, and the abundance of seafood would ebb for the duration of winter's short visitation to the Gulf coast.

Mamie made sure there was a picnic table cleared for Luke, and her face beamed a delighted grin when he told her his parents were meeting him here. Billy Jack arrived with a pitcher of beer and a frosted mug even before Luke took his seat.

Luke filled his mug from the pitcher. Several friends stopped by his table to speak. Tommy Granger was there, moving to the beat on the dance floor with one of his "broadies." Scotty Dillard sat at the table next to Luke's, feeling his oats and munching on tidbits of hushpuppies Odessa Barlew stuffed in his mouth.

Old friends from high school welcomed Luke home and inquired about his absence. It was good to be back. He had intentionally arrived ahead of his parents. It was like old times, almost. However, there was one thing he found somewhat odd. In a town like Pemrose Key there was no doubt they all knew of his marriage to Lisa. Several present here today had even been at their wedding, yet no one asked where Lisa was or even mentioned his marriage. Was it because they didn't know her at all...or because they knew her so much better than he did?

When there was finally a lull between friends, he poured himself another beer and glanced out across the bay. His eyes wandered over to the old dilapidated pier off to one side of Mamie's dock. Runabouts crowded the perimeter, and several larger fishing boats filled the few available slips. Many people had come by water, taking advantage of the day's warmth. There was even a sailboat in Skip Traylor's slip, its tall mast towering above everything else, including the tin roof of Mamie's Place.

A sailboat. Luke pushed the screened door open and walked slowly down the dock towards the boat slips, dodging the holes and loose timbers of the pier. He was drawn towards that sailboat, and as he got closer, he could see the rolled spinnaker. It was bright, turquoise blue.

"You want something?"

Luke turned to face a man about his own age, though larger and more muscle-bound. He was clean shaven and sported a close-cropped military crew cut. A skin-tight, white T-shirt with rolled up sleeves exposed well-worked biceps, and an anchor tattoo decorated one arm.

"Just admiring your boat. I guess it's yours. Right?"

The man eyed Luke suspiciously. "Yeah, its my boat. What about it?"

"Nothing. Nothing. Just had some time to kill before meeting some people here,. Thought I'd look at the boats. What is it? About a twenty-five footer?"

"Uhhh, yeah, that's what it is." The man looked over his shoulder towards the cabin. "So what?"

Just then a second man emerged from the cabin and walked towards them. He stopped just behind the young man. Spectacled eyes stared sullenly at Luke, and a well-worn navy cap was cocked at an angle atop bright red tufts of curly hair. When he stepped forward, Luke saw that he worked a piece of line he held in his hands. The middle finger of his right hand was missing. Luke stared back at Munsen Wales, but directed his conversation to the younger man. "Nice talking to you, buddy. Nice boat." The boat was at least a thirty-six footer.

When Luke opened the screened door to go back in, a woman hurriedly pushed her way past him and headed down the pier. She had long dark hair and exotic eyes. She was an older woman, but in spite of her age, which he judged to be at least fifteen years older than himself, she fit her white T-shirt and denim bell-bottoms very well. He was struck by the fact that she bore a remarkable resemblance to Lisa. Once inside he turned and looked back at her. Amazingly, she could pass for Lisa's older sister. Good looking woman, too. No wonder both of the men at the sailboat still stood where Luke had left them, watching the woman's approach. Luke watched as the woman maneuvered her way along the pier, and realized with surprise that the sailboat was her destination. When she reached the boat, the younger man extended a hand and helped her aboard.

Meg and Ryan had arrived and Mamie wasted no time in getting them seated at Luke's table.

His mother stood to hug him. "Luke, we're glad you're home."

His dad shook his hand and directed him to the position beside Meg.

"We were surprised when you called from Los Angeles and said you were coming home early. What gives, boy?" His father eyed him narrowly, seeking an answer in Luke's eyes.

"Nothing, really. I guess we both missed Pemrose Key. Lisa was anxious to get back to the new condo and start playing house, you know. By the way, thanks for everything." Luke sought to avoid making contact with Ryan's eyes by peering into his beer and jabbing his finger at an imaginary speck floating atop the suds. He glanced out across the pier. The woman with the long, dark hair still stood aboard the *Que' Pasa*, engrossed in conversation with Munsen Wales. The younger man was nowhere in sight.

Mamie scurried forth, Billy Jack ever at her heels. He placed large platters before them and Mamie stood close by, wielding her wooden spoon until they had each filled their plates to her satisfaction.

"Where is Lisa, Luke? Anything wrong?" Ryan's fork paused mid-air, his bushy eyebrows were lowered in a frown.

"Everything's fine," Luke lied. "She just had to see Edna after being gone for so long. You know how women are, Dad."

"Now wait just a minute," Meg interjected. "Don't you two go generalizing. If I had just returned from my honeymoon, you know I'd be right by Ryan's side, stuck like glue. He couldn't get rid of me if he tried. I don't know about this younger generation, you young people seem to have more independence than we did at your age. With the exception of his work, your father and I have been inseparable, Luke."

"Your mother's right. Are you sure everything's okay, Luke?"

"Yeah, everything's fine, I told you. I'll be ready to start back to work bright and early Monday morning." Luke was ready for the conversation to shift.

"That's what it is. You still aren't happy working with me, are you, son? I had hoped, given a few months time, that would change. I know you like the work. I know it's not that. It's the other that you want to do, right? You just can't get it out of your craw, can you?" Ryan didn't wait for Luke to answer. "I understand, Luke, and I'm going to see what I can do about it, if you're really that unhappy."

"Don't worry so much, Dad. Everything's fine the way it is. I really don't mind the work." His heart wasn't in the words, but he tried to sound convincing. "I'm outdoors. I don't have to be confined to an office. You've made it easy for me, and I sure can't beat the job security." Right now, until he knew more, he didn't need to make any changes in his life anyway. When the time came, the first major change he would make would be to get rid of Lisa. More than anything he wanted to be free from his job and her, but right now other things came first. He'd given his word to Joe Lianoho.

As they finished the last of the mullet, Mamie came over and seated herself on the bench beside Ryan.

Mamie, that was wonderful." Ryan pushed his plate away to the middle of the table. "We've stayed away too long, Meg and me. Actually, I really don't need to come around here too often." He patted his extended belly with the palm of his hand, then eyed Mamie seriously. "How are you, Mamie? I mean how are you, really?" Ryan seemed to be earnestly concerned for Mamie's well-being.

"Everything's fine, Ryan. Just fine. I miss my boy. I'm thinking about taking them scoundrels up on selling this place. I was really keeping it for him, so's he'd have something one day. I didn't want things to be so hard for him. He just got so mixed up, so angry at Lord knows what, he didn't even seem to know himself. Guess part of it comes from never having a daddy to help raise him—never knowing who his daddy was. Guess that's my fault. I reckoned he'd be better off not knowing, long as his daddy weren't living with us. That's a choice I made, not Toby's daddy. It was him wanted us to be a family. He wanted to be there and help raise his son, but there were reasons why I made the choices I did. You just never know if choices are the right ones, until it's too late.

"Who'd have known all those years back that my being so independent would hurt my child in the long run? Can't do nothing about it now. And who knows? Might've been worse if I'd made the other choice, then he might've been mad about something else. I figured he'd grow out of some of them feelings, though, and come on and take this place over. It's a decent living, and I saved enough so he would've been plenty comfortable, what with my other properties and all, but he didn't know it. Now he never will."

Luke and his parents listened quietly, allowing Mamie to open up. It was the best way they knew to help her.

"I just wanted him to learn how to work, and appreciate what he could do for himself, first. Like you done raised this fine boy of yours to do, Ryan." She reached across the table and squeezed Luke's hand.

This was the most any of them had ever heard her say about Toby's father. Through the many long years, there had been no other man in Mamie's life as far as anyone in Pemrose Key knew. None. Not since the father of Toby, whoever he might have been. She had to have loved him, with the abundance of love she had for others, she had to have known love at least once in her life. She had to have experienced that bonding with another human being in order to have acquired those attributes that were so admired in her by others. She seemed to be so complete and happy with herself as a woman. Surely, without love, she could never have given so generously of herself to those who filled her world.

From time to time over the years, Luke had heard his mother ponder the question of who Mamie's lover might have been, and what might have happened to him. Ryan always told her to quit wondering and that if Mamie wanted her to know, she would have told her. Romanticist that she was, Meg couldn't help speculating, but there was no solving the mystery, for Mamie had always kept her secret locked in her heart, and Meg had too much propriety to question.

Meg broke the silence that followed Mamie's verbal musings. "Mamie, you're so wonderful with people, and you seem to love this place so. What would you do if you ever sold Mamie's Place?" Meg leaned across the table and encircled Mamie's large, clasped hands with her strong, slender ones in a motherly, protective fashion. She searched Mamie's eyes for the truth that lay buried within. Those wise, brown eyes of Mamie's reflected the warmth and love that was always visible, and which now served to veil the pain. Those who knew her also knew there was a weariness there which was surely borne of her loss and the many restless nights it must have caused her. The weariness and fatigue had to be what compelled her to consider selling.

Luke knew what his mother was thinking. They all knew Mamie would regret selling. It was her lifeline. There was nothing else she could do that she would love so and that would make her feel so useful. The people, her friends, the customers, they were her lifeblood.

After telling Mamie goodbye, Luke and his parents said their goodbyes in the parking lot.

"Don't forget, son, we'll be hosting a fund raiser for Peyton in a few weeks, right before the November election. We're going to have Opry stars from Nashville and barbecue from Dreamland. A real foot stomping hoedown. We'll have a big time, and help Peyton out in the bargain. I'm doing this for his daddy. Baines Fuller has always been ready to help me when I needed it, and in spite of his bluster I believe him to be an honest man who has looked out for his constituents fairly. We want you and Lisa to be there. 'Course I know you will, what with you and Peyton being friends."

"You know we'll be there, Dad, and pleased to do anything we can to help." So cordial. So proper. He said all the right and expected words. He sounded so confident, knowing full well Lisa wouldn't do anything to help. There was no guarantee he could even find her the afternoon of the party. All he could do was wait and see. If she didn't go with him, he'd worry about making excuses when the time came.

Luke stood in the parking lot and waved his parents off with assurances he would bring Lisa by real soon, and wouldn't wait for Peyton's party before coming around.

It was still light, still a little time before sunset to go by Oyster Bay and see what was going on. Maybe he would run into Trotter.

Luke strolled down the pier towards the *Shady Lady's* slip. Three slips away, tied to the outskirts of the dock, was a black and white Tiara, with a black Bimini top covering the bridge and a black stripe running the length of the hull. There didn't appear to be anyone around.

Luke stepped aboard the *Shady Lady* and Trotter's grinning face peered out through the cabin door. "Lucas, what you up to, boy?" Trotter had an engine part in his hand and was covered with grease, as usual. "Come aboard. I'm just about to finish up in here." He laid his crutch outside the cabin door on the cockpit floor and maneuvered the step-up from the cabin. With his muscular arms and facilitated by his one good leg, he dragged himself the short distance across the cockpit floor and lowered his torso into the engine hold. He disappeared below only for a few moments, then swung his body up and out.

"Done!" He rubbed his hands together briskly, relishing the completion of the task, oblivious to the grease he was ingraining even deeper into his palms.

Luke's deck chair sat facing the black and white boat, and Trotter commented on Luke's repeated glances towards It. "That's the *Mari Jane Too*. You know, Skip Traylor's boat. You seem mighty interested in her."

Luke nodded while continuing to stare at the boat. Skip Traylor's boat. No, he hadn't known. This was not the boat Skip Traylor owned in Luke's pre-Vietnam days. The *Mari Jane* had been the predecessor of the *Mari Jane Too*, and Luke remembered her well, a thirty six foot Chris Craft, almond colored, not white and black.

Trotter closed the hatch to the engine hold and pulled up a deck chair beside Luke. He reached into an ice chest that sat beside the cockpit door and retrieved two cold beers, passing one to Luke and popping the top on the other for himself.

The sun was setting and the breeze was beginning to die down a bit. Oyster Bay patrons strolled up and down the pier, cocktails in hand. This was the time of day to be sitting in the cockpit of a boat at Oyster Bay Marina, sipping a cold beer and admiring the sunset. It was nearly enough to make you forget your troubles, Luke thought, and silently renewed his vow to one day have a boat on the water.

"How was the honeymoon?" Trotter's face was deadpan, and his tone of voice revealed nothing.

Why was it, then, that Luke had a suspicious feeling he knew everything? Luke ignored the question. "I'm gonna' need your help with something, Trotter."

"You know you can count on me."

"I want you to dive with me tomorrow."

"I'm your man."

It was settled. No questions asked.

It was dark now. Music drifted from the loudspeakers. People strolled to and fro, up and down the piers, waiting for their names to be called to a table.

The position of Luke's chair provided him with a clear view of the cockpit of the *Mari Jane Too*. The cabin door opened and a slender woman with long, dark hair emerged. She stepped up onto the pier and Luke watched as she hurried past the *Shady Lady*, never once looking in his direction.

Trotter saw her, too. He looked down uncomfortably and studied his beer can. "You didn't know about those two?"

"I found out recently. Our days are numbered anyway, and it has nothing to do with Skip. Maybe in a round-about way it does, but there's a lot more to it than that."

Trotter puckered his lips thoughtfully and affected a slow, understanding nod.

From his position aboard the *Shady Lady*, Luke also had an unimpeded view of the parking lot. He waited for Lisa to drive out through the gates of Oyster Bay before rising from his chair. "Be seeing you, Trotter. Got to get home and act like I'm married. See you tomorrow?"

"I'll be here."

When Luke arrived back at the condo the front door was slightly ajar. He slipped in quietly. Lisa had to have arrived only minutes before him, yet already he heard her rummaging through the whiskey cabinet.

She seemed startled when he walked into the kitchen. "Did you enjoy your visit with Edna?"

Lisa poured from a full bottle of bourbon. She didn't answer. She was in another world and probably couldn't carry on an intelligent conversation with him anyway. Tomorrow she probably wouldn't even remember where she'd been.

He opened the sliding glass doors to let the sounds of the ocean in, then went to bed. Just before he fell asleep he heard the lock click on the door to the guest bedroom.

Luke woke before sunrise. It had been an early night and he had gotten a good night's rest. He felt good. He threw some gym shorts on, chugged a glass of orange juice and was out the door and pounding the beach within minutes of arising. The white sand sparkled along the shore; tiny bits of sea algae glowed in the light of dawn. Morning. What a glorious time to be up and on the beach, the fresh new dawn presenting its gift of a new beginning. His soul absorbed the sounds and the smells of the sea; the salt and the sand and the elements induced an inner strength, supplying the power to conquer not only this day, but the balance of life.

When Luke returned to the condo for a quick shower and shave, his efforts not to disturb Lisa were successful. She was still sequestered in the other bedroom when he quietly left for Oyster Bay.

It was only six-thirty when Luke stepped aboard the *Shady Lady*. He knew he didn't have to worry about Trotter not being there this early. Trotter was an early riser, too, and the apartment he occupied was located just across the parking lot of Oyster Bay Marina. The docks of Oyster Bay were practically in his front yard and sure enough, before Luke had planted both feet firmly in the cockpit, the cabin door flew open. He was met with the smell of coffee and the distinct aroma of fresh fish frying.

"Man, that smells good!" He patted his belly and remembered he'd gone to bed without any supper last night.

"Mullet. Jumped in the skillet not more than twenty minutes ago. How about some breakfast?"

"I could use some, right after I sample that swamp water you got brewing over there."

"Hey-y-y...I make danged good coffee. Watch out or you won't be getting any."

"Believe me, it's better than what I'd get at home."

They sat across from each other on padded benches at the galley table. Trotter had prepared a breakfast fit for a king.

Luke surveyed the spread. Stacked high on a ceramic platter were golden fried mullet, much more than two hungry men could eat at one sitting. Beside the mullet sat a bowl of pungent 'mater gravy made for spooning over the creamy white hominy grits that were already swimming in butter. Another platter held a half-dozen fried eggs, exactly the way Luke liked them, crispy on the outside, with the bright yellow yolks left just runny enough for soppin' with one of Trotter's homemade buttermilk biscuits. When the eggs ran out, there was a quart jar of natural clover honey for drizzling over the balance of the biscuits.

"You trying to give Mamie some competition?" With the bottom of the gravy ladle, Luke fashioned a well in the middle of his grits, then filled it with the reddish-brown sauce, thick with chunks of fresh tomatoes and sautéed onions.

"There ain't no competing with Mamie's cooking." In spite of his denial, Trotter clearly enjoyed the compliment. "I always make breakfast on the boat. Somehow being on the water makes it better. Know what I mean?"

"I do know what you mean. I know very well what you mean..." Luke left it open. He knew that neither his words, his voice, nor his eyes could conceal the longing. He wanted so badly to change his life, to be back on the water again doing what he wanted to do. For Luke it wasn't fishing. That's where he and Trotter differed. He had to have more of a challenge than that, but he knew what he could do, and what would make him happy, if ever he had the opportunity. One day, maybe.

"Let's go diving." Trotter smacked his hand against the table, signifying that he was sufficiently stuffed and breakfast was over. He cleared the table almost as soon as he laid his fork down across his empty paper plate. "What've you got in mind, Luke?"

Luke chugged his last drop of coffee and swiped the back of his hand across his mouth. "You'll see. Just head for the pass."

"It'll take us awhile to get to the pass. That means it'll be a couple of hours before we go down."

"Good thing, too, or I'd sink after that breakfast you just fed me. That is the object, though, isn't it?"

Trotter laughed.

Luke finished KP duty and battened down the galley while Trotter went above to get the engines revved and chortling.

They would be underway soon. Luke hoped he could find the spot where he had witnessed the rendezvous of the two boats yesterday. Of course, with no markers in the water all he could do would be estimate in relation to his vantage point from the beach, and the few landmarks he had taken note of: a large, ancient piece of driftwood half buried in the sand, save for three gnarled limbs that pointed skyward; the angle and degree that he had noted the boats to be in relation to Pemrose Pinnacle; and a windsock that topped a pole perched in the middle of a sand dune that rose between the beach and the road.

Trotter turned the controls over to Luke and he steered the *Shady Lady* through the pass. She hit the open waters with a penchant, moving fluidly across the minor swells. With only the slightest coercing from him, she accepted his gentle guidance, submitting herself to him, a woman stroked by loving hands, moving in accordance with his will. They moved as one, the rise and fall of her bow carrying them swiftly to their destination. He looked towards the shore. Pemrose Pinnacle rose above all other high-rises, rising higher even than the pale pink, stuccoed walls of the Hilton, which was perched grandly on the banks of the channel of the pass. He attempted to position the *Shady Lady* at the angle he had observed Skip Traylor's black and white Tiara to have approached from. From there he tried to estimate at what point and what distance the sailboat had relieved itself of a portion of its cargo. As they neared the shoreline, he could clearly identify where he had stood on the beach. He had broken off one of the driftwood limbs and staked it in the ground at the spot where he witnessed the unloading of the cargo. Luke noted with relief that it stood in the same spot. He had not been sure he could expect it to still be there at all, someone might have moved it, but his chances were greater, he knew, since school had started in early September and the beaches were nearly deserted. As the distance increased between the shoreline and the *Shady Lady*, he could still see the limb very well, his vision facilitated by the binoculars Trotter kept on board.

While Luke attempted to pinpoint at least an approximate area, Trotter busied himself below, getting into his short, one-piece wetsuit and checking his oxygen tank. Luke was a good diver, but Trotter was a pro. Trotter's diving expertise was a result of the winters spent diving for oysters around Appalachicola. Trotter would go down first.

Luke pulled the throttles into neutral, slowing the boat. When the boat came to a complete stop, save for bouncing about with the waves, he lowered the anchor slowly to the bottom of the sea. It had to have been somewhere around here. His gut feeling told him he must be close. If the "object" had been weighted enough, they just might find it. If not, it could have drifted to China by now. The current on the ocean floor had been known to produce strange results when in control, taking possession of all in its path.

Trotter leaned against the rails of the boat, keeping his crutch within close proximity. Luke helped him on with his tank. Trotter swung his torso around on the rail. Exhibiting an expert balancing act, he lowered himself to the platform and slithered into the water, disappearing beneath the surface.

Luke had described the object as best he could, having seen it only from a distance across the water. It appeared to have been covered or wrapped in something dark and he had noticed that what seemed to be the end of a rope trailed off behind it as it hit the water.

Luke waited. He sat back in a folding chair and propped his feet on the railing, hoping to appear to be merely relaxing should anyone observe their boat in this particular area. They decided not to raise the diver's flag. There were few other boats on the water today, thus lessening the danger the absence of a flag might present.

The hour that passed seemed interminable to Luke. He wasn't one given to sitting still for any length of time, anyway. It was with disappointment and relief that Luke regarded Trotter's reappearance.

It was time for Trotter to surface, and Luke always got nervous during those last few minutes of anticipation. As happy as he was to see Trotter's safe return, his disappointment was keen over the failure of the dive to produce any concrete evidence of what he had witnessed. Perhaps he would have better luck himself. He was sure Trotter had covered plenty of ground, so to speak. They would relocate the boat a few degrees to the west of their current position, maintaining the same lateral but moving closer to Pemrose Pinnacle.

Luke could have been off in his estimation. After all, that's all it was, an estimation. He hadn't fully expected to find anything, but it was worth a shot. Something had been thrown off that boat, God only knew what, and he intended to do his utmost to find whatever it was, as impossible as the task might seem. He was in his wetsuit and ready to go as soon as Trotter surfaced. He helped Trotter aboard and waited until he could help him with his tank.

"No luck, huh?"

"Nope, clean as a whistle down there. Sorry, Luke." Trotter replaced his prosthesis before assisting Luke with his equipment. "It's been a while for you. You going to be okay?"

"I'll be fine. It's one of those things like riding a bicycle, you know?"

"Yep." Trotter gave Luke a slap on the back for luck. "I'll wait here for you."

"Yeah, thanks, do that. I'd appreciate it." Luke stepped over the rail and out onto the platform. He paused only for a moment before lowering himself into the water. The water was clear today. On the surface it had been that beautiful, translucent, emerald green that sparkled in the sunshine on blue-sky days.

Below the surface, Luke made his way slowly. It did all come back to him, but he didn't want to take any chances. He relished a thrill, true, but when he engaged in thrilling pastimes, he also was deliberately cautious, the results of which had yielded a spared life in Vietnam, and he didn't intend to part with that life yet.

It was beautiful below. At first he simply enjoyed the scenery, nearly forgetting why he was down here, but once he had orientated himself, he began to search in earnest for the parcel the *Que' Pasa* deposited yesterday. Their new location yielded more than the smooth bottom Trotter had encountered. He was closer to the pass now than Trotter had been, and he extended his search in that direction. There was an old submerged fishing vessel that had lain on the ocean's bottom for more than a hundred years, just east of the pass. During their high school days, Trotter and Luke had explored it numerous times on diving expeditions. Many tales surrounded it, including one that detailed how the ghost of Admiral Wilder Beauregard Pemrose walked the waters of the pass on stormy nights. His figure illuminated by flashes of lightning—a bolt of lightning being what had set his boat afire and taken it down, along with his entire crew only minutes before they would have arrived at their homes across the bay, and their anxious, waiting families. The dramatic tale made for many an exciting adventure for two boys with active imaginations on sleepy summer days when the *Shady Lady* had been hauled for hull cleaning and maintenance and repairs, or when the tourist trade had been so insignificant as to not warrant taking her out for lack of customers.

Seeing the shadowy profile of the old hull as he made his way towards it brought back memories of those carefree summer days. Luke slowed his approach, moving with caution. There was always a great variety of sea life hovering around the abundant feeding ground the wreckage of the old boat provided, and he remembered eels, stingrays and octopi were among the numbers. Nothing to really worry about, but down here alone it was prudent to use caution. His senses were heightened, and he was alert to everything around him.

There it was! A long object wrapped in a canvas tarp and trailing a rope. The current had wrapped the rope around the boat's upended rudder and was caught there. The canvas bundle was suspended over the boat, floating and bobbing about, like a kite above the beach on a gusty day, tethered by its kite string. They obviously had unloaded their cargo in a hurry, and had not taken the time to weight it properly to insure its eternal burial at the bottom of the sea. Sloppy work if it was something they wanted to hide. He would know soon enough. The object must have drifted rapidly with the current once in the water. It had been submerged enough for its trailing rope to catch hold of the rudder, otherwise, without proper weighting, it would have drifted indefinitely, suspended just above the ocean floor, until it washed ashore. Luke tugged on the rope, pulling the object downward a bit. It seemed too heavy to be a body, unless there was just enough weighted material in it to make it feel so, but not enough to serve its intended purpose of resting on the bottom of the sea forever.

Luke was excited and anxious to get the object to the surface and aboard the *Shady Lady*. He tugged again, concentrating on freeing the rope and forgetting for only a split-second to monitor his surroundings, but a split-second was too long. He looked up from his task and stared into the face of a shark. He didn't move and the shark turned its attention to the canvas clad bundle, poking at it curiously. As the shark's interest intensified, he seemed ready to vie for his prey. Luke's objective was to get the object to the surface. Now that he'd found what he was looking for, he wasn't going to readily let the shark pilfer his booty. The shark apparently wasn't very hungry at the moment, but given what he knew of a shark's disposition, that was subject to change with the slightest bit of agitation. Also, the shark outweighed him by at least a hundred pounds.

The shark got tired of poking and viciously, without warning, his large, highly visible teeth tore into the canvas. Luke panicked, not for fear of the shark so much as for the potential loss of whatever the canvas contained. A few mouthfuls on the part of the shark would obliterate whatever was in there, especially if it was a body. Now Luke was torn between his usually prevalent cautiousness and good sense, and the desire to know what was in that bundle. Looking around, he wondered what it would take to scare the shark off. His hopes sank when he saw two more sharks swimming swiftly towards him. Before he could make them out clearly, the waters around him bubbled and swirled frenziedly, and through the tumultuous waters he just could make out the dark, shadowy bodies that were stirring up the turmoil. His good sense prevailed and he lowered himself to the depths of the rudder and wedged himself as best he could under the edge of the hull. He stayed there, scarcely moving, until the waters were once again calm. Tentatively, he reached for the rope that was attached to the rudder and gave it a tug. He couldn't see well enough through the stirred up silt to tell if the canvas object was still intact, but the weight he felt on the other end of the rope told him it just might be. He began to follow the line upwards through the water and towards the object. He would know soon enough if the sharks were still there.

When he saw the bellies of two sharks propelling themselves towards him, he fought to contain his fear lest it evolve into foolish panic. After the ruckus that had just transpired, they wouldn't be too friendly. His eyes darted back down to the ship, seeking a course of action, a route of escape. Within seconds the sharks were in clear view, close enough for him to reach out and touch. In that instant his emotions plummeted from one extreme to the other—from a fiercely overpowering peak of fear to a gushing flood of relief— which momentarily drained his body of all strength. The two sharks were not sharks at all. They were porpoises, and they were friendly. They had apparently chased the shark away in a frenzy of pommeling him with their snouts. It was likely they had discovered the parcel earlier, and for some unknown reason had been guarding it, waiting for its owner to retrieve it, and they had not taken kindly to the shark intervening and attempting to destroy it. Luke couldn't laugh outwardly with his mask on, but inwardly he laughed hysterically.

He proceeded with the task at hand, this time unhampered by the carnivorous fish. Every now and then the porpoises swam protectively past him, seemingly happy to have assisted him and strangely aware that they had. The first thing he had to do was free the rope from the rudder. Now that he could finally attempt it, it wasn't too difficult to do, aided by the small dagger strapped to the outside of his right ankle. He checked his watch. Not much time left, but he should be able to do it. Don't want to cut it too close. Once released, he fastened the rope to his waist and began to swim towards the partially tattered canvas, winding the rope between his thumb and forefinger, lasso-like, as he progressed.

The rope was secured to one end of the object. He created a halter by unwinding the end he held in his hand and hurriedly securing it to the other end. This gave him a handle so that he could pull the bundle behind him with one hand while he made his way to the surface with the other. He kept a close eye on his watch; there was no time to lose. He had no choice but to surface immediately. Trotter was watching the waters closely, nervously, Luke knew. When he saw Luke, it took him only moments to raise the anchor and idle the boat nearer to Luke. In his rush to surface, Luke had not secured the rope as well as he should have when attaching it to the winch Trotter lowered to him. That end of the rope came loose and the canvas went tumbling back into the water. Luke's heart fluttered to the pit of his stomach as he saw it falling past him. Luckily, one end of the rope was just trailing off the winch. Luke lunged forward and grabbed at it with both hands. It was a lucky catch. Following the canvas down into the water, he was able to stop its submergence and once again maneuver it back to the surface, this time tying it securely to the winch. Trotter hoisted it through the air and up into the cockpit.

Luke was next. With Trotter's help he pulled himself onto the platform and rested there a moment before stepping over the rail into the boat.

Luke approached the canvas roll that lay across the deck of the cockpit, and he was reminded of the night they had pulled Toby's body from the water. This bundle was shaped exactly as a body might be were it wrapped in canvas and secured by a rope. He and Trotter looked at each other across their "body." It was up to Luke. It was his find. With some trepidation and a certainty that it was a body, he began to sever the rope at several points with his dagger. Trotter stared incredulously as Luke unfurled the canvas. Falling to the deck with every turn of the canvas were rifles, automatic rifles, and handguns, maybe eight or ten, at least. Still they weren't at the heart of what was concealed beneath that canvas. The weapons obviously served as an anchor for the object.

Luke slowed his unwrapping as he neared the end of the canvas. He took a deep breath, and with one final turn of the canvas, a body wrapped in plastic rolled onto the deck. They could see well enough through the multi-layered plastic. It was definitely the body of a man. Luke used his dagger to slit the plastic wrapping from the base of the neck up to the hairline, taking care not to cut through the face. Carefully, he parted the plastic with the tip of his dagger. Large, brown eyes stared up at him. He knew those eyes. Even the dark hair was in place, a fringe of bangs cut smoothly across the brow line, Buster Brown fashion. The revelation was shocking. It was Stephen Pau, far from the shores of Hawaii. The last thing Stephen Pau had said to Luke on that distant shore at Fort DeRussy Park was that he had memorized his face, and that when they met again, he would know him.

The plastic had preserved the body, along with the outer canvas wrapping and the now cooler temperatures of the water. Luke figured that Stephen had been killed when the boat was only a few miles out. The murderers probably bagged the body and stuffed it in their cooler until they had time to dispose of it properly. They must have considered the boat's anchors too indispensable to use for weights, or they were just too stupid to think of that, so they employed the use of their cargo. Without being properly weighted, there was the possibility of the body being beached on a nearby shore, or floating around in the water and being spotted by another boat.

With the tip of his dagger, Luke applied pressure to the plastic and it slit easily from the neck down to the abdomen, exposing a dark, bloodstained circle in the middle of the chest, discoloring the madras plaid shirt Stephen Pau wore.

"Poor Stephen." Luke remembered the danger warning Joe Lianoho had given, and he knew Stephen Pau had received no less of a warning himself.

"You know him, Luke?"

"I met him before."

"He's not from around these parts, is he?"

"Hawaii. He served on Logan's boat, once."

"Under your father-in-law?" Trotter cocked an eyebrow.

"Guess we ought to call the Coast Guard. They'll want to poke around down there, too. We may as well just sit tight until they get here."

Trotter stepped down through the open cabin door and went to the interior control station. Just as he was about to speak into the radio mike, Luke stopped him.

"Wait. Don't want to alert the wrong people on the open airwaves. We'll go to the Coast Guard. Let's record our location."

"Right." Trotter replaced the mike in its cradle, then turned his attention to the Loran, making a notation of their latitude and longitude on a navigation chart that lay beside the control station.

Realizing they had stumbled onto the trail of the gun smugglers didn't generate a great deal of excitement in Luke. The activities of this one little sailboat had already been discovered—by Stephen Pau. Had Munsen Wales also been aboard? When Luke had seen him yesterday when the *Que' Pasa* was docked at Mamie's, he hadn't appeared to be in too much danger. Having seen the *Mari Jane Too* escort the *Que' Pasa* through the pass pretty much confirmed, in Luke's mind, Skip Traylor's involvement. This certainly came as no great surprise. The FBI was after bigger fish, Luke knew. It shouldn't be difficult to find out who owned the *Que' Pasa*. That revelation ought to tell him where the guns came from. At least it would be a start.

The Coast Guard station was in close proximity to the pass. Within a matter of minutes Trotter had navigated the pass and traveled the short distance through the inland channel. When he eased the *Shady Lady* up to the docks, they were met by a uniformed Coast Guard officer. Once again, they found themselves explaining how a dead body came to be aboard their boat.

"You say you went out looking for this body and you just happened to stumble across it in the middle of that great big ocean out there? And you didn't even know for sure it was a body you were looking for?" The officer stood aboard the *Shady Lady*, both hands on hips, straddling the corpse and voicing his incredulity. He had weathered his share of storms. He shook his gray, crewcut head, again expressing his disbelief. "Guess it could happen. I'm going to call the sheriff. It was in local waters, and he'll want to be involved in the investigation. We have paperwork to do before this fellow can be removed from your boat, Mr. Blackwell."

When the sheriff arrived, he took a hard look at Luke and Trotter. "Boys, is this a coincidence or just a favorite pastime?"

"We're not bounty hunters, Sheriff. We just happen to be in the wrong places at the right times." Luke felt uncomfortable. He couldn't explain his knowledge of the role the two boats played.

He couldn't reveal that there was a connection to the body and the weapons and Vietnam, or that it was all part of an even greater scope of smuggling, and the illegal transportation of weapons. He couldn't even reveal the identity of Stephen Pau.

At least Trotter knew not to talk. Luke could only imagine the questions he must have regarding his failure to identify Stephen Pau to these men. Trotter wouldn't ask, and he wouldn't volunteer information.

After apprising the sheriff and the Coast Guard investigator of the few pertinent details they could reveal, Luke and Trotter were dismissed, but they were informed that they should stay available in the event they were needed for further questioning.

Trotter didn't look at Luke, and he made sure they were out of earshot of the two men as they made their way down the concrete ramp to the boat dock. "I ain't asking."

"Good." Luke didn't look at Trotter as he began untying the lines while Trotter made his way up to the bridge.

It was late afternoon when they arrived back at Oyster Bay Marina. Luke was relieved to find that Lisa wasn't home. He could probably thank Skip Traylor for that. It would give him a chance to place a call to Joe Lianoho. He must talk to him, let him know that Stephen Pau was dead. Poor Stephen, he had seemed like a nice guy. Luke refused to allow himself to dwell on the probability of whether he had a family, or kids.

Luke removed a card from his billfold and dialed the number on it.

"Federal Bureau of Investigation," a woman's voice on the other end informed.

"Joe Lianoho, please. This is Luke Callaway."

After waiting a mere second, he recognized the voice that greeted him from the other end.

"Luke, how are you?"

"I'm fine, Joe, but I'm afraid Stephen Pau is not. I met up with him much sooner than I expected. He's dead." No wasting words, Lisa could come home any minute. "I pulled his body out of the Gulf of Mexico today. I didn't tell the Coast Guard or the sheriff who he was. I thought I'd better leave that up to you."

There was a reverent silence on the other end of the phone line. That silence conveyed Joe's anguish.

"They must have found out who he was. He was to infiltrate their operation, find out what he could, and contact you with instructions on how you could help him on that end. There were some guys he'd served with on Logan's boat. I wonder how they found out he was working for us?" He answered his own question, "He was careless." He then admonished Luke, "Don't you make that same mistake, Luke. I told you this could be dangerous. These people play for keeps. They have too much at stake not to. Damn!" Silence again.

"You did right not telling the sheriff. We can't take any chances at this point, and I don't know if your local boys would fully respect the magnitude and possible ramifications of blowing this deal. Like I told you before, there are some big guys ramrodding this investigation. If we don't pull this off I know I won't have a job anymore, and at my age I don't intend to blow my retirement. Do you know this sheriff of yours?"

"Fairly well. I think he's okay, but I wouldn't want you to make any decisions based on what I say about him. Check him out for yourself. He's been around these parts for a long time."

"We have. I just wanted your opinion. Eventually we will need the help of your local constabulary, but I think we had better take it one step at a time. The sheriff needs to know who Stephen is so the body can be sent back here, to his family."

Luke didn't want to know the family profile.

"I don't want you to be the one to tell him, Luke. I'll work that out. The fewer people who know you're working with us, the more valuable you can be to us. Also, it lessens the risk you take."

"I saw Munsen Wales yesterday, Joe. He seems to be a lot healthier than Pau. He didn't acknowledge that he recognized me."

"He recognized you. Was he with someone?"

"He was—and they were on the sailboat that dumped Pau's body into the Gulf." Luke detailed the events of the day for Joe Lianoho and briefed him on what had happened yesterday that led up to the body search.

Lisa came in just as Luke was hanging up the phone. Her clothes were disheveled, her hair was mussed and she reeked of bourbon. She greeted Luke with surprise and unconcealed dismay that he had arrived home before her. She kept her distance from him, pausing in the shadows of the hallway and hurriedly escaping to the bathroom. Luke heard the shower water running for almost an hour.

It was a long time before she came out and when she did, she had her robe on and her hair was wrapped in a towel that hung down over one side of her face. She didn't have much to say and she wasted no time getting into the kitchen and breaking the seal on a fresh bottle of whiskey she took from the cabinet. She poured it straight into a short glass, polished it off neatly and refilled the glass before replacing the bottle cap. She left the bottle close by and readily available on the counter.

Luke stood in the doorway of the kitchen, watching her. It was getting dark outside, so he turned the kitchen lights on.

"Don't." Lisa slammed her hand down against the counter top. "No lights." She reached for the light switch, swiftly recovering the darkness she so desired.

Luke reached for the switch, again filling the room with light. "It's getting dark in here, Lisa, keep the lights on."

"I said no lights, Luke!" Her voice trembled with anger and once more she reached for the light switch. When she did, the towel that wrapped her head and concealed one side of her face fell down her back. She grabbed for the towel and attempted to reposition it on her head and across her face. It was too late, Luke had already seen what she tried to hide.

"Lisa, what happened to you?" He took her chin in his hand and tilted her face to the light as she tried to turn from him. There were red, swollen streaks across the left side of her face, clearly the imprint of a hand, and the corner of her eye was black and blue. "Who did this to you, Lisa? I want to know. Tell me!"

"None of your business! I slammed on the brakes and hit the dashboard...the steering wheel. I slammed on the brakes and my face hit the steering wheel." She turned her glass up and finished its contents, then faced Luke defiantly, her eyes full of contempt.

"Lisa, what have I done to fill you with such hatred for me?" That was the one question that summed up all the questions he'd had about all the things that had happened since they got married. It wasn't only the booze that caused her to behave so, and it wasn't just Skip Traylor, or Edna. There was something more. He had to know about the utter hatred he faced. "What have I done to you? You wanted to marry me, for God's sake. What is all the anger about?"

He didn't expect an answer. She did not, would not and could not take responsibility for any of her actions. Mostly it was the booze, and she refused to admit that she was an alcoholic—a bonafide, card-carrying alcoholic. It was a sickness, Luke knew, but there was also that underlying, venomous hatred she harbored that seemed to stand on its own, apart from the alcoholism. He was frustrated and furious with himself for not seeing it before he married her.

Lisa didn't bother pouring. She glared defiantly at Luke, turned the bottle up and chugged the whiskey without benefit of a glass at all. "I do hate you! I hate you!" She spat the words in his face, her voice raised to a shrill, hysterical pitch. "You and your high and mighty rich family. Your mama who's so perfect and your daddy who's so grand. What about poor Edna? She loved you, but you wouldn't have anything to do with her. She was poor and had to take care of her sick mama all the time. She had to hide her mama from everybody. She couldn't be like the other kids. She loved you more than anything on this earth, Lucas Callaway. Your friends taunted her and you made fun of her and you wouldn't give her a chance. She told me everything. I hate you for hurting her—for what you did to her. I never loved you anyway. It was Edna, I did it for her, to get even with you."

Lisa's eyes widened with the realization of what she had revealed. "Ohhh!" she gasped. Fearfully, she clapped her hand over her mouth. "Oh, so help me, that's not true. I don't mean it...I don't mean it...I don't mean it! Don't tell Edna, please, don't tell Edna. I didn't mean it!" She closed her eyes and turned the bottle up to her lips and took great gulps, as if the liquid in the bottle could eliminate from sight the world that tormented her mind. "Please, please Luke, don't tell." She dropped to the kitchen floor and like a crumpled doll, sprawled limp upon the glossy linoleum, her robe fanning out around her, arms folded across her lap, cradling her head and sobbing hysterically. "Don't tell...don't tell...don't tell," she cried uncontrollably.

Luke stood frozen, looking down at her piteously. He was struck with the realization that this was right where Edna wanted him to be. Lisa's words merely repeated part of the conversation he had overheard between she and Edna at the airport, but they answered the question, to a degree, of why Edna instigated his relationship with Lisa. How twisted and warped both of their minds, and how terribly sad for Lisa to be so needy for love and attention to allow Edna to manipulate her so completely. For a time Luke had envisioned himself as her savior, dashing to her rescue. She was beyond redemption. Edna had brainwashed Lisa, shrewdly taking advantage of her illness to satisfy her own unquenchable thirst for revenge.

With hindsight, the truth rang clear. Using Lisa as her instrument of revenge, Edna had devised a plot to get even with him, and for what? For ignoring her when they were kids? With clear conscience he could declare unequivocally that the act of ignoring her had been the extent of his cruelty to her. He had never made fun of her or laughed at her as others had, but by simply avoiding her he had hoped to extinguish the flame she professed burned in her heart for him. He had found avoidance to be the kindest method in dealing with her infatuation. Now, it seemed she had succeeded in her efforts at retaliation. He knew Edna wasn't through with him yet.

Edna had sought to inflict pain upon him, and he could picture her now, after the encounter he'd had with her at Mamie's Place on his first day home—plotting the whole scenario in her mind, arranging his "chance" meeting with Lisa, and coaching and coercing Lisa into the role of irresistible temptress, using Lisa as her weapon against him. It was clearer now than it had been at the airport, Lisa had never cared for him. She never could have. It was all an act. Lisa was as much the victim as he was, though maybe even more so. The only depth of feeling she was capable of was reserved for the bottle, and those who facilitated her habit.

"I won't tell on you, Lisa."

She was pathetic. A victim from birth—of her parents, her family, and of Skip Traylor, who probably had used her more deplorably than Edna. Her's was a fate pre-destined by the circumstances of her life, and the absence of a loving, nurturing family. Luke wanted to have more compassion for her, and to have the desire to help her as he once had. Instead, he found himself hoping that this gaping wound that now lay open between them wouldn't hamper his investigation. He was as disgusted with himself as he was with her. The need to distance himself from her was overwhelming. He turned and left Lisa sobbing in the middle of the kitchen floor, her bottle beside her—her life in jeopardy—his life in shambles.

22

Luke sat across the desk from his father.

Ryan removed his reading glasses and looked up from a stack of legal documents he had been perusing. "These are yours, Luke." He slid the papers across the desktop towards Luke.

Clipped to the top of the documents was a slim stack of gilt-edged certificates. Luke stared incredulously at the papers. He knew what they were and it scared him, for his father's sake. He looked from his father to the certificates and back again, knowing what this must mean, yet trying to fathom the reasoning behind it all.

"I've sold out, Luke, to Jeremy Mason, over in Alabama. He's well-known there and in Tennessee. He's done a few jobs around the panhandle and he felt like this would be the right time to get into the Florida market. He's trying to expand his operation."

"I've heard of him." Luke didn't like what he was hearing. He remembered that Jeremy Mason had won out over Callaway Construction on the shopping center job over on Main Street, with an "eleventh hour bid," according to Edna. Edna's Shopping Center, to hear her tell it.

"Mason has approached me before about selling. Said when I got ready to retire to let him know. I always told him not to hold his breath, that my boy was coming in right behind me."

Luke winced at that remark, but Ryan continued.

"Mason's a younger man than me. Smart, too. He can keep this company going. That's one thing that is important to me."

Luke stared at his dad in disbelief. "I don't understand. You're still young, too young to retire."

"Well, I won't exactly be retiring just yet. Part of the deal is that I stay on and run the operation here for the next year, with a five year option after that, if we both mutually agree. No changes, really. I just won't be the big boss-man anymore. As far as my duties go, I will continue to run things just as I always have, but I won't be calling all the shots or making the final decisions. It'll be a relief—less pressure—less stress. Let somebody else make the decisions for a change." When Ryan spoke these last few words, his eyes darted from one corner of the room to the other and his hands fidgeted with the corners of some papers on his desk in an obvious attempt to avoid looking Luke in the eye.

Luke was skeptical of the arrangement. He knew Ryan couldn't work under those conditions. "But...why? You don't need the money. I am here now, right behind you as you said. Aren't you satisfied with the work I've been doing? Hasn't my being here helped ease your workload?"

"Luke, you haven't fooled me one iota. I know how unhappy you've been. This has nothing to do with what kind of job you've done. You're the only one I know who could do the job to my satisfaction. I know that your unhappiness here can cause problems in your marriage. I know that being forced to work here to support Lisa properly can make you build up resentments towards her. I don't want to be the cause of any problems for you. Everything I've ever done was because I loved you, and now if it causes you nothing but heartache, none of it is worth it."

"You can't do this, not because of me. I won't let you. My life's going fine." Luke experienced a desperate, suffocating pressure on his chest. His father's life revolved around this business.

"Luke, it's already been done. The deal hasn't closed, of course, but I've agreed to the terms verbally, and you know my word is as good as any piece of paper there is. I can't back out. You needn't feel any guilt about it. You know I make my own decisions. If you're not happy here, it would defeat my whole purpose of wanting to insure your happiness. I've been selfish. I thought I knew what was best for you and your bride. I tried to impose my will on you, but I was wrong. I don't need to continue to run this business by myself. It's gotten to be too much to handle at my age. Callaway Construction has grown more than I ever imagined. If you liked the business and wanted to be more a part of it, that might be different, then you could ease some of the burden for me, but let's be practical, there's no sense your being miserable the rest of your life, like I would have been had I done what your grandfather wanted me to do. I want nothing but happiness for you, whatever it takes to achieve it, as long as it's legal and healthy."

For the first time in many years, Luke felt like crying. The parameters of that protective shell of his were limited, and apparently did not extend far enough to cover family love and emotions, only the death and destruction of Vietnam. Now the veneer began to crumble, and the revelation that he wasn't such a tough guy shook his being to its depths. Everything Ryan had ever worked for had been for his wife and son. Handing these papers over to Luke was the culmination of that sacrifice, that love. In the early years he'd used his brawn, working hard, struggling for every cent he ever made. Finally, with the sweet victory of success, he used his wits to build a business that would be a legacy for his only son. With the stroke of a pen that legacy would be placed in the care of some stranger. To Luke, this action contradicted the creed Ryan had long maintained, that a man's work created life's meaning. Without meaning to life, life was not worth living.

The silence was penetrating as both men grappled with their emotions. Seeking relief from the uncomfortable pause, Ryan's voice boomed louder than usual, "Do you remember, Luke, when you were just a scrap of a lad? Why, you couldn't have been more than nine or ten years old. Do you remember how you got all scrubbed up one day, put on your Sunday suit, and slipped out and got yourself a job at the Sunset Hotel?"

Luke laughed at the memory. "I do. I remember spending summers on Pemrose Key before we moved here from Mobile. Mom and I would be here all week long enjoying ourselves, and you came over on Friday nights and spent weekends with us. Come Monday morning, you had to get up early and drive the two-and-a-half hours back to Mobile to work. Guess I figured if I went to work, too, you wouldn't have to work so hard, and you could spend more time with us at the beach."

"You were some kid, looking out for your old man," Ryan recollected fondly. "You knew you had something to offer. I remember the desk clerk saying you strolled right up to that front desk with all the confidence of a Harvard graduate and asked to see the man who was in charge of the hotel. The manager was so amused and impressed by such a small boy's ambitions, dang if he didn't give you a job! Of course when you told him your father stayed in Mobile and you needed to make some money to help your family, he did sort of misinterpret that. Your mother was horrified when he called her expressing his indignation over the fact that her sorry husband had left her and her young son to fend for themselves. He told her he would be happy to give her fine young boy a job helping the older boys set up beach chairs and umbrellas." Ryan's eyes glistened as he reminisced.

Luke winced. "I remember. Mom was appalled. She thought I'd gotten the job by telling him my father was a bum and that we were destitute. When they finally figured out that Mr. Rhodes misunderstood my explanation for wanting work, he got such a laugh out of it he gave me the job anyway. Guess I did look pitiful. I'd had a growing spurt since the last time I'd put that suit on. My trousers looked like flood britches and my coat sleeves were practically up to my elbows. Since I walked down the beach to the hotel, I wore my tennis shoes with my suit. I took myself very seriously, you know. I got into your hair cream, and I figured if a little bit would do, a lot would do a heck of a lot more. My hair was so slicked down it took me two days to wash it all out. I'm sure I was a sight." Luke laughed, recalling the image he must have projected.

No matter that the umbrellas were bigger than he was, he had managed very well. Every summer after that he had a job at the hotel, doing whatever was needed.

By the time Luke turned twelve, Ryan had expanded his business to include Florida, and he moved his family to Pemrose Key permanently. Luke was able to get on at the marina, working with the charter captains cleaning fish and washing down the charter boats, and then finally doing what he really loved, crewing aboard the *Shady Lady*. That lasted until he had to go to work for Callaway Construction the summer of his sixteenth birthday.

As Ryan had watched his son grow, he began to delegate more and more responsibility to him, grooming him for a future with Callaway Construction. He knew the boy missed being around the docks and on the water, but he figured he would grow out of it. Luke never did.

Finally recognizing that fact prompted Ryan to take action, and it was with great pride and much love that he now offered up this symbol of his life's work.

Luke picked up one of the certificates. "Dad, these have my name on them. Callaway Construction belongs to you and Mom. These aren't mine. These are worth a great deal of money, but it's your money. I'll make my own way."

"Luke, look at the dates on them. They were gifts, many years ago. Secret gifts. Your mother and I started putting away Callaway Construction stock in your name a long while back. These were birthday gifts, Christmas gifts, graduations, milestones-in-your-life gifts.

We were entitled to give our only child birthday and Christmas presents, weren't we? You wouldn't deny us that, now, would you? They weren't worth as much back then as they are today, but they're yours just the same. We were all very lucky that their value increased. It will take a few months for the deal to close, but until I sold the company, you couldn't do much with them, anyway, and we wanted to wait till you were mature enough to do the right thing by them. When we close the deal and this translates into dollars, I trust you'll use yours wisely. You do know the value of work, and I don't think this is going to cause you to get lazy and fail to pursue your goals. Maybe this will just help you get there a little bit sooner—and you won't have to pay that loan back you've been trying all over town to get."

"I should've known I couldn't keep any secrets from you around this town. That effort was before I decided to go back to work for Callaway Construction. It hasn't been so bad working for Callaway, Dad, really. I'm grateful to you for everything."

"You can't fool me. You might have been okay with it, but you haven't been happy. Now you can realize that dream of yours that I've heard so much about. You and Lisa will have all the security you need while you get that business of yours underway, and maybe start a family of your own. Who knows, maybe I'll be working for you one day!"

At the mention of Lisa's name, Luke stared in stony silence at his father, lest his expression reveal what he was not yet ready to tell. Lisa would never willingly give him a divorce now, and if she did, she would want a large share of his proceeds from the sale of Callaway Construction. Luke remembered the conversation he'd had with her only yesterday. Once more he'd tried to appeal to her to get help, even though he'd sworn she was hopeless. During one of her sober moments, he tried to talk reasonably with her. As gently as he could, he tried to get her to recognize the fact that she had a drinking problem and that it didn't have to be this way for her.

His motives were not entirely unselfish, knowing it would be a lot easier to leave a stronger, rehabilitated Lisa than the sick, pathetic fragment of a woman who greeted each day with no greater hope than to wish for a well-stocked whiskey cabinet. She had lashed out at him angrily, rejecting his suggestions, declaring that she had no problem, and vowing to never quit drinking.

Luke reflected on the hopelessness of life with Lisa, and as he stared across the desk, he witnessed in his father's face the great pride he took in the bestowal of this gift upon his son. Luke clearly realized that allowing Lisa to claim a portion of what this man had worked for would be a travesty unto him. Not even for his freedom could he cast aside so callously this gift his father offered. It wasn't the money that mattered. It was the lifetime of back-breaking work, and the love of a man for his family that it represented. Lisa, who had never even been a wife to him, and who had married him, by her own admission, not out of love, but in acquiescence to her cousin's will, had no right to any of Ryan Callaway's legacy to hard work. Lisa was many things, but she was not Luke's wife. He leafed through the certificates and pushed them back across the desk to his father.

"What is it, son?" Ryan replaced his reading glasses and looked down at the papers, puzzling over what the problem might be. "What's the matter?"

"Dad, would you do something for me? Keep these in safekeeping for awhile, and don't tell anybody about it. I can't explain right now, but there's a lot going on that this could affect. Please don't ask me what, just trust me. I can't take these right now. I don't know how long it'll be, but I don't want Lisa to know about my share in the company just yet."

"Luke, what have you got in mind? This sounds like something I should know about." Ryan leaned across the desk closer to Luke, as though to better exam what his son was concealing. "You and Lisa haven't been married long enough to be having problems. You should still be on your honeymoon. What is it, Luke? What's wrong between you two?"

"Dad, don't ask. Please, just respect my request. There's more here than a problem between me and Lisa."

"Well, thank God for that. For a minute there I was afraid you and that pretty little thing weren't going to make it."

"All I can tell you is that there are going to be some changes in my life. I can't speculate on exactly when, but I want you to hang on to these for the time being. I know it's hard to understand, but if it's any comfort, I assure you that I'm not doing anything illegal."

With deep bewilderment, Ryan peered across the top of his reading glasses. "I thought I had it all figured out. I thought it was the job that was making you unhappy. Whatever else it is, I'm sure you'll get it worked out. Living with that divine little creature you're married to can't be too bad. If it is marriage problems, well, you two are young, there's a lot to learn. We Callaways don't run from our problems, we tackle them. I feel confident you'll handle everything prudently."

This was difficult. Luke couldn't stand to see the concern on his father's face when his generous offering should have sparked a cause for celebration. How ungrateful Luke must seem to not even offer a logical explanation, but he had no choice. A full explanation would touch on the investigation, and he was sworn to secrecy. Even if he were not, his father's knowledge of the situation would only make things more difficult. Ryan would want to help.

Luke knew it was with little insight into what his life with Lisa was really like that Ryan and Meg welcomed Lisa into their home on the afternoon of Peyton's party. With a show of affection, they welcomed her with open arms, into their home, and seemingly into their hearts. They'd had little contact with Lisa since she and Luke had married, and there had been little opportunity for them to get to know her. Luke found himself avoiding visits with his parents, and the few times he had seen them, he had been alone. His mother graciously attributed the scarcity of their visits to their busy social life, while Ryan, somewhat less delicately, kidded Luke about it being because of a prolonged honeymoon status. He still didn't want to accept that there could be a serious problem.

Before their wedding, Lisa had frequently insisted that Luke take her to visit his parents, often when he would have preferred spending time alone with her. In retrospect, he could most certainly confirm it was an ulterior motive on Lisa's part, an avoidance to spending time alone with him—that, and a contrivance to ply his parents with her charms, enlisting them as allies in recruiting Luke into Ryan's business, thus securing her own financial future, and support of her habit. This exploitation of Ryan had not required great mental exertion on Lisa's part other than having to refrain from imbibing in prodigious quantities of alcoholic spirits while in his parent's presence. Miraculously, Lisa had pulled it off with a greater degree of sobriety than Luke could now fathom she was capable of. Ryan had welcomed the opportunity to reinstate his offer to Luke that he come back to work for Callaway Construction. Luke had accepted. Almost everyone was happy.

On the day of Peyton's party, more than two-hundred people promenaded along the shores of Pemrose Bay. What a festive sight it was, all those Southerners masquerading in the finest Western garb money could buy. The turnout was as much in deference to Ryan, and Meg's reputation as an exceptional hostess whose parties were the talk of the county, as for any desire to get Peyton elected. Considering the position the Callaway's maintained in Pemrose Key, and Senator Fuller's status, Peyton's nomination and ultimate election was pretty much a given.

For Luke, the party was a refreshing departure from the marital tensions that inflicted themselves upon him daily, diminishing his very existence.

Many of the county's elite came to pay homage to Senator Baines Fuller, write a big check for his son, hobnob with his Washington cronies and stuff their faces full of barbecue. The barbecue alone was reason for a party. The succulent pork was roasted slowly for hours over hot coals of hickory chips. Gallons of pungent barbecue sauce simmered over the coals and permeated the air with an enticing aroma. In keeping with tradition, baskets of white bread flanked the huge platters of hickory smoked pork, and large bowls of Mamie's cole slaw, baked beans and Black Bottom pie rounded out the menu. Peyton stood a real good chance of being elected.

Interestingly enough, Edna Sinclair did not leave Peyton's pudgy little side. That was curious. Luke knew they had to know each other, given the size of Pemrose Key, but he didn't think they had ever been very chummy. From what he observed, they now appeared to be pretty thick. If they had not known each other well before this day, their familiarity was deceptive.

Edna behaved charmingly, obviously on good behavior for Peyton's sake. Lisa was charming. Luke watched with amusement the sharp eye Edna cast Lisa's way throughout the afternoon. Somehow Edna managed to be attentive to Peyton's on-going oratory and at the same time monitor Lisa's every move. She appeared to be succeeding at both. Fascinated, Luke found the influence Edna had over Lisa absolutely amazing. Lisa's good behavior was an immense relief, and by keeping his distance, Luke was actually able to enjoy himself. When it was time to go, Lisa sweetly kissed both the older Callaways goodbye.

While Luke drove in silence, Lisa hummed to herself all the way home.

Luke unfastened the pearlized snaps on the sleeves of his plaid, western shirt, readying himself for bed. From the kitchen he heard the door to the whiskey cupboard close with a muffled thud. The evening had gone almost too well. Lisa's behavior had been impeccable, a rare moment with her, for sure. She had not even come close to inciting a riot. The Lisa his parents had been exposed to tonight would make it all the more difficult for them to understand the failure of his marriage. He agonized, in part, for what could have been and never would, and in part for his decision to go ahead and ask Lisa for a divorce. It was becoming nearly impossible to continue the charade around his friends and family. If she didn't fight the divorce, he need never disclose his financial holdings. Soon, he would test the waters. As for Joe Lianoho, Luke felt he would understand.

He didn't see how divorcing Lisa would jeopardize his mission when thus far, staying married to her had in no way facilitated an investigation of Cole's Bayou, nor had it produced any useful concrete evidence against any Logan or Sinclair family member. He would talk to Joe in the morning and if he concurred, Luke would tell Lisa tomorrow, when she was sober—IF she were sober.

Lisa entered the room and stood silently, drink in hand, watching Luke undress.

"What is it, Lisa? What do you want?" Luke asked irritably. Her silence unnerved him, as did her presence in general.

She sipped from her drink and continued to stare at him from beneath her dark eyelashes, her head tilted slightly sideways, a coy smile on her lips. He watched as she ran her fingertip around the rim of her glass, over and over and over again, round and round and round, still not uttering a sound, just smiling and staring and sipping.

Damn! "What is it, Lisa? What's the matter? Why don't you talk to me?" He made no pretense of concealing his aggravation.

When she spoke, she didn't sound drunk, "Lu-u-u-c-a-a-s, guess what I know." She drew his name out slowly in her best ever

Southern drawl. "We're going to be rich, I know we are! We're going to be rich, Lukey, we're going to be rich as sin." She danced a little jig, holding her glass high, swaying it in her hand.

Luke scarcely breathed, waiting for Lisa's next words.

Lisa continued, "Senator Fuller was talking to Sheriff Gravlee tonight at the barbecue, and do you know what the Senator said? He said rumor has it that your daddy sold his business for a great big whopping amount of money. Senator Fuller asked the sheriff if he knew anything about it." She paused, watching Luke's reaction closely.

Unbuttoning the front of his shirt, he turned away from her and walked towards the sliding glass door to the balcony of their bedroom, avoiding her scrutiny.

"Sheriff Gravlee said your daddy was already incredibly rich. 'Course everybody in Pemrose Key already knew that anyway, and the Sheriff laughed out loud when Senator Fuller told him the rich just get richer. Then he told the Senator that was something HE was sure as hell unfamiliar with, but that he was sure the Senator knew what he was talking about. Anyway, when they saw me standing there, Senator Fuller turned to me and said, 'Well, pretty lady, you are going to be very rich yourself, you know' and I said, 'Whatever do you mean, Senator?' Then he strolled out to the terrace with me and told me your daddy really didn't need all this money he was supposed to be getting for his business, that nobody needed all the money in the world, and that handsome young husband of mine would surely be getting a goodly portion of it. He said you would likely be powerfully rich in your own right, Lucas, and of course I was just thrilled. He said he was surprised I didn't already know about it. I told him I was sure you just wanted to surprise me.

"You didn't tell me your daddy sold his business, Lucas. Edna says these are the kind of things a husband should always tell a wife. Why didn't you tell me, Luke? It's true, isn't it? We are going to be filthy rich, aren't we?"

"You told this to Edna?"

"Of course I did. And why shouldn't I? Edna is very happy for us, Luke."

Now that Lisa knew, it could spoil everything. He supposed in this town it was only a matter of time before everybody knew, especially since she had discussed it with Edna. What had made him so stupid as to think he could keep it from her? His plans for tomorrow, for telling her he wanted a divorce, would have to be postponed.

The November elections came around soon enough. Peyton won. Maybe the barbecue had paid off. Certainly the Callaway's support had some influence. When the victory celebration was held at the Civic Center in Pensacola, Luke still had not asked Lisa for a divorce.

Lisa informed Luke daily of the plans she and Edna were making about what to do with all that money. Wasn't it wonderful, Edna being such a smart business woman and all? She knew exactly how they should invest their money, and it would sure behoove Luke to pay attention to her. Oh, and the things she would buy for herself, as soon as his daddy closed the deal.

Thomas Logan called much more frequently these days, just to check on his *darlin' little girl*.

December passed, and with it, the celebration of Christmas, which had been a mockery to Luke. He went through the motions—buy Lisa an expensive gift; put on the good front. Go to the parties, but make sure Edna was there, too, to keep Lisa in tow.

Lisa had a grand time Christmas shopping for herself and running up incredible amounts on Luke's charge accounts in anticipation of the finalization of the sale of Callaway Construction. Her booze brands had been upgraded considerably.

Luke was glad when December ended, but still, he had not asked Lisa for a divorce.

23

January brought good tidings. The card read:

> *Visiting Mobile in a few weeks and coming to Pemrose Key.*
> *Hope to see the two of you. Please save some time for me around the middle of February. Will call you from Mobile.*
>
> Luv, Cooper

The short message was scrawled on a picture postcard of the Statue of Liberty, but it was postmarked Minneapolis.

Luke read it again and again. He stared at her signature and closed his eyes, visualizing her face—her smile. *She was coming...she was coming.* How could he endure the few weeks until her arrival? He hadn't seen her in months, but every day he had to concentrate hard on pushing aside the thoughts of her that possessed his mind. Thinking of her was how he got through each day of his life, but extinguishing those same thoughts was how he endured his marriage. Thoughts of being with Cooper would drive him mad were he to dwell at any great length on that prospect. He had to force himself, at times, to banish those thoughts from his brain, and place them in a rational perspective. After all, not even Cooper had guessed his passion for her. He had attempted with great difficulty to maintain discretion and conceal his sentiments.

He left the card out on the kitchen counter for Lisa to see. It was addressed to her, too. He knew she didn't know or care how he felt, and he had long since discovered that the jealousy she had demonstrated in Hawaii was merely a tantrum of the vanities, an expression of an egotistical self, and her self-imposed competition between the fair skinned beauty of Cooper, and her own dark, exotic features. It had to do with rival good looks, and the incomparably sweet goodness of personality that Cooper possessed.

The few weeks passed, and still the card lay where he'd placed it. Lisa had not uttered a word of acknowledgment about Cooper's visit, but on the calendar that hung by a magnet on the side of the refrigerator, five days in the middle of February were X'd out. Could it be that Lisa anticipated Cooper's visit as a means of reconciliation, perhaps giving her the chance to play the role of the perfect wife and hostess?

It was one of those rare moments when Luke and Lisa actually sat down in each other's presence for lack of anything else to do. It was Saturday and an unseasonably warm day. Both had returned from their daily activities. Luke had spent the day with Trotter, and God only knew where Lisa had been. At any rate, their timing had coincided and Lisa was not yet too strongly under the influence. They had settled comfortably on the balcony and were enjoying the blessings of winter's reprieve—the warmth of the sun on this glorious February day.

Luke decided to take advantage of Lisa's mellow mood and attempt to persuade her, for perhaps the hundredth time, to accompany him to Cole's Bayou.

"Lisa, why don't we go visit Edna and her mother?" Maybe he could pull it off if he conveyed the attitude that this was an unselfish act on his part, a conciliatory offering. "They are your family, and I've never even met your aunt since she was sick at the time of our wedding. A family gathering might be fun."

He hated his own hypocrisy, but the investigation depended on it. Luke needed to check out Cole's Bayou to see if he detected any telltale signs of illegal activity. Joe was pressing for more information about the family and Thomas Logan. Their interest in Logan seemed to have evolved from lukewarm to somewhat toasty.

If he could get the information Joe needed, he would find a way around his divorce and Lisa's greed. If he had to, he would try to "buy" her out on the slim chance she wouldn't try to take everything if he was generous with her. At times he was so desperate he felt he would give her anything she wanted if that's what it took, but thoughts of his father's years of toil, and the inequity of it all, would quickly rein in that idea.

"We could take some food over there, maybe have a drink, and I can get to know these people of yours. What do you say?"

Lisa gave him an icy glare. "No Luke, I don't think so. Aunt Ruth's not well. No, I don't think so. It's not like that with my family, you know."

He felt like a heel, but he relentlessly pursued his quest. "No, I don't know, Lisa. I don't know at all because you all have never invited me to come around. I'm not even sure there is an Aunt Ruth." He had to find out more. He persisted, "Come on, let's run over there. Call Edna and tell her we're coming, and that we'll bring something to eat. We'll get a pizza or some barbecue or something." He desperately needed that opportunity to look around Cole's Bayou, check out Shank's Landing, and unless there was a good reason to be up in there, a stranger poking around would be too conspicuous.

"No, Luke. We can't." Lisa fidgeted and began chewing on her fingernails. She got up and stepped inside the doorway. "I'm going to get something to drink. You want something?"

"No, I'm fine." Let it rest for awhile. Sometimes she was more pliable after a few drinks. Trouble was, you never knew which way it was going to go, tantrum or tranquility.

The sliding glass door was left open and Luke could hear the phone ring. When Lisa answered, her voice was flat and non-expressive. "I don't know. Talk to him about it, he makes all the plans. Hold on a minute." She called out to him. "Luke, telephone."

As Luke entered the kitchen, Lisa was already finishing the drink she had gone inside to fix. "Who is it, Lisa?"

She turned her back on Luke and poured from the bottle again. "Your friend, Cooper DeLaney."

He was glad Lisa's back was turned when she spoke Cooper's name, so that she couldn't read the obvious in his face.

He drew in his breath and held the phone over his heart for a moment before placing the mouthpiece to his lips. "Cooper, how are you? Good to hear your voice...are you in Mobile yet? ...That's great...When did you get there?...Yes...we look forward to seeing you, too." He modulated his voice as best he could, so as to not show any emotion or reveal the tremendous excitement he experienced at the sound of her voice. "Well, when will be a good time for you?...Okay, I can reschedule some things. See you Monday, then. We both look forward to it."

He hung up the phone. "Lisa?"

She still had her back to him, but she waved her hand loosely in the air, signifying agreement with what he'd said. Except for the hand-wave, she stood motionless, evidently engrossed in her own thoughts.

Luke fought to maintain control of his voice. "Cooper...she'll be here Monday. She tries to come every year to the beach. This time she wants to come to Pemrose Key. We'll take her out to dinner, maybe go to the Marina Cafe. We can go to Mamie's for lunch one day. She'll be here at least a week. My parents will probably want to have all of us over one night—appreciation for her helping me get home after Vietnam." He'd never mentioned Cooper's name to his parents, nor the fact that she had helped speed his journey home, but he had to say something. He wanted to shout, he wanted to laugh with joy. Cooper was coming. He wanted to divorce Lisa, but for the time being, he grimly acknowledged that he was still married to her. "What do you say, Lisa? It'll be a good departure from the winter doldrums for us."

"We'll see." Lisa poured another glassful of bourbon, her third as far as he had counted. She filled the glass more this time than before.

The green monster again. That self-imposed competition. Was that it? He couldn't figure it. She didn't care about him or being his wife, she'd told him so, but she didn't seem to want him to have friends, not even Trotter. It was the alcohol. It was already beginning to tell on her. Dark circles had appeared beneath her eyes and he was surprised to notice that her previously flat tummy now protruded slightly. She was still very beautiful, physically, but Cooper much more so to him, with her sweet nature and genial personality.

"Have you decided about going to Edna's? Shall we call her now?" Luke sought to change the subject, get her mind off Cooper.

"No, Luke, I think I'll go out for awhile, though, if you don't mind."

"Fine. Go, have a good time. I've got some reading I want to do tonight, anyway."

Lisa grabbed her purse off the sofa and was out the door in a flash, her bottle stuffed inside a brown paper sack, glass in one hand, keys in the other.

It was a relief to have her gone. They had lapsed into a courteous marital maintenance since the day Lisa had confessed her hatred for Luke, and since the night they came home from Hawaii, there had been no further effort on either of their part to engage in any sexual activity. Luke bided his time, imprisoned in a sort of private hell until the day Lisa no longer inhabited his world. Lisa had permanently established quarters in the guest room, and they led separate lives. Lisa merely seemed to exist on a daily basis. Six months into their marriage, she just seemed to be living in limbo, as though she were waiting for something—but what? His inheritance? She seemed to take their relationship, or lack of one, in stride, not anxious for any changes and expecting nothing from Luke as a husband—beyond financial support, and the proposition of wealth. As long as he left her alone with her bottle, she never complained about anything. It seemed strange she never questioned, never wanted more, never mentioned divorce. It was as though she assumed this was what life was about—that this mere existence was marriage and, he speculated, based on the little he knew of her parent's marriage and the absence of her father, this was all she knew of married life.

With Lisa gone tonight, Luke felt at peace, a rarity for him these days. He lay on the sofa listening to the tranquil music of the ocean casting its hypnotic spell while day's fading light gave way to darkness, and the February chill crept into the room through the open terrace door. He didn't move to turn the lights on or to draw the door on evening's chill. *Cooper*...his thoughts of her ebbed and flowed with each breaking wave. *Cooper...Cooper.* She would be here soon, but he couldn't hold her and he couldn't tell her and she wouldn't know. She would fly away again, and she wouldn't know of his love. At least he would see her, her joyous spirit buoying him—offering a glimpse of a world beyond the agony of the life he shared with Lisa—providing nourishment for his soul for the months ahead, the months he would spend away from her, waiting until he could see her again, and not knowing how long that might be. It was his life that was in limbo, but with thoughts of seeing Cooper again playing in his mind, he drifted off to sleep with a greater contentment than he had known for some time.

On Monday it was raining. Nasty weather. The rain came down in sheets. *What a glorious day! She was coming today.* Luke would see Cooper in a few hours. He worried about her drive over from Mobile in this downpour, but he knew that wouldn't stop her. He already knew that much about her, she was steady and predictable and true to her word. No game playing.

Luke was glad Lisa was still asleep. He wanted to spend this time alone, thinking, planning, dreaming, relishing a life without Lisa, maybe even...a life with Cooper. If Lisa awoke, he thought he might go for a run on the beach, even in the rain and the cold, simply to get out of the house, away from her. He fervently hoped she would sleep a bit longer.

The doorbell rang. His heart skipped a beat, several beats. She was at least an hour earlier than he had estimated. Before answering the door, he paused a moment to collect himself by taking a long look through the glass doors, beyond the gray, pelting rain to the turbulent waters of the Gulf. Strange as it seemed, the white-capping waters had a calming effect on his own turbulent, inner-self. He couldn't believe he was so nervous. He opened the door and beheld her radiant smile.

Cooper hugged him warmly. "Luke, I've missed you—and Lisa—where is she? I'm anxious to see her, too."

"Cooper..." He held her at arms length, his hands on her shoulders. "...it's so good to see you." Their eyes met and held, and for just one moment, one fleeting moment, Luke thought he saw in her eyes what he felt in his heart.

Cooper instantly averted her eyes. She looked past him, surveying the room.

"We didn't expect you quite so early. Lisa had a late night. She's still asleep. That must have been an exhausting drive over for you."

"Oh, it wasn't bad at all. I hope I'm not too early. I left earlier than I had planned because of the weather, but there wasn't much traffic at that early hour. Even taking it a bit slower than usual I made good time. Maybe the rest of the week won't be this wet. I was hoping to spend some time walking the beach and rejuvenating my soul. There's nothing more exhilarating than a brisk walk on the beach and satiating the sinuses with salty air in the middle of winter, especially when you live in Chicago—in February."

She had a joy about her that was so infectious. "Come in, get warm and make yourself comfortable. I'm sure Lisa will be up soon. Meanwhile, we can visit." He couldn't take his eyes off her, and he didn't even try to conceal his pleasure at seeing her. "It is so good to see you, Cooper. I know you go to the beach often, but there's a lot we can show you in Pemrose Key." The "we'" was deceptive, he knew.

"Luke, it's very good to be home, to the coast, I mean…" She smiled warmly and warmed her hands on the coffee mug he handed her. "…back down South. I've missed this place. Chicago's fantastic, but the good Lord knows, I get so homesick sometimes. We get the seasons down here, and just enough winter to let us know there is one, but Chicago's winters are relentless. Once in awhile I get weary of scraping snow off my windshield at five a.m. in ten degree weather in order to make an eight a.m. flight, and not knowing for sure if I'll make it to the airport at all. Then I don't know for sure if my flight can even take off, or if I'll have to go home just to turn around a few hours later and go back to the airport because conditions have improved. I really do love flying, and I guess those kind of uncertainties keep life exciting, but I just need to come south every now and then for R & R. Do you know what I mean, Luke?"

"More than anything. Vietnam did it for me. There's just something about this place. Blame it on the moon, the sun, the tide…

whatever. It's almost bewitching, what she can do to you. I loved it always, but I never knew how much until I left. There's that undeniable magnetism that pulls you back, regardless of how long it's been. You have to come back, eventually."

"That's it! Although it's an intangible, without my annual Gulf infusion, my shot of vitality, I become totally drab and exactly the color of winter in Chicago. Just being here is an invigorating experience, and it gets me through the balance of winter." She laughed easily and walked to the terrace door. She spread her arms as if to embrace the stormy skies and white-capping waters of the Gulf, as if to be filled with its magnificent power similarly as Luke had sought its strength just before opening the front door to let her in.

Strange, they were so much alike. It was so good to have someone understand his feelings, someone to relate to on his own level. He'd kept so much inside for so long. Everything she said was injected with vitality. He couldn't believe she was actually here. He watched her movements, taking note of every detail, like the curve of her back as she stretched her arms. The white cashmere sweater she wore fit the contours of her body nicely. Her shiny, coppery hair fell softly around her shoulders and cascaded down her back. She'd let it grow longer since Hawaii. Nice. He could reach out and touch her, if he dared. No, he could never do that to her. He respected her too much. He was married, in her eyes. He knew she was the kind of girl who couldn't live with herself if she thought she had any influence at all on his pending divorce, the divorce Lisa didn't yet know about. For now, he could only be Cooper's friend. Was there more for her? Did her feelings run as deeply as his? He cared so much, and there was such chemistry between them, surely she felt at least some of what he felt. It had been there on the day they met, he knew, but he had been the one who had not been ready to pursue the initial attraction. The magnetism had been there, the electricity had been there, but he had pushed it aside and for days after his return home, he had felt an emptiness, a longing to talk to her again that tugged persistently at his heart. A few weeks later he had transferred those emotions to Lisa, and her sexuality seemed to fill the gap.

Cooper turned from the window, hugging herself with happiness as she walked back across the room. Just as she settled in comfortably on the sofa, they heard a door open in the hallway.

"Luke...Cooper." Lisa spoke matter-of-factly, as though finding Cooper in her living room were an everyday occurrence. She stopped in the doorway and leaned her shoulder against the door frame. She was sleepy-eyed and subdued. She stood tugging at the sash of her robe, pulling it tighter around her waist. Her voice was flat and inhospitable, but it wasn't belligerent. She seemed bothered not at all by the fact that Luke and Cooper sat alone in the living room, snuggled down cozily amongst the pillows, Cooper on the sofa, Luke on the love seat, both sipping steaming mugs of coffee and chatting intimately about things that didn't interest Lisa in the least.

"Lisa, join us. I'll get you some coffee, if you'd like. Cooper got here earlier than we expected. I've got breakfast started, biscuits are in the oven." He sought an appearance of normalcy with the pretense.

"That's alright, Luke, I'm going to have a 'milkshake' for breakfast, if you don't mind, and then I have some things I need to do, but don't let me stop you and Cooper from having a good time. These next few days are packed for me, and I'm sure Luke will be more than happy to show you around, Cooper. Don't mind that I won't be able to join you. There just never seem to be enough hours in the day."

She sounded more like Edna every day. Funny that he never noticed it much before he married her.

"Lisa, it's good to see you." Cooper's words were sincere. She rose and greeted Lisa with a warm hug. Ignoring Lisa's lack of response, she took Lisa's hands in her own. "I'm afraid I've just barged in without giving you much notice. Please don't worry about me. I was going to be here anyway. I'm staying at the Hilton, and if you and Luke get a chance for us to go out to dinner or something, just let me know. I don't want you to change your plans or anything, you two just go on about your business as usual and if you have some time for me, great. We'll have some fun."

"I am going about my business. I've got things to do and I'm telling you, I won't be changing my plans for you. Don't worry about me and I won't worry about you." Lisa glanced defiantly at Luke, then quickly looked away. "You and Luke can have some fun together. Right, Luke?" As these words were spoken Lisa looked back at Luke and focused her eyes unwaveringly on his. "I won't feel like you're upset by my absence and I can go right on and do what I was going to do."

Well, at least she was honest about that. He had misinterpreted the X's on the calendar. Apparently she was reserving those dates for herself, and they coincided perfectly with Cooper's visit. He was mildly curious about what she might be up to.

Cooper seemed embarrassed by Lisa's rudeness. "I-I feel like I'm imposing. Like I said, I'll be at the Hilton, and if we have a chance to get together, that's great. Don't either of you change your plans on my account. I mean it."

"Cooper, you would be doing me a favor if you let Luke show you around." Lisa sounded exasperated now, and she spoke sharply. "I told you, I have other plans. I know Luke can show you a real good time."

Cooper's eyes conveyed her plea to Luke, *please, get me out of this. What's going on here?*

Luke eyed Lisa skeptically, but his desire to spend time alone with Cooper prevailed. "You can hardly say no to that kind of persuasion, Cooper."

Lisa had something up her sleeve, but what more could Luke ask for? It didn't matter that he knew there was an ulterior motive. Lisa's gesture had cleared the way for them to relax and enjoy being together for the duration of Cooper's stay, that is if Cooper found herself to be so inclined.

"Well! That settles that." Luke stood and rubbed his hands together. "Breakfast is almost ready, Lisa. The bacon should be about done and I'm sure the biscuits are. How would you like your eggs?"

"I told you, Luke, I'm having a milkshake," Lisa reiterated crossly. She went into the kitchen and just as Luke had seen her do so many times before, she began her morning by reaching into the cupboard and pulling out a bottle of gin, then she took the orange juice from the fridge and splashed a small quantity into her glass before filling it with booze. Lisa closed her eyes and took a sip, then drew her breath in deeply before speaking. "Got to get cleaned up. Ta-ta, folks." She lifted her glass to them, oblivious to the fact that she sloshed a goodly portion of its contents on the floor around her. She then disappeared down the hall and into the bathroom.

Cooper looked uncomfortable. She shrugged and spoke hesitantly, "Well, I'm not sure if I should take up too much of your time, Luke. Like I said, there's plenty to occupy me here, even if it's just walking the beach. I thought that as long as I was going to be in Pemrose Key, it'd be fun to get together. I like to get an early start, but I suppose I really got here too soon." Cooper reached for her purse.

"It was my idea, Cooper, and I'm delighted you did. I've already arranged for time off, and you heard for yourself, Lisa wants me to entertain you. She'll feel bad if I don't. Stay, please." Luke took her purse from her hand and laid it back upon the sofa.

Cooper conceded and followed Luke into the kitchen. He felt her eyes on him as he moved deftly about, buttering biscuits and breaking eggs in the skillet.

They planned the day over a leisurely breakfast. First he would go to the Hilton with her and help her get settled in. Then he would show her around Pemrose Key, HIS Pemrose Key, not the tourist version of Pemrose Key she'd only heard about. He had other plans, too, and he was glad Lisa wouldn't be accompanying them.

24

After Cooper checked in at the hotel, Luke took her sightseeing around Pemrose Key, and then to a late lunch at Oyster Bay Marina. They were lucky to get an upstairs table beside a picture window that overlooked the dock, providing a clear view of the Intracoastal and the boats in the harbor. Once seated, Luke placed an order for a pitcher of Bloody Mary's and two dozen baked oysters. When he turned to hand the waitress the menu, a hand clamped down firmly on his right shoulder.

"Callaway, I thought that was you coming up those steps. What's with goofing off on a Monday?" Trotter nodded at Cooper and finger-tipped the brim of his soiled captain's cap. "Ma'am, how do?" He slid into a vacant chair beside Luke, the cap still perched on the back of his head.

"Trotter! I'm glad you're here." Luke rose half out of his chair and gripped Trotter's hand. "This lady helped me get home to Pemrose Key after the war, from Chicago, that is. Cooper, this is the meanest, slyest, slitheringest old snake this side of the Mason-Dixon line...and the best friend a man could ever have. Trotter Blackwell, meet Miss Cooper DeLaney."

"Mr. Blackwell, it is a pleasure to make your acquaintance." Cooper's green eyes peered steadfastly into Trotter's brown ones as she warmly offered her hand.

Luke watched Trotter with amusement. Trotter was momentarily taken aback. He wasn't used to women the likes of Cooper DeLaney. She was straightforward and sincere, and it was evident he liked her immensely, especially when she shook his hand with gusto.

Trotter always went for the eyes. Luke could read him like a book, too, and he was pleased with Trotter's assessment of Cooper. His actions signified to Luke that he knew instantly Cooper could be trusted. Luke had never wanted to know what Trotter thought of Lisa. With Cooper, everything was different.

There was an easy camaraderie amongst the three of them. Cooper fit right in, as though she had always belonged here. She seemed to bring out the best in both Luke and Trotter. Trotter did not inquire about Lisa's absence.

With no particular place to go and no hurry to be there, the three lounged back in their chairs and sipped leisurely from the icy cold mugs, talking quietly, laughing frequently and offering an occasional toast to one another. It was a peaceful, relaxing day. Outside, the sky was gray and heavily overcast. The pelting rain had ceased, but a constant drizzle speckled the water and kept the pier wet and slippery. It was a good day for staying in and doing exactly what they were doing. Even the frequency of passing boats had dwindled. Only an occasional barge made its way slowly through the channel at the insistence of a powerful little tugboat churning mightily behind.

Luke found it a very pleasant way to while away the time, with his best friend and the woman he loved beside him, sharing good food and drink and merriment. The weight of the world, his world of the last six months, was lifted. *The woman he loved*. No, Cooper didn't know, but he was certain Trotter did.

Cooper was easy to talk to, and a good conversationalist, whereas Lisa relied on her Barbie-doll looks and had never shared one intelligent conversation with Luke. Cooper enthralled him and he watched her every mannerism and inflection as she talked animatedly with Trotter, describing some of the many wonderful places she had visited since going to work for the airline; inquiring about his boat; sincerely interested in his love for fishing.

Luke's constant comparison between the two women had to cease. It was becoming an obsession with him and interfering with the present. For a long time, whenever Lisa would come home drunk or wouldn't come home at all, he could do nothing but sit and dream wistfully about the day when he and Cooper might finally be together. Now she was here, and he was obsessed with comparisons. Or were they justifications? The comparisons only made things worse. It made him despise Lisa all the more. There was nothing he could do yet, but he would soon take steps to alter his situation.

All three watched with curiosity and an aesthetic appreciation for the beauty of a sleek, seventy-five foot Hatteras as she cut through the choppy waters and slipped into position against the outer dock for fueling. The harbor master and dockhands rushed to attend the gleaming yacht and cater to her needs.

From their vantage point, the trio observed with humor the frenzy of activity generated by the arrival of the stately ship on such a lazy, rainy day, and they speculated on who the boat might belong to.

Luke's laughter ceased when he looked across to the opposite pier and saw Lisa exiting the cabin of the *Mari Jane Too*. She was attired in white, skin-tight, hip-hugger bell bottoms, a sheer, navy blue blouse with a neckline cut nearly to her naval, and red clog heels. Skip Traylor exited behind her, grabbed her wrist, and spun her around to face him. She jerked herself free from his grasp and he instantly smacked her across the face with his hand. She spat at him, then walked precariously down the pier towards the yacht, leaving Skip casting angry gestures behind her.

Luke assessed Lisa's summer attire on this chilly day in February. Judging from the amount of fuel the yacht seemed to be taking on, it could make its way to a more tropical climate.

It was clear that the X's on the refrigerator marked Lisa's rendezvous with the yacht, also clear was the source of the marks Luke had previously seen on Lisa's face.

Lisa clogged her way up to the boarding gate of the big boat, then turned and signaled to a dock hand standing nearby. The young man retrieved three large suitcases and a duffel bag from inside the fueling station. Lisa was helped aboard by a silver-haired man wearing a white turtleneck sweater, navy blazer, black leather gloves and a white captain's cap emblazoned with gold braid. As the dock hand struggled aboard with Lisa's luggage, the silver-haired man brushed Lisa's lips with his and handed her a filled champagne glass.

There was an embarrassed silence at the table. Luke closed his eyes and rubbed his forehead with the palm of his hand. He looked up at Cooper and glimpsed the sudden awareness in her eyes. Trotter absently folded and refolded the corner of his paper placemat and cleared his throat.

They continued to watch as a few lines were released and the boat pulled away from the dock. Revving its engines at full-speed once past the no-wake zone and churning water rapidly, the boat made its way down the Intracoastal towards Pensacola Pass.

The pity and embarrassment Luke had seen in Cooper's face changed instantly to anger as she kept her eyes on the departing boat. To fill the silence, Luke read aloud the words that were inscribed in gilded letters across the transom. "The *Captain Hook*. She must be new around these parts. That's a fine ship."

"Not a great day to be going out," Trotter contributed.

"Nope, not a good day...to be going out, that is." Luke poured from the pitcher, filling all three mugs and raising his own in a toast, "But a good day all around. Cheers, and welcome, Cooper, to Pemrose Key."

Cooper raised her glass, touched it to Luke's and silently searched his eyes with hers before lifting the glass to her lips.

Witnessing Lisa's departure aboard the *Captain Hook* brought an early end to the day. The ambience quickly faded and it was difficult to recapture the mood. Trotter excused himself, and Cooper seemed uncomfortable over what she had witnessed. It was still light outside when Luke returned Cooper to her hotel. Exercising great restraint, he said his goodbyes in the lobby.

25

*L*uke arrived at the Hilton to meet Cooper in the coffee shop promptly at six a.m. On this glorious Tuesday morning following the day of Lisa's departure from Pemrose Key, Lisa still hadn't returned home. Perhaps if Luke hadn't witnessed her departure yesterday, it would be easier to be worried about her absence.

Luke and Cooper downed a quick breakfast of sausage and biscuits and consumed several coffee refills before hitting the road. Luke had a mission. He intended to do some snooping around to see what he could find out about Scranton Peabody. The best place to start would be to check out his weapons parts manufacturing plant.

Luke had persuaded Cooper to drive with him up to Baseline, Alabama, to try and locate the plant. With Cooper along, it would be a pleasant drive, and he would have her to himself, away from Pemrose Key and all the people there who knew him. He didn't expect to find out much, but at least being familiar with the plant's location was one of those little chunks of knowledge he felt he needed to acquire.

Of course he couldn't tell Cooper about the investigation, thus his mission must serve a dual purpose. They would drive to Masonville, Alabama, to check on a job for Callaway Construction. To get to Masonville they had to pass through Baseline, Alabama, the home of Red Dawn Manufacturing.

Masonville was a fishing town where Callaway Construction was overseeing the development of a lake resort, and construction of a fishing camp motel. The project wasn't Luke's responsibility and his presence wasn't required on the job, but it was a good excuse to pass through Baseline.

"This is a fine thing, Luke. I come all the way from Chicago to Alabama, drive through pouring rain to get to Florida and as soon as I get here, you take me right back across the state line to Alabama. Are you trying to get rid of me or something? Dump me back on Alabama, maybe?" Cooper laughed as she pushed billowing strands of hair back from her mouth and eyes.

Luke had the top down. He turned the heater on to spite the chilly February air and to warm their toes. Cooper seemed to love it. Even with the slight chill, it was a heat wave compared to Chicago this time of year. The sun warmed the day, and she looked happy as they sped along, the wind in her face, blowing her hair about. It was fine. Her coppery hair shimmered golden in the sunshine.

They were on the outskirts of Pemrose Key when Luke began braking the car. He pulled off and stopped on the side of the road.

"Luke, where are we? Why are we stopping?"

"Mango Junction. Look."

Before them was a little makeshift stand with a large sign that proclaimed in red, hand scrawled letters, *HOT BOILED PEANUTS*. A withered old woman wearing a scarf and a worn, torn, overcoat stood beside a great iron kettle that was raised up off the ground by some concrete blocks. She busied herself around the kettle, stoking the fire beneath with a few scrawny sticks.

"Who is she, Luke? Do you know her?"

"Perky Bittle. Just look at her. She's at least a hundred years old they say, and still working out here along the roadside. That's bound to be what keeps her going. Mamie checks on her now and then, making sure she has food and that she's okay. You don't know Mamie yet, but you will. We'll go to Mamie's Place tomorrow."

A few cars whizzed by as Luke and Cooper walked the short distance along the edge of the highway to Perky Bittle's stand. He held Cooper's hand in a protective gesture. It felt perfectly natural to touch her and for outward appearances, signified nothing other than friendship.

"Why, Lucas Callaway." Perky's voice was tremulous and crusty. "You came all the way out here to see me, boy. Bless your soul." She spoke slowly, stopping frequently to catch her breath. The coat was a large bundle for her tiny frame. To even be here at all, the old woman must have a strong constitution, but physically, beneath the great, brown tweed coat, she appeared to be thin and frail.

"Perky, I brought a friend to meet you. We want to buy some of your fine peanuts. Miss Perky Bittle, meet Miss Cooper DeLaney."

"Missy," she greeted Cooper with a shaky inclination of her head.

Cooper returned the greeting with a nod and a smile.

"It's been a few years since I've seen you, Perky. How've you been? How's business these days?"

Perky's stand had once stood in the heart of Pemrose Key, on the vacant lot across from Keefer's Drugstore, but for many years now Perky hadn't ventured far from Mango Junction.

"I'm fine, Lucas. Skip Traylor just passed by here. Bought four bags from me. Taking 'em to some friends up at Baseline, he said." She squinted at Luke with amazingly clear blue eyes. The clarity of her eyes belied her age and looked to be the only remnant of youth.

What did she know? Mamie and her friends and all the many passersby must surely keep her well informed. Or perhaps she had "the gift" like all the kids said when Luke was growing up in Pemrose Key. Some even ventured that she was a witch. Peering into those wise old eyes gave Luke cause to wonder. Was the mention of Skip Traylor merely coincidence?

"Funny thing is, his friend, Scranton Peabody, already done gone the other way, down the canal towards Pensacola on that brand new yacht of his. Makes one wonder who Skipper's taking all them peanuts to. He's always told me they was for his old friend Scranton. I reckon he knows Scranton ain't there today." She peered into Luke's eyes as she spoke, as if waiting for a reaction from him. She stared. She just stared with those piercing blue eyes, those old eyes that looked so young, but had undoubtedly seen much in her long years of living in the panhandle.

Luke looked across the road, noting the distance of the Intracoastal canal from the highway. It must be at least a quarter of a mile across a tangled parcel of scrub and underbrush to the banks of the water. Identification of boat traffic through the channel would require tremendous vision acuity. How good could Perky Bittle's vision be at one-hundred years of age?

"We'll take two bags, Perky."

Gnarled, bony fingers gripped a large, slotted, wooden spoon, and with a surprisingly steady hand dipped into the steaming vat. With unhurried motion, she drained the water from the hot peanuts as they cooled in the crisp air, then ladled them into plastic bags. She tucked the plastic bags into brown paper sacks and folded the tops of the bags down around the bundles before handing them to Luke.

Luke felt the warmth through the bags as he held them in one palm while fishing in his pocket for coins. He paid her double and when her back was turned, he stuffed a wad of bills into the coffee can beside the kettle.

They bid Perky farewell and walked along the roadside to the car, the gravel crunching beneath their shoes.

Before opening the car door, Luke looked back. Perky held the bills up in her hand and waved them at him. "God bless you, child. You're a good boy, Lucas Callaway. Missy, you hang on to him. You hear, Missy?"

Luke knew she wasn't a witch.

Cooper smiled and waved back at her. "Oh, Luke, she's so special. Who is she? Does she have any family?"

"I've never heard of any, Cooper. I hate to say it, but she's been such a fixture around these parts for so long, I guess I've kind of taken her for granted and never really learned much about her."

One thing Luke had learned from Perky was that the boat they saw Lisa board yesterday, the *Captain Hook*, must belong to Scranton Peabody. From the looks of it, Scranton's "old friend," Skip Traylor, hadn't been invited, and from the little scene on the pier with Lisa, it appeared he hadn't been too pleased about it either. Luke found it to be an amusing irony—two men vying for his "wife."

With Cooper along, the two-hour drive to Baseline was most pleasurable. Red Dawn Manufacturing was out in the boondocks, away from all civilization. It was surrounded by a high, chain-link fence with a gated entrance. The tight security was something Luke hadn't planned on. While he pondered the situation, what appeared to be a delivery truck pulled up to the gate from the inside. When the electronic gates parted to allow the truck to exit, Luke seized the opportunity and entered into the enclosed parking area. The driver of the truck waved down at them as they passed.

"I want to get some directions from here, Cooper." Luke wheeled into a parking lot in front of a low profile brick building. "I'll be back in a few minutes." He was out of the car before he finished speaking.

Luke surveyed the layout of the buildings. The low brick building before him likely housed business offices and from Luke's perspective, seemed to stretch endlessly toward its rear. Between one side of the building and the high chain-link fence that surrounded the property ran a rutted dirt lane. Down the lane and behind the office building, Luke sighted several tall, concrete block buildings that looked more like manufacturing and warehousing facilities, and they looked exceedingly more interesting to him than the office building.

Assuming an authoritative attitude, he strode boldly down the dirt lane towards the rear of the building. There were no windows located on this side, just brick that seemed to stretch forever to the rear. At the end of the building, the dirt lane opened to a large, asphalted area. On the front side of the building, everything had appeared still and quiet, but around the warehouses, he found just the opposite. Several forklifts moved back and forth across the lot in a flurry of activity, and four large tractor trailers were backed up to a loading dock. Luke watched as men loaded crates aboard the trailers. Two of the trucks had the familiar markings of the *Speedy Eagle Freight Lines*, while the other two bore the placard, *Pemrose Produce*.

Luke had never heard of *Pemrose Produce*. One would be hard-put to make a living growing produce in the salty sands of Pemrose Key. He started across the asphalt towards the loading docks, moving purposefully, trying to appear as though he belonged here. Quickly, his eyes scanned the trailers, looking for an opportunity to get close to one. His moment came when one of the men left his post at the rear of one trailer and joined in a discussion with two men positioned behind another trailer. The man who was left loading the first trailer mounted a forklift and disappeared into the warehouse. Luke picked up his pace and when he reached the trailer, he hid on the inside of a wheel until he was sure the three men were absorbed in conversation. Satisfied that he hadn't been seen, he hoisted himself up inside and discovered its nearly full cargo load to be stacks of boxes stamped Red Dawn Manufacturing. Luke wedged himself in behind one tall stack of the wooden boxes, making him less vulnerable to detection. He must get one of these crates open. If his hunch was right, they contained more than weapons parts. The heavy, wooden boxes were securely nailed down. Luke frantically sought a means of prying one of them open. He must work fast before the cargo handlers returned.

All he had to work with was his pocket knife. He quickly acknowledged that it would take a day to penetrate one of these boxes with such an inadequate instrument. His concentration was disturbed by the sounds of an approaching diesel engine.

A voice near the rear of the open trailer shouted, "Hey! Hold it. We're not through back here. Watch it with that cab! These boxes are not secure."

As Luke saw the forklift approaching with another stack of crates, there was a tremulous jolt as the rig evidently attached itself to the trailer. That jolt set the taller stacks of crates into motion, including the one Luke hid behind. Without hesitation, he decided to risk discovery by pushing with all his strength against one of the stacks of swaying boxes. It worked, and two of the crates on top tumbled end over end to the floor, smashing against one another. The force of the fall busted the lid off one of the boxes and rifles fell to the floor, confirming Luke's suspicions and providing him with information Joe Lianoho was looking for. Red Dawn was producing more than weapons parts. Now Luke must seek a means of escape. The commotion he'd created was sure to instigate an investigation. He dodged behind the boxes and crouched down low, out of sight. Sure enough, two cursing men entered the trailer and quickly began repacking the rifles in the box from which they had fallen. Stealthily working his way between the pallets of cargo to the rear of the trailer and seeing no one else in sight, Luke jumped to the ground and ran.

He made it as far as the driveway on the side of the low brick building when suddenly he came face-to-face with the barrels of three vicious-looking automatic rifles, like the ones he'd found in the boxes. He hadn't seen the riflemen as they'd moved in from behind.

"Hands up, mister." One of the three grizzly thugs growled.

In a flash, Luke's mind transported him to another time, another place, when he'd been confronted similarly by three Viet Cong in the middle of the jungle in Vietnam. The faces of those men seemed indistinguishable from these. This trio of unshaven, back-country faces, and those three dead men whose youthful, Asian features were permanently etched in Luke's memory, seemed to be one and the same. In the jungle, Luke had taken all three of them out with his bare hands and the repeated thrusts of his dagger. Now, when he moved his hand instinctively to reach for that dagger, it wasn't there, and these old men were quicker than those Vietnamese boys had been. Here, Luke had been unprepared. The barrel of a rifle was shoved hard into the side of his face. The guns were the same as those in that other place in time. He felt one barrel push firmly against his breast bone, and another between his shoulder blades. He raised his arms slowly and the guns backed away, but all three were still trained directly on the center of his heart.

"Where you going, mister? You can't come back here. What business you got here, anyway? This here's a high security area, and we got our orders from Mr. Peabody that nobody who ain't authorized to can come back here." The old codger spoke through clenched teeth and a packed jaw of chewing tobacco. He had greasy, thinning, black hair, narrowed, beady eyes and a most unpleasant frown on his face.

"I was trying to find somebody who could give me some directions to Masonville. A truck at the front entrance let me in. Nobody told me I wasn't supposed to be here." Luke had no way of knowing if they knew of his discovery or not. They didn't seem like the brightest of Alabama boys. If they knew Luke had penetrated their security, it was likely they would keep it to themselves lest their boss figured they weren't doing their job.

"Can't nobody back here tell you nothing. We'll go up to the front office, and that woman in there'll tell you whatever she wants you to know. Now get on with you." With the tip of his rifle, the man who had spoken directed Luke to move along. He must be the spokesman for this brilliant trio. The other two remained silent. The man lowered his gun to his side and followed Luke to the front of the building while the others maintained their positions at the rear.

When Luke and his captor reached the entrance, the man stood aside and directed Luke through the door. He was just an old country boy. Jobs were probably scarce in these parts and this man's fear of losing his had possibly saved Luke's skin. Even though the old man had likely never killed anything larger than a squirrel, Luke was glad he didn't test his rifle on him.

"Go on in there, now. They'll help you get to where you're going." The man nudged Luke between his shoulder blades with the barrel of the rifle.

Luke entered through double doors into the lobby of Red Dawn Manufacturing. Scranton's prosperity was evident here. Luke was impressed with the lavish furnishings and millwork of richly finished woods. A glass encased collection of pricey antique weapons adorned one wall. It was surely meant to impress visiting dignitaries, such as those responsible for Scranton's lucrative contracts. Luke's eyes fell from the collection of antique weapons to a leather wing-back chair beside it. His pulse raced with fear when he saw Cooper sitting silently in the chair. Her eyes widened, indicating surprise and relief over Luke's appearance, but she said not a word.

A soft-spoken, immaculately groomed woman appearing to be in her mid-forties, manned the gleaming, mahogany, circular desk in the lobby. The woman's dark hair was pulled back severely and braided into a bun at the nape of her neck. Dark eyes peered at Luke through large, round, tortoise shell glasses. Luke had an uncanny feeling he knew her or had seen her before. In spite of the fitting interior decor, she looked out of place here in the middle of the boondocks, but her austere glamour imparted class.

"May I help you, Mr. Callaway?"

Luke felt like she knew exactly what he'd been up to, but no mention was made of his exploration at the rear of the building, or of his encounter with the Mountain Boys.

"We wanted to get directions to Masonville."

"So your friend, Cooper, told us. We thought she might be more comfortable waiting for you here inside. I've already drawn up directions for you." She courteously provided Luke with a piece of paper containing typewritten instructions.

Luke glanced at the paper. "Glad to know I'm not too far off the beaten path. Thank you for the directions, Mrs..., Miss...?"

"Miss Lydia Rhinehart. I'm happy to have been of assistance to you, Mr. Callaway." Miss Rhinehart cast her eyes down to the stack of papers before her and proceeded to pencil notations in the margins.

Luke ignored the dismissal. "Hope we haven't interrupted you too much, Miss Rhinehart." He noticed a ceramic mug of steaming coffee on the front edge of the desk. Beside it was an open sack of still-damp peanuts and a little silver case about the size of a pillbox, or a snuff box. It was attached to a short piece of halyard line spliced together to form a continuous circle, like a keychain. The shiny silver and the piece of rope contrasted oddly, Luke mused, but the line added a masculine element to the delicate silver. The abandonment of these items indicated to Luke that his intrusion had interrupted somebody.

Without looking up from her paper work, Miss Rhinehart responded, "Not at all, it gets almost too quiet out here sometimes." Having said that, she laid her pencil down, pursed her lips and took a sip from a delicate china teacup that sat to her right. Obviously the chunky ceramic mug wasn't hers.

"So you make guns here, do you?" Luke asked in a tone he hoped sounded innocent enough.

She removed her glasses and unsmilingly leveled her gaze at Luke. "Not exactly. We make weapons parts—not guns, Mr. Callaway—weapons parts."

Luke forged ahead. "You're not from these parts, are you, Miss Rhinehart? Not with that accent."

"I'm from California. San Diego."

"California? If you don't mind my asking, how would a Californian wind up in a small Alabama town such as this?"

Talking about herself, her demeanor became less guarded, almost animated. "Well, actually the owner and I go way back. A number of years ago we worked for the same company in California. When he started Red Dawn, he made me an offer I couldn't refuse, and since I wasn't totally unfamiliar with this part of the country, I took him up on his offer. I lived not too far from here when I was a child, but that was many years ago. One thing I've learned, you can never really go home. So, here I am, in exciting Baseline, Alabama."

Interesting. This lady must be one heck of a receptionist—or something—for her boss to make it lucrative enough for her to move here from California.

Miss Lydia Rhinehart took another sip from her teacup, picked up her pencil, and once again looked down at her paperwork. "Well, I hope you two don't have any trouble finding Masonville. I've got to get back to work. Good luck."

The dismissal was firm this time. Throughout the exchange Cooper had remained silent, but she now rose from her chair and took her place beside Luke. Together they walked to the door and she called out as they exited, "Thanks for your help, Miss Rhinehart."

Outside, as they descended the steps, something compelled Luke to glance back over his shoulder. When he did so, he got a glimpse of a man watching them through one of the glass sidelights that flanked the door. The man ducked out of sight too quickly for Luke to get a good look at him.

Cooper saw him, too. "Who was that man, Luke?" She asked when they reached the car.

"I don't know, Cooper. I don't know who he is, and it looked like he didn't want me to know, either. I guess he works here." Despite Luke's composed demeanor, the hairs bristled on the back of his neck, and he knew it was time for them to take their leave of Red Dawn Manufacturing.

The gate was wide open, and Luke hastily headed for Masonville. The gate closed automatically behind them.

With time now to reflect on the preceding events, Luke felt a surge of relief at having safely escaped an experience that could have had dire consequences. It had been foolish to bring Cooper along. Joe Lianoho had warned him of the danger he might encounter in this investigation. He thought of the close call he'd had, and of the long, steel barrels that had been aimed at his heart. He shuddered to think that Cooper might have had to face those rifles. Luke knew he had seen those rifles before, rifles with identical markings. Replaying the incident in his mind, he remembered where. They were the same American-made rifles which he, in a wild, uncontrollable rage, had savagely smashed against a tree, attempting to destroy them when they had fallen from the hands of three dead Vietnamese boys.

"How was it that you ended up inside, Cooper?"

"I was sitting there waiting for you to return when all of a sudden, this man appeared beside the car and asked me to come in. He didn't act like he was giving me much of a choice. I think it was the same man who was watching us leave."

"What did he look like, Cooper?"

"The most noticeable thing was his red hair, and he was bald on top. Actually, he kind of scared me, but when we got inside he disappeared into the back somewhere. Miss Rhinehart seemed like a nice lady, so I wasn't too worried—except for wondering what happened to you."

"I'm sorry about that, Cooper. Did this red headed fellow have a gap between his teeth, or a missing finger, or any other noticeable features?"

"Not that I noticed, Luke. Why? Do you think you know him?"

"He sounds like somebody I've met before."

"Is there something you're not telling me, Luke? I thought we just stopped for directions."

"Cooper, did you notice anybody else while you were waiting for me? Did you see any other people, or anything? What all did Miss Rhinehart have to say to you?"

"She didn't say much to me at all. She asked me who I was with and what we were doing here. I told her. At least I told her what I thought we were doing there. I'm not so sure, now. I did overhear her talking on the phone to a senator in Washington, Luke. She asked him how the weather was there and she told him it was so beautiful here, that 'he,' whoever 'he' is, had taken his newly acquired girlfriend and his newly acquired yacht for an extended cruise. She told this senator that everything was operating smoothly, and she assured him that 'he' wouldn't be coming back for a long time. Luke, do you think she was talking about the same man your friend, Perky Bittle, was talking about?"

"Cooper, did you hear the name of the senator?"

"No, Luke, she never called him by name. She only called him 'Senator.'"

"Hey, can you imagine being from San Diego, and winding up in a place like Baseline?"

"Look at us, Luke, how far we've traveled. And look where our hearts lie, in Mobile, and tiny Pemrose Key."

"I get your point! The lady did mention she'd lived around these parts as a kid, but still, I find it a bit curious. Granted, the Gulf of Mexico has captured our souls, but what enticement might Baseline offer?"

"Well, home is where your heart is?" Cooper presented the statement as a question. She shrugged her shoulders, lifted her palms upward and looked around at the woods that surrounded them. "Maybe she likes to hunt!"

"Right, woman!" Luke leaned across the seat and tousled her hair. "Manhunt, maybe! I have a feeling it was more like her heart is where her boss is."

"How far is Masonville, Luke?"

"Less than fifty miles. We'll be there in an hour. We'll have lunch in Masonville before going out to the job. Bet you're getting hungry."

"I'm okay, Luke, but are you? You seem to be worried about whatever you see in that rear view mirror? Is it someone you know?"

"You don't miss much, do you, Miss DeLaney? I don't know. There's a black sedan behind us that just seems to be staying kind of close, but not close enough for me to get a look at who it is. Perhaps it is someone I know."

"You mean like that red headed man? Why don't you speed up and see what they do?"

He looked sideways at her and grinned. "Reading my mind, now?" The little thunderbird raced ahead of the black sedan and the pressure Luke applied to the gas pedal placed at least a half-mile between them. With a glance in the rear view mirror, Luke eased off the gas and slowed to a more comfortable pace. "That got him off our backs." He leaned to turn the heat down and the radio up.

"Look again." Cooper snapped shut her compact after freshening her lipstick. A glance in her compact mirror had revealed otherwise.

Luke tensed when he peered in the rear-view mirror and saw the gap between the two cars narrowing rapidly. Cooper's safety was in his hands. The black sedan barreled towards them at breakneck speed. "Hang on." he instructed Cooper. "Here we go."

Luke put his foot down hard as he expertly guided the car around the turns and curves along the heavily wooded road, but the black sedan stuck like glue, now less than fifty yards behind them. They came into a clearing and the road ran straight and narrow through a flat, open field. The little thunderbird took to the open road like a streak of lightning, leaving the sedan more than a hundred yards behind. The black sedan seemed intimidated and began losing momentum. Luke wouldn't slack off this time. Instead, he took advantage of the sedan's slower pace, and left it behind for good.

Because of Cooper's presence, Luke was still shaken by the experience as they came into Masonville. He was relieved when a familiar landmark just inside the city limits came into view, Palmer's Cafe. Of the few times he had been to Masonville, he had narrowed his culinary experience down to the best of the only two restaurants in town.

"You okay?" He patted Cooper's hand on the seat beside him.

"I'm fine, considering. How about you?"

"Just some nut back there, probably trying to show off his driving skills. Let's eat!"

The restaurant was packed. They arrived right at lunch time, and apparently most of the local business luncheon crowd had discovered, as he had, that Palmer's was the best place to eat.

After filling up on a meal of turnip greens and cornbread, butter beans, fried green tomatoes and quart sized glasses of sweet tea, he felt better able to put the experience of the black sedan into proper perspective. Probably just a bunch of kids out joy riding. The events of the recent past with Toby and Stephen Pau must have left him a bit paranoid, and Lisa's shenanigans of late had him on edge. The luncheon respite did much to dissolve his apprehension, and he was ready to head for the outskirts of town.

"Ready?" Luke took a final swig of tea and pushed back from the table.

"Ready. That was wonderful! I haven't had good old southern cooking like that in ages." Cooper blotted at her lips with her napkin.

"It was good, but wait until we go to Mamie's tomorrow. She'll want to adopt you and fatten you up. One thing about Mamie, she equates food with love. She feeds the people because she loves them and if they don't eat, she feels like they don't love her!"

"That I can live without! They won't let me on an airplane after this trip." She walked ahead of Luke to the door.

"You have nothing to fear, from where I stand." He offered admiringly as he followed her out the door.

Gun shots exploded around them, piercing the quiet streets of the little country town. Cooper screamed and turned back to Luke, her arms around her head. The glass front of the restaurant shattered. People within screamed hysterically as fragments of glass pelted their clothing and their skin, and everyone scrambled to the floor. Instinctively, forcefully, Luke pushed Cooper to the sidewalk. "Get down!" he shouted. It was Vietnam all over again. He covered her body with his own. Shots rang out repeatedly and Luke located their origin when he saw a black, Buick sedan pull away from the curb across the street and speed off towards the boundary of the city limits. He didn't get the license tag number, but he identified it as a California tag.

Cooper trembled uncontrollably beneath him.

"They're out of here. Are you okay?" He helped her to a sitting position and placing his arms around her, he held her close. He looked around, surveying the damage. People in the restaurant were beginning to rise to their feet and a little girl cried, but thankfully, everyone seemed to be okay. A sheriff's patrol car screeched to a stop in front of the restaurant, and three uniformed deputies piled out, weapons in hand.

"What the heck happened here?" A large, pot-bellied guy with a lopsided badge pinned to his pocket stood before Luke on the sidewalk, waving his pistol around dangerously. Evidently patrolling the quiet streets of Masonville had provided him little experience with firearms. This had to be the most excitement Masonville had witnessed since Wisteria Creek exceeded its bounds and flooded the town in 1951, as the framed newspaper article in the restaurant proclaimed.

"We're okay here, Sheriff," said Luke. Then, with tongue firmly planted in cheek, "You got here just in time, though." Luke stood and brushed his pants off.

Cooper gave him a reproachful look as he helped her to her feet. Her hands were like ice and she still trembled, but her sense of humor was intact, and she was unable to conceal the slight upward turn at the corners of her mouth. "Shame on you," she reprimanded him in a low voice.

"Let's get out of here." Luke pulled his keys from his pocket.

"Not so fast, son." The sheriff's deputy shook his gun at Luke. "Nobody leaves here 'till we know exactly what happened."

"Yessir, we just have to be somewhere real soon, but we'll be glad to tell you what we know." Luke squeezed Cooper's hand.

"We couldn't really see who they were, probably just some kids playing with their new hunting gear or something. Anyway, just as we came out of Palmer's they started practice shooting. Lucky nobody was hurt."

"Ever see 'em before?" The sheriff asked.

"Never saw them before today."

"You not from these parts, are you?"

"We just came over from Pemrose Key. My name is Luke Callaway, and this is Cooper DeLaney. We came over to check on a project Callaway Construction is completing on Senator Hart's fishing resort."

At the mention of Senator Hart, the deputy seemed satisfied that Luke had told him all he knew. "Well, that's about it, then. Thanks for your cooperation." He dismissed them with a wave of his gun, then had a parting comment, "DeLaney, huh? Speaking of Senators, you wouldn't be any kin to Senator DeLaney up in Washington, would you, Miss?"

"Yes, sir."

Luke stared at her. Of course! Why hadn't he connected the name? Senator Macon DeLaney was from Alabama, and Luke recalled now that Cooper had mentioned to him before that her father spent a great deal of time in Washington. Many times he'd heard his own father mention the name of his childhood friend, Macon DeLaney.

"If we need anymore information from you, we'll call you in Pemrose Key. I bet either one of the senators would know how to get in touch with you. Meanwhile, we'll be on the lookout for those kids." This time the deputy tipped his hat and turned to join the other two deputies inside the restaurant.

Cooper collapsed in the front seat of Luke's car, still very visibly shaken. Not until they were back on the road, heading in the opposite direction of the black sedan's route, did she speak.

"Kids, huh?" The two words conveyed all her apprehension, all her fear, and all her skepticism. They asked all her questions and told Luke she knew that he knew all the reasons, maybe not all the answers, but the reasons why. "I'm still in shock, Luke. I've never been shot at before."

Luke glanced at her and squeezed her hand.

"It's complicated, Cooper. There is more to it than I told you, but I can't tell you or anyone else about it right now."

"I'm not sure if I should, but I trust you, Luke. I don't know exactly why, but I do. I don't know you all that well, I guess, but I know you very well."

Luke countered her remark with silence. He glanced frequently in the rear-view mirror and was relieved to finally turn off the main road, onto the freshly graded, red clay road that led to the resort area along the lake. Luke reflected on the events of the morning. It had been a close call, and not one he relished a repeat of anytime soon.

The construction site was a beehive of activity. Most of the men grinned and waved at Luke, then continued with their work. Luke really didn't need to do much other than kick the dirt around a little and talk to the supervisor. At least he was making an appearance, lending validity to his reason for coming up this way, even though by now, Cooper more than suspected otherwise. There wasn't much to see, yet. They'd only begun to pour the foundation for the lodge, and the lake wasn't very pretty right now, muddied as it was from all the construction. Having seen everything there was to see, Luke headed for Florida, and home.

The drive back through Masonville and Baseline was uneventful. Nearing Perky Bittle's stand, Luke saw that something was wrong. The closer they got, the more uneasy he felt. He began slowing the car even before he saw the huge kettle overturned on its side, lying in the smoldering coals. Water had run in a stream out to the road, and peanuts lay all around the kettle.

"Wait here," he told Cooper when he stopped the car and got out.

He reached to right the kettle, it was still warm. He looked around for Perky. He didn't have to look far. Bahia grass grew tall and golden beyond the roadside clearing and there, nestled in the grass, he saw the brown, tattered, overcoat that Perky Bittle wore. As he neared the coat, he saw she still wore it. She lay prone in the grass, blood oozing from her mouth, her lifeless blue eyes staring into the blue sky. Her frail, twisted fingers clutched the collar of her coat and held it close around her neck with both hands. She must have lain there for some time, unable to move, trying to stave off the chilling wind that rustled the grasses she lay upon. How much evil someone must possess to take the life of someone so old and fragile, leaving her to die alone in the cold. Luke closed his eyes and lifted his face heavenward. He offered a silent prayer. How tragic that her long life should end so violently. She was so innocent, so harmless. First Toby, then Stephen Pau, and now Perky Bittle. Never had Pemrose Key seen such senseless tragedy.

Who would be next, and who was responsible? He and Cooper had nearly been on that list, only hours before. What was the connection? Had someone seen them stop at Perky's stand earlier in the day? Did it have something to do with his appearance at Red Dawn Manufacturing? He recalled the day's events. He had discovered what Red Dawn really manufactured, and they had been chased, and then the shooting. How was all this connected? God forgive him if his actions had contributed to Perky's death in any way. He would have to move faster now to get to the bottom of this, before more lives were lost.

Absorbed in his thoughts, Luke never heard Cooper approach. He felt her presence, though, even before she placed her cold hand in his. She stood beside him and squeezed his hand tightly and tears filled her eyes.

A housewife with a carload of kids passed by, and Luke flagged her down. Without his going into great detail in front of the children, the woman quickly comprehended and volunteered to call for help when she got down the road to a phone.

Sheriff Gravlee came himself. "Damn shame!" He walked around with a clipboard notepad while his men gathered evidence. "We got us somebody bad on our hands, Luke. I reckon it ain't just coincidence that we've had three murders in Pemrose Key within about six months of each other. We ain't had no good leads on those other two. Poor Perky. She didn't deserve this. I hate to be the one to tell Mamie right here on the heels of Toby being killed. She really cared about this old woman, probably more than anybody else in Pemrose Key. They been friends a long time."

With nothing left to do in Mango Junction, Luke took Cooper back to her hotel. He would return later and take her to dinner. At Cooper's insistence, he promised that if Lisa had returned home, he would bring her along, too. Ever the dutiful husband. Cooper wouldn't have it any other way, he supposed. Everything on the up-and-up. Not merely for appearance sake, either, but out of that profound sense of morality Luke knew Cooper to possess.

Darkness fell, and still Lisa had not returned.

Luke splashed aftershave on sparingly and combed through his still-damp hair. He donned a pale blue, open collared shirt, khaki trousers and a navy sport coat, meeting and exceeding the usual Pemrose Key dress code along the beach, unless, of course, a specific occasion called for more formality. He studied himself critically in the full length mirror and decided he looked passable.

Luke arrived at the hotel and called Cooper on the house phone. She elected to meet him in the lobby. Luke watched from across the room as the elevator doors opened and Cooper exited alone. She paused momentarily to scan the lobby in search of him, then smiled happily when she saw him waiting for her. She wore a soft-yellow, cashmere dress and to Luke, she looked like an angel floating across the lobby towards him. Her coppery, golden-flecked hair was piled atop her head and a few graceful tendrils escaped to frame her face. Luke noticed others turn in her direction and eye her appreciatively as she crossed the room. This was a lady.

Luke proudly offered Cooper his arm and escorted her to the restaurant. The hotel sported an excellent restaurant, somewhat more elegant than most of the restaurants along the beach, attributable mainly to the attraction of the hotel for business conferences and conventions.

To make the evening special, Luke ordered a bottle of expensive champagne, which they sipped slowly. Luke was in no hurry for the evening to end. Being a week night it wasn't crowded and the service moved at an appropriate pace. Luke didn't care who saw them. After all, had not Lisa given them her blessings, right before she embarked on her journey?

Luke looked around at the other tables. On the opposite side of the room, at a corner table, he saw a red headed, balding man and a striking, dark haired woman maybe in her mid-forties. Curiously, the two appeared to be staring at Luke and Cooper. The woman was exotic looking with dark eyes and thick dark hair that curled and fell across her shoulders. There was something familiar about her. No one had to tell him who the man was. It struck him that the woman looked like an older version of Lisa and suddenly, he realized where he had seen her. This was the woman he'd seen board the *Que' Pasa* right after Stephen Pau's death, and he realized now that he had seen her again—today.

Cooper turned and followed his gaze. "Luke, that's the man I saw at Red Dawn this morning."

"I know it is, Cooper, and that's Miss Lydia Rhinehart with him."

"Well, I guess it is. I almost didn't recognize her with her hair down."

"It's her. The hair is different, and she wore glasses today, but it's the same woman. The man is Skip Traylor. He's a friend of Lisa's. He's the one who tried to stop her from going out on that yacht yesterday." He didn't tell her Skip was having an affair with Lisa, until yesterday—he didn't have to.

"Oh." Cooper cast her eyes downward, embarrassed for Luke. "What a coincidence that they should show up here, Luke. Do you think they might have anything to do with our being chased and shot at today?"

"In spite of my not telling you anything, Cooper, you've about got it figured out for yourself, haven't you?"

"Not entirely. Not yet, anyway. Luke, you don't think he could've been the one who killed Perky Bittle, do you?"

"From what I know about him, I would say he was capable of it. There are other things he's rumored to be involved in." Luke pushed his chair back and stood. "I'll be right back, Cooper. I believe I'll go speak to Miss Rhinehart and her unscrupulous companion."

As Luke crossed the room to the table in the corner, Skip Traylor scrutinized him undauntedly. His behavior was much bolder than that Luke had witnessed in Hawaii, when all Skip could do was hide in the shadows and turn tail and run. Now that Lisa seemed to be linked to another man, perhaps Skip felt he had nothing to hide from Luke.

Luke inclined his head gallantly. "Miss Rhinehart, nice to see you again. I found my way to Masonville very easily today, thanks to your directions. What a coincidence seeing you here tonight."

Skip Traylor continued to glare at Luke. After a moment he snarled, "Why did you need directions to Masonville? Seems to me you already knew your way there, seeing as how Callaway Construction has a job going on at Senator Hart's place."

Luke ignored Skip's remarks. "I believe you're Skip Traylor, right? It's been a few years. I wouldn't have recognized you if my wife hadn't identified you in Hawaii."

Skip slapped his palms down loudly against the table top, rattling silverware and glasses and shaking the table violently as he pushed himself to a standing position. "Look here, you dandy, I ain't taking nothing off of you. You Callaways think you're so high and mighty. It ain't none of your business where I was a few months back." The man was shouting now, and Luke recognized the fact that he was totally inebriated. Restaurant confrontations were getting to be an unpleasant pastime. People at other tables were staring. The waiters and the Maître'd were in a huddle, probably taking a vote on which one had the nerve to approach the two.

Skip Traylor's fist came up fast, popping Luke hard under his chin, and snapping his head back painfully. Luke recovered from the blow, drew his fist back and met his mark, matching Skip's swing with one of his own and bringing him to his knees. The waiters followed this cue, and with Skip at a disadvantage, they moved in quickly and grasped him by the elbows, one on either side. Under the Maître'd's supervision, they removed Skip from the restaurant.

Lydia Rhinehart remained cool. She took a sip of her wine, then stood and offered Luke her hand. "Mr. Callaway, I'm so sorry for the trouble. I fear Mr. Traylor had a little too much to drink tonight. Not much harm done, I hope. Enjoy your evening." She was gone in a flash, across the room and out the door, presumably in search of Skip Traylor.

It all happened so quickly, before Cooper could come to Luke's aide. Now that he had returned to the table and seeing that he was okay, she feigned aloofness, pretending that nothing had happened out of the ordinary.

"Madame." Luke bowed cordially before Cooper, rubbed the palms of his hands together and took his place across from her. He rubbed his chin and grimaced. "Ouch!"

"You big baby, see what you get for trying to cause trouble. I have no sympathy for you. You're lucky it wasn't worse."

"Like a bullet hole through the chest?"

"Exactly! But don't even joke like that at this point. Considering today's events, that isn't funny in the least."

"You're right. Sorry. You may be on to something, though. Skip Traylor may well have had something to do with what happened today. Matter of fact, it's beginning to look highly probable. My, you are beautiful this evening. Did I tell you just how lovely you were when you stepped from the elevator tonight. You looked like a dream—MY dream."

"Oh, stop it. I think you're heady from the champagne and that blow to the head." Her voice softened, "How do you feel?"

"Like I've had a blow to the head, but I'm sure the chateaubriand will do wonders for that. And I don't intend to apply it to my face." He couldn't take his eyes off Cooper. *Cooper...if I could reach across this table and touch you the way I want to. If I could only hold you. If I could only tell you.*

26

On Wednesday, intermittent, cloudy weather cast a dreary shadow on the day. It also proved to be a bad day for going to Mamie's. Mamie wasn't there. She was taking care of the burial arrangements of her old friend, Perky Bittle. The crowd was sparse and spirits were lagging. It wasn't the same without Mamie's lively laughter. The knowledge of what she was doing and the pain she was experiencing further served to dampen spirits.

Luke and Cooper enjoyed a small sampling of Mamie's fare, then strolled the antiquated docks. One sailboat was tied to the pier, but no one was aboard the thirty-six foot Catalina. It was the *Que' Pasa.*

"Let's go check out Oyster Bay, Cooper. Maybe Trotter will be there." He guided her around the holes in the pier and back towards Mamie's, but before they reached the door, Luke heard the engine of a boat approaching the dock. He turned to see a small, two-passenger skiff pulling up next to the *Que' Pasa.* A red-headed man got out and boarded the sailboat, but not before throwing a blatantly conspicuous glare Luke's way. Luke stared back until the man controlling the engine of the skiff sped away across the bay, and the red-headed man disappeared into the *Que' Pasa's* cabin.

When they got to Oyster Bay, the *Shady Lady's* slip was empty. "I guess Trotter had some charter customers. It's a fairly decent day for going out. Fishing's not too good this time of year, but sometimes people just like to get out and try their luck anyway." He spied Scotty Dillard on the opposite pier.

An idea began to formulate. He wouldn't want to do anything to endanger Cooper, but what could happen? He knew these waters like the back of his hand. So did Scotty. So, he rationalized, there could be no harm done with the two of them. "Come on, Cooper, we're going to try our luck, too."

"What do you mean, Luke? Try our luck at deep sea fishing?"

"No. inland fishing. Actually, we'll just go sightseeing. There's Scotty Dillard. See that little boat he's messing around with? Scotty's an inland fishing guide. We're going to get him to take us for a ride around the bay."

Scotty's boat was recognized by everyone around these parts for his frequent fishing of these inland waters. This was the way to go into Cole's Bayou. Luke didn't know what the venture might yield, but he felt like some of the answers could be found there. Since he had never been able to manipulate Lisa into taking him, he would go on his own, just a little ways in, so he could get the feel for things, then he would come back another time without Cooper.

"Hey, Scotty, I haven't seen you around in awhile."

"Yeah, I know. I been working, trying to get through this winter. Been doing some oyster diving. Pay's okay when they ain't no charter business." Scotty looked down and studied his feet. His beard was still a sloppy stubble, and he kept winding and unwinding a small piece of twine around his hand.

Luke remembered how shaken Scotty had been at Toby's funeral—how shaken they all had been, but in particularly, Scotty. Before finding Toby's body, Scotty seemed to have more confidence, and he seemed unscathed by the world, kind of innocent, like a kid. Luke was sure Odessa Barlew had educated him on certain aspects of worldly pleasures, but he just looked so much like a kid with that baby face. The Toby experience had definitely changed him. Outwardly he'd always looked innocent, but now he seemed more timid, more fearful, than he had before.

"Scotty, this is Cooper DeLaney. Cooper is a friend of mine from Chicago."

"Mobile." Cooper chimed in, winking at Scotty, sensing his uneasiness.

"Mobile AND Chicago." Luke corrected himself. He knew Cooper was making an effort to put Scotty at ease.

"That's better! Imagine a friend not even knowing where you're from, Scotty." She pulled Scotty into her realm with her friendly manner, making him an ally.

"Mobile AND Chicago? Well, you sure do get around, Cooper." Scotty giggled childishly. He was warming up to her. He was particularly shy around women he didn't know. Apparently Odessa Barlew had neglected to teach him the social graces, or more likely, had taught him all she knew.

"We'd like to hire you to take us out, Scotty."

"Today?" Scotty stared incredulously at Luke. He looked at the sky. The sun was momentarily peeking through the clouds.

Fishing the bay wasn't typical of Luke. When Luke fished, he generally went for the larger game.

"What's wrong with today? I thought we might cruise around the bay. Do a little sightseeing...show Cooper around. She's been here since Monday and hasn't even been on the water yet."

"Well, okay, I guess we could do that. We won't be catching too many fish today, though. It's going to be getting dark soon and the wind will be picking up. I reckon you won't be keeping this lady out too late once that chill starts setting on the water." Scotty was already loosing his lines and making the boat ready for departure. "You should have started sooner, Luke."

"You're right, Scotty. Let's just call this a sightseeing trip, and we'll come in whenever we're ready. Why don't you head over by Cole's Bayou?"

"If that's what you want, Luke. Y'all c'mon aboard."

The little boat bounced through the choppy waters, with Scotty navigating from the helm at the center of the open cockpit.

Luke and Cooper sat aft, huddled together for warmth. Cooper laughed in spite of the icy wind in her face, and Luke drew her closer to his side.

She was so close to him, so beautiful in the sunlight that trickled through the clouds. He touched her face, then tilted her chin and pressed his lips to hers. He kissed her tenderly, deeply, and she yielded to his kiss. He buried his face in her hair and his cheek felt the warmth and softness of her skin next to his; he wanted more.

Cooper's eyes were closed and she breathed a sigh before putting her hands on his shoulders and gently pushing, placing some distance between them. She looked at him sadly for a moment, then cast her eyes downward.

He tilted her chin up with his fingertips again.

She turned away. "No, Luke."

"Look at me, Cooper. Please, look at me."

Her eyes glistened and he wanted to kiss the tears away, but instead, he pulled her to his chest and cradled her head against him, holding her quietly for a moment.

She spoke softly, but firmly, "I'm leaving tomorrow, Luke, and I won't be coming back."

Inwardly, he panicked. He may never see her again. Through his own disappointment, he could see she was hurting, too. He wouldn't argue with her. Maybe she did want him, but she was also torturing herself with guilt. What he had done had not been fair to her, and he didn't want to hurt her anymore than he already had. Why had he acted so foolishly? He must be a complete idiot to risk something so precious to him as her love. This would only serve to push her farther away.

"Hey, you two, we're here." Scotty slowed the boat at the mouth of Cole's Bayou and shouted back over his shoulder, "Where'd you want to go, Luke, anywhere in particular?"

"Not really, Scotty. Just cruise along the bank, not too close in. Thought we might get a look at the old fishery, Shank's Landing." Luke thought it should be safe enough there. Any farther in towards the back of the bayou might be risky, but Shank's Landing was on a wider span of water, and not too far into the Cove. There were houses around there, including Edna's. What could happen, he reasoned.

Scotty's eyes grew larger. "Shank's Landing? You sure you want to go in there, Luke?"

"I don't think we have anything to worry about, Scotty. We're not going ashore. Besides, the fishery's closed down and that place is deserted now, isn't it?"

"I don't know, Luke. They say some bad guys still hang out there, but if you really want to, we can go a little ways in." Scotty hesitated, waiting for Luke's response. He would trust Luke, but his voice indicated he wasn't overly confident.

"You might be right, Scotty. We won't go to Cole's Bayou today. Maybe another time. Why don't you head back. It's getting late, anyway."

Before Scotty had a chance to respond, Cooper interjected, "No, Luke. Let's go to Cole's Bayou. I'm not ready to go back yet, please. I'd love to see the old fishery. Is it much like those in San Francisco?"

Luke laughed aloud at the comparison. "No, Cooper, I'm afraid not. And after what happened yesterday, I don't want to risk putting you in danger again."

"Oh, please. I'm leaving tomorrow and I don't want to miss seeing a thing. What more could possibly happen after yesterday?"

"Well, I think it would be okay, but I just don't want to take any chances with you. Scotty's right, we should just forget it."

"But I really want to see it, Luke. The bayous have such a flavor all their own. I would love to experience Cole's Bayou—see what it's like. That's all part of the intrigue of travel. I'm not afraid, and I won't hold you responsible for anything that might happen."

"I AM responsible while you're with me." He melted under her gaze, and it was difficult to deny her anything, besides, his own curiosity compelled him to relent. "I guess it wouldn't hurt to go just a little ways in, if you really want to."

She seemed so enthusiastic about everything. The adventure might serve to take the edge off what had happened. He wanted her to leave Pemrose Key with happy memories, not feelings of remorse because of his stupid actions.

"Okay, Scotty, do it."

"If you say so, Luke." Scotty glanced skeptically back over his shoulder at his passengers, then pushed slightly forward on the throttle.

Cooper pulled her jacket snug around her and tried to smooth her disheveled hair.

"It still looks nice." Luke winked at her and smiled. She had distanced herself from him. He knew it was what she had to do. He could kick himself. He would let her pretend nothing had happened. He would pretend nothing had happened—as best he could. He loved her more than ever, and he wanted more than ever to touch her again.

They approached Shank's Landing, Scotty staying at what he deemed to be a safe distance from the bank. The water was calmer inside the cove than it had been out in the bay. The cove still held the eeriness, though, that it had on the first night Luke had taken Lisa home. Even from the water side there was just something about this place. The clouds had quickly consumed the sunshine, and the sky was gray and foreboding. Weathered cypress trees that grew in a dense grove along the shoreline cast a more intense darkness along the bank. Tangled webs of Spanish moss thickly encased the trees and snaked out along their branches, draping the boughs with long, wispy tendrils that cascaded down and dangled just above the water's surface. The wind droned forlornly through the trees, stirring the Spanish moss into motion. The ever present smoke drifting from hobo camps that had been occupied the night before created a misty haze along the shoreline.

Cooper wrapped her arms around herself and pulled her jacket tighter. "It's so beautiful in here, Luke, so uniquely Southern in a mystical kind of way."

"Slow down, Scotty. Let's see what that is up ahead. Looks like there's been some activity here, after all. There, up on the dock by the fishery. It looks like boxes or crates of some kind. Do you see that?"

Scotty slowed the boat. "I see it, but I can't tell what that is, Luke. Sure looks like a lot of stuff, though. Thought you said this place closed down a long time ago, Luke."

"It did, as a fishery. Looks like somebody might be using it for a warehouse of some sort, though. I'd like to get close enough to see what it's all about. Why don't you see what you can do." The docks looked deserted. It seemed safe enough to approach from the water. He was pretty sure he knew what the crates were, but he wanted to get close enough to verify it.

Scotty idled the boat nearer to Shank's Landing. Wooden crates appeared to fill the old fishery, and many were stacked outside the building along the dock itself.

Take her in closer, Scotty. I'm getting out. Let me off at the dock, then you take Cooper and head on out of here. Wait on the far bank until I signal for you to come get me. If you don't see me within ten minutes, take Cooper back to Oyster Bay, and see that she gets back to the Hilton. I'll make my own way back."

"Are you sure you want to, Luke?" Scotty's eyes were wide, but he eased up next to the dock.

"Luke, maybe you shouldn't." Cooper was genuinely concerned and although nothing had happened, she seemed to realize this wasn't just a lark anymore.

The imprinted words on the stacks of crates were visible now, RED DAWN MFG. Luke stood to catch hold of a piling.

There was no warning. The earsplitting blast of a shotgun exploded nearby, and the barrage of shell pelted their boat and splashed in the water around them. Luke pushed the little Whaler away from the dock, and pushed Cooper to the floor.

"Let's get out of here, Scotty...!"

Before Luke had completed the sentence, Scotty had the boat in gear and the bow out of the water. Suddenly, Scotty's hands flew to his face, and he collapsed to the floor of the boat. The boat spun around wildly and raced out of control across the water towards the opposite bank.

"Scotty!" Luke shouted, trying to make his way forward. He stepped over Cooper, then the propulsion of the boat threw him to the floor. They were nearing the shoreline at high speed, headed straight for an embankment and the cypress trees.

Cooper succeeded in getting to her knees and crawling forward. Seconds before the boat would collide with the bank, she was able to reach around Scotty and pull back on the throttle. The boat shuddered and miraculously turned at the same moment it slowed, bouncing in its own wake and drifting beside the bank through the dangling moss.

"Good girl, Cooper." Luke spoke more to himself than to her as he made it to the transom of the boat and took the wheel. He idled the boat out away from the shore and cut the engines. When they were a safe distance from Shank's Landing, he let the boat drift freely so they could take care of Scotty.

"Is he dead?" Cooper asked, her eyes full of fear as she helped Luke turn Scotty over.

Scotty's face was bloody, particularly around the eyes, and Luke couldn't see his pupils. He'd been hit in the head. Luke felt for his pulse. "He's still alive. His head looks like a bloody sieve, though. We've got to get him out of here, fast. You stay with him, and I'll get us there."

The nearest dock was Mamie's Place. Luke headed the boat in that direction. He radioed ahead, calling for an ambulance to meet them at Mamie's.

Cooper sat in the floor of the boat beside Scotty.

"Here, take this and use it for his head." Luke gave Cooper his jacket. She folded it and placed it across her lap, then gently cradled Scotty's bloody head.

It seemed an eternity, but within ten minutes they arrived at Mamie's. Luke pulled up to the dock beside the screened door. As they were pulling in, he got a glimpse of the ambulance arriving in front. By the time he tied their lines the stretcher was beside the boat, and two able-bodied men were lifting Scotty onto it.

Mamie was waiting for them on the pier, along with a small group of curious patrons who had wandered outside. Mamie paced back and forth, wringing her hands and fretting. "All this trouble we been having, something bad sure has come on Pemrose Key."

On the radio Luke had identified Scotty as the one who was injured, and Odessa Barlew had been summoned by Mamie. As Odessa climbed into the ambulance beside Scotty, she asked Luke if he would mind taking Scotty's boat back to Oyster Bay.

Before leaving, Luke introduced Cooper to Mamie. It didn't take long for Mamie to proffer a full appraisal of Cooper. "I like her, Luke! It's good to have lots of friends."

That natural-born instinct of Mamie's, she seemed to know everything. *Friends.* Luke knew he hadn't fooled her for a moment, not about his feelings for Cooper, not about his marriage to Lisa, not about much of anything, ever.

When they departed, Mamie hugged Cooper and squeezed Luke's hand. She gave him an owlish look as though she were seeing right through to his brain.

Perky's name had never been mentioned, even though Mamie knew Luke and Cooper had found Perky's body.

It was a quick trip to Oyster Bay. Luke took the controls while Cooper sat aft, snuggled in a blanket Mamie gave them. At the Marina, Luke secured the little fishing boat to it's pilings.

Cooper was quiet as they drove away from Oyster Bay. Luke reached across the seat and took her hand. "What is it, Cooper? Still mad at me?"

She ignored his question. "Luke, it's a good thing I'm leaving tomorrow. I came to Pemrose Key for R & R, but it hasn't been such a healthy place to visit. So far I've stumbled upon the brutally murdered body of a sweet old lady; my escort for an evening was embroiled in a restaurant brawl; I've been shot at twice, admittedly once because I insisted on going where we shouldn't have, and because of it I've seen a man downed by gunfire. I've had a close encounter with a married man, which I deem to be the most dangerous situation of all. All I have to say is, get me home to Chicago! I think it's a bit more civilized there. She tempered what she said with a smile.

"We're friends, Luke, and you're very special to me, but friendship is all it can be." Her lower lip trembled almost imperceptibly, but he noticed.

She was okay. The old Cooper seemed to be emerging. Luke vowed not to make the same mistake again.

"Cooper, I wouldn't hurt you for anything. Friends it is." *For now.*

When they got to the hotel, Cooper begged off for the evening. She had to pack. She told Luke she would see him at breakfast in the morning, if he would like, before she left for Chicago.

With Cooper opting for the night off, Luke planned his evening as he drove the short distance home from the hotel. Much as he wanted to be with her on her last night here, he hadn't pressured her. He would take a run along the beach, and after a hot shower he would call the hospital to check on Scotty. Maybe they would know more about his condition. The initial prognosis by the medics who had treated him at Mamie's hadn't been as bad as Luke had feared. Though serious, Scotty's injuries didn't appear to be life threatening, but he had experienced some shock and trauma. Following surgery, he was expected to be placed in intensive care. Scotty would be sedated most of the night. Odessa Barlew and her friends would be there. Luke would call the ICU and talk to Odessa before going to see Scotty tonight, if she told him not to come until tomorrow, he would settle down with a good book for a few hours before hitting the sack. At least he would get to see Cooper in the morning before she left.

When Luke got home, he wasn't too surprised to see Ben Gravlee waiting outside the door to his condominium.

"Hello, Sheriff. What can I do for you?"

"I want to talk to you, Luke. Can I come in?"

"Sure, come on in. Guess it's about Scotty Dillard, huh?" Luke held the door open for Sheriff Gravlee to enter.

"No, it's not about Scotty Dillard, Luke. Not right now, anyhow. Scotty's going to be okay, you know. He lost an eye, but he's alive. That's more than we can say about some of our other neighbors of late. We picked up the radio call to Mamie's, and one of my men was at the hospital waiting for him. They had to operate on him, but we'll find out what happened when he gets out of surgery. I figure he was probably out over somebody's oyster beds, and they didn't take too kindly to it. Is that what happened, Luke?"

The sheriff's gaze didn't waver, and Luke didn't flinch.

"Something like that, Sheriff."

In these parts shootings were infrequent, but not uncommon. The back bay areas and the oyster beds were sacred turf for some, and off-limits to outsiders. Intruders were unwelcome, and the sheriff frequently had to look the other way. It was the unwritten law of the land. The oyster growers kept their beds fed and fertile, and illegal harvesting was often met with a bombardment of shotgun blasts, or worse.

If Gravlee knew what was going on at Shank's Landing, he didn't want Luke to know he knew. If he didn't, Luke didn't want him to know. The wrong move by local law enforcement officers could throw a wrench into the entire operation and create nothing but confusion, making it an impossibility to get to the top of the heap. Both men understood each other, but it wasn't clear exactly what each understood.

"Have a seat, Sheriff."

"Don't need to, Luke. This won't take long." Sheriff Gravlee had removed his hat upon entering the room and he stood now, turning the brim round and round in his hands. He watched Luke's every move as he told him what he had to say.

"Got word from the Coast Guard, Luke, about three hours ago. There was an explosion offshore this morning, some thirty-five miles out from Pensacola Pass—a boat named *Captain Hook*. It didn't take the Coast Guard long to get there. There wasn't much left of the boat. They're still looking for survivors. They found two bodies right off. Seems your buddy, Trotter Blackwell, saw it happen. Don't rightly know exactly how many were on board. The boat belonged to Scranton Peabody. No sign of him, yet, but his office up in Baseline says he was on board."

Luke turned his face away from the sheriff's scrutiny and looked out across the ocean through the glass doors.

"Your wife, Lisa, was one of the bodies they found, Luke."

"Thank you for coming in person to tell me, Sheriff. Does anyone else know?"

"No, not about your wife. Of course Scranton Peabody's company may have known who all was on board. We figured you'd want to tell her family yourself."

"I'll tell you what, Sheriff, I'm not in real thick with her family, and if you wouldn't mind, I would appreciate it if you would tell them for me. Edna Sinclair and her mama are all the family she's got in Pemrose Key, and we're not what you would call 'close relations.' I don't know where Lisa's father is. Edna should know how to get in touch with him. From what I understand, he's been in Europe; Hawaii; Newport News. The only time I ever met him was at our wedding. If you could contact them for me, I would appreciate it. I'll tell my family, of course, and make any funeral arrangements that need to be made. Do they know what happened?"

"They haven't determined for sure, but they said it might have been a fuel explosion. They will salvage what they can, and naturally they'll conduct an investigation."

"I'll be anxious to hear what they find."

"We all will. I'll tell Edna and her mama for you, Luke."

"Thank you, Sheriff."

Luke closed the door and locked it. It was over. For a long while he stood and stared out the sliding glass doors, seeing nothing, not even the water, for now. What he felt was a combination of sadness and relief, and fear. Is this what he had wanted? He had not loved her, but the possibility had been there once. He hated her for destroying that possibility. Lisa was beautiful, but she had been on a suicidal plunge, spiraling downward, and bringing him down with her. She was a little girl, but she was a tramp and a self-destructing alcoholic. Months ago he gave up on her and on their relationship. Could he have done more to help her? He knew that question would always haunt him. Even in death, in giving him his freedom, Lisa had left her mark on him.

His parents must be told, before they heard from someone else.

Ryan and Meg were sitting at the kitchen table when Luke entered from the anteroom. His unannounced visit surprised them. The news stunned them. Luke knew their grief was genuine, but he suspected much of it had to do with their concern for him. The Callaways were caring people, but how deep could grief run for someone you had never really known? Lisa had been so elusive after the wedding that their efforts to reach her on a more personal level had fallen far short of success. Meg had wanted to be a mother to her, but Lisa had maintained her distance. Luke had shielded them as much as possible from her shenanigans, and neither Ryan nor Meg ever understood her. They came to regard her merely as their son's wife.

Luke knew they must question why Lisa was aboard the *Captain Hook* and not at home with her husband. Surely they had sensed his unhappiness, and it was likely Ryan realized his son's marriage was in trouble when Luke asked him to hold on to his share of Callaway stock.

In his mind, Luke defended the lack of grief he experienced, but there would be no public pretense. The real tragedy of Lisa's life was not her death, it was whatever causes had driven her to waste her life on alcohol. The bottle had dictated her life and generated the irresponsible actions that placed her in the position that led to her death.

It was late when Luke left his parents, nearly midnight. He drove directly to the Hilton. Cooper would probably be asleep by now. He would call her from one of the house phones that was situated opposite the front desk.

Only one desk clerk was on duty, and he looked like he was about to nod off. Luke noticed a young couple leave the coffee shop and stroll slowly across the lobby towards the hotel's main entrance. The lobby was otherwise deserted.

He rang Cooper's room repeatedly—room number *Seven-Hundred*. There was no answer. He was sure it was *Seven-Hundred*. How could he get confused over such a simple number as that? He hung up the phone and approached the desk clerk. "Can you help me, sir? A friend of mine is staying in number *Seven-Hundred*. She doesn't answer. Could you verify that room number for me?"

The clerk appeared irritated at having been disturbed at this late hour. He must have been sleeping with his eyes open. He grudgingly checked the records and informed Luke that Miss Cooper DeLaney was registered to room number *Seven-Hundred*.

"Thanks, Mister. Hope I didn't disturb you too much." Luke drummed his fingers once on the counter and turned on his heel towards the elevator and pushed the button for the seventh floor. Room *Seven-Hundred* was at the end of the corridor on the seventh floor. Luke rapped on the door, softly at first, then louder when there was no immediate response. He knocked again, and again. There was no answer. The thought of losing her when he finally had his freedom panicked him.

There was nothing to do but return to the lobby. This time the desk clerk's elbows were propped on the counter and his chin rested in his cupped palms. He was sure enough in deep slumber now. Luke decided not to wake him just yet. Instead, he strode across the empty lobby and through the massive glass doors that opened to the terraced pool area. In daylight the beach and ocean were visible beyond the pool. Tonight, all Luke could see was an occasional whitecap where the ocean was supposed to be. He could hear the loud, incessant rush of the ocean, though, and a low pitched murmur of voices nearby.

To his right, he noticed the faint glow of a cigarette. There, in the dark shadows of a partially shrub-enclosed section of the terrace, two people sat at a patio table. Luke saw her before she saw him. She was facing him, and a man occupied the space across from her, his back to Luke. As he neared the table, the man turned to see who might be approaching, and Luke recognized his friend.

"Trotter! What are you doing here?"

"Luke!" Clearly surprised to see Luke, Cooper spoke before Trotter had a chance to.

"I've been looking for you, Cooper. I was worried, I thought you were going to pack and go to bed early tonight."

"I was, Luke, and I did, until Trotter called my room looking for you."

"Sit down, Buddy, I must've just missed you after you dropped Cooper off. I tried you at home first, then I came here." Trotter took a deep tug off his cigarette before tossing it to the ground and grinding it beneath his foot. "There's something I got to tell you."

"I've got something to tell both of you. I suspect our news is the same."

"You know about Lisa." Coming from Trotter it was more a confirmed statement than a question. "It's a tough break, Luke." Trotter's voice lacked sincerity, but he placed his hand sympathetically on Luke's shoulder. The gesture itself seemed sincere.

Cooper interrupted the moment. "I'm sorry, Luke. I'm so sorry. I wanted to be Lisa's friend, too." Cooper knew Lisa least of all, perhaps that's why her expression reflected genuine sympathy.

"I know, Cooper, and you tried. I heard you were out there, Trotter. Want to tell me what happened?"

"I hauled some junk out to my reef, and there was this other boat dead center over where I was headed, right on top of my hole. At first I thought it was one of the other charter boats fishing my spot. Ticked me off, so I headed towards them, intending to put a stop to it. The closer I got I could see that it was bigger than most of the boats around here. It was the *Captain Hook*, the one we saw Lisa go out on. That made me even madder, and you know how I am. I had to have a better look. When I got up within shouting distance they came out of the cabin. Lisa started waving her arms and hollering something at me. Of course there was no way I could hear her, but I'm sure it was choice, judging by the sign language she was using. I cruised in real close to let her know I saw her. I waved and used a little sign language of my own, then I took off. Without any warning that jerk she was with pulled a shotgun out and started blasting at me. I ran the *Lady* hard and put some distance between us before he did her too much damage. When I got out a safe distance from them, I turned around, thinking I might taunt them a little bit. At that distance I knew that even that fine ship couldn't outrun the *Shady Lady*. Right before my eyes the *Captain Hook* blew sky high. They were gone—just like that!" Trotter snapped his fingers. "It was like when it happened at Mamie's cabin. I radioed the Coast Guard and they had a boat there in about ten or fifteen minutes, but by the time they got there a half-dozen other boats were already scavenging the area. I was trying to dodge debris and do what I could to look for survivors."

"Ben Gravlee said they thought it was a fuel leak. He said that's what the Coast Guard was looking at."

"Not anymore. It wasn't a fuel leak, Luke. They think it was a bomb."

"A bomb?" Cooper's hand went to her heart and she looked from Trotter to Luke.

Luke listened as Trotter continued. "That's what it looked like to me, Luke. The way it came apart...the way it blew. There were two explosions. The initial one looked like it came outward from the bow, and I figure that was the bomb. The second one must've been the fuel tanks. That's when everything else blew. That's what really finished her off. The Coast Guard picked up two bodies and they gathered up a few body parts and a lot of debris."

"Oh, poor Lisa." Cooper let out a sob.

"Did they...speculate over who might have planted a bomb on board, Trot?" Luke looked cautiously at Cooper, hoping to not upset her further.

Cooper's eyes brimmed with tears. "Luke! What are you saying? Do you mean you really believe it could've been a bomb? Do you think that somebody wanted those people dead?"

"Cooper, listen to me. I think people wanted *us* dead. It's not difficult to believe somebody wanted them dead, too, is it?"

"I don't know, Luke. I've never had to think about murderers and murdering."

"I'm sure you haven't, and I should never have placed you in the kind of dangerous situations we've been in. I'm putting you on a plane back to Chicago first thing in the morning, just as you'd planned."

"No, I'm not going. I've changed my mind. I'm staying here. You've just lost your wife. I don't know what else is going on in your life, but I'm your friend. I want to stay here and help you in whatever way I can."

Dear God, if only she could.

Trotter had an observation, "That might not be such a good idea, Cooper. I know it ain't none of my business, but, no sir, I don't think that'd be too smart."

Luke and Cooper had been so absorbed in their conversation and each other, they both looked at Trotter now as though he had suddenly materialized.

"Luke, your wife got killed today, probably murdered, and there are people out there wanting to know who did it. Maybe some even wanting to kill you, too, for whatever reason. Cooper might be just a good friend of yours..." Trotter looked down at the unlit cigarette he toyed with between his fingers. "...if you don't mind my saying so, though, I see it as something more than that. Might be that other folks do, too."

"Trotter!" Cooper was indignant.

"What are you saying, Trotter—that I'm suspected of planting that bomb onboard the *Captain Hook*? Is that what this is about?" Luke's voice didn't conceal the anger he felt.

"I'm just pointing these things out for your own protection, Luke. I don't think it would look good for you if Cooper is hanging around here."

"Have you lost your mind, Trotter? You act like you believe I had something to do with this."

"Think about it, Luke. Forget about your personal position and view this thing as an outsider might. You got a wife you want to divorce, right? And on the very day your wife is killed, you're seen running all over God's creation with this beautiful creature here."

Luke didn't look at Trotter. He directed his words to Cooper. "I have never told Trotter, nor anyone in Pemrose Key, that I wanted a divorce, not even Lisa. I intended to. Our marriage never had a chance. Lisa's only love was for the bottle, and she seemed dedicated to destroying herself and our relationship. You both knew what she was like."

"I suspected as much, Luke, but I hoped for so much more for you two. I wanted you to have your share of happiness. Until today, I never thought that anyone could ever construe our relationship to be anything other than friendship."

"Today I made a mistake, Cooper. You made that clear."

"Trotter's right, I know my being here could cast you in a bad light, Luke."

"I want you out of here, Cooper, but not for that reason. Do you think I killed Lisa, Trotter?"

"There've been times when I thought you had cause to kill her, Luke. Others may see it that way, too. Think about it. The bomb must have been planted on board the *Captain Hook* before it left Pemrose Key. Think about this, too, I'm your best friend and I just happened to be there to witness it."

Luke peered upward, into the night sky.

It was two a.m. before the trio broke up, Trotter leaving Luke and Cooper to contemplate the 'morrow. The desk clerk was awake as Luke escorted Cooper to the elevator. He seemed surprised to see someone in his lobby and eyed Luke with ill-concealed disdain. Luke couldn't resist throwing him a snappy salute before taking the elevator up with Cooper.

Luke wasn't taking any chances where Cooper was concerned. She was too precious to him. He would see her to her door and make sure she was safely in her room.

"I'll take a rental car to the airport tomorrow, Luke."

"I don't want you to do that, Cooper. I'll take you."

"No, Luke. It can't be that way. You heard Trotter. I feel very strongly about this, so please, don't try to talk me out of it. Besides, I'm sure you'll have your hands full. I wish I could stay and help you, but Trotter's right, my presence would only harm you, so I'll say goodbye now."

Luke put his arms around her and held her close, merely as a friend, for now. "Call me from the airport and let me know you got there."

"I'll call you." Cooper looked up at him with innocent eyes and she gently pulled away from his grasp. "You have to go now, Luke." She closed her door and disappeared from his sight.

He stood there until he heard the lock click on her door. He was tired. It was hard to think straight about the events of the day, but his mind was perfectly clear on one thing, he loved Cooper DeLaney with all his being.

27

The seldom-closed, heavy draperies were pulled snugly across the windows. Luke swatted at his alarm clock, knocking it off the nightstand. The annoying bell kept ringing. He groped in the dark, feeling around on the floor for it. The numbers on the Baby Ben glowed—eight o'clock. He'd gone to bed around three a.m., but he couldn't sleep. Not until an hour ago had he finally closed his eyes and dozed off.

The ringing was persistent. It wasn't the alarm clock, he realized, raising himself to a sitting position. It must be the doorbell. His head felt thick and fuzzy, "Who is it?" he called out. There was no response. He thought of Cooper. She would already be on her way to the airport. Ring...ring...ring. "Alright, alright...I'm coming."

Luke retrieved a bathrobe from a chair and shoved his arms into it. When he opened the door, he was face to face with Ben Gravlee and two other men. One wore a Coast Guard uniform, the other, a plain brown dress suit.

Luke didn't try to conceal his surprise at being visited by this threesome at such an early hour.

"I know you're surprised to see us, Luke, but these gentlemen just want to ask you a few questions about your wife. Can we come in?" The sheriff was almost apologetic.

"Sure, come on in. I'll put a pot of coffee on if you'll just give me a minute. Have a seat and I'll be right back." Luke was nervous. He fumbled in the kitchen with the coffee pot. He could hear the men talking in the living room, but he couldn't hear what they were saying. In a horrifying rush, everything Trotter had said last night came back to him. He remembered the accusations that Trotter said might be likely; the implication of Cooper; the fact that they had been seen around town together this week. He felt a knot in his gut.

While the coffee brewed, he dashed into the bedroom and threw on a pair of Levis and a sweatshirt. When the coffee was done, he put the pot and four mugs on a tray and carried it into the living room. The men helped themselves. The two strangers were introduced to Luke as Mario Dios, an investigator for the Coast Guard, and Jackson Cummings, an agent for the FBI in Pensacola.

"Mr. Callaway, we just have a few questions for you. We'd appreciate it if you would cooperate in helping us determine what might have happened aboard the *Captain Hook*." Jackson Cummings slowly stirred his coffee with a spoon. Round and round and round he stirred.

"I'll assist you in whatever way I can, gentlemen. What would you like to know?"

"Do you know anyone who would have had any reason to kill your wife?"

"No, I don't."

"Did you know this Scranton Peabody, the fellow who owned the boat?"

"No, I didn't. I vaguely remember hearing his name as a kid before Mamie bought his place, but to the best of my knowledge, I've never met him."

"And you don't recall seeing him around Pemrose Key since you got back from Vietnam?"

"No, sir, I do not. If I did, I didn't know who he was."

"When is the last time you saw your wife, Mr. Callaway?"

"I saw her Monday."

"Monday?"

"Yessir."

"Monday...and that was the last you saw of her?"

"That's right."

"Did you have a conversation with her on that day."

"I did."

"And what did you discuss?"

"Small talk, mostly."

"I guess she told you she was taking a trip aboard Mr. Peabody's yacht, right?"

Luke hesitated and repositioned himself in his chair. "No, she didn't."

"You're wife left town for several days and she didn't tell you she was going?"

"I'm afraid that's right, Mr. Cummings. She didn't tell me she was going."

"And you didn't report her missing? Did you know at all where she was? Did you even wonder? Weren't you worried about your wife, Mr. Callaway?"

Luke stood and walked to the glass doors. It was evident the direction this conversation was taking did not make him look good.

Mr. Cummings waited.

"Mr. Cummings, my wife frequently strayed. No, I wasn't worried about her in the sense you are implying, I knew where she was. That is, I knew her general whereabouts. I saw her Monday afternoon boarding the *Captain Hook*. I saw a man who might have been Scranton Peabody, but I don't know for a fact that it was him."

"Did you have words with her when you saw her, Mr. Callaway?"

"No, I didn't. I don't suppose she even knew I saw her."

"Well, you said you spoke with her on Monday. Was that before you saw her at the marina?"

"Yes, it was. It was that morning."

"Did you have words with each other? Did you have an argument? Is there anything you can remember that might have compelled her to leave without telling you?"

Luke was exasperated. This was not going well. How could his marriage be explained to anyone who thought on a rational level. Everything, from the first moment he met Lisa to the day she died, everything about their relationship, was beyond the comprehension level of the normal person.

Before Luke could answer, Mr. Cummings fired away, "Do you know a Miss Cooper DeLaney, Mr. Callaway?"

Luke fought the lump in his throat. "She's a friend, but there is no reason to involve her in any of this."

"I'm afraid she may already be involved, Mr. Callaway. Maybe you and Miss DeLaney are just friends, like you say, but let's suppose that your wife thought otherwise. That would be possible, wouldn't it? A lot of wives are jealous. Some even go to extremes because of jealousy. Say, for example, your wife was real jealous of you and this Miss DeLaney's, uh, 'friendship.' If she were an irrational person, she might even try to harm herself, to get your attention, or to end it all if she thought there was no hope for your marriage. That does happen from time to time, now, Mr. Callaway.

"Don't you think it's possible that your wife may have boarded the Captain Hook with explosives loaded in her bag, and the determination to end her young life in a dramatic way? Does that seem at all likely to you?"

Luke was amazed. Did they actually believe Lisa had done this? As Luke stood there absorbing what Jackson Cummings had just said, the idea began to intrigue him. How fascinating that before implicating him, these men would think Lisa had killed herself. It was preposterous, but who was he to argue with them? The only other suspect might be himself, as Trotter had warned him, unless they knew about the activities of Scranton Peabody's company. That could likely have placed Scranton in the position of being a target for foul play. There could be many implications there, but Luke wasn't going to be the one to inform them. Jackson Cummings was with the FBI. Certainly it could be assumed that the news of Joe Lianoho's investigation had reached as far as Pensacola.

"We're exploring the possibility of murder, but some of our strongest evidence suggests a suicide by your wife."

The telephone rang out shrilly.

"May I?" Mr. Cummings reached for the phone without waiting for a reply. "Hello? ...Sure, he's right here. May I tell him who's calling? ...No, this is not Trotter. Hold on just a minute, Miss DeLaney, he's right here." Jackson Cummings looked at Luke from beneath lowered eyebrows as he handed him the phone. "It's, ah-h-h...a Miss DeLaney."

The implication intended was not lost on Luke. "Cooper...No, everything is okay...there are just some people here talking to me about Lisa. You got to the airport okay...That's good...I'll talk to you later...Have a good trip." He cut it short.

Now it was the Coast Guard's turn. The man called Mario Dios had not spoken until now.

"Did your wife have any knowledge of explosive devices, Mr. Callaway, as far as you know?"

"I would say no, Mr. Dios, Lisa certainly didn't have any knowledge of explosives."

"Do you know anything about explosives? I understand you returned from Vietnam less than a year ago. What were your responsibilities while there, Mr. Callaway?"

"I was involved in Special Forces. What I did remains classified information. I'm not at liberty to tell you, Mr. Dios. There's still a war going on. I'm sure you can appreciate that."

"Of course."

"Well, we will keep you informed, Mr. Callaway. I'm sure you are as anxious as we are to get to the bottom of this. Our investigation will continue, and we'll let you know what we learn." Mr. Cummings led the way as the three men filed out the door.

Ben Gravlee was apologetic, "Sorry we had to wake you, Luke. See you later."

The Coast Guard said nothing.

Mr. Cummings had a parting shot, "Oh, yeah, our condolences to you."

When they left, Luke put in a call for Joe Lianoho. He had to tell him what he had found out this week at Baseline and at Cole's Bayou yesterday. He had to tell him about Lisa, and there was still that newspaper photo he'd found at the Los Angeles airport.

Joe Lianoho was out of the country. Luke left his name, and was told he would be contacted by someone soon, but he had the feeling he was being put off.

28

The month of August, 1969, brought to Pemrose Key the usual sweltering heat of August days. The relentless southern sun had seemingly dissipated the Gulf breezes in its wake, leaving the panhandle to survive the sultry days and feverish nights sluggishly, with no sign of relief. The torrid heat created a general apathy amongst the townspeople, and seemingly everyone did only what was necessary to get by. Tourism was down, fishing was poor, and the only excitement in town was that generated by the establishment of a new boat manufacturing plant on the outskirts of Pemrose Key. The old Seafarer plant at Mango Junction had been refurbished and reopened under the name Windward Boats.

The formation of Windward Boats was the realization of Luke's dream, finally made possible by his share of the proceeds from the sale of Callaway Construction.

It was six months since Lisa had been laid to rest. With the summer heat, the investigation of her death had virtually come to a halt, as had the investigations of Toby's and Perky's murders. Nothing concrete had been determined, and no suspects had been named. An indifference evolved with the passage of time. People seemed to want to put the unpleasantness behind them. The murders were a blemish on the previously unsullied complexion of Pemrose Key and could ultimately affect their valued tourist trade. Scranton Peabody's body had never been recovered, but no one seemed to care. No more murders had occurred, and the general consensus was that it was best to just let sleeping dogs lie. Once again, greed would prevail.

Since Lisa's death, Luke's only communication with the FBI had been his visit from Jackson Cummings. Joe Lianoho had been consistently unavailable whenever Luke had tried to reach him. Luke had not been formally dismissed from his responsibilities, but since he was no longer Thomas Logan's son-in-law and Cole's Bayou seemed even more inaccessible to him now, he assumed they no longer deemed him to be of value to their cause. Whether they needed him or not, he would continue with his own investigation, as a personal quest. He heard that acquaintances of Scranton's had been interrogated, but nothing more had come of that, and he discovered that Red Dawn Manufacturing continued to operate, providing weapons parts for the United States government, based on the premise that Scranton Peabody would someday return.

In spite of his fears, Luke had heard little from Edna. She had received the news of Lisa's death very calmly and unemotionally. He had prepared himself for her to pounce. He figured there would be lots of wailing and gnashing of teeth and accusations made, but amazingly, nothing of the sort had happened.

The funeral had produced a sizable, and greatly disproportionate, turnout. Heavy attendance on the Callaway side, a mere handful on the Logan side. A scarcity of sincere sorrow was prevalent on both sides. A few crocodile tears were shed. A meager few Callaway acquaintances had ever met Lisa. Duties prevented Thomas Logan from returning for his own daughter's funeral. Luke received a telegram from him, which he read with disgust. Logan explained that, regrettably, he would not be there. There was a war going on, he declared, and much as he had loved his little girl, there was nothing he could do for her now. However, he wanted Luke to be assured he shared his sorrow and grief and would visit Pemrose Key and pay respects to his daughter's gravesite as soon as he returned stateside.

Luke got on with his life. Within weeks after Lisa's death he had moved into action, mobilizing his long-laid plans. The availability of the old Seafarer plant and the recruitment of Trotter enabled him to smoothly implement the establishment of Windward Boats. The summer heatwave had enticed Trotter to accept Luke's offer. The heat was too sweltering for tourists to be inclined to spend a day at sea aboard a fishing boat. With business down, Luke's offer came at a most opportune time. Luke wished he could also have the benefit of his father's business expertise. He could use his help, too, but Ryan had agreed to stay on for at least a year at Callaway Construction to assist in the transition of the transference of power. Luke didn't know how Ryan would react to such a proposal, but he played around with the idea. He would keep it in the back of his mind and hope that his father didn't pick up the five year option.

Luke's days and nights were filled with plans for the Ariadne. The Ariadne—My Dream. She had long been his dream, and her final design had evolved over many years of visions in his mind. Modifications and improvements to her design had occupied his thoughts during the hellish years of Vietnam. The anticipation of returning to Pemrose Key and realizing that dream had been the impetus for his survival. The Ariadne would do wondrous things in reaching unprecedented heights in performance. Now, given another six months time, he would be ready for full-scale production. The first prototype would be ready sooner, and with all the kinks worked out, he'd have her rolling off the assembly line in no time.

Life was good—as good as it could be for the present, and better than it had been in a long time. Time, brief as it had been, had done much to heal the wounds of his devastating marriage to Lisa. He kept the condominium at Pemrose Pinnacle, but he bought the *Sea Spirit,* the boat Trotter had once told him about, and moved aboard. He docked her at Oyster Bay, inside the U on the pier opposite Trotter and the *Shady Lady.* He rarely returned to the condo at Pemrose Pinnacle, spending most of his nights on the water, sleeping aboard the little thirty-six footer, and taking his meals there. This was now home, much more so than Pemrose Pinnacle. This reconnection with life on the water brought him a degree of peace.

The images of the holocaust of Vietnam were subsiding, but there was one other thing that constantly nagged at him. For all the fulfillment of his longed-for dreams, the one he longed for the most had yet to be realized, and in all likelihood, might never be. The absence of Cooper left an emptiness in his life. Only Cooper could complete his world, but she remained adamant that they shouldn't see each other. The one moment of passion, when he had been so inept at concealing his feelings, had been on the very day Lisa had been killed. Such bad timing on his part had left Cooper with unappeasable guilt. From time to time Luke received a card from her, dashed off between her trips from one side of the globe to the other. She was keeping herself busy, she said. When not working, she was traveling, trying to see as much of the world as she could.

For now, the Ariadne served to occupy his mind, and his passion for the boat and her forthcoming inception was able to displace, to a degree, the emptiness that possessed him during the long, still nights as he lay awake in his berth, contemplating his need for something more. The emptiness borne of the more needful part of his soul, that which required a reciprocal love from another human being, plagued his days and tormented his nights. The two loves of his life were vastly different, but he needed them both, Cooper and the Ariadne. Without one or the other, his life was not complete. Cooper alone could not even have satisfied him had the Ariadne never been conceived. He had learned his lesson. He knew that with Cooper, he could find happiness, but not the total inner peace that always seemed just beyond his grasp. Now, he knew that even with the Ariadne, without Cooper he could never be content. His ultimate aspiration was to have both of them in his life.

One day in the middle of August, Luke had worked himself to near exhaustion. He was driven to meet his production deadline and the goals he had set for himself. He was a hard taskmaster and would spare himself no slack, putting in twelve and fourteen-hour days or more. As time passed, the more consumed he became with the pursuit of Cooper. The more he thought of her, the harder he pushed himself. He labored endless hours, not only to achieve his goals for the Ariadne, but in an attempt to oust the thoughts and visions of Cooper from his mind.

On this particularly exhausting day he had worked at a furious pace, working out details, tackling production problems, some of which seemed insurmountable at times. He left the plant late, driving the distance between Mango Junction and Oyster Bay, wanting nothing more than to get home and relax aboard the *Sea Spirit*. When he arrived at Oyster Bay, it appeared that every tourist who had invaded Pemrose Key during the heat of August had flocked to Oyster Bay to promenade along the docks and sip a cool tropical beverage while waiting for their name to be called to a table.

Tonight, Luke couldn't abide the throngs of people and their noisy laughter, or the blaring music of the loudspeakers. He decided to take the *Sea Spirit* and anchor out to get a good night's rest. The little *Sea Spirit* slipped through the night, navigating the still waters of the Intracoastal, and the peaceful waters soothed his soul and calmed his overwrought nerves.

He would anchor in a place he knew well. He and Trotter had spent countless nights camping on the beach of the tiny island whose namesake was that of the old deserted Civil War fort, Fort McBain, the only landmark on the island. The island was uninhabited and so geographically small it held in its confines only the remains of the old fort. It lay right beside the mouth of the pass and in days gone by served to protect the shores of Pemrose Key and the surrounding territory and waters. Fort McBain had once been a lookout station for enemy ships attempting to invade the harbor. Stone remnants remained across the island. The pilasters were pocked and weathered and half covered with sand that had washed and blown through many a storm and had piled high against the stone. He had fond memories of his boyhood and playing pirate amongst the ruins with his friends; and of the many nights telling ghost stories and frolicking in the water's edge after dark, trying to stay cool on a hot summer's night; of catching a mess of fish and throwing them in the skillet over an open fire on the beach and going to sleep happy, with a full belly and not a care in the world. How far they had come. Too far to ever go back.

Now, this place was nearly forgotten, save for providing a trysting place for lovers, a romantic hideaway for those boaters consumed with passion—a deserted beach on which to spend a sunny day together.

Luke would spend a restful night here, alone. A slight breeze stirred the waters of the bay—much to his relief. He cast his anchors and cut his engines once he'd readied his boat for the night. He retrieved a cold drink from his ice chest and set up a folding chair in the cockpit. Leaning back comfortably in the chair, he propped his feet up on the railing. It was getting late, but he could unwind best by sitting here, sorting his thoughts and recounting the day's events, absorbing the peacefulness before going to bed.

An hour passed, perhaps, and still he sat in silence, his thoughts embracing his mind. The quiet was broken only by the occasional splash of an unseen mullet jumping, and the water lapping intermittently at the side of the boat as it rocked occasionally in the timid breeze. He had anchored in fairly shallow water in a familiar, protective cove only yards from the beach where he had spent so many nights with Trotter.

Luke heard the voices before he saw the sailboats, two of them, silhouetted in the light of the moon on the far side of the narrow island. The masculine voices cut into the still darkness, but not clearly enough for him to decipher the words. When one of the boats lowered its mainsail, Luke quietly retrieved his binoculars from the cabin. He was at an advantage up in the cove. Part of the ruins of the old fort served as a backdrop and concealed his position from view. He heard the low whir of a trolling motor. Aided by the binoculars, he could see the profile of a dinghy skimming across the water, motoring away from one of the boats towards the beach.

Luke removed his outer garments and Docksides and slipped on a pair of water shoes. He strapped a dagger around his calf, stepped over the transom to the swim platform, and quietly lowered himself into the water. He skimmed through the water, barely causing a ripple as he made his way to the beach.

Luckily, the moon was bright enough tonight to guide him as he moved stealthily across the island, staying close to the ruins and darting between sand dunes and rocks. When he came to open beach area, he had gone as far as he could without exposing himself to the visitors. It was far enough. Luke hid behind a section of brick and stone and had a good view of the little dinghy, which was now beached on shore. No one was in the boat. He lay still, afraid to move, fearful that his own breathing might give him away. He could hear voices out on the sailboats more clearly now; both boats had lowered their sails. Who had been in the dinghy, and where had they gone? It seemed like hours that he lay there, not moving a muscle and determined to know what was going on. Finally, two figures appeared from some undetermined point along the shore and headed towards the little boat, struggling with a crate-like object they carried between them. He watched them lower the cumbersome item into the dinghy and walk back in the direction they had just come from before suddenly disappearing. Luke rubbed his eyes and squinted, trying to focus better in the dark. Still, he could not see where they had gone. He crouched there, waiting, trying to hear what was being said aboard the two sailboats. There was no shouting or loud voices, merely what seemed to be casual conversation. He still couldn't make out the words. After about five minutes, the two men on the beach reappeared, loaded down with another crate, which they lowered into the little boat. Just as before, they turned and walked a short distance before disappearing again.

Luke counted a total of three trips to and from the little boat. When they were done, they pushed the boat off and motored back out to the dark side of the nearest sailboat. Though Luke couldn't see, he heard what sounded like cargo being transferred from one boat to another. After awhile the dinghy headed back for the beach and the entire process was repeated.

There were two sailboats and Luke deduced they were both taking on cargo, in which case this procedure would likely go on for the remainder of the night. He had a heavy day tomorrow, and it was nearly two a.m. He might as well get back and get a little sleep, unless he wished to expose himself and have a confrontation with these fellows. He did not believe this would be the wisest or healthiest thing to do at this time, particularly since he was outnumbered. He needed to come back when these guys weren't hanging around, after the dust had settled, and do some investigating on his own. He knew the cove side of the island well, and he knew the tunnels and corridors of Ft. McBain were extensive, but he had not spent a great deal of time on the side of the island where the boats were now anchored. He couldn't fathom where the cargo was coming from, unless there was an entrance he didn't know about.

When Luke shifted his weight to turn away from the wall, a loose brick tumbled noisily across the stonework and fell to the ground with a thud. He instantly crouched lower and when a beam of light scanned the spot where he had stood only moments before, he knew they had heard. His position was precarious, balanced as he was on the pile of brick and stone that was stacked against the remains of the wall. In order to regain his footing he would have to stand partially and risk being seen, but if he didn't do something soon, he would likely dislodge more bricks, and possibly slip and fall. His heart raced as he stood. The beam darted dangerously close and he didn't know if he'd been caught in their light. The beam crisscrossed the wall once more, apparently still seeking the source of the noise. Luke stayed low, scarcely breathing. Finally, perhaps satisfied nothing was there save for maybe a wild critter, they extinguished the light and turned their attention back to their task.

Luke had an unpleasant vision of what these strangers would have done to him had they caught him. Back aboard the boat, he couldn't sleep. He checked frequently to see if the boats were still there. They were, all night long. Finally, somewhere around daybreak, he watched the boats sail away in the morning light.

As soon as the boats were specks on the horizon, Luke started his engines, pulled anchor, and returned to Oyster Bay. By six a.m., after a quick shower and shave, he was at work.

Luke's day was full, and he was too busy to think about how tired he was, but when day was done he headed straight for Oyster Bay.

Aboard the *Sea Spirit*, Luke went to bed without giving any thought to dinner or the events of the day, or the night before. He was asleep within minutes of hitting his bunk, and the only thoughts that entered his mind in those few waking moments before he drifted off to sleep were visions of Cooper.

Several days passed, and Luke had given much thought to how he should approach the far side of Ft. McBain. He felt certain that what he had seen was relevant to the FBI's investigation, and he was sure that it was something somebody didn't want him to know anything about.

Luke decided to tell Trotter what he had witnessed. Typical for Trotter, he didn't jump to conclusions. He was a lot like Luke in that he had to see for himself, so the two of them laid their plans. They decided to go back out to the island that night.

Luke and Trotter left Oyster Bay at midnight, headed for Ft. McBain aboard the *Shady Lady*. They bypassed the cove, going directly to the far side of the island. There was no full moon tonight. When the island was in sight they slowed their pace, rigged some lighting, and directed the beams to the shore. Scanning the shore revealed nothing immediately. They concentrated their efforts on the area where Luke had seen the dinghy, but saw nothing. Trotter adjusted his beam, accidentally shifting it to the right of the beach. It skimmed across the water of the bay and out to the Gulf, catching in it's light the bright white of a sail. In one swift instant, the revving of a powerful engine was heard. From nearby, a spotlight mightier than the *Shady Lady's* was directed towards the *Lady*. A powerful, blinding light rushing towards them, illuminating the *Shady Lady*—lighting the night that surrounded her, and making her vulnerable. Vicious sounding engines revved on a high powered boat as it tore across the water towards them, like a demon from the deep

"Let's get the hell out of here!" Trotter shouted. He had the *Lady* in gear and headed across the bay before the speeding boat could travel the distance. All they could see was the blinding light, but it could only be a high-powered speedboat in such hot pursuit and it could easily overtake them.

Trotter cut all their navigation lights, found the main channel and headed for the Pass. They figured the open waters of the Gulf would be the safest, biggest place to hide and they didn't want to get trapped in the channel or lure the speedboat back to Oyster Bay. The plan worked. It didn't seem they were being followed. Trotter headed her out towards the open sea, circumventing the sailboats. Once they were a safe distance out from the Pass, Trotter turned the *Lady* back towards the shore and worked his way along the beach towards the next closest pass, which was in Alabama waters.

"Did you get a look at them?" Trotter shouted above the roar of the engines.

"Couldn't see them. I don't know how you managed to get us out of there, but I'm sure grateful to you." Luke was frustrated with the end their mission had met, but he experienced the familiar rush over being back in action again.

"Do you think they recognized us, Luke?"

"They did if it was somebody we know."

"How could we ever determine that?"

"They'll let us know."

Luke decided to back off his investigation during the week that followed. There was apparently too much activity surrounding the island at this time, and there was much to do at Windward Boats.

Exactly one week from the night they had the *light* encounter, Luke rose at dawn to get an early start at the plant. As he was going out to the parking lot of the marina, he saw Trotter on the pier by the *Shady Lady*. Luke knew he would see him shortly at work, but something about Trotter's bearing compelled him to veer from the direction of the parking lot and stop by the *Shady Lady's* slip.

"What's up, Trotter?" Even before Luke got the words out, he knew there was a problem.

Trotter stood looking down at his boat, holding one of his fuel tank caps in his hand. His expression was one of total devastation. "You said they'd let us know, Luke, and they have...they spiked my fuel with sand."

Luke knew there would be no consoling Trotter until he had revenge on whoever was responsible for wrecking his engines.

To somebody, there was something on that island worth hiding. Luke and Trotter's investigation had turned up nothing, but it had increased Luke's determination to find out what it was all about. Now he had another reason.

With the *Shady Lady* out of commission, Trotter devoted more time than ever to his responsibilities at the plant. There'd been no insurance on the *Lady*, and he didn't have the resources to replace both of her engines. Luke sought to find a way to help, but Trotter was too full of pride to accept monetary assistance. That would be charity. The humility he'd experienced as a child when his mother was forced to repay "charity" she accepted on behalf of her children, had left its mark on Trotter. Nothing came without strings, he maintained. Thus his assertions had precluded any semblance of charity or assistance from Luke, even though Luke tried to convince him he was responsible, since they had been on his mission. Trotter was adamant, he would take care of this himself.

The first prototype was nearing completion, and she was a honey. Luke was on a high. They still hadn't forgotten about Ft. McBain, but with the culmination of the Ariadne drawing nigh, they were forced to put other problems on the back burner for a few weeks.

29

Cooper was coming. She had finally agreed to see Luke, and she was coming for the launching of the first Ariadne.

The first Ariadne would be christened the *Morning Star.* As bright as a star and as fresh as a newborn day—the *Morning Star*—she would fly across the water with the utmost efficiency and the quietest of engines. The interior appointments were soft leathers and rich, highly polished teaks. She was truly a dream, Luke's dream, as was Cooper. Maybe he would have a chance to make both of them a part of his life. Telling Cooper he loved her had become most urgent. Now that she had agreed to come to him, perhaps he could convince her before it was too late—before she found someone else, or tired of his attentions. He must be careful not to scare her away forever. Letting her know how much he truly loved her could have a significant impact on his life, whatever the outcome.

Everything in his life finally seemed to be falling into place. The only thing that could make it more perfect would be Cooper's acceptance and reciprocation of his love. He was as happy as he could ever remember being. He'd been irrational in his feelings for Lisa, and in spite of his strong desire to be with her in the beginning, that underlying current of danger had always been the driving force. He recognized this flaw that had propelled him into marriage, and how he had mistakenly identified those feelings as happiness.

Happiness, then, had eluded him. But that was all in the past. It had taken the tragedy of Lisa's life—and death—to get there, but his own life was now like a rebirth. He had been through much anguish and self-reproach, but had finally come to terms with his feelings of guilt. He'd been given a second chance, a reprieve from the mistakes of his past. This time he'd make the right choices, and try not to screw up his life. The future had bright possibilities and Cooper had the capacity to fill his life with pure joy. He would make her happy. He would cherish her and fill her life with love.

It was Friday. The weekend loomed ahead and with everything at the plant coming together so perfectly, there wasn't much to do. He and Trotter could take the weekend off. It would be a good opportunity to go back out to the island, this time during daylight hours, do a little further snooping. He would take the *Sea Spirit*. They would just poke around, see if they could tell anything from a safe distance. Safe. The concept of the word had been typically foreign to Luke. He had always been cautious, but he'd never shied away from danger. Now he astonished himself at his inclination to avoid a hazardous situation. It was about Cooper. He wasn't sure he wanted to put himself in danger before he had a chance to tell her how he felt. This is what he'd lived for. She was coming, and his entire life lay ahead of him—a life to possibly be shared with her.

Luke had been anxious to get back out to the island, but one thing seemed to have led to another and time got away. Now he chastised himself for his procrastination, but he was determined to do something about it today. With the prospect of Cooper coming, and that one little sentence on that one quickly written postcard: *I'll see you in September, I'll be there for the launching of the Morning Star*, his entire world had changed.

He held the postcard once more in his hand. It was a picture of the Eiffel Tower. It was easy to envision Cooper there, standing beneath the famous edifice amidst a group of friends, laughing and talking, her cheeks aglow and her long, copper colored hair blowing in the summer breeze that caressed Paris. He turned the card over and read the line again, *I'll see you in September. I'll be there for the launching of the Morning Star.*

He put the card in his middle desk drawer, and there, inside the drawer, was the folded piece of newspaper he had stuffed in his pocket when he and Lisa had waited in the Los Angeles airport on their return from Hawaii. He had all but forgotten about it these past months. He unfolded it now and looked at it. It was worn from being folded and unfolded so often when he had first returned from Hawaii. He had stared at it in speculation many times. Months ago he had even contacted the *Washington Post,* and they had given him the name of the Memphis based photographer who had taken the photo. At first Luke thought he might be onto something. He had been successful in reaching the photographer, and although the photographer did not know the names of the people in the photo, he was able to give Luke the name of the organization that had been formed following Martin Luther King's death. With a little digging, Luke had even discovered a contact for the organization. Only two of the seven people in the photograph could be identified. The dead-end finally led Luke to rule as impossible the assumption that had prompted him to pocket the photo in the first place. He folded the bit of newspaper once again and placed it back in the drawer. He started to close the drawer, but instead, he unfolded the paper one more time and stared hard at it. His assumption was preposterous, he knew, but nevertheless, he would send this by mail to Joe Lianoho today. Maybe this would gain him a response from Joe.

Luke jotted a quick note, pulled Joe's business card from his billfold and copied the address on an envelope. He stuffed his note and the folded news page in the envelope and sealed it, then placed the business card in his desk drawer, alongside Cooper's postcard.

After locking his desk, he set off in search of Trotter. On the way out he dropped the envelope in the mail box. The postman would be here any minute now, his secretary informed him.

Trotter was supervising the production line. He was skillfully overseeing some mechanical adjustments to the *Morning Star*. His innate affinity for engines and anything mechanical led him to follow very lovingly and painstakingly Luke's blueprints, and to make necessary suggestions and improvements with Luke's concurrence. The Ariadne line that Windward Boats would build was almost as much a part of Trotter now as it was Luke. Together they were fulfilling their childhood fantasy.

Luke didn't want to interfere with what Trotter was doing. He wouldn't want to slow progress. Instead, he caught Trotter's eye. A one-word exchange was all it took, "Tomorrow?"

Trotter nodded an affirmative and turned back to his work. Luke returned to his office, but before he had a chance to even sit down, the receptionist called him on the intercom. "Mr. Callaway, there are some gentlemen here to see you."

"Thank you, Mrs. Anthony. Send them in."

Luke stood to greet his visitors. He was surprised when Ben Gravlee and Jackson Cummings entered, and he experienced a sense of foreboding. A deputy sheriff, one Maynard Skinner, followed the two and stood in the doorway of Luke's office, resting his right hand on his holster.

Jackson Cummings wore the same plain brown suit he'd worn the last time Luke saw him, the day they declared that Lisa must have been responsible for her own death. After an all around exchange of pleasantries, the insipid Jackson Cummings informed Luke that they no longer believed Lisa had killed herself.

This came as no surprise to Luke. He waited for Jackson Cummings' next words.

"New evidence has come to light, Mr. Callaway."

As he stood before Luke, the man in the plain brown suit pulled a white envelope out of his inside coat pocket. He removed the contents from the envelope and held the piece of paper so that Luke could see the words as he read them aloud. Very poorly typed in red ink, the note proclaimed:

Dear Lucas,

When Cooper arrived this morning, I didn't know what to do anymore. She's so beautiful and you seem so in love with her, the way you used to be with me. I remember our first night together Luke, the night we met. I loved you so from the very beginning, and now this other woman has come into our life. I know you say you're only friends, but I can tell by the way you look at her that she has taken my place in your heart. If you want a divorce, Luke, I'm afraid I can't oblige you. I don't think I could ever let you go, I love you too much. We have to work through this thing with Cooper. We have a love that's worth saving and I could never, ever, let you go. We'll make it work, Luke, I promise. Our good friend, Scranton, has offered to let me go out with him for a few days aboard his yacht, to do some praying and thinking. He's a good man, Luke, as you know, and he wants us to be happy. He's like a father to me. He wants to help both of us. He likes you a lot. He said to let you spend this time with Cooper and that you should let her know there could never be any future for the two of you because you still love me. I know it's true, so I'm giving you this time to get things out of your system and send Cooper back to Chicago. I can't stay around while she's here. I can't face the situation between the two of you, so, I'm off for a few days and when I get back, I want to start fresh, Luke. I'm determined we're going to have a good life together. I can make you happy, you'll see.

I love you My Precious,
Lisa

The signature was the only part of the letter that was handwritten. It appeared to be Lisa's signature.

Jackson Cummings looked blandly at Luke. "Not exactly the words of a woman ready to do herself in, would you say, Mr. Callaway? Looks to me like you had probable cause to do away with your wife."

Luke was stunned. "Where did you get this? Where the hell did you get this letter? I never saw this. Lisa didn't write this."

"Do you recognize her signature, Luke?" Ben Gravlee interjected calmly. "Take a look at it...is that Lisa's signature?"

Luke took the letter in his own hands. He stared at it, horrified. There was no doubt, the signature seemed to be Lisa's—but the words—in the limited conversation Lisa had participated in with Luke—the words didn't sound like something she could begin to string together.

"This is all a lie. Nothing written here is the truth."

"You're under arrest, Luke, for the murder of your wife, Lisa Callaway, the murder of the hired captain of the Captain Hook, Johnny Lowe, the murder of the deckhand, Bruce Stenholme, and for the unrelated murder of Toby Washington."

Luke was numb when they placed the handcuffs on his wrists. His mind went blank.

The next few days were a blur as he was poked and prodded and questioned and fingerprinted. Slowly, his fury began to surface. His confinement and his inability to control what was happening in his life brought with them a recurrence of the nightmares of Vietnam. There were explosions, always explosions, that woke him in the night. And water—a great body of water, and fragments of a boat and body parts, and he would be in the middle of it all—and all the pieces would rain down on his head and he would awaken, his mind tortured and his body drenched with sweat. The nightmares were particularly hellish whenever he thought of Cooper. He'd never held her close and told her he loved her, and now that possibility had slipped from his grasp forever. What could he tell her now? What could he offer her if he were found guilty?

Meg and Ryan spent every minute that was allowed visiting Luke at the jail.

'We'll get you out of here, honey...soon, too." For once the stress showed on Meg's face. Her voice wavered, and Luke knew she cried for her son every time she left him.

His father had expressed great difficulty in dealing with the fury he encountered over the injustice. Luke feared for Ryan's health, as he knew Meg did. Her worry for Ryan served to double her stress. He just wasn't handling this well at all. He was used to being in control. He'd raised a fine, honest boy...a war hero already, and at such an early age...had fought for his country...had been commended for his actions. This wasn't supposed to happen in America, where generations of Callaways had fought for their country, himself in World War II and his father in World War I. His grandfather had even fought in the Spanish-American War. Luke had been arrested and charged with murder, and there wasn't a damn thing Ryan had been able to do about it. This wasn't fair. Where was justice? Was it merely a word?

Luke bore the weight of tremendous guilt—guilt for the shame and pain he'd brought upon his family. The guilt kindled his fury at himself. His passion had been his first sin. Driven by lust, he had plunged head-on into a perilous situation by agreeing to marry Lisa. His lust had won over the power of his sensibilities. Now, he found no peace, and the inability to change things tortured his mind. He'd been callous about Lisa's death, even relieved by it. His reaction had been honest, but it was coming back to haunt him.

Luke's nightmares culminated with visions of a casket lying on the grass, partially shrouded in a mist, like that in Cole's Bayou— like a sub-tropical haze. As he drew closer to the casket, the mist would part so that he had a clear vision of its contents.

He saw himself lying there, upon a sheet of white satin stained with blood. He was dressed in a navy pinstripe suit, white oxford cloth shirt and red, paisley print tie. Every detail was perfectly clear, even down to the starched white handkerchief that peeked out of his breast pocket enough to reveal the tiny, neatly embroidered initials in one corner: LRC—Lucas Ryan Callaway. His eyes were not closed. They were wide open, as Perky Bittle's had been, but they were glassy, like shiny marbles gazing vacantly at the dark, gray sky. Not unlike other eyes he had seen before, not unlike the eyes of Teddy, the boy Luke had held in his arms as he died in the jungle of Vietnam—the boy who had once saved Luke's life. If Luke were convicted of any of the murders, he would be put to death. He, too, would be dead, like Teddy, and Perky and Stephen and Lisa.

Luke stared in the mirror at an image he barely recognized as his own. He was reminded of an earlier time when his youthful eyes glimpsed the savage reflection of a man full-grown. A man who roamed the jungles of Vietnam alone, fulfilling a mission with a single purpose, detached from all feeling and emotion. He'd been shocked, then, by the image of his own vanishing youth.

He wrote Cooper, then he tore the letter up. He had to try and forget her. She was out of his life forever.

When Meg and Ryan visited, he saw the anguish in their faces at his changed appearance. They beheld a stranger, as he himself did—hollow cheeks, deep dark circles beneath veiled eyes set in an expressionless face, wavy blonde hair now as closely cropped as a recruit, or a convict. He'd requested the cut himself, hoping to relieve some of the sweltering heat in the jail, now the style emphasized the hollowness of his cheeks.

Ryan was strangely subdued. He, too, was at a loss. For all his influence, all his powerful connections, and all his money, there was nothing he could do to help his only son. Luke suspected Meg must have used her persuasive powers to elicit a promise from Ryan not to react in anger in Luke's presence, so as to not increase Luke's burden. They both tried to conceal the strain they felt, and in the face of their stoicism, Luke could not reveal the deep love and devotion he felt for them. The inner battle he was waging with his own emotions conflicted with his ability to express anything at all. To reveal himself would cause him to experience a depth of feeling he could ill afford. The wall had been erected, but teetered fragilely on the verge of collapse. His very survival depended upon the strength of that wall.

"We're gonna' get you out of here, boy. Don't you worry, it won't be long. They've set your preliminary hearing for next Wednesday. Hopefully the judge will set bond, and we'll have you out of here in a flash."

Luke nodded, "That's fine, Dad." He wasn't convinced.

Today was the big day. Luke's mother went to the condo he still maintained at Pemrose Pinnacle and selected her favorite suit for him to wear. A navy blue pinstripe with white oxford cloth shirt and red, paisley-print tie. She also saw to it that he had a fresh white handkerchief for his breast pocket. When she visited him this last time before the preliminary hearing, he noticed that she had taken one of his handkerchiefs for herself. She held it tightly in her hand, intertwined around her index finger, recognizable to him by the tiny, black stitched initials that peeked out from one end of her tightly clutched palm. Clutching the handkerchief stilled the fingers that would characteristically be drumming away at a time like this.

Meg's determination to maintain a modicum of grace and dignity tugged hard at Luke's heart—there was a crack in that wall he had erected. She was the real love of his life, and that she had to be put through this nearly killed him.

"Your father didn't come, Luke. He wanted to, but he couldn't."

"He's disappointed in me, I know, and I understand. I'm sorry for hurting you and Dad. It's too late to say so, but I should have listened to you. If I could only go back to that day you tried to tell me. I've let you down." Pieces of the wall began to fall away, and Luke experienced a terrible ache in his chest.

Luke started to say more, but before he could speak, a guard held the door open and Ryan Callaway entered the room. Ryan briefly cast his eyes downward, as though ashamed for not being there sooner. He slowly crossed the room to take his place beside his wife. His pain and his shame was more than Luke could bear.

Everything about Ryan's bearing was out of character. He looked old and defeated, and his voice strained when he spoke. "If God had blessed me with many sons, my only hope would be that they could all be as fine as you. You've fulfilled all the dreams a father could ever have for a son. You've never given your mother and me a moment's trouble, Luke. If only my father could have been as proud of me."

Meg placed one hand over the top of Ryan's and held it there. She closed her eyes prayerfully, touched her fingertips to her lips and blew her son a kiss.

A guard came and asked Meg and Ryan to leave. Luke had to get dressed for the hearing.

With a whisper and a prayer, Luke entered the courtroom, handcuffed and flanked by two sheriff's deputies.

Ryan had hired the best legal minds money could buy, over Luke's protests. Luke's means were considerably more modest than his father's after sinking a goodly portion of his funds into Windward Boats. He wanted to hire a local attorney, one he could afford, but in the end, Ryan had his way. He'd gone outside Escambia County, all the way to Washington, D.C. Martin Daugherty and Patrick Mullican were tops in their field. They sat together now, on the far side of Judge Peyton Fuller's courtroom, at a table with notepads and books piled before them and one empty chair that was reserved for Luke. The deputies shepherded Luke across the room to his seat beside Daugherty and positioned themselves nearby.

For Daugherty and Mullican to be such keen legal minds, Luke questioned the scarcity of their meetings with him, and it was with some trepidation that he entrusted his life to them. He had met with the two of them only twice, and the first meeting had seemed to Luke to be merely a determination of whether they wanted to take on his case. The third meeting had been with Patrick Mullican alone, and had been a fact-collecting mission. It was a lengthy meeting, and Luke had been encouraged to bare his soul, to hold nothing back. At the conclusion of that particular meeting, his attorney admonished him severely and threatened to quit when Luke failed to tell him about the visit to Red Dawn Manufacturing, and being shot at by the black sedan.

How had they found out about that? Luke was angry and had to struggle to maintain self control when he was informed that Martin

Daugherty was on his way back from Chicago that very moment, where he had spent the previous day interviewing Cooper DeLaney.

Okay, so he should've told them about that, but the hard part was explaining the reason for going to Red Dawn Manufacturing in the first place. Not even to his attorneys could he betray the confidence entrusted him by Joe Lianoho. He would not reveal information regarding the suspected illegal weapons activity, or his involvement with the FBI investigation. In Luke's estimation that would be tantamount to treason, and to do so might blow the entire investigation. There might be something Joe could do if Luke could get in touch with him, but perhaps Joe assumed him to be guilty of killing Lisa.

As the prosecutors presented the evidence in Judge Peyton Fuller's courtroom, it was revealed that traces of explosives material had been found in Lisa's unlocked car. This discovery led to the initial assumption that she had committed suicide. Actually, anyone could have planted that evidence there. It was an unfailing habit of Lisa's to leave her car unlocked and the keys under the mat, but now, Luke was the primary suspect responsible for the evidence found in Lisa's car.

Luke took the witness stand to answer the charges against him.

The prosecutor was a large man, taller, and weighing at least sixty or seventy pounds more than Luke. His bald head was so shiny it appeared to be polished. He had ruddy red cheeks, no eyebrows and beady little eyes that looked like glassy buttons stuck in the middle of a high forehead. Apparently aware of the threatening effect his size had on most people, he used it to his advantage and pounded away unmercifully.

"Luke, you are a Vietnam veteran, is that correct?"

"That's correct."

"What was your rank when you completed your last tour of duty?"

"Captain."

"You were in Special Forces, correct?"

They had done their homework, but he wouldn't let this guy intimidate him.

"I was."

"You worked with the CIA?"

"I did."

"And what were your responsibilities in Vietnam?"

Luke cringed, inwardly. "I was a member of Special Tactical Forces."

"We've established that fact. WHAT did you specialize in, Mr. Callaway?"

"I can't answer that. It's classified information."

"Suppose I answer that for you? The United States Marine Corps has cooperated splendidly with our investigation, Mr. Callaway. They take a dim view of decorated ex-Marines applying those skills which the Corps taught them, in order to commit murder in civilian life."

"Objection, Your Honor." Mullican now justified his existence.

"Sustained."

"Mr. Callaway, you were the last to see Toby Washington alive. Where did you see him?"

"I don't know that I was the last to see him alive. I drove him to one of the cabins by his mother's restaurant a couple of weeks before it was blown up. That was the last I saw of him."

"It's a well established fact in Pemrose Key that you retrieved Toby Washington's body from Pemrose Bay, did you not?"

"I retrieved a body from Pemrose Bay. I was later told that it was Toby Washington. Others were with me." Luke looked towards Peyton, but Peyton was too busy penciling notes on a pad to notice.

"How was he killed, Mr. Callaway?" The man was relentless in his quest for the "truth."

"In the explosion of that cabin, I assume."

"And how was your wife, Lisa Callaway, killed?"

"In an explosion...aboard a boat."

"I have here a document I would like for you to examine. It is official, you can rest assured. What does it say you did in Vietnam, Mr. Callaway?"

Luke felt more defeated than he had in his entire life.

"I specialized in demolitions." It was all there before him, in black and white. "I targeted specific enemy locations and saw to it they were obliterated."

"And in what manner were those demolitions executed, Mr. Callaway?"

"Through the use of explosives."

"In other words, Mr. Callaway, your job demanded that you kill, in cold blood, through the expert use of explosives."

"Objection!"

"Overruled!" True to his position, Peyton remained impartial, friendship be damned.

If sufficient evidence was found against Luke, he would have to go to trial before a higher court.

Luke looked out at the familiar faces that filled the courtroom. Many were there, he knew, to lend support. Many others were curiosity seekers, there merely to witness the bloodshed, the mangling of the gladiator, the fall of the ruling class. They were the ones who emitted an audible gasp that rippled through Judge Fuller's courtroom, the ones who were titillated by his answer, and longed for excitement in Pemrose Key.

"Quiet!" Judge Fuller pounded his gavel. "There will be silence in this courtroom or all spectators will be removed at once!"

Luke was relieved when Peyton adjourned the proceedings until Thursday morning. As a friend of Luke's, Peyton had refused to recuse himself as Judge based on the fact that he claimed he knew just about everybody in Pemrose Key. He wouldn't be sitting on the bench if he recused himself of every case in which he was acquainted with somebody involved.

The advent of the proceedings on Thursday morning did not bring a change-in-tide as Luke had hoped. Lisa's letter that had incarcerated Luke was read aloud, providing a case for probable cause, and Luke was questioned in-depth about his relationship with Cooper. His discomfort was immense. Even his parents had not known about Cooper, though technically, there was nothing to know. His passion for Cooper remained locked in his heart. In spite of the prosecutor's badgering, Luke was able to honestly portray his relationship with Cooper in a positive light, with her reputation remaining intact. How could anything about Cooper come across as less than good and pure? She had never allowed whatever was between them to progress beyond friendship, and she had been genuinely happy for Luke when she first learned of his marriage to Lisa. She was a good person. Beyond Luke's one indiscretion, he had been careful to conceal his love from her. Although she hadn't known the nature of his intentions, they had been completely honorable, and not merely lustful. Very simply, he loved her.

Scotty Dillard was the first witness called to the stand. In a strange way, he seemed proud to bear the patch over one eye. It made him look less baby-faced and seemed to bolster his confidence, but Luke was consumed with guilt knowing that he had been the one responsible for the loss of Scotty's eye.

Scotty recounted the day of the boating incident, the day he took Luke and Cooper out to Cole's Bayou, the day Lisa had been killed. He only told the truth. With the prosecutor's talons in him, everything he said made Luke look guilty and refuted Luke's description of his relationship with Cooper. Luke's efforts to illustrate a merely platonic relationship were instantly nullified.

Poor Scotty, his swagger was a bit comical and he seemed to have no idea how damaging his testimony was to Luke. He had seen Luke kiss Cooper, and Scotty couldn't lie under the intense examination of this axe-man. Luke didn't expect him to. Luke had foolishly exhibited his passion. In spite of his immediate regret at having done so, the tenderness of that kiss had lingered, and never could he have imagined that his regret would be this profound. That one magical moment had now been examined and dissected in public; sullied, like so much dirty laundry, allowing the entire courtroom to draw a false conclusion about Luke's relationship with Cooper.

From his lofty position, Peyton seemed to listen with relish as the prosecutors extracted non-related particulars from Scotty. They twisted and turned everything Luke said into a fabrication, painting an image of a torrid affair between Luke and Cooper, attempting to taint Cooper's reputation.

Luke was incensed and to his surprise and great chagrin, the next witness to be called was the hotel desk clerk who had been on duty the night of Lisa's death. The very same desk clerk Luke had disturbed in the wee hours of the morning. A few hours later, the morning paper had featured the headline: PROMINENT PEMROSE KEY FAMILY MEMBER KILLED. The article began, *Wife of Decorated War Hero Dies in Mysterious Explosion in Gulf Aboard the Captain Hook*. It was accompanied by a picture of Lisa, and her husband, Lucas Callaway.

Luke remembered the little desk clerk's annoyance at being disturbed that night. Now, relishing the limelight, the unpleasant little man seemed delighted to inform the court that on the very day of Mrs. Callaway's death, Mr. Callaway had come calling on the beautiful lady, Miss Cooper DeLaney, who had been a registered guest of the hotel since early in the week. Miss DeLaney abruptly canceled the remainder of her stay and departed hastily the morning that headline appeared.

Toby's name wasn't mentioned on Thursday. Luke was curious as to how they planned on connecting him to Toby's murder, but he wasn't at all anxious to find out.

On Friday, Mamie appeared in the courtroom for the first time since the beginning of Luke's preliminary hearing. Luke knew this would be a painful day for her. Doc Bauchet, ever the attentive doctor, was at Mamie's side. Poor Mamie, she would have to relive it all again.

Doc Bauchet was called to the witness stand first. He was asked to tell the story of the day Luke showed up on his doorstep, cradling a badly wounded Toby in his arms. Luke avoided looking Mamie's way, ashamed that he had concealed this information from her.

Luke listened as Doc told of the care he had given Toby, and of the day Luke came and took him away against Doc's advice. The questions the prosecutor asked were convoluted, and he twisted Doc's answers and portrayed Luke as the villain. He intimated that Luke had savagely done away with Toby, and implied that in very short order he would reveal the motive for Luke's actions.

In recounting his time spent with Toby, Doc Bauchet broke down and sobbed. He said he felt God had presented him with that opportunity, that time alone with Toby, to reveal some truths to him. The opportunity had been lost, however, because of a pledge he had made long ago. He had now been released of that pledge, and in memory of Toby, Mamie had agreed, finally, to allow him to reveal the identity of Toby's father.

For the next half hour the court was held spellbound as Doc gave a running commentary. The story that unfolded before the silent crowd was a most remarkable accounting of Doc's life. In an unprecedented action the judge allowed the story to be told, and even the prosecutors did not object.

Many years ago, as a young man in medical school in his hometown of New Orleans, Doc had been given an internship at a hospital in Mobile, Alabama. While there, he took a room at a nearby boarding house. A serious student intent on his studies, he had never had time in his life for romance or boyish pursuits. His aging, French immigrant parents had a dream that their only son would someday become a great physician. They ran a small bakery, and what little money was left after the family's immediate needs were met was put aside for their son's education. Doc worked very hard to contribute his share towards his education, with the hope of someday bringing pride and prosperity to his family.

In the boarding house where Doc roomed, a beautiful and kind young Negro woman resided in exchange for preparing meals for guests and tenants. No one could have been more surprised than himself when he found he was falling in love with her. For a long while she dodged his amorous advances, but he was young and virile, and she alone quickened his pulse. He did not have time to waste. He would be leaving Mobile eventually, and just as he had been serious in his studies, he was even more serious in his pursuit of her. She eventually succumbed to his zealous ardor and secretly, they maintained a passionate love affair. Had they been discovered, this young woman, Mamie Louise Washington, would have been without a much needed job. The young man quite possibly could have been kicked out of medical school, because of the bigotry that prevailed amongst some of the professors.

When the time came for him to return to New Orleans, Doc begged Mamie to go with him. He wanted a wife, and he wanted no other woman but her. She declined. She was adamant that his career, his life-long desire to become a physician, take precedence in his life. She promised him that if he were fortunate enough to obtain the position he sought up North, she would at least consider coming to be with him—she didn't promise that she would—simply that she would *consider* it. Doc spent six months at Charity Hospital in New Orleans and then, the much desired appointment at one of Detroit's most prestigious hospitals came through. He wanted to tell Mamie in person.

"I wrote her that I was coming back to Mobile, that I had something important to tell her. When I got to the boarding house, she was no longer there. She had disappeared without a trace. Mrs. Moriarity, the landlady, told me she left one night after dinner—just left a note saying she was sorry, but that for certain reasons she had to leave immediately. In the note, she thanked the landlady for all the kindness she had shown her.

"Just as I was leaving, Mrs. Moriarity told me something that changed my life. I remember every word. She said, 'It must have something to do with the fact that she was with child. Guess she figured it wouldn't be too long before I noticed. Heck, I noticed weeks ago,' she said. 'I just didn't say anything about it. Figured she'd come to me for some help sooner or later.'" Doc paused and licked his lips before continuing his recitation of Mrs. Moriarity's dialogue. "She said, 'She was the best cook I ever had. Heck, most of my guests stayed here because of Mamie's cooking. She was a smart gal, too, except for getting herself in that way. You know, it's funny, but she never had no boyfriends calling on her or nothing. Pretty girl like that one was, it seemed a bit strange. When she had a day off, mostly she just stayed in her room. Can't figure who the young fellow was that got her that way. I would've sure noticed if there'd been any colored boys hanging around here, yessir, I would've noticed that.'"

Not a sound was uttered in the courtroom, and Peyton allowed the doctor to continue to speak.

Doc dabbed at his eyes and continued his story, "I was devastated. I was going to be a father, and I had no idea of where to even start looking for Mamie. I had to be in Detroit in a week. I didn't want Mamie to have to raise our child alone. I loved her and already I loved the little one that was growing inside of her. Then it struck me she might have decided to do something foolish. That was a thought I couldn't allow myself to dwell on. I knew she was probably ashamed and desperate, but I felt I knew her well enough to know she would not destroy her unborn baby, our child that was conceived in love. Even so, the slight possibility of that happening made me more desperate to find her quickly.

"I never did find her before I took my job in Detroit, but every chance I got, every vacation, every long weekend, I returned to Mobile and continued the search. For ten years I searched for her. I tried to remember every clue she had ever given me of her origins, but she was nowhere to be found. One day I passed by a construction site on a corner of Government Street in Mobile. There was a big sign on that site that said, CALLAWAY CONSTRUCTION. Well, that name sounded familiar, and I played with it over and over in my mind that night. Something told me if I could just make the connection, there was something in that name *Callaway* that might give me a clue to where Mamie was, and hopefully, my child. That night in a dream it came to me. Mamie had mentioned a family named Callaway. She told me she had learned to read because of the generosity of a young boy named Ryan Callaway, whose family she had once lived with and cooked for. In their kindness, when she had been much younger, the Callaway family took her and her aunt in, and for room and board and a small salary, she had cooked for the family for several years before finding her way to Mrs. Moriarity's boarding house.

"Finding Mr. Ryan Callaway, a prosperous man with a son of his own, was not difficult. He was a pretty prominent figure around those parts, and Mr. Callaway did know Mamie Louise Washington's whereabouts. Fact is, as coincidence would have it, he was pretty much responsible for her whereabouts. Seemed that she had recently relocated from Mobile to right here in Pemrose Key. He told me she had just begun an enterprising venture. She had acquired a restaurant and was single-handedly running that and raising a fine young son. What Ryan Callaway didn't tell me was that it was because of his faith in Mamie, and his generosity and friendship, that she was able to start that restaurant. He was the one that gave her the loan she needed to buy Mamie's Place. Through hard work and determination she soon began to show a profit, which enabled her to repay her debt and acquire additional property." At this proclamation, Doc beamed his pride in Mamie.

Luke turned around in his seat and saw that Ryan's countenance had softened, and he looked humbled as Doc spoke of his gratitude to him for seeing that Mamie and his son had been taken care of. Luke had never known his father had been the one to help Mamie. Now, Doc's words filled him with an even greater respect for the goodness in his father's heart.

Doc barely paused. "I found Mamie. She was right where Ryan told me she would be, but she wasn't too happy to see me."

Doc went on to tell of his discovery that his feelings for Mamie had remained intact, and he fell in love with the precocious child, Toby. Mamie had gotten on with her life, and she'd done what she felt was best for the boy. For Toby's sake, she made Doc swear never to reveal their secret. No, she could not leave the South and her beloved Mamie's Place. She could not move to Detroit, and she could not marry a white man. Yes, she loved him. Always had. Always would. And there would never be another man in her life, but the fact remained that the two of them just couldn't be. Her boy came first, and that's the way it was. Doc would just have to accept that.

Doc left town, returning to his lifelong dream, his prestigious position as a medical doctor at the fine hospital in the big city. As promised, Mamie sent him letters apprising him of little Toby's progress in school, and photographs of each milestone in his life. Doc was broken-hearted. His parents had since died, and Mamie and Toby were the only *family* he had. The pressures of his work, his love for rich foods, and loneliness for his family brought on heart problems. He always believed the loneliness was the primary cause for his ailments. He cared for his patients, but not for himself.

Before too many years had passed he was forced to retire from his practice at the hospital. A colleague of his, a heart specialist, recommended a warmer, more relaxed climate and a small, private practice. Doc headed South. He assured Mamie he would keep his vow of secrecy only if she would let him see his son from time to time.

"I felt better just being in the same town with them. At least I would be here if they ever needed me. But Toby's gone now." Doc paused briefly, his lower lip quivered and he closed his eyes for a moment. The courtroom was quiet. Everyone seemed to be holding their breath for fear the judge or the prosecuting attorney might put an end to the story. "And he never knew who his father was...and he never knew his father loved him. I did love that boy, and it might have made a difference in his life if I had only told him when Luke brought him to my house and I had to glue him back together. If I had only told him when I had the chance..." Doc's voice trailed off and his last words were barely audible. "If I had only told him..."

"A-hem." Peyton cleared his throat and slammed the gavel down hard. "All right, is there other evidence to be presented here regarding the murder of Toby Washington?"

"There is, Judge." Daugherty rose from his chair beside Luke and walked to an easel positioned at the front of the courtroom. "I have a hunch, Your Honor, that Toby Washington is still alive."

Luke stared at him in amazement. Did Daugherty have proof of what Luke had suspected?

The courtroom was abuzz with disbelief and astonishment at Daugherty's bold assumption. Luke saw Mamie cover her face with both hands. Doc had resumed his place beside her and placed his arm around her shoulders.

Luke's suspicions had been based on a minute shred of evidence that he mostly deemed coincidence, and therefore dismissed as wishful thinking and a far-fetched possibility. He had been the one to retrieve the body, and he recalled that even then, he had his doubts over it being identified as Toby. When he heard the coroner's report, he had still been more than slightly skeptical, but he couldn't argue with the coroner's office. Somebody had wanted Toby out of the way badly enough to try and do him in, as witnessed by his condition the night Luke first found him at Cole's Bayou.

Luke watched with interest as Daugherty lifted a blank white page on the easel to reveal an enlarged black and white glossy of the very same newspaper photo Luke had mailed Joe Lianoho. This was the shred of evidence that had nagged at Luke since his return from Hawaii, the shred of evidence he had deemed to be impossible in the face of the coroner's report, and the lack of any contradictory proof. For some reason, Luke had been compelled to drop it in the mail to Joe the day he had been arrested.

In the newspaper photo there appeared a young man who looked for all the world like Toby Washington. It was a bit fuzzy, but now, seeing the original it had been reproduced from at a greatly enlarged size, there seemed to be no question.

Daugherty turned another page. The next photo focused in only on the presumed Toby—it had to be him. Even the tiny birthmark on his left cheek, the one positive identifiable feature, was highly visible.

The courtroom was now in complete chaos, and Daugherty had to raise his voice to a shout to be heard above the crowd and the pounding of Peyton's gavel. "We have determined that there is strong evidence suggesting Toby Washington may still be alive, Judge. The photographer who took this photograph has been contacted, as well as others who have been positively identified in this scene that day. At this time we ask permission for an exhumation of the body that was found in Pemrose Bay, and purported to be Toby Washington."

"Oh, my good Lord!" Mamie stood alone at her seat, unable to contain her emotions. She walked down the aisle slowly, toward the photograph of Toby, uttering softly, "That's my boy, that's my boy. Praise God, he's alive." Her hands were trembling as she touched the photo, seeking to embrace it as though it were a living, breathing, human being—as though it were the son she so grieved for standing before her. Doc followed and gently took her by the hand and led her back to her seat.

Luke looked across the room at his own mother and saw her dab at the corners of her pale blue eyes with his handkerchief.

"Order! Order!"

Pandemonium prevailed, and there seemed to be nothing even Peyton could do to quiet the crowd. He, too, had to shout to be heard in his own courtroom.

"We agree with the defense that there may be a reasonable assumption made that this is a photograph of Toby Washington, but we have NOT established a date for the photo. Counsel, was this photo taken before or after Toby Washington's presumed death?"

"After, Your Honor." It was Mullican's turn, and he was ready. He leapt forward now, with the actual newspaper that contained the photo and the accompanying article that listed the date of the rally that was to take place. There appeared to be no question, now.

A hush fell over the courtroom as all awaited the judge's comments about this remarkable turn of events. "I'm satisfied, I suppose, that this photo was taken after Toby's death. However, we still do not have proof, beyond a shadow of a doubt, that this is Toby Washington."

"It's NOT Toby Washington, Peyton. It can't be. He is dead. I know he is!" The shrill voice shrieked from the center of the courtroom, interrupting Peyton's assessment of the situation.

Luke recognized Edna's voice before ever turning to see her literally hyperventilating. She was jumping up and down and emphatically shrieking that Toby was indeed dead. Strange assertion for Edna Sinclair to be making.

"No, I'm not dead, Edna." A voice from the rear of the courtroom proclaimed loud and strong, "I'm not dead at all, Edna, but don't you wish I was?" And through the opened doors of Judge Peyton Fuller's simmering courtroom, on a hot August afternoon in Pemrose Key, strode a light skinned black man, very much alive, in the persona of Toby Washington.

The doors banged shut behind him, and the crowd was uproarious as Toby made his way down the aisle to the front of the courtroom. Peyton spewed and sputtered and repeatedly pounded his gavel, demanding silence of the rowdy crowd. The closer Toby got, the more Peyton looked as if he had seen a ghost.

Mamie screamed and struggled to get to her feet. With Doc on her heels she made her way to the front of the courtroom where Toby now stood.

Toby addressed himself first to his mother, "I'm sorry, Mama. There are reasons why I couldn't get in touch with you. There's a lot to tell you." Then to Peyton, "It's really me, Peyton...Judge. For the record you can say that I didn't know I was supposed to be dead. Guess you could say I was just missing, but here I am, right alongside the living, and I don't know what else I can say except that Luke didn't kill me. He didn't even try to kill me. He's never been anything but a friend, and all he did was try to help me. I was just too stubborn to realize it at the time." He looked directly at Luke, and his eyes signaled an apology for his anger the day Luke took him to the cabin from Doc's.

Toby turned to embrace his mother, then put an arm around Doc's neck.

"You heard?" Doc asked the question anxiously.

"I heard. I heard."

"Order! Order! Silence in this courtroom, and I mean SILENCE!" Peyton emphasized with his gavel, then continued to speak, but the noise abated only slightly. "In light of this startling revelation, and with the evidence surrounding the bombing of the *Captain Hook* being mostly circumstantial at this point, I have no choice but to release Luke Callaway on bond. Bail is set at $100,000."

Luke heard Peyton over the din, as did his attorneys and Ryan Callaway. It was true, Peyton had no choice. Considering Peyton's actions during the proceedings, Luke wondered if Peyton would have released him had he been given a choice.

Ryan's booming voice now filled the courtroom. He was back to his old self and very much in charge, "The money will be here in less than fifteen minutes, Peyton. I want my son out of this place. NOW!" No longer appearing the pussycat, he roared his command.

Peyton gave up on trying to quiet the crowd. He grabbed some papers off his desk and retreated to his chambers in a huff.

30

reedom. To Luke, the feeling was akin to his first night home from Vietnam. He stayed with his parents at The Magnolias, not wanting to see or talk to anyone just yet. He knew it comforted them for him to be here, safe, under their roof, and he allowed them to indulge their parental instincts of protectiveness, a small compensation for what they had been through.

All three gathered round the kitchen table, marveling over the events of the day, afraid to even mention what might yet happen regarding the other murders. They skirted around that particular issue, but there was one item they didn't avoid. Luke's mother looked at him across the table, her gaze level, her fingers stilled for now. "You love her, don't you, Luke?"

"How did you know? I never told you about her."

"I knew the moment you spoke of her in court the other day. This one I knew was right...this time."

Luke recalled another conversation they'd had at this same table a little more than a year ago, also about a woman in his life, a woman his mother perceived he didn't love.

"Cooper had nothing to do with the failure of my marriage to Lisa."

"I know that."

"She doesn't know how I feel about her."

"I know that, too."

"I'm not going to tell her."

"I know." Meg reached across the table and took Luke's hand lovingly in her own. "One day it will happen."

Ryan wasn't going to be left out of this conversation for long. "Senator DeLaney and I have been friends since we were boys together in Mobile. He's a fine man, a true gentleman, and I'm sure he has a fine daughter."

"She's a very special lady, but as I said, we're only friends. There's been nothing between us, much as I would have liked for there to have been. She's not to know otherwise, not now, not until I get out of this mess."

"I know, son, and you will...you will...wait and see."

When Luke went up to his room, he tried to phone Cooper in Chicago. There was no answer. It was probably just as well.

Luke hung around long enough to have breakfast with his parents. He knew his mother was still worried about him in spite of her words.

"You look better already, Luke. Did you sleep well last night?"

"I slept great, Mom. It feels good to be home." Great—except for agonizing over Cooper—before much needed slumber overtook him.

He couldn't conceal his impatience at wanting to get on with his schedule at Windward Boats, or, unknown to his parents, wanting to get on with the investigation.

Anxious to get home aboard the *Sea Spirit*, Luke left shortly after breakfast. He wanted to change clothes and open his mail before heading for the plant. Mostly junk mail had accumulated in the pile he picked up at the post office on his way to Oyster Bay. There were two envelopes that aroused his curiosity. One was a small envelope addressed to him in what appeared to be a woman's handwriting. It looked familiar, like the handwriting on the cards Cooper had sent before, so he opened it first, and immediately wished he hadn't.

Dear Luke,

I hope this letter finds you well. I'm so sorry Luke, for any complications my friendship and presence in your life may have caused you. Things have not been easy for you, I know. I wanted to help you in some way, but your attorney, Mr. Daugherty, said that would not be the wise thing to do. It was the same thing Trotter said all over again, and so I stayed away. Do you remember, Luke, when I told you I had always wanted to live in Hawaii? Now I have my chance. By the time you get this, I will probably have already moved. I'm looking forward to it. Next to Pemrose Key, Hawaii is my favorite place in all the world, so you can imagine my excitement when I learned that my transfer request had gone through. Take care, Luke. I hope your life is wonderful. I know everything will be straightened out soon.

Fondly,
Cooper

Luke stared blankly at the letter. Cooper's personal letterhead told him the letter was really from her, but he couldn't believe it. Across the bottom, a single line was drawn through the address, indicating she could no longer be found there. His panic at losing touch with Cooper surpassed the hopelessness he'd experienced in jail. Cooper had told him she had friends in Hawaii. Perhaps there was a man involved. Perhaps her move had been predicated by a romantic interest Luke didn't know about. He couldn't bear to think about that possibility. He re-folded the letter and put it aside.

The next envelope he opened with less hesitation, but he wished he hadn't opened this one, either.

Greetings from the law firm of Biggins and Slater came in the form of a *petition to sue* on behalf of Lisa Logan Callaway's estate. They sought what she would have been rightfully entitled to as his wife had she lived, the purpose being primarily for the future and lost support of the child, Tabitha Logan.

Luke read it again, trying to comprehend, not sure he understood the words before him. Who the heck was Tabitha Logan? Lisa would have been a child herself when she gave birth. Edna had to be at the bottom of all this. His first inclination was to pick up the phone and call her and tell her what she could do with her law suit. Only through the employment of great restraint did he resist. That wouldn't be a wise course of action, he finally reasoned. Okay, let it simmer for awhile. He didn't believe there was anything that could be done just yet. He hadn't been convicted of Lisa's murder. If he was and Lisa did have a child, Lisa's *estate* might possibly have a chance. Her heirs would be entitled to some sort of restitution if he were found guilty of her death.

He wasn't interested in reading the rest of his mail. He stuffed it all, including Cooper's letter and the petition to sue from Biggins and Slater, into his briefcase.

Luke was anxious to check on the business. That would help take his mind off the bad tidings he'd received in the morning's mail. Besides, he'd been away far too long. Trotter assured him he had things under control, but Luke had to see for himself. If he was lucky, the production process of Windward Boats had not suffered as a consequence of his incarceration.

Luke relished each moment of freedom. As anxious as he was to arrive at the plant, he drove slowly out to Mango Junction. His daily drive to work was a reminder of Perky Bittle, and he often thought of her as his route took him past the place where her peanut stand once stood. Today, instead of passing by, he pulled off on the shoulder of the road in about the same spot he and Cooper had parked on the day they found poor Perky dead. Gone was the big kettle, but the ramshackle, open-air shed still stood, such as it was. The two-by-four poles served to support a square of rusty, corrugated tin for overhead protection. For Perky, there had been no protection against what had ultimately and needlessly concluded her century-old life. Luke reflected back on that chilly day that seemed like an eternity past. So much hurt to so many. How senseless Perky's murder had been.

Feeling much anguish at all that had transpired since his return to Pemrose Key, Luke silently renewed his vow to get to the bottom of this. The resurrection of Toby eliminated at least one vindication to which he had sworn, and for this he was thankful. Toby owed him some answers, though. Luke would give him time to get through this reunion period with Mamie and Doc, then he would expect more details. He suspected there was more to all this than Toby had indicated in court yesterday, and he determined to make scheduling a meeting with Toby a priority.

Luke absently kicked at a few rocks that lay in the dusty roadside beneath his feet. When he did so, he heard a metallic sound as something rolled with the rocks. A round, disk-like object surfaced, and as he leaned to pick it up, something else caught his eye. It was a short piece of plaited line such as that used for flag halyards or awnings. Both the piece of line and the metal object were encrusted with mud. When he rubbed the dust and the dirt off with his fingers, he held a small silver snuff box in his hand. One side was inscribed with the initials ST. He turned the box over in his palm. Engraved on the other side were the initials LL. He turned the box over and over in his hand, contemplating the obvious and wondering if those initials had been inscribed before or after he married Lisa. What a fool he'd been. He studied the broken line. The unlayed ends indicated a short splice that had been worked out. At one time the ends of the piece of line had been spliced together to form a continuous circle. For such a small, lightweight object, care might not have been given to the splicing, and even a weak tug or a strain could easily have severed the splice.

He had seen these items before. He tried to remember where, tried to visualize the place in his mind where he had seen the silver box and that bit of rope and then it came to him—he could relate the items to a specific day, a specific time, and he knew that in his hands he held the key to Perky Bittle's murder.

When Luke arrived at the plant he was greeted enthusiastically by the small group of clerical workers he employed. They offered tidbits of news and encouragement about the production deadline. If the deadline could be met, the Ariadne would be introduced to the general public at the Miami Boat Show, an important event in the boating industry that could be a tremendous assist in marketing the Ariadne. It appeared Luke's small staff had done a tremendous job of generating interest in the Ariadne through press releases and trade publications.

If Trotter was moving his end accordingly, they could make that deadline. Luke went outside and crossed the yard to the huge concrete-block building that housed the heart of Windward Boats—the machinery and tools and dies and fiberglass molds that were the things his dreams had been made of for so many years. He looked around the yard with pride at that reality now, and at what had been accomplished in such a short time. He had set uncompromising standards in the hiring of his work force, and it was now paying off. Over the years he had absorbed much from his father regarding the pitfalls of running a business. You don't cut corners where the quality of your product is concerned, and you don't get respect from your employees if you don't hire the kind of employees you can respect. There was much more to running this business than an innovative design and a desire to succeed.

Luke was met at the entrance to the building by Trotter. Behind him stood the men in his production crew. Typical for Trotter, he had grease on his face and held an oversized wrench in his hand. He didn't smile when he greeted Luke. None of them did.

"Follow me," Trotter commanded grimly.

At first the damage wasn't evident, but upon closer inspection, Luke saw the sand that filled the motorized workings of the cutter. He looked around and saw the bent shaft on the gears of a forklift and the smashed and dented sides of the mold for the Ariadne's hull.

The sight nauseated him. His eyes stung with the fury of this unspeakable action. He stood motionless, consumed by anger and reluctant to speak until he had his emotions in check. He had presence of mind enough to know that his selection of words was crucial to the morale of his men. What he said could make or break them. His mind raced for a solution, and when he did speak, it was with conviction, "It can be fixed. Trotter, find out what it's going to take to replace or repair this machinery. How about the die...what kind of shape is it in?"

"They didn't get to it."

"Good! We'll make another mold. Order whatever materials are necessary, and if you have to pay extra to get them expedited, do it! We're going to meet our deadline. We'll be putting in some long hard hours, but I'll make it worth your while. There'll be bonuses all around for everybody when we're done." He knew his men would earn their bonuses, and he'd see to it that Trotter's bonus, as foreman, was profitable enough to replace the *Shady Lady's* engines. "We are going to make the Miami show as planned." And he believed it.

Boosting morale didn't diminish Luke's anger. He would leave work early this afternoon. He knew what he had to do and he was going to do it, but first he would have a word with Toby. Maybe Toby could enlighten him and hopefully, provide him with some information that would help before he implemented his plan. He dialed Mamie's number.

Toby would meet him tomorrow at four o'clock aboard the *Sea Spirit*. Luke couldn't think of a better place. He'd motor out in the bay, and they would have complete privacy.

Next on the agenda, deal with Edna, find out what this blasted lawsuit was all about. He knew what he had to do there, too. He had married Lisa, and though it had been a marriage in law only, she had taken the Callaway name. Her illness had consumed her, and her short life had been wasted on the abuses that stemmed from the ravages of a pathetic childhood. She had a child that needed to be taken care of, and Luke would do all in his power to keep that child from the pitfalls that had destroyed Lisa's life, and nearly destroyed his own. If money would help place her in a loving home, then he would provide it. He would accept financial responsibility for the child, Tabitha.

He pulled several files from the file drawer in his desk. He looked at the numbers. The sums had been far greater before the realization of Windward Boats. He had sunk a great deal into his belief that he could make a go of it. He had no idea what Edna and her attorneys had in mind. They could go easy on him, or they could wipe him out. With the figures before him, he only hoped there was enough to appease them. He personally had been relying heavily on the success of Windward Boats. Paid in one lump sum, the cost of raising a child over a twenty year period would put a hefty dent in his cash reserves, monies that could be critical to the growth of the business. There were some other holdings, various stocks and bonds he hoped he wouldn't have to get into. The money he would propose to contribute would have to be a hefty sum or they wouldn't buy it. They would likely reject his offer and pursue litigation, whether he was found guilty or not. That sum of money, held intact over the next twenty years, could make a great deal more money for Luke, but the undesirable aspect of a twenty year relationship with Edna, if she became the child's legal guardian, prompted him to look at the lump sum aspect. Twenty years of paying the piper was something he couldn't handle. Edna would be just the type to try and make him dance to her tune. In the long run he would pay and pay and pay. No, he wouldn't do that.

Luke ran his index finger down the *S* list in his Rolodex until he found the number listed for *Sinclair, Edna*. It stood out from the others. Lisa's hand had scrawled the number there. For once he was actually thankful it was Edna's voice he heard on the other end of the line, and not batty old Mrs. Sinclair.

"Edna, this is Luke."

"Well, Lukey, darling, I've been expecting to hear from you. Got my little message, did you?"

"I need to meet with you, Edna. We need to talk about this in person. Maybe we can settle on something out of court."

"Maybe we can, and maybe we can't, Luke. I hope you realize how much it costs to raise a child these days. Lisa was doing a pretty good job of it before you...before she got killed."

"I don't know how that could have been, Edna. Lisa was never with the child, and the only source of income she had was what I gave her."

"Maybe that's true, Luke, but she went without a lot of things herself to do for the kid. The fact is, she was your wife, and she's no longer here to take care of this child, thanks to you."

"Edna, I won't defend myself to you. If I accept responsibility for this child's support, it has nothing to do with how Lisa was killed. My reasons for doing so, Edna, would be beyond your comprehension. Anyway, I'm prepared to make an offer to settle, pending certain conditions being met. If you want to meet with me, I'll go over it with you. If things are agreeable to both of us, you can have your attorneys draw up the necessary papers and we'll be done with it."

"Of course I'll meet you, Luke. Just tell me where and when?"

"Tomorrow afternoon...three-o'clock...my boat." What he had to say wouldn't take long. She'd be out of there before his meeting with Toby. His morning would be free to spend at the plant.

"I'll see you there, Precious. Ta-ta." Click.

When Luke left the plant, he drove over to The Magnolias. He knew his parents wouldn't be home. They, too, were trying to get on with their lives after the interruptions of the past few weeks. With their son in prison, their world had been turned upside down, and many things had been put on hold. Ryan had to go to work, and Meg was fulfilling some charitable obligations that she had neglected lately.

Maria was in the kitchen when Luke arrived. "Good to see you, Luke. We so glad you're out of the jailhouse. Nobody think you did it, you know?" The frown on her face and her furrowed brow indicated she had been sincerely worried about Luke and his parents. She lifted one hand out of the dishwater, and with it still dripping wet she pushed her coarse, slightly graying, dark hair off her forehead.

"Thanks, Maria. I need all the support I can get."

"You don't look so good, Luke." She took both hands out of the dishwater, dried them on her apron and turned to face Luke. "We need to fatten you up. Look at you," she scolded, clucking at him like a mother hen.

He could always count on Maria being honest. She was a plump, matronly looking Cuban woman in her late forties or early fifties. She'd been with the Callaway family since they moved to Pemrose Key when Luke was only twelve years old, and she'd helped raise Luke. Now she earnestly expressed her concern for him.

"What can I do for you, Luke? Your mama and daddy, they not here."

"I know, Maria. I just came by to get something. I'll be right back." Luke took the stairs two at a time. His room was neat and orderly. The bed was made, and the dirty towels had been removed from the hamper. He went directly to his bedroom closet, reached to the top shelf, and pulled down an old shoebox. He knew what he was after and he wasted little time in getting it. He set the box on the bed and removed the lid. The .45 he'd used in Vietnam had rested safely there since his return. He opened the top drawer of his dresser and reaching to the back of it, lifted out a metal safe-box with both hands and placed it on the bed beside the shoe box. When he opened it, he examined the contents for a few moments before reaching in and taking out several .45 clips and transferring them to the shoe box. Beneath the clips, old coins, and miscellaneous trinkets dating back to his childhood, lay a slightly yellowed envelope that must have been there for several years. On the outside of the envelope his name was typed in red ink. The envelope's seal had never been broken. Curious, he decided to open it. The envelope contained a graduation card that looked as new as though it had been stuffed in the envelope that very day. The message inside was typed—in red ink:

Dear Lucas,

Happy Graduation. You're going away now and I won't see you for a long time. You've made a mistake, Luke, your rejection of me is your loss. I had so much to give. You'll see, one day, what it's like to love someone and not be loved in return. Then you might learn what pain is all about. Beware, Luke, you better be watching over your shoulder for I WILL get even with you one day. Not as long as I live will I forget the mockery you and your friends have made of my love and I will get even! I will stop at nothing to destroy your life! It may be a long time from now, but I can have patience. I can have lots of patience because I will

*never love anyone but you and I will see that you're
never happy with anyone else. I promise.*

All my love and hatred,

E.S.

The hairs on the back of Luke's neck bristled! He had the uncanny feeling that his destiny had been predetermined by Edna. He had been warned those many years before. In his hands he held the prophecy. The fate of his predestined future had now come to pass. He remembered that day, graduation day. Edna had stuffed the card in his hand, and he had in turn given it to his mother to keep for him during the ceremony. His mother had placed it on his dresser at home, and there it had remained for days before he absently stuffed it in the box with other items of junk, never bothering to read its contents—never caring what Edna might have had to say. Now he returned the card to its envelope and placed it back in the shoe box.

Could his knowledge of the contents of that card have made a difference in his life or affected the decisions he had made early on regarding Lisa? Would he have been on guard and more aware of Edna's manipulation of the relationship? This was further proof that it had been a devious scheme from the start, and that Edna had instigated and executed her plot with a vengeance and a purpose, employing Lisa's weakness as her weapon, all because Luke had spurned her advances.

He returned the safe-box to its place in the drawer, stuffed the shoe box under his arm and headed back down the stairs.

"I'm gone, Maria. See you later," he called out from the foyer, hoping to escape before she saw him.

No such luck. Maria appeared in the hallway. "No, not so fast, you. I fix you something to eat. I got good ham sandwich ready for you. You got to put some weight back on."

"Not now, Maria, I can't. I'm in a hurry."

"You not in too big a hurry to eat. You got to eat anyway, right?"

"I guess you're right, Maria. I tell you what, you wrap it up for me and I'll eat it later. How's that?"

"That's better than no eating at all. You wait right here. I be right back."

In a flash she returned with a brown paper sack, which she shoved at Luke's chest, forcing him to take hold of it. Judging from the weight of it, there had to be more in there than one sandwich. The whole bag of potato chips that peeked out from the top of the sack confirmed that. She had stuffed the sack full.

"I tell your mama I feed you. She'll be so happy." Maria smiled and reached up and patted Luke's cheek. "You good boy, Luke."

"I tell you what, Maria, let's don't tell them I was by here. They'll be upset that they weren't here. Okay?"

Maria squinted her eyes at Luke. "What you mean not tell them you were here?" Her eyes darted to the bundle he held under his arm. "What you got in that box, Luke? What you don't want your mama and daddy to know?"

"Nothing, Maria, I just don't want to worry them anymore than I already have. I've got to go now. Thanks for the lunch, Maria. See you."

Maria stood in the front doorway, hands on her broad hips, shaking her head back and forth and clucking as she watched him drive away.

Luke went directly to the *Sea Spirit*. Once aboard, he settled in for the night. Tomorrow was going to be a big day. He got out a notepad and began his proposal to Edna. He pored over some figures and calculated and recalculated. He certainly understood where his father had been coming from when he chose construction work over accounting. Luke would be forever thankful for having other resources and talents to fall back on. While he worked, he munched on the contents of the sack Maria had pushed off on him. It came in pretty handy, after all. He must remember to thank her.

Before stuffing the papers in an envelope, Luke added one last stipulation to his proposal: He must be provided with copies of Tabitha's birth records, and proof that Lisa was her mother.

With the decision made about Tabitha Logan, Luke felt like he had one worry behind him. Tomorrow would tell. Aboard the *Sea Spirit,* he slept better than he had in a long time. Things just might work out, he told himself before he dozed off to sleep.

31

*L*uke woke to an overcast sky. He stood in the cockpit and surveyed the clouds while he chugged his second cup of coffee. If they didn't break by noon, it could throw a kink into his plans.

It was early when he got to the plant—and quiet. Thankfully, the balance of the day was that way, too. Everyone's attention was focused on repairing the damaged equipment.

Luke sought to have a word with Trotter before going to meet Edna, to let him know he wouldn't be in tomorrow. He found him in the plant, hunched over the engine of the forklift.

Trotter looked up with a grin. "We've just about got this one, Boss."

Luke gave him a thumbs up.

Trotter wiped his hands on his coveralls as he climbed down from the lift. "What's up?"

"I just wanted you to know, I won't be in tomorrow."

"What's the deal? I thought you couldn't stay away from this place?" Trotter gave him a sideways look.

Luke turned away and stared out the entrance to the yard beyond. "I got some business to take care of. I know you can handle things here. You've been doing a pretty good job of it, anyway." He frowned at Trotter, worry lines creasing his forehead. "Trotter, with all that's been going on, if anything happens to me, I've got to ask you to do three things for me—help my parents get through it; see that the Ariadne makes it, and..." On this last one he stumbled. He looked back towards the entrance and noticed the sun trying to break through the clouds. When he turned back to Trotter, he met his gaze squarely, "...and tell Cooper I loved her, and that I didn't do it."

"I don't think that last one's necessary."

"More than anything, I want to tell her myself. But if for some reason I can't, I want her to know I said it. I want her to know for sure."

Trotter said nothing.

Luke turned and walked out into the sunshine.

When he left to go meet Edna, he stopped his car in front of the plant and took a long look at the sign over the entrance that read: Windward Boats, A Callaway Corporation.

Edna was late. He should have known she would be. Luke sat at the table in the galley and queried over the old photograph he held in his hands. It wasn't the primary reason for this meeting, but he was anxious to ask Edna about the photo he'd recently found among Lisa's possessions. The resemblance to Lydia Rhinehart was uncanny, and Luke believed it to be her when she was younger. She looked even more like Lisa then than she did now. Perhaps Edna could shed some light on it. He put the photo aside and took one last look at the papers he had prepared before stuffing them back in the envelope. He sealed the envelope and with large, loose script, penned Edna's name on the outside and left it lying in the middle of the table. Three-thirty! Where was that woman? He should have known better than to count on Edna.

"Yoo-hoo! It's me, Luke. I'm here."

He grimaced at the sound of her voice. When he peered out the cabin door he saw Edna standing on the finger pier that ran alongside his boat. Stupidly, she had worn high heels and a business suit out on the dock. Now he'd have to help her aboard.

"Come on in, Edna. This won't take long. Here, let me help you." He extended his hand to her. She teetered for only a moment before catching her heel between the boards of the pier. When she tried to pull her foot loose, she swayed backwards and did the prettiest free-fall right into the water.

Luke stepped up onto the pier and looked in the water on the other side. Edna was flapping around, shrieking and hollering. When she saw Luke peering down from the pier at her, she started yelling, "You pushed me, Lucas Callaway. You pushed me! So help me, I'll get you for this."

Luke couldn't help himself, he hadn't laughed so hard in years. Edna's wet hair hung down over her face, covering her eyes, and all you could see was her nose. She continued to shriek even after Luke threw her a life preserver. Her shrill voice soon began to draw a crowd, and several of the other boat captains came running to help. The sight of Edna in the water, sitting in the middle of a life preserver with her legs all akimbo, was all it took. Her skirt was up to her waist and billowing out around her, revealing loosely dangling garter belt clasps. The sight was hilarious, more because of WHO it was rather than WHAT had happened. It began with a few chuckles, but soon evolved into full blown belly laughs. Grown men lined the pier, holding their sides, bending over double with laughter. The more Edna shrieked, the harder they laughed. Lisa wasn't the only one well known around the marina.

When they finally fished her out, Edna attempted to recover her dignity. Now shoeless, it was easy for her to step aboard the *Sea Spirit*. As she did so, the crowd dispersed and Toby appeared on the outside dock. When Edna saw Toby standing there, her eyes rolled back in her head, and she started hyperventilating as she had done in court.

Luke watched this amazing transformation with curiosity.

Toby seemed to take it in stride. "Edna. How you doing? Did you have an accident?" The question was innocent enough, or so Luke thought.

"Aiee-e-e." Edna emitted an ungodly howl and went after Toby with both arms flailing, trying to reach him from the cockpit of the boat.

Toby laughed and dodged her efforts. "Whoa, woman. What did I do?" He laughed again. "Am I early, Luke?"

Luke looked at his watch. "No, I just need to settle something with Edna here, and we've had a slight delay. Would you give me a few minutes, Toby?"

"I'll take a walk. Be back shortly."

"Come on in, Edna. I've got a towel in here you can use." Luke stepped aside.

Edna entered the cabin with her nose in the air. She took the towel from Luke and began rubbing her hair and blotting her face. "Thank you, Luke."

She almost sounded human, Luke thought. Poor Edna, she brings it upon herself, and she just can't seem to do any better.

"Sit down, Edna. I found some more of Lisa's things at the condo. Photos, books, things like that. You can have them." Luke handed Edna a grocery sack that was folded down at the top. "Maybe that kid of hers will want them someday. I was curious about this picture, though. Do you know who this woman is, Edna?"

Edna took the photo from Luke's hand and stared at it. "That's my Aunt Lydia. The last time I saw her, I was five years old, but I remember her."

"She's Lisa's mother?"

"*Was* Lisa's mother...she's dead. I guess Lisa told you, her mother died when she was a baby."

"She's not dead, Edna."

"How the heck do you know that?"

"I met her, and she lives not too far from here."

"Oh, God, if my mother ever finds out about it, she'll try to kill her if she recognizes her. So would Thomas Logan."

"Why would they want to kill her, Edna?"

Lydia Rhinehart was becoming even more of a mystery.

Edna stared at the photograph and seemed to be contemplating her answer.

Luke pushed. "Edna, what is it about this woman? Why can't you tell me? I know where to find her. I'll ask her myself if you won't tell me."

"I hate that woman." Edna glared at Luke and spoke through clenched teeth. "Thomas Logan is my father, too. She stole my daddy from my mama and me. My mama's own baby sister stole her husband from her."

"So Lisa was your half-sister."

"She might be. My daddy always said he never was sure she was his. I think she was. It nearly drove my mama mad when he left us, and she started drinking. She hasn't been the same since. I think Lisa had the taste for the drinking in her blood, just like my mama. I took after my daddy."

"What happened between he and Lydia?"

"She liked to party. After she had Lisa she wanted the party to continue, so she took off. Left Lisa for him to raise. Married some guy out in California, Daddy said. Then one day her husband went out fishing in the Pacific Ocean and never came back. They never even found his boat. For awhile they thought Daddy had something to do with it. He said they never suspected anybody as pretty as Lydia could do anything like that, but Daddy had his own thoughts. The police didn't know her the way we knew her. Later, Daddy told us Lisa's mama had died. Now you're telling me she didn't, and that's a real shame, Luke."

"So you're really Edna Logan, not Edna Sinclair?"

"My real name is Edna Logan. Mama was a Sinclair. She changed her name back after he left her, but he said he wouldn't send her any money for me if she changed my name. Daddy said that I was the only thing he knew for sure was really his. Even though he couldn't be here because of his job, he said he always knew where to find what belonged to him, but Mama never wanted the name Logan mentioned in our house again, so she called me Edna Sinclair. Mama's not well. Her mind just ain't right no more. It's all Aunt Lydia's fault. Mama didn't even know who Lisa was, or she wouldn't have allowed her in our house. I wouldn't have either, except Daddy wanted it. I did it for him—not for Lisa."

"Lisa didn't know you were sisters?"

"Daddy didn't want her to know. Like I said, he never really believed she was his, but he said he didn't have any choice but to raise her. Everybody felt sorry for him when Aunt Lydia left him and the baby. Daddy said if he didn't keep Lisa, it could hurt his chances of advancing in the Navy. I really think he wanted her to come live with us when she started growing up, just to get her out of his sight. I think she reminded him too much of Lydia, with her wild ways."

Luke's disgust for Thomas Logan had never been greater. Nor his pity for Lisa, and he wondered if Lydia had ever tried to find the daughter she'd cheated out of knowing a mother's love. Grudgingly, he pitied Edna, too, but he didn't intend to turn this into a social occasion, and it was already going to be more of a charitable event than he had ever bargained for.

"Okay, Edna, here it is." Luke wasted no time now in getting to the point of the real reason he'd called this meeting. "Pending certain conditions being met, I'm accepting responsibility for contributing to Lisa's estate, which means her child. If it weren't for the child, I wouldn't be so philanthropic. This is in no way an admission of guilt. Perhaps the money is needed to support the child, but there are guidelines here. A trust will be established in this child's name. I will do what I can to help place her in a good home."

"Wait a minute, Luke. I'm going to raise this child. After all, she is flesh and blood, you know."

"Edna, do you think you can give this child the kind of love that Lisa was denied? Think of her needs. More than money, she needs a mother. Can you raise this child alone and be a good mother to her?"

"I'm raising this child, Luke, and that's final!"

"Understand, Edna, the money is not for you, and if that makes any difference in your wanting to raise her, consider that now. The trust will be established, but there will be no more after this. This is a lump sum settlement, one time only, and you will agree to terms to that effect. Is that understood?"

"You can't talk to me like this, Luke Callaway. You're not quite in a position to be so high and mighty now, are you?"

"Edna, I'm done with you! Take this envelope and get off my boat. I've said all I intend to say." Luke held the door open for her.

She snatched up the envelope and the brown paper sack that contained the only remaining pieces of Lisa's life and went up the steps and out into the cockpit. Before she ascended to the pier, she reached up and retrieved her one shoe that lay on the dock beside the boat. "I'll send you a bill for my dry cleaning and my shoes."

"Send it along with the baby's birth certificate verifying Lisa's the mother. That's one of the terms, Edna."

Edna tossed her wet head, sniffed the air with her nose and stomped down the pier towards the restaurant.

When Edna had cleared the scene, Toby sauntered down the pier, grinning broadly. "Man, it's busy around here today, aint' it? What's with Edna?"

"You know Edna." There was nothing more Luke cared to say about her.

Toby wouldn't let it rest. "Edna and I got to know each other pretty well before Nam, you know."

Luke thought he comprehended what Toby was trying to tell him. "Really?" He tried not to act surprised. *Toby and Edna? Poor Toby.*

"Yeah. Didn't last long, though. I found out why you were always running from her back in high school. Thing about it is, the only reason she gave me the time of day was because of what she wanted from my mama."

Luke listened as he loosed the lines. "What did she want from your mama?"

"Her place."

"Yeah, I was around one day when she tried to put it to her, now that you mention it. She doesn't give up, does she?"

"She had me going for awhile. I ain't proud of it. I talked to Mama about selling her place and realized it wouldn't be the thing for Mama to do. When I told Edna that's how I felt, she looked like a barracuda hit by lightning on a squalling night. Man, her hair stood straight up on end when she came at me. She realized she'd wasted all that attention on me, and still didn't get what she wanted. Boy, was she mad!"

"I've seen her that way before, too." He couldn't help chuckling at this image of Edna. "It's good to see you again, Toby. You came back to life at just the right moment. Great timing for me, anyway. How about taking a little cruise with me?"

Luke waited until they had pulled away from the dock before asking. "Okay, friend, what gives?" Now he wanted some answers.

They idled along through the Intracoastal canal.

"Luke, I was going to have to talk to you anyway. You know Joe Lianoho?"

Luke's expression revealed nothing of his astonishment.

Toby kept talking, "Okay, I know you're not going to tell me. I know Joe, too. I been working for him. He knows I'm telling you now. It's a long story, man."

"Let's hear it."

"When I was in Nam, I got myself messed up with some bad dudes. They were smuggling pot in and selling hashish. I was their errand boy, for a few bucks and an occasional joint. I figured, what the hey, what could it hurt? We're all big boys here. Smoking a weed now and then seemed to make things come out better. Especially on the days when somebody you knew got killed out there. I got caught. I wasn't too smart in more ways than one. I didn't get discharged 'cause of a bad back, like Mama thinks. I had to cooperate with the law or get put in the hooch. I became an *informant*. Seems that the bad dudes were badder than I thought. There'd been a couple of guys killed in Saigon in their little operation. It wasn't just *harmless pot smoking* that was going on, I found out. Anyway, I helped put 'em away and the authorities thought it'd be best for my health if I got out of there, so they worked up another deal for me. They would let me come back to Pemrose Key if I would cooperate with the FBI in an investigation. I proved myself, I guess, by helping them in Nam. Now they trusted me a little more. On my way home, I stopped off in Honolulu for a couple of weeks and got fully briefed by Joe Lianoho. When I got back to Pemrose Key, things fell into place better than I thought they would. Some of Scranton Peabody's boys hired me on."

"What were you sent home to investigate, Toby?" Toby seemed willing to talk, and Luke had to be sure they were working for the same cause.

"Gun-running—in Vietnam. Even today illegal weapons are being smuggled in and delivered to the Viet Cong. You know where they think some of them are coming from—Pemrose Key. The government is looking at all their contractors that supply weapons to the military."

"Or weapons parts?"

"You got it. Red Dawn Manufacturing is at the top of their list. Scranton Peabody got greedy. He started using inferior alloys in the parts he supplied to the government, saving himself some big bucks. He didn't know Uncle Sam was on to him. Now that they've started looking at Red Dawn a little closer, the FBI suspects they might be acquiring additional parts from other manufacturers to put together relatively inexpensive weapons that the Viet Cong will pay premium prices for, and that China and the Soviets are happy to acquire for them. So far the proof has escaped them."

"I might can help them there, Toby, if I can ever get in touch with Joe Lianoho. I saw the weapons. I was at Red Dawn."

"Joe needs to know that. I'll be talking to him this afternoon, you don't mind if I tell him for you, do you?"

"Have at it."

"Joe's been keeping up with you, Luke. You got shot at one time too many. He let you cool off on purpose, to keep you out of trouble. Jackson Cummings helped railroad you, for your own good. They don't think you killed Lisa, but I don't think they're one hundred percent sure. Joe said after meeting her in Hawaii, he couldn't much blame you if you had. He said it looks better that you're being watched by the Feds rather than working with them. With that being the case, now, he thought it'd be safe to let you out. Nobody will want to bother you right now. With Scranton out of the way, he decided it was time for me to come on home and help you out. So, here I am."

"But we still need to find out how high the involvement goes... who's at the top."

"That's where they hoped your connections would come into play, Luke."

"I haven't helped them much there, I know. I have found out there's a senator involved. I have my suspicions on who it is, but I don't have any proof yet. What happened out there at Cole's Bayou, Toby, the night I found you?"

"When I infiltrated Scranton's operation, I started asking too many questions. I guess Peabody's contacts made it easy for him to have me checked out. They worked me over and left me for dead. They threw me overboard at the mouth of Cole's Bayou. After you took me to Mama's cabin, I slipped over to her place one night after she'd closed and called Joe Lianoho. He told me to get out of there and lay low. I left the same afternoon they blew up the cabin. It was just coincidence, and an awful shame, that some poor fisherman got caught in the crossfire. When it was believed the body was mine, Joe decided it was best we let it stay that way for awhile, so he moved into action and put me under protection. The coroner's office here cooperated, of course, since it was the FBI asking the favor. I couldn't tell nobody I was still alive or where I was, not even Mama. I went down to New Orleans for a spell, and then up to Memphis. I didn't know my picture was being taken when my face turned up in that newspaper along with them others. I guess for you it's a good thing it did. After you sent it to Joe, he mailed it to your attorneys. Thought they might could put it to good use after your cooling off period."

"What about Skip Traylor?"

"Guilty as sin. No proof of who he's killed, though."

"I think I've found proof he killed Perky Bittle."

"Man, you been busy, Luke. Maybe Skip will lead us to others. I was just getting hot on him when I had to blow."

"Aptly put, Toby."

"Well, that's about the size of it. I know your father-in-law—EX-father-in-law—is suspected to be involved somehow, and he's one of the reasons they recruited you. He's either pretty slick, or has one heck of a hold on his men. They ain't none of 'em talking. Pau did, and look what happened to him. All the activity that's going on in Cole's Bayou, and your wife being who she was, I think they thought Logan just might try to recruit you into the 'family' business. Thought that might bring him out in the open. I was making my first run in there the day they got me, so I never had a chance to see much. I think we were hauling guns in those crates labeled Red Dawn Manufacturing, not just weapons parts. I was trying to pry open one of the crates when I got caught. They were already on to me so they were watching me closer than I knew. They figured it wasn't none of my business what was in them boxes."

"Now we know what was in those boxes. Thanks, Toby, for coming to help me. You realize you might still be in danger?"

"I know. I couldn't let you take the rap, though. The FBI knew you didn't kill me, but just on the chance you killed Lisa they didn't want it screwing up their operation. That's what's most important to them—not me, not you, not Lisa, but the investigation. They had to let it play through, not only for your own safety, but to keep you from screwing things up anymore in case you had gotten ticked enough at your wife to do her in. Jail was the safest place for you right then, for all concerned."

"Yeah, I'll have to thank Joe for the favor."

They cruised through the Intracoastal back to Oyster Bay. Luke guided the *Sea Spirit* up next to the dock and let Toby off. What was most surprising to Luke about Toby's entire revelation was the bit about he and Edna. He would've never guessed.

32

It was nearly five o'clock. The sun flirted through breaks in the clouds. There would be a few more hours of daylight if the cloud cover didn't increase. The early hour should facilitate Luke's arriving at his destination before it became too crowded.

Once past the NO WAKE zone, Luke pushed forward on the throttles and headed for Fort McBain. He thought he knew what the activity was he had witnessed. It was probable that whoever had been on that island was responsible for the damage to Trotter's boat and at the plant last night. By morning he should know.

The bow of the *Sea Spirit* rose and fell with the swells as she skimmed lithely across the bay under Luke's experienced hand. He had a plan. He would return to the cove, laying low until dawn. He would then make his way across the island on foot as he had before, only this time he wouldn't retreat. He was determined to discover the mysteries the old fort harbored. He had weighed the risk involved, but he had taken risks before.

When Luke arrived at Fort McBain, he was relieved there were no other boats in sight. That would give him the advantage. He anchored out at his hiding place in the cove. After dining on canned tuna and mayonnaise atop soda crackers, he selected a book from the shelf in his small berth and sat outside in the cockpit reading until dark. He lay the open book on his lap and watched the fireflies flit beneath the few weather-beaten scrub oaks on the island.

He'd made up his mind to do this. He would not dwell on it—he would just do it. After a long while he closed the book and went to bed. Dawn would be here soon enough.

The wind whipped up the waters and whistled through the cove. The rocking of the boat awakened Luke. He lay there for about an hour, listening to the choppy waters smacking against the hull. The weather very likely provided him with an unexpected advantage, forestalling any activity at the point, enabling him to poke around freely without risk of detection.

Famished after the evening's lighter fare, he grabbed a package of jelly rolls from a stowage area in the galley and gobbled three, washing them down with a carton of cold milk. No coffee this morning—too rough to try to brew any. The milk would have to do.

He pulled on his bathing trunks and reviewed his checklist. He didn't intend to return to the boat before he found out what he wanted to know. He was thorough. He always had a list when he had a plan.

> *Dry Clothes*
> *Tennis Shoes*
> *Field glasses*
> *C-rations*
> *Canteen*
> *Dagger*
> *Flashlight*
> *Weapon/ammo*

The duffel bag was already packed. He checked its contents against his list. Everything was there. The clothing was rolled around the field glasses and gun. If this turned into war, he would be fighting for his life. He would not go in unprepared.

At the first light of dawn, Luke battened down the hatches aboard the *Sea Spirit*. He took his bundle with the supplies he had prepared and walked around to the bow of the boat. He had nosed in as close as he could to the island. The *Sea Spirit* drew about forty-two inches of water and now she lay sixteen to eighteen feet from shore in about five to six feet of water. He had a strong right arm and he was confident he could make the pitch that far. Much farther might be iffy considering the weight of the bag and the direction of the wind. The exact distance to shore was just an estimate, so all he could do was try. First, he tied a line to the strap of the duffel bag. What was supposed to be a waterproof tote didn't look to be a hundred percent so, and he didn't need to get his gear wet. The line was an added precaution, at least he could retrieve the bag if necessary, wet or not. Next he took the other end of the line and tied it to a bow cleat. The line was long enough to allow for plenty of slack, which he would need for the throw. He stretched his right arm up over his head, then rotated it with his fist in the air, limbering his muscles. He picked the bag up and held it with both hands, aiming it towards the shore, then transferred the bag to his right hand and hurled it aloft with all his might. The rope followed, uncoiling rapidly and snaking through the air. It met its mark and landed on the sandy shore within three feet of the water line. He loosed the line from the bow cleat and let it dangle in the water while he returned to the stern. Clad only in his trunks, he dove shallowly into the water, circled around to the bow of the boat, retrieved the loose-hanging line and swam to shore, line in tow.

Luke pulled his shoes and dry clothes from the bag and put them on. He loaded his gun and concealed it in a holster strapped around his shoulder beneath his loose fitting shirt, then he followed the overgrown path to the closest entrance of the fort, the part of the fort he knew, the part he had explored many times in the past.

The remaining items, including the flashlight and field glasses, were stuffed in a pouch belted around his waist. He concealed his duffel bag in a niche that had been a secret hiding place for him and Trotter in days gone by. It had been a place for hiding discoveries and trinkets and imagined treasures, the place where they had left secret messages for each other, and had provided a safe haven when they were being chased by pirates—and other boys. He reflected momentarily on those times long ago, and marveled to himself at the very different set of circumstances that brought him to this place now. When he emerged from the fort, a misty fog had rolled in and it had begun to drizzle. So much for dry clothes. He mused wryly at the painstaking care he had taken to insure the bundle got to shore without getting wet.

Over time, the winds and waters had heaped the sands against the ruins, making it easy for Luke to climb up on a wall section of the decaying fort. From atop the wall, even through the mist, he had an open view to the side of the island that fronted the Gulf. No boats in sight yet. That would enable his plan. He hastened down from the wall and took the most direct path around the ruins to the location where he had first seen the skiff come ashore. Luke looked to the water's edge for any signs of a boat launch. It was barely detectable, but he spotted a place where crushed shell and pebbles that covered this part of the beach parted slightly to define a worn path where a boat or boats had been pulled from the water repeatedly and launched again. The rising tides covered most traces, but farther from the water's edge the path became more discernible. Luke's eye followed the direction of the path. It led to an area of dense, overgrown foliage. From where he stood, scant sections of a concrete wall could be seen beneath the growth. As he neared the wall, he saw what looked like the remains of one of the many batteries that had fortified this area of the panhandle in days gone by. Wildly uninhibited vines scaled huge sections of the concrete, and scrub-brush climbed the walls, concealing what remained of the battery that had once existed here. Luke hacked at some of the vines with his knife, but it would take more than his small dagger to make any headway. He backed a few yards away and scanned the portion of the wall that lay directly ahead of the somewhat obscure path and then he saw it. The dense growth camouflaged a crevice in the wall. When he pulled at some of the vines, they parted readily, leaving a neat opening that provided easy access to a dark, cavelike tunnel. He noticed nothing unusual immediately, nor any reason why the tunnel might hold an attraction for the occupants of the boat he had seen before. He ventured in, looking for openings along the wall that might lead to offshoot tunnels. Still he saw no hint of what might have generated the activity he had observed around the island.

Farther into the tunnel, two corridors angled off in opposite directions and another one went straight ahead. He directed his flashlight along the sand-covered floor and noticed that the most trafficked route veered off to the left. He had not ventured far into the corridor before he came upon a long aluminum skiff turned on it's side against the wall, bottom side out. The discovery of the boat confirmed that he was on the right track, but he must find what cargo the flat-bottomed boat hauled to and from the great sailboats that came in the night, and where they were hauling it. If his plan went as hoped, he would also discover who was doing the hauling, and maybe who was in charge. Deeper into the tunnel-like corridor he moved, exploring every opening with his flashlight. The rooms were small and uninteresting, revealing nothing.

Luke worked his way back to the entrance and started down another corridor, which consisted only of solid stone on either side. At first the sounds outside were barely detectable, but then he realized he was hearing the unmistakable sounds of a speedboat's rapid approach. As the engines groaned louder, he ran back towards the entrance. He could go back down the first corridor and into one of the empty rooms, but he wouldn't be able to observe any activity from there. He could hide behind the aluminum boat that leaned against the wall and observe the entrance, but that would be too great a risk in case they utilized the boat, yet it appeared to be the only place that would provide any cover near the entrance. The speedboat had already maneuvered through the jetties and now neared the island. The engines slowed as the boat's occupants readied to pull into the launch area.

Luke hadn't yet explored the third corridor. This last hope yielded a room in which he could successfully hide and still observe the entrance.

As Luke ducked into the nearest opening, he searched the room with his flashlight. Holes pierced some of the walls from the bottom to the top. These were possibly barracks where bunks, long since dismantled, had been bolted to the walls. Luke noticed words and letters chiseled into the rough concrete between the holes, and as he extinguished his flashlight, he wished he had time to examine this graffiti left by soldiers in days gone by. He flattened his body against the wall where other young soldiers had left their mark, then he remembered he had failed to pull the vines back in place to cover the evidence of his presence. He assessed his predicament. If he ran from the tunnel, they would see him for sure. If he stayed put, they were likely to look for him, knowing that someone had disturbed the entrance. He cursed his stupidity at making this potentially deadly mistake.

He could retreat back into the darkness of one of the corridors and hope they wouldn't find him, but his unfamiliarity with this part of the old fort put him at the disadvantage of not knowing if these tunnels dead-ended, as many did that he had explored in the past, or if they honeycombed to other tunnels that might provide an outlet for him. He had to know who the occupants of the boat were. This was what he had come for. He would stay put and try and get a look.

Luke watched from his hiding place as the pilot cut the engines and raised the motor tilt. He cut the engines just right, and their momentum propelled the boat into the launch area, beaching it neatly on the shore. Luke had to admire his expertise. Two men piled over the sides of the boat and began coming towards the opening. They were still too far away for Luke to identify them. There were only two and when they got close enough for Luke to see who they were, he was astonished. One was Peyton Fuller; with him was a balding red-headed man. If the man was Munsen Wales, Luke could presume Peyton to be innocent. After all, Toby had surprised him only yesterday with the revelation that he worked for the FBI. It could be that Peyton did, too. As a judge, he was involved in law enforcement. On the other hand, if the man was Skip Traylor, there could be no doubt as to Peyton's involvement, or his daddy's.

Luke watched furtively from the darkness of the bunk room, fearful that they would notice the entrance had been disturbed. His fears were realized when Peyton stopped running and pointed towards the opening. The red-headed man pulled a pistol from a holster strapped openly to his chest. It was then that Luke saw— all the man's fingers were intact. The realization was a huge blow. Peyton and Skip Traylor were conspirators, accomplices in whatever misdeeds they conspired to commit.

"Somebody's been here," Peyton's blustery voice carried.

The two men walked slowly towards the entrance, examining the evidence of an intrusion.

"Did you forget to cover the hole last night, Traylor?"

"It had to be Larry, I left before he did. I told him to put the boat away. He must have forgotten to close up shop."

"Larry's not what you'd call a genius, is he?"

Whoever Larry was, maybe the guy with the tattoos, Luke was relieved that Peyton seemed to be buying it instead of initiating a search for an intruder.

"He's not a genius, but he sure can heft those crates. He ought to be here soon to help me move the rest of them out for tonight's pickup."

So, more were coming. Luke would lay low and see what else he could learn, and who he might be able to round up. If they were transferring cargo and it was the illegal weapons, he would catch them red-handed.

"If that idiot is this careless, we'll have to get rid of him, *after* he finishes taking care of business tonight."

"Logan won't like that. Larry is his boy. He thinks he's the only one he can trust on this end."

Luke watched with fascination as Peyton pressed against the concrete facing of the entrance with his palm, easily loosening a concrete panel that revealed a hidden cubbyhole.

"I don't give a rip what Logan doesn't like. We don't need him, either, now that we have our Commie contacts. I'm in charge of this operation, now." Peyton removed a leather-bound binder from the hiding place as he spoke.

"Hah! You think! Your old man's the only one that's ever been in charge, even before he decided to have Scranton killed for double-crossing him, he was the one really in charge."

Unruffled, Peyton didn't look up as he studied pages of the notebook he held. He pulled a pen from his pocket and began to scribble notes on the pad, like an accountant keeping records.

"Let's see what we did last night. With that shipment gone, we can start counting our cash. It divides up nicely now with Scranton out of the way." Peyton paused and looked up from his figures. He stared unsmilingly at Skip, and his expression was more threatening than Luke had known Peyton to be capable of exhibiting. "You and Lydia killed Scranton."

"Yeah, after you caused all the trouble by introducing him to Lisa. I ought to kill you for that. You knew what you were doing. You wanted Scranton gone, for your daddy. It wasn't enough for you to handle all Scranton's legal business, you wanted it all. Once Lisa and Scranton had been together, they both had to die."

Peyton laughed an ugly, undignified snicker. "Poor Lydia, after she waited all these years for that double-crossing Peabody to marry her, he runs off with a younger woman." Peyton laughed again. "She sure blew them out of the saddle, though, with your help. Lisa never had a chance once she got Lydia's dander up."

The revelation jarred Luke. He had been accused of killing Lisa, when in truth, the mother who had never wanted her had been her murderer.

"Shut up. You egged it on. I told you it wouldn't take much for me to kill you with my bare hands, even if you are the all-powerful Judge."

"Like you did that poor, helpless old woman?"

"Everybody felt sorry for that old woman, but I know she's the one told Callaway he could find me at Red Dawn that day. I know he came snooping around looking for that Hawaiian fellow. They must've been friends because the fellow had Callaway's name in his wallet. That old woman was a witch. She told me I had the devil in me, and that I wouldn't ever find no peace as long as I was on this earth. She was trying to hex me and she just plain ticked me off, so I killed her. It was easy. Just like this, I broke her scrawny neck." Skip demonstrated by putting his two closed fists together and making a snapping motion. "It was just like wringing a chicken's neck. Cluck, cluck, cluck." Skip laughed and clucked insanely, seeming to get a kick out of the recollection of his feat and watching Peyton's reaction.

Luke winced at the memory of Perky and the fatal blow she had been dealt. He put his hand over his shirt pocket and felt the flat silver case beneath the fabric. Skip's words confirmed what Luke had suspected to be true. After Skip chased him and Cooper to Masonville, and failed to kill them, he must have circled back to Mango Junction and taken his anger out on Perky. Even as old as she was, it was evident Perky had put up a struggle, grasping at the already frayed leather cord around Skip's neck as she fell to the ground. When Skip ran to his car, it fell away from him and lay by the roadside until the day Luke found it. Luke would kill Skip Traylor with his bare hands if he got the chance.

"You know, Judge, we only hired that Hawaiian on because he said he was on Logan's boat in Vietnam. Logan figured he was a snitch when he showed up in Pemrose Key wanting to work with our boys. Logan wanted me to give him a job so we could keep an eye on him, and eventually, get rid of him."

"You should've gotten rid of him sooner than you did, like when you radioed in and I told you to do it right then. That was a big risk you took. You thought I didn't see you throw him overboard when I met you in the *Mari Jane Too*."

"I told you, when that storm blew in out there, we needed every hand we could get. He helped save the Que' Pasa."

"Shut up, Traylor! Somebody's coming." Peyton cocked his head sideways, straining to listen.

"I don't see no boat out there."

"Precisely. Now listen." Peyton swatted his hand in the air, silencing Skip.

Luke watched as the two men moved stealthily to the entrance, one crouching on either side. Skip Traylor drew his gun. Luke, too, heard the slow, uneven footsteps crunching in the hard-packed, shell covered sand. Skip was right, there was no boat. Whoever it was must have come the same way Luke came in, from the cove on the far side of the island, where the *Sea Spirit* was moored.

Luke watched and waited as quietly as Peyton and Skip. When the footsteps slowed near the entrance, Luke recognized Trotter's profile in the opening.

Instantly, Skip's raised hand came down hard against Trotter's head, knocking him unconscious with the butt of his pistol. Trotter crumpled to the floor, and Skip aimed the gun at his head.

Luke started to shoot, but remembered that their accomplices might now be in the vicinity. He replaced his weapon and instinctively, he let out a howl and lunged from his hiding place. In one swift movement, he viciously attacked, thrusting his body against Skip Traylor's side and knocking him to the ground. Luke pounded Skip unmercifully—for Stephen Pau, and old Perky Bittle, and even for Lisa. He thrust his fists repeatedly against Skip's head and his chest and his gut. He would kill him. Over and over he pounded until his fists were soaked in the blood that covered Skip Traylor's face, and until a shot rang out.

Peyton had retrieved Skip's pistol that had flown from his hand and he now stood over Luke, the gun aimed directly at him. Trotter still lay lifeless across the sandy floor. Luke raised himself to a standing position.

"Luke, w-wh-what are you doing here?" Peyton stammered.

"You had me fooled, Peyton. I wouldn't have suspected you or your daddy of any of this."

"You heard, did you? That's too bad, Luke. We've been friends a long time." Peyton looked like he could cry.

"You're no friend, Peyton."

Peyton was angry, and his voice quivered. "Help Traylor up!" Even brandishing a gun, Peyton didn't appear to be much of a threat. He'd always seemed a bit of a ninny with his blustery stammering, his pudgy face and his soft skin.

Luke helped Skip to his feet and leaned his limp body against the wall. Skip rubbed his hands over his face and let them slide down across the front of his shirt, smearing blood all over himself. Luke wished he was as bad off as he looked.

"I'll kill you, Callaway." Skip gurgled the words.

Peyton silenced him. "Shut up, Traylor. We got to figure out what to do with these two."

"I know what to do with 'em."

"We won't kill them here. I want them disposed of in Pemrose Key, so their bodies can be found and nobody will come poking around out here looking for them. Where's your boat, Luke? Over in the cove?" Peyton knew the cove and that side of the island as well as any of them did. "Maybe we'll just put both of your bodies on that boat of yours, then light a fire and put her adrift."

"I like that, Judge. Let's do it." Skip shuffled closer to Luke.

"Shut your mouth, Traylor. Let me think about this. I don't kill people the way you do, without thinking things through first. That can get you in trouble." Peyton was huffing and puffing from all the excitement. Luke had never seen him sweat. It was Peyton's brains, not his brawn, that had gotten him his judgeship. "Go get that line over there off that flat-bottomed boat and tie them up."

Skip staggered his first few steps before steadying himself. He soon returned with a heavy, coiled rope. He rolled Trotter on his side, then tied his wrists and one ankle together behind his back. Luke knew he was next. There was enough line left on one end to tie Luke in the same fashion and lash he and Trotter together.

"Get down there with your buddy," Skip growled, and shoved Luke in the chest with both hands. "Move it!"

At the thrust of Skip's hands, Luke took a few steps backwards, into the tunnel. Peyton still held the gun in one hand, with the other he pulled a flashlight from his pocket and lit up the narrow area just beyond the opening.

"Still afraid of the dark, Peyton?" Luke taunted, recalling the few times Peyton had spent the night on the island with a group of the boys.

"Why you..." Peyton puffed up his chest angrily.

At that moment, Luke saw beyond them to the launch area where a small skiff bearing two occupants was pulling ashore beside the speed boat. The timing was perfect.

A voice called out from the beach, "Hey, who's in there? Is that you, Skip?"

Flustered and thrown off guard, Peyton turned to see who had arrived. Luke took the opportunity to push him to the ground. The gun and flashlight went flying. While Peyton tried to recover and pick himself up, Luke and Skip scrambled for the gun. Skip's already outstretched hand seized the gun first. Peyton's flashlight bounced along the ground and blinked off, and then the gun went off.

Peyton groaned and Luke heard the sandy gravel crunching beneath his body as he fell to the ground with a thud. As Skip tightly clutched the gun and stared at Peyton's lifeless body, Luke backed into the darkness of one of the tunnels. Skip took aim and fired. Luke was trapped. All he could do was retreat, and hope to find an exit. He turned and ran blindly, not knowing where the tunnel would lead him. The deeper in he got, the darker it became as the balance of light the entrance provided began to wane. He heard footsteps running behind him, and voices. Nothing to do but forge ahead. The light from the opening soon became nonexistent, and he was forced to stop. He fumbled for his own flashlight, shining it ahead of him, looking for the direction of the tunnel. He looked around frantically for a hiding place. There were none. Sheer concrete and stone surrounded him on each side. He ran farther into the tunnel, coming into a wide, open area. If he could find an exit, he could circle around and help Trotter.

Luke's light had been seen. Shots were fired and a bullet hit his flashlight, knocking it from his hand. A spray of bullets ricocheted off the walls and something pierced Luke's thigh. Searing pain shot up his leg, through his groin and into his guts, and probing with his hand he felt the torn flesh of his inner thigh. He sucked in his breath sharply and his body shuddered involuntarily. He clenched his fist in an effort to thwart the pain, and with certain death at the hands of Skip Traylor his only alternative, determined to go on.

Luke pulled his gun from beneath his shirt and fired back in the dark in the direction of the gunfire, hoping to discourage their advance. He listened, not knowing if his bullets had met his target. His gun was empty and there was no time to reload. He turned and ran, hobbling and dragging his wounded leg, hoping to find an exit. He knew the tunnels catacombed subterraneously throughout the island. There had to be an escape, and he was going to do all in his power to find it.

The pain was excruciating. Luke used the wall for support to pull himself along with his arms, lessening the weight placed on his leg.

Terror gripped him, not just the familiar fear he had experienced many times before. He was boxed in like a caged animal, and he knew with a certainty they would spare him no mercy. Peyton, if he was still alive, was no friend, and Skip was after blood. They were ruthless killers.

The rush of adrenalin targeted every muscle and nerve-ending in Luke's body and struck with force, empowering him to move forward, seeking a crevice he could escape to long enough to ease the pain if only for a moment. He tried to control his breathing, but it seemed to echo off the damp, stone walls. It seemed louder than the footsteps he heard coming closer, heavy shoes grinding in the sand that covered the floor of this part of the old fort; squeaking and grinding, getting louder, coming closer. How many of them could there be?

He waited silently, poised for whatever danger presented itself. His hands were like bricks—heavy, taut and ready to strike, capable of destroying. Split-second scenarios of what might or might not occur in the next few moments of his life played rapidly in his mind as his brain frantically sought a successful course of action against whatever evil might await him.

He reached behind him to gain greater support from the wall. His hand struck something metal. He groped in the dark. It felt like iron. It felt like a handle. He turned to feel with both hands, and then fought to contain the cry that welled up in his throat. With his left hand he found hinges. It was a door!

He pulled on it with both hands. It wouldn't budge. He tried again and again, pulling with all his might. There must be a latch. *Calm down....slow down....you have time.* He found the crack of the door opening. The door fit so snugly and flush against the wall, the crack for the opening was almost imperceptible, but he found it by the location of the handle. He felt very carefully, and followed the line of the opening all the way to what he perceived to be the top of the door, based on the height of it. It was there, a hard, flat piece of metal wedged into another piece of metal that fastened to the wall.

They were coming closer. He knew the brightness he had seen was the distant glow from their flashlights. As he struggled with the latch, he glanced over his shoulder. The light was brighter. He couldn't see them, but he saw the light. With all his strength, he pushed on the steel rod, attempting to dislodge it from its position in the steel clasp that held it fast. With one desperate shove it gave way and fell to the sandy floor.

A beam of light from behind him lit up the door. They were here, and they saw him. With a surge of strength borne of fear,

Luke grasped the handle and thrust open the heavy, stone door. As the door opened, a nauseating pain engulfed Luke. It pierced the small of his back, right above the base of his spine. He fell to his knees, momentarily paralyzed. But then, with reflex action, his hands drew up in defensive fists. Before he could react or get to his feet, the boot-clad foot took aim again and gored his left shoulder, knocking his body against the wall and to the floor. Before he could recover from that blow, the boot came down hard in the pit of his stomach. The single-mindedness that Luke had been capable of calling on in Vietnam came into play. It was the only resource he had. Through the pain, he saw clearly that he had only minutes to live. Drawing on all his strengths, he erected that wall that had shielded him and empowered him while at war, enabling him to focus only on the task at hand, disregarding all else. With more luck than calculation, when he made a reach for the boot as it withdrew from the middle of his gut, he succeeded in throwing whichever of his assailants possessed it to the ground with a groan and a thud.

"You son-of-a…I'll kill your arse!" The voice growled at him.

It was the unmistakable cockney accent of Munsen Wales. The flashlight lay on the ground, half buried in the sand, providing only a dim light. The other assailant moved quickly to lift his accomplice from the ground. "Get up, dammit! Help me! Don't just lie there."

Munsen's struggle to get to his feet gave Luke the time he needed to raise himself off the ground. There was no stopping them. Luke didn't know what was on the other side of that door, but he had to get through it. It was his only hope; his only possibility for survival.

One of them went for the flashlight, and Luke pushed the door the rest of the way open. The flashlight, successfully retrieved by one of his assailants—Luke still wasn't sure which—was aimed through the opening of the door and lit up the room beyond, revealing an arsenal of weapons of war. There were opened cases of handguns, automatic rifles, ammunition, and case upon case of identical sealed crates, all stamped with the words, RED DAWN, MFG.

"Thank you, Scranton." Luke muttered aloud and fought the urge to cross himself. He reached for one of the rifles with both hands. It wasn't likely to be loaded, he knew, but he grasped the barrel securely, then turned and swung with all his might, striking the butt forcefully against his attacker's head. The flashlight fell from the man's hand just before he fell to the floor, but not before illuminating the blood that spewed from his ear. With one glance at the man's hands before he crumpled to the floor, Luke ascertained it was Skip Traylor. Luke could see from the faint light that Skip's twin was coming towards him now, gun in hand. This one was, indeed, Munsen Wales.

Luke had to know. "Munsen, why? You betrayed your country, our government, your adopted land that you professed to love. You nearly gave your life for this country. Why the betrayal now?"

Munsen came closer to Luke, the gun aimed at Luke's head. Was this the last vision of life Luke would glean? Munsen snorted. He was semi-frothing at the mouth now. Dimly, Luke saw the flicker of insanity in his eyes.

A light shone from somewhere. A gun went off, and Munsen Wales grabbed the front of Luke's shirt, dropping his own gun in the process.

Now, face to face, Munsen gazed into Luke's eyes, clinging to Luke's shirt all the while...clinging to life.

Munsen grinned, exposing his toothy gap that matched his twin brother's and then gave his answer, "Blood's thicker than water, eh? 'e's my brother, you know, ehhh..." These were Munsen's final words before he slid the rest of the way to the ground, his arms outstretched, his hands releasing Luke's shirt as his body fell to the floor.

It was, in the end, not for love of country, not for love of life in America, but because this hard-headed, stubborn brute of a man who had given so much for his country, had finally given his life for the love of a long-lost brother.

It was Trotter whose aim pierced the heart of Munsen Wales.

"I figured you were playing possum back there, Trotter. I didn't think anybody could take you down that easily, but what took you so long?"

Trotter grinned as he loped unevenly towards Luke, his prosthesis dragging only slightly in the sand. "Are you alright, Luke? That leg needs some attention before you end up like me."

"I'm a lot better now than I was a few minutes ago, friend. How'd you get yourself free?" Luke removed his loose-fitting shirt and fashioned a tourniquet around the top portion of his leg. The pressure helped ease the pain a bit, or at least Luke wanted to believe it did.

Trotter slapped the thigh of his artificial leg. "This is the leg that idiot tied. Working it just so, it came right off, giving me enough slack to free my hands. That's one good thing about having a peg leg. All I had to do was strap this thing back on and I was on my way."

"How did you know I was in trouble, Trotter, or where to find me?"

"It didn't take a genius to figure it out, Luke. When you left the plant the other day, I pretty much knew what you had on your mind, but I figured if you wanted me to know, you would've told me. I got Tommy Granger to bring me out to Fort McBain in his runabout. It didn't take a lot of snooping around to find your boat up in the cove. I had an idea you'd gone on foot over to where we saw the boats that night. I figured I could do the same. After we checked on board *The Sea Spirit*, Tommy nosed into shore and let me off. I got him to radio the sheriff, and he went to meet them at the pass to show them where to go. Peyton was bleeding like a stuck pig, about like you are. He thought he was dying and he asked me to help him. I told him help was on the way, and Sheriff Gravlee would be here any minute. Boy, was he ticked. He tried to get that big fellow there that I just sent to heaven—or wherever—to stop and help him, but he ran right past us, looking for his brother. I thought it was Skip at first. There was another joker with him, but when he saw Peyton was down he turned tail and ran. He shoved Peyton's speedboat out a ways and climbed aboard. Guess he liked it better than the one he came in. Last I saw, he was drifting around out there trying to figure how to make it run without the keys."

"Good thing you came looking for me, Trotter." Luke took the flashlight from Trotter's hand and directed the beam on the crates. "Take a look at this—what we did here today may help a few more of our boys survive a confrontation with the Viet Cong."

Trotter whistled. "So that's been helping them wipe us out in Nam."

Luke illuminated the walls with the beam of light. He remembered the bunk room and wondered if this room had once held more of the same. He steadied the light in one corner of the room where a wooden stairway rose steeply towards the ceiling. "I wonder where that goes."

Trotter shrugged. They would soon know. Luke took the steps slowly, pulling himself along, trying not to place too much pressure on his wounded leg, while Trotter followed behind in a similar manner with his one leg and his peg. The steps were unusually steep and tall, made of thick, rough-hewn timbers, and as they ascended, Luke saw a faint sliver of light above. At the top of the stairs, they discovered that the source of the light shone from beneath a door.

"Dead end, Trotter."

The door was locked, but then Luke saw from the light of the flashlight that a deadbolt was attached to the bottom of the door and secured to the tread of the top step. It lifted easily, much more easily than the last lock he had forced open.

Luke pushed against the door. At first it didn't budge, then he leaned his shoulder against it and pushed again and the door opened to a room in which aged wood-and-steel tankards lined the walls.

"Where are we, Luke?" Trotter asked from his lower position.

"I'm not sure, Trotter. Let me give you a hand." Luke cleared the door opening and helped Trotter ascend the final steep step.

Luke spotted another opening. "Let's see where that goes." He stopped short of the opening and was amazed at what he saw. Through a not-too-distant doorway he saw the back of a man standing at a counter wielding a knife. To one side was an area that contained several refrigerators and stainless steel sinks. Trotter pulled his gun and they eased in closer, until the man came into clear view. The knife the man held poised above his head came down sharply, with a thud. Luke heard the hammer click on Trotter's pistol. When the man spun around, they were amazed to see Billy Jack, holding a cabbage half in each hand. Billy Jack stared at them from where he stood by the stainless steel sink, every bit as astonished as Luke and Trotter.

"Mamie's Place!" They voiced in unison.

"How did we get here?" Luke wondered if he might not be hallucinating from the loss of blood.

Trotter started laughing.

Mamie came through the door, her spoon at rest in her pocket, her eyes wide with astonishment. "Where on God's earth did you boys come from?" She quickly appraised their appearances. "And where in dear God's name have you been? Luke, you look like you been hurt bad, baby."

Toby appeared behind his mother and went immediately to Luke, helping lower him to a bench positioned against the wall. The seeping blood had begun to cake and Luke loosened the tourniquet. The bullet would have to be removed soon.

"I know where they came from, Mama. Billy Jack, call an ambulance."

Luke winced at the pain.

"Don't you worry, Luke. They'll be here soon. You're going to be okay." Mamie stood helplessly by, wringing her hands and not appearing to be convinced.

Luke clinched his teeth and forced the words out. "I think we just figured out why Edna wanted you to sell your place, Mamie. Scranton Peabody has a weapons arsenal down there. Evidently, he was her 'secret' investor. That tunnel must run under the channel to get here from Ft. McBain. Right, Toby?" Talking would take his mind off the pain.

Toby understood. "I think you hit it on the head, Luke. It ain't far at all out Mama's back door here, through the keg room and into the fort, as you just found out. This place would have been perfect for Red Dawn's operation. You can see forever out across the bay and tell if anybody's snooping around. I used to try to get that door open when I was a kid, but I never could. Scranton told Mama when she bought this place that it just went to a cellar that always had water in it, so he had it sealed up. Too bad he didn't have enough foresight when he sold this place to Mama to realize that this tunnel could someday be valuable to him. His road to making millions would have been that much shorter and a little more lucrative. By the way, Luke, I spoke to Joe Lianoho yesterday after we talked, and again a couple of hours ago. They moved in on Red Dawn this morning and closed them down. What you saw and heard out at Red Dawn confirmed their suspicions. Baines Fuller was arrested at his Washington office this morning, and they caught up with Thomas Logan at Pearl Harbor. He was being wined and dined by some fat Commie pig; caught him red-handed accepting a big pile of cash."

"And I just thought you were trying to build boats, Luke. Of course nothing you do surprises me, buddy. Toby, you have surprised me. We all thought you were a lost cause." Trotter expressed his wonder at the role his two friends played in a major espionage game. "The sailboats we saw, Luke, what was that all about?"

Luke focused on his words, trying to ignore the increasing pain. "The Gulf side of the island had to be their point of departure for their smuggling operation. It looked innocent enough, like sailboats anchored out off the island for the night, a pretty common sight around here. I suspect you had it figured out as to what Skip was doing, Trotter, when you said he was making runs to Mexico, only instead of hauling drugs, he was hauling weapons to the Viet Cong."

"You going to make it, Luke?"

"I'll be okay, Toby. Tell us more."

"From what Joe says, the CIA had already figured out their route some time ago. They knew the goods were surfaced across Mexico to the Pacific coast, then delivered to Russian fishing vessels in international waters. It was the Russians problem to get the stuff into the hands of the Viet Cong. They were likely delivering to Macau or Hong Kong, or some other neutral country. Coordinating the entire effort and negotiating with his Communist buddies, was one Commander Thomas Logan."

"I saw Red Dawn crates being stored out at Shank's Landing, too. What was that all about?" Luke clutched the bench tightly and was thankful for the distant siren he heard. What in fact had been only ten or fifteen minutes had seemed like an eternity.

"They had to have somewhere to unload by truck."

"You mean Pemrose Produce trucks, Toby?" Luke could hear the siren getting closer.

"That was their cover. Since the smuggling runs were two and three months apart, the goods were kept there until motorboats could haul them across the bay, through the pass and around the jetties to Fort McBain for storage until the sailboats arrived again. All that trafficking around an uninhabited island was an added risk, sooner or later somebody was going to notice, but Cole's Bayou is too shallow at times for a sailboat, so they couldn't ship from there. Likewise, the bay side of Fort McBain, ever since the Corps of Engineers dredged the canal and all that sand was pumped along Fort McBain's shoreline. Sailboats were less suspicious and more economical to run. Fishing boats don't have enough stowage space, and they run out of fuel. Cargo boats would get too much attention from the Coast Guard. Scranton could have saved himself a lot of risk and money by unloading his goods here and taking them through that secret passageway over to the fort."

Mamie had ceased wringing her hands and was silently listening to the conversation when she spied the gun in the holster that hung low on Trotter's hip.

"What is that you got hanging around your waist, Trotter Blackwell? You get that gun out of here. Can't you read? Don't you know what that sign says on my front door? It says NO FIREARMS ALLOWED INSIDE, and I mean it!"

Luke tried to laugh, but he couldn't, and his voice was weak. "Now, Mamie, what would've come of me if Trotter hadn't been handy with that weapon?"

"I tell you what, if it wasn't for weapons, none of this would have happened in the first place. Not even that war in Vietnam, and that's the God's honest truth. Ain't that right, Lucas?" She winked down at Luke, but she looked worried.

Toby stood beside Mamie and reached out and placed his arm around her shoulders. She smiled, but a single tear streamed slowly down one cheek.

Luke's leg was numb. He felt no more pain. The room began to spin around and suddenly, everything went dark.

33

"**I** must be in heaven," Luke murmured. He recognizes Cooper. She's staring at him, and through depths of darkness, her coppery hair is shimmering in an aura of light. Cooper has come to him at last, and to Luke, she looks like an angel. He desperately tries to reach out and touch her, to tell her he loves her. But he's so sleepy, so groggy. "My special angel..." he murmurs, struggling to lift his arm, to reach out and touch the face that peers down at him. "...I love you."

The face backs away. "Hey, don't touch." The voice is masculine. "We're good friends, but I don't know about this love business."

Luke's vision begins to come into focus and he recognizes Trotter.

"You ain't in heaven, Buddy, that's for sure. Not yet, anyway."

"Trotter...where did Cooper go?"

"I think you're hallucinating, Luke. You've lost a lot of blood. Cooper ain't here, and I sure ain't no angel. They let me come in here for a minute before you go into surgery. You're at Baptist Hospital in Pensacola. Your folks were just in here. I'll tell them you're awake now."

"Is Cooper here, Trotter?" Luke's lips felt thick as he formulated the words and his tongue felt as relaxed as his body.

Trotter's voice was gentle. "No, buddy, she's not here."

An orderly wheeled in a gurney. "Time to go, Mr. Callaway. You can see everybody after we get that bullet out of your leg."

"I think he'll be fine, Mr. and Mrs. Callaway. We got the bullet out okay and all strategic parts seem to be intact. We just want to watch him for a day or two, since he lost so much blood."

Luke hears the words, but he doesn't recognize the voice. He tries to open his eyes to see who is talking about him, but he can't. Regardless of his efforts to stay awake, he feels himself slumbering off again. He wrestles with this for some time, it seems, before finally recognizing the people who are with him.

"Mom..."

"Yes, Luke, Darling, we're here."

He reached his hand out to his mother. Another face came into focus. "Trotter, is that you?"

"It's me, Luke. You made it, and you got to keep your leg."

"Dad." He focused on his father and he saw, reflected in his father's eyes, the terror of having witnessed what could have been the final moments of his son's life. Not a word had to be spoken as they looked at each other. All the love Luke had known as a boy, and all the reasons why his father had fought him, suddenly came to light more clearly than ever before.

Luke's mouth was dry and his tongue felt like sandpaper, but he got the words out slowly. "I'm going to live, am I?" He looked from one to the other.

"You made it, son. You lost a lot of blood, but they've patched you up good as new. They said you were going to keep trying to go to sleep on us, but they want you to wake up now, so we're going to stay here and bother you. How's that?" Ryan joked, but his usually gruff, gravelly voice was gentle.

Luke laughed a little. "Oww." He held his hand over his stomach. "It hurts to laugh."

"Then we'll try not to be too funny." Ryan chuckled.

Meg picked up Skip's snuff box off of Luke's nightstand. "What is this, son?"

"That's how I knew Skip Traylor killed Perky Bittle. Ironic, isn't it?" He formulated his words slowly. "After Lisa's death she gets revenge for her murder. Her gift to Skip was the clue that gave him away."

Sheriff Gravlee tapped on the frame of the open door.

"Could I talk to Luke for a minute, folks? You can stay if you like."

"I'm going to head out, Luke. We're still trying to meet that Miami Boat Show deadline. I'll get back with you later." With those words, Trotter was gone. Luke didn't blame him for not liking hospitals, he'd spent his share of time in them.

"How do you feel, Luke?"

"They say I'm going to make it, Sheriff. What about Peyton?"

"He's here in the hospital, too. We've got a man posted outside his door. They say he's going to live. He may not want to, though. The rest of his life will be spent behind bars, if he doesn't get the electric chair. He sure did throw away a first class chance at a good life. Baines Fuller had a fatal heart attack after he was arrested this morning. I thought all of you would want to know, especially since he was a friend of yours, Ryan."

"I considered him a friend, at one time. Amazing how you can know somebody your entire life and not really know them. I've seen a lot of corruption in business over the years, but what I guess has really surprised and disappointed me the most is Baines Fuller's involvement with this. When Scranton Peabody sold Peabody's Pub to Mamie, to get a little capital to open Red Dawn, he aimed to go after those government contracts with the aid of Senator Fuller.

I introduced them, never imagining that the two of them would eventually conspire to commit treason against our government. I talked to Macon DeLaney a short time ago. He said that Scranton had a lucrative legitimate operation going at first. Red Dawn manufactured weapons parts and hauled them by truck to the Navy base here in Pensacola, where they were transported by the Navy for assembly. He was doing good with his government contracts, until he started passing off bum goods."

Luke's heart lurched at the mention of the DeLaney name. Certainly Cooper's father would know where to find her.

"You talked to Senator DeLaney, Dad?"

"That's right, Luke. I'm sure you'd be interested in knowing that Senator DeLaney spearheaded the investigation. I believe you are acquainted with another DeLaney family member." Ryan teased and his eyes twinkled.

Luke groaned aloud and he wondered if Macon DeLaney knew how close he'd come to getting his daughter killed. He probably would never want Cooper to see Luke again, if Luke could ever even find her.

Ignoring Luke's pain, Ryan continued. "When the federal government found out that an Alabama company was using inferior alloys in their production, Macon DeLaney was appointed to head up the investigative committee. He suspected Senator Fuller was somehow involved, knowing he was always lingering in the background whenever Scranton stood to get a government contract, but he had to be sure. It's tragic that Baines Fuller allowed himself to be consumed by greed, and more tragic that he brought his son into it."

Luke had questions for Ben Gravlee. "Did you know about the smuggling operation, Sheriff?"

"I've been working with the FBI since right before you were arrested, Luke. Toby says he explained to you that going to jail was for your own good."

"Yeah, so he said. Thanks a heap!"

"I suspected something was up with Peyton awhile back. Right after he was sworn in as Judge he got himself one of those expensive, high powered speedboats. He just didn't seem like the type, and we started getting reports of it being out on the water a lot after dark. Young Peyton seemed like a right busy Judge. Guess he needed a little extra income to keep up his expensive habits. He got that boat to impress Edna Sinclair. Seems he's sweet on her. Fancied himself to be a playboy of sorts, evidently." The sheriff rolled his eyes heavenward at this unlikelihood.

"I had my boys watching him. Guess we weren't watching him close enough. It wasn't natural the way he kind of seemed to turn on you in court when he was supposed to be your friend. That's what cinched his guilt in my mind. I figured he was tangled up somehow in this mess. An honest judge would have removed himself from the case from the beginning. Since it was more like a kangaroo court anyway, we decided to give him enough rope to hang himself. We had it all planned for Toby to come into court and come back to life the way he did. I watched Peyton real close then. The look on his face was priceless."

"Edna and Peyton, huh? Amazing. That woman must have hidden talents. Was she involved, beyond trying to get Mamie to sell her place to Scranton, her 'secret' investor?"

"Oh, yeah. According to Peyton, she was involved alright. If Peyton's in trouble, he want's everybody to be in trouble, so he's been running his mouth. Edna's the one put it in Peyton's head to fix Lisa up with Scranton. He had told Edna about this woman who had been wanting Scranton to marry her for years, even followed him across the country to Baseline. He said Scranton was probably scared to marry her because she'd already been suspected of doing in one husband. That put ideas into Edna's head. It appears that the hatred Edna had harbored for years for a sister she had never known kindled a curiosity that led her to agree to take Lisa in until she finished high school. She had always wanted a closer relationship with her old man, so she agreed to keep his secret about Lisa being her sister. If the Navy had gotten hold of that one, he would have never made Commander. When she finally met Lisa and saw how beautiful she was, she hated her even more. Guess she figured if Scranton's girlfriend had killed once, she'd kill again. She could get Lisa out of the way and have her daddy to herself without even getting her hands dirty. She had no idea Scranton's girlfriend was really her long-presumed-dead, Aunt Lydia, and Lydia had no idea Lisa was her daughter. Edna egged Peyton on about getting Lydia to kill Lisa. It worked. My men are looking for Edna now, for conspiracy to murder."

Luke was in much better shape when Trotter returned to the hospital the morning following his surgery. Luke still didn't have all the answers.

"Have they found Edna, yet, Trotter?"

"Nope. She done flew the coop. Ben Gravlee and the FBI are still looking for her. They tried to talk to her mama, but she was completely incoherent, kept babbling about a baby."

"A baby?"

"Yeah, maybe it's the Tabitha kid those attorneys mentioned in those legal papers we found in your briefcase."

"Whoa. When did you find papers in my briefcase?"

"When Tommy took me out to the cove and we found the *Sea Spirit*, with your briefcase on board. We thought it might contain a clue about where you went. We didn't just open it without talking about it first, for a full five seconds, we even took a vote on it, real democratic like, and it was unanimous that we should take a look at what was inside. Looked like some heavy reading there. Found some interesting correspondence from Biggins and Slater, and a settlement proposal to Edna. I know it probably ain't none of my business, but knowing Edna, you better think about that one a bit more, Luke. Edna's going to be arrested, and nobody can find any trace of any kid."

Trotter paused, seeming to gauge Luke's reaction before continuing. "I found a letter from Cooper, too, Luke. I only read it because of what you said to me before you went out to the island, about telling her you didn't do it and stuff, you know."

"You mean that I love her?"

"Yeah, that stuff."

When Luke didn't say anything, Trotter went on, "I'm sorry Luke, about her moving, and about reading the letter. I hope you didn't mind. Her old address was on the bottom of that letter, so I tried to get in touch with her while you were in surgery. I talked to her ex-roommate. She told me Cooper's already moved, and that she didn't have a forwarding address for her yet."

Luke was certain the pain he felt came from his heart and not from his wound.

It was evident Trotter wasn't comfortable talking about Cooper because of the pain it seemed to cause Luke. "I brought your boat back around to Oyster Bay."

"Thanks, Trotter. I appreciate that. I appreciate everything you've done. If it weren't for you, I wouldn't be here talking about it."

Trotter didn't try to hide his relief when a nurse came in and told him he'd overstayed his visitation time. Luke needed his rest.

When Trotter left, Luke tried to sleep, but as soon as he began to doze, the phone rang.

"Hello?"

"Luke, is that you?"

Luke bolted as upright as was possible for the shape he was in. "Edna, where are you?"

"Well, I ain't that stupid, Lucas Callaway. Do you think I'm going to tell you when Ben Gravlee's got the entire Sheriff's department of Escambia County out lookin' for me?"

"No, I guess that wasn't a very intelligent question, Edna. Why are you calling me?"

"I want to see you, Luke. There's something you need to know."

"Edna, in light of everything that's happened, I rescind my proposal. You're in a lot of trouble, you know. Whatever I do for this Tabitha kid, if there is a kid, will have nothing to do with you. It looks like all of Lisa's heirs—you, Logan, Lydia Rhinehart—will all be behind bars."

"You think I don't know that, Luke? I ain't stupid! I don't have but another minute and I've got to go. When are you getting out of the hospital, Luke?"

"Tomorrow."

"Good. I want you to meet me at Mamie's Place at three o'clock tomorrow afternoon. I want Mamie and Toby and Doc there, too, you hear? And tell Ben Gravlee to be there, but not to bring every danged idiot in his department."

"I hear, Edna. I'll see what I can do."

There was silence on the other end, then a dial tone.

Luke's hand was still on the receiver when the phone rang again. "Yes, Edna?"

"No, not Edna, Luke, Joe Lianoho here."

"Joe, how are you?"

"How are you?"

"Vietnam didn't do me in, this won't either."

"Sorry it seemed like we bailed out on you, Luke. I had a man keeping an eye on you there."

"You mean the Plain Brown Wrapper?"

Joe laughed. "You know Jackson Cummings."

"Yeah, he took good care of me. I guess Munsen Wales was a disappointment?"

"Munsen Wales did what we expected of him. He helped lead us to the others. What we didn't expect was that he would kill your wife."

"I thought Skip Traylor and Lydia Rhinehart killed Lisa."

"Munsen Wales not only served under Logan for awhile, he got involved in munitions and explosives in a slightly different way than you. Traylor offered to pay him for making the bomb that blew up the Captain Hook. A little money was all it took to effect a reconciliation between the two brothers. When Miss Rhinehart was apprehended and told that Lisa was her daughter, the baby she left behind in California many years ago, she broke down. She confessed that the bomb had been her idea. Traylor planted it in one of Lisa's suitcases and Miss Rhinehart paid a dockhand to stow it aboard the Captain Hook, along with Lisa's other luggage."

Luke's parents were at the hospital to pick him up at noon as he requested. He was anxious to be released, and he knew as soon as the doctor made his rounds he would be a free man again. This time it meant real freedom. When the doctor appeared, he dismissed Luke with a clean bill of health and orders to get his surgical wounds cleaned once a week by Doc Bauchet for the next few weeks. The relief was evident in his parent's faces. Now they could all resume some normal semblance of life. Things seemed to be coming together again, and Luke thought that soon he might even try to find Cooper. A lot had happened. He didn't think he would have a chance with her now, but he intended to find out.

Ryan now appeared to be okay with Luke's independence. He seemed to understand, finally, the part of Luke that was so much like himself. No one on God's earth liked a challenge better than Ryan Callaway, except maybe his son. Luke had come by that trait honestly, had he not? Ryan was excited for Luke about the potential of Windward Boats.

Having already recognized that Ryan could be a valuable asset in the business, Luke made his father a proposal. Ryan accepted. Ryan would complete his one year of tenure at Callaway Construction, and then he and Luke would finally be partners in the new "family" business, Windward Boats. Luke wasn't fooled by his mother's placid smile when Ryan accepted the proposal. Luke knew his mother well enough to know how important that decision was to her. When their eyes met, he saw the abundance of his mother's love, and her joyful peace in knowing that the bond between her two Callaway men was indestructible.

When they left the hospital, Meg and Ryan protested when Luke asked to be taken to Mamie's Place, and they protested louder when he asked them not to come in, and told them he would get a ride home. They obliged him, though.

There were not too many people in Mamie's this time of day. It was the in-between hour. A few tired fishermen sat at stools at the bar. Other than that, it was quiet. Mamie greeted him at the door. Doc was at her side, and Ben Gravlee was there.

"Where's Toby?" Luke asked.

"He's in the kitchen. He'll be right out." Doc nodded towards the door to the kitchen. "There he is now."

Just as Toby entered, in walked Edna, holding a small child in her arms. The child looked to be around two years old, or thereabouts.

Edna got right to the point and addressed herself to Ben Gravlee. "Sheriff, I understand your boys are looking for me. I'm here to turn myself in. I don't have no choice, I know. For once in my entire life, I'd like to do something right." She turned to Bauchet next. "Doc, you remember a few years ago I tried to get you to give me an abortion? You wouldn't do it, so six months later you delivered my baby. You didn't know whose baby it was, and I was grateful you never asked."

She turned now to face Toby. "Toby, you remember when I tried to get you to talk your mama into selling her place? I was doing it for Peyton. He asked me to. He knew how badly Scranton wanted to get it back, but he didn't know just how low I would stoop to get it back for him. He didn't know I would sleep with somebody else to get what I wanted. I don't know why, but Peyton trusted me, and he didn't want me sleeping with nobody but him. Peyton hadn't never been with no other woman before, and I told him I hadn't ever been with a man before. I used you, Toby. You found that out, and then you went off to Vietnam. All I got out of it was pregnant...her name is Tabitha." She looked at the little girl and stroked her dark curls with one hand.

Mamie instantly grasped what Edna was saying, and her hands trembled as she reached for the child. "My grand-baby, this precious child is my grand-baby." Mamie cooed, "She's so beautiful."

Mamie took the child in her arms, and Edna's eyes glistened as she handed her baby over to her.

"*Our* grand-baby." Doc beamed. "And I brought her into this world."

Toby had to recover from the shock before he spoke, but when he did it was with pride and wonder. "*My* daughter? I have a little girl? You mean this is my little girl?"

"Tabitha Logan is her name." Edna looked at Luke now. "She's not Lisa's, she's mine. Edna Logan is my legal name, like I told you, but when Lisa was killed, it was the perfect way to absolve myself. I was afraid if Peyton knew, he wouldn't have nothing else to do with me. When I started showing, I broke up with him 'till after the baby was born. Then when we made up, I had to hide the baby from him. From you, too, Luke, whenever you came out to Cole's Bayou to pick Lisa up. What made my plan even more perfect was that it'd be a way to get back at you, Luke—for rejecting me, for never loving me—by making you have to pay.

"I know I'm going to jail for a long while. I never could be the kind of mama she needs, no more'n my mama ever was to me. She needs lovin'. Everybody does, and I know she'll get it from you, Old Woman." Edna actually smiled. "She's got your doe eyes, Mamie, and she's got some of you in her, too, Doc. I started noticing that after you told us in court you were Toby's daddy. Toby, I know you can be a good father if you'll listen to your mama! When this little girl grows up, let her know her mama did love her for the little bit of time she was with her. She'll need to know that, and that it ain't her fault she was born just a little too soon in this old world."

"She wasn't born too soon for us." Mamie held Tabitha in her arms and rubbed her soft cheek against Tabitha's. Tabitha murmured something indecipherable and pulled at the kerchief that wrapped Mamie's head.

"She'll do just fine, Edna," Doc assured her. "This is one child I'm going to see to it has everything she wants in life. After all, I'm a grandpa, and I can spoil her if I want to."

"C'mon, Edna, let's go." Sheriff Gravlee placed handcuffs on Edna and led her to the door.

"Mama...Mama." Tabitha stretched her tiny arm out and reached towards the door, opening and closing her little hand.

Edna didn't look back.

"Here, baby, let Mamie get a look at you, you sweet thing, you."

As the door closed behind Edna and Sheriff Gravlee, Tabitha patted Mamie's cheeks with both hands and rubbed her nose to hers and giggled.

34

efore leaving for the Miami Boat Show, there was one more loose end to tie up. The birth of the Ariadne would have much more meaning for Luke if Cooper were here to share it with him. He was introducing his life-long love to the world, but he fervently wished that Cooper, the love of his life, could be by his side. Luke called Cooper's old number repeatedly. No one was ever home, not even her former roommate Trotter had claimed to have talked to. He would keep trying from Miami. He refused to accept as a finality the letter she had sent him.

The Miami Boat Show was thrilling. The Ariadne won top awards for innovation and design and received acclaim far beyond even Luke's expectations. It would take at least a year to fill all the orders they received. Windward Boats, a Callaway Corporation, was on it's way, with Lucas Callaway at the helm, and Ryan Callaway taking a comfortable position as Second Mate.

"You did it, Luke. You did it!" Trotter beamed as though he were a mother who had just given birth.

"*We* did it, Trotter. This wouldn't ever have happened without you." Luke handed Trotter a sealed envelope. "This is for you. You're the First Mate of this operation."

"What is it?"

"Open it."

Trotter fumbled with the seal then finally ripped the envelope open. His fingers thumbed through the brand new bills and he looked at Luke.

"It's the bonus I promised you."

Trotter didn't comment on the money, but he pulled out a single folded piece of paper that was nestled in between the bills. "What's this?" He stared at the official-looking document.

Windward Boats is as much yours as it is mine, Trotter. She was your dream, too. This is part ownership in Windward Boats. You earned it."

Trotter's lips formed a thin line and he drew in his breath. Luke could have sworn he saw a tear fall from the eye of this tough guy who Luke knew to be as mean as a stick of dynamite and quick as a snake.

Luke turned his face away, towards the crowd, to save Trotter the embarrassment of knowing he had seen. What he saw then was a vision coming towards him, seeming to float through the crowd, standing out from the masses with shimmering, coppery hair and a radiant smile. Luke blinked. It couldn't be. Even he, in all his efforts, had been unable to find her. She wouldn't have known where to find him. Unless... He elbowed Trotter, afraid to take his eyes off the vision for fear it might evaporate. She came nearer, the dimples deepening playfully at the corners of her mouth, her green eyes flashing mischievously. "Trotter, I-I think I'm hallucinating again."

Trotter laughed. "That ain't no hallucination this time, Luke. That's the best looking woman I've ever seen, and unless I'm hallucinating, too, she's coming for you."

35

"Who gives this woman in marriage?" The question lingered in the air and for a moment, no one spoke. Father Mallory's resonant voice filled the sanctuary and bounced off the tall, cathedral ceiling of the Episcopal church.

"I do." The loving father, the silver-haired, dignified Senator from Washington, Senator Macon DeLaney, took one step forward. Before releasing the arm of this, his only child, his precious daughter, before entrusting her care and well-being to the young man who stood beside her, his eyes met Luke's.

One look was all it took. The Senator's penetrating gaze revealed much, as in Luke's estimation, was intended. He had the same sincere, green eyes of his daughter, and they reflected respect and trust that Luke would do his utmost to never violate that trust; to never again place his daughter in a position of jeopardy. In that one split-second, a bond was formed between these two good men, with Cooper as the common denominator.

As the final vows were spoken, Luke lifted Cooper's veil. Her eyes bespoke love and joy, and he kissed her tenderly, and the small congregation murmured satisfaction and approval.

Luke wanted to be the first to say it. "Mrs. Lucas Callaway." His lips still close to hers, he murmured the words before they turned and walked hand-in-hand back up the aisle and through the doors of the sanctuary.

Luke swept Cooper up in his arms and carried her across the threshold of their suite at the Royal Hawaiian. Cooper had resided in Hawaii for such a brief period of time, they chose to spend their honeymoon there so that they might create their own Hawaiian memories—together.

Luke poured champagne and toasted the only woman he had ever truly loved. He was filled with pride at the joy he saw reflected in her smile, knowing that it was for him that her happiness shone through. "Do you love me, Mrs. Callaway?"

"I believe I loved you from the first moment I met you. I love you with all my heart." Her warm breath whispered in his ear the words he had so longed to hear.

He embraced her tenderly, protectively, vowing silently to never let her go, and when he kissed her, she responded passionately. It seemed he had waited an eternity for this moment. Very slowly they undressed each other, playfully teasing and kissing, touching and laughing.

Being with Cooper was more than Luke ever imagined it could be during those long months of wanting and waiting. He felt he couldn't get enough of her. He wanted to drink her in slowly—to consume her—body and soul. He devoured her with his eyes, then he encircled her waist with his hands and as he moved them down across her body, her hips moved willingly beneath his touch.

She was his special angel. She gave of herself unselfishly, the sweetest love he'd ever known, a gift to him, her husband. It felt so good to love...to be loved, and loving Cooper was unlike anything Luke had ever experienced. With the blending of their passions, the melding of their souls, they both discovered complete happiness, and the consummation of their union was borne not of lust, but of a deep, abiding love.

Cooper lay beside Luke, cradled in his arms. He never wanted to lose the joy he had finally captured. His life was now complete. He touched her face, tracing every feature with his fingertips, loving her with his eyes, losing himself in hers. He adored her.

"I love you, Cooper, and I'll love you till the end of time." For Luke, those spoken words released years of stifled emotions. He could express his feelings again. The fortress that had imprisoned his emotions had finally crumbled, and he was free to feel again the things that had been welled up inside him, the things that made life worth living—compassion and love and pleasure.

They laughed together, and they were filled with a joy that went beyond sexuality, the joy of friendship that would bind them forever. Luke wanted to protect her and cherish her and share all of his life with her, the way it should be with man and wife.

This was the secret his mother possessed. This was what it was all about, what she had tried to tell him marriage and love should be like on that day that seemed so distant now. This, then, was love.

The End

About the Author

McAuley Huffman grew up in Alabama in close proximity to the Gulf of Mexico, swimming in the ocean, playing on sand dunes and fishing and crabbing from old piers with her siblings while watching beautiful sunsets on the water. As a child, her imagination was fueled by the many books she devoured, which led to writing short stories and keeping a journal of her life and the exploits of family and friends.

After attending a small university in a small Alabama town, she satisfied her wanderlust by traveling the world as a flight attendant for a major U.S. Airline. Everyone she met had a story. Lives and stories intermingled with her imagination and storybook characters were born; fictional tales were spun.

Pemrose Key is a fictional work inspired by the majesty of the Gulf along the Alabama-Florida panhandle and the colorful, southern characters who inhabit these shores.

Pemrose Key is McAuley Huffman's first novel. Watch for her second novel, *Forever, My Love,* to debut soon. McAuley resides in Birmingham, Alabama, and spends her time traveling to the coast and penning new works of fiction.

Made in the USA
Columbia, SC
14 January 2022